WITCH, INTERRUPTED

A WICKED WITCHES OF THE MIDWEST MYSTERY
BOOK THIRTEEN

AMANDA M. LEE

WINCHESTERSHAW PUBLICATIONS

PROLOGUE

12 YEARS AGO

"And how does that make you feel?" Dr. Mitchell Jordan, Walkerville High School's lone guidance counselor, steepled his fingers as he rested his elbows on the desk and regarded me with cool eyes.

"I have no idea," I gritted out, refusing to look away from his pointed stare despite the fact that he made me uncomfortable. "How is it supposed to make me feel?"

"There is no 'supposed to' in all of this, Bay," Jordan replied. "All that's important is what you feel ... and why."

"Okay." I licked my lips and spared a glance for the two teenagers sitting in chairs across from his desk. They looked as annoyed and nervous as I felt. "I feel we're being persecuted, and I don't like it."

"Yeah," my cousin Clove agreed as she leaned forward. "We're being persecuted, and we don't like it."

"We definitely don't like it," my other cousin Thistle concurred, her eyes flashing. "It makes us angry ... and you aren't going to like us when we're angry."

I shot Thistle a quelling look. "Knock that off." Aunt Tillie, the reason we were in this lovely mess, had taken to showing us old

1

episodes of *The Incredible Hulk*. Other than some glaring plot holes and quaint effects, the show was fairly entertaining. Unfortunately, Thistle had taken to emulating and she was thirty seconds away from ripping off her shirt and growling as she flexed.

Thistle rolled her eyes. "Don't tell me what to do. I don't like it when you tell me what to do."

"You don't like it when anyone tells you what to do," Clove pointed out. "You have attitude when anyone bosses you around."

"That's because I'm fifteen," Thistle snapped. "I don't need anyone to boss me around. I'm an adult."

"Fifteen is not an adult," I countered.

"That's a very good point, Bay." Jordan adopted a practical tone. "Fifteen is not an adult. You're seventeen. You're almost an adult. Why don't you tell me what sparked this little ... incident?"

I didn't immediately answer, his words and tone grating. Thankfully, I didn't have to spend much time debating whether I should answer. Thistle took the decision out of my hands ... and launched into a tirade.

"It wasn't a 'little incident,'" Thistle barked. "What's going on in your pants is a little incident."

I was mortified. "Thistle!" My cheeks burned.

Jordan's eyes flashed with impatience for the first time since we were called into his office to discuss the altercation in the hallway. It was clear Thistle's jab hit its mark, which was exactly what she was hoping for. My cousin was nothing if not thrilled when she hurt someone's feelings. "I think you're walking a precarious line, Thistle," Jordan warned. "You might want to watch yourself."

Thistle narrowed her eyes, a not-so-subtle warning that she was going to push things to the limit. I wasn't in the mood for detention or suspension, so I cut her off.

"Thistle is simply upset because we were called into your office even though we were the aggrieved party," I interjected quickly.

"Your vocabulary is quite impressive, Bay," Jordan noted, slowly shifting his eyes to me. "I can see why you're excelling with the newspaper. That doesn't change the fact that Thistle is acting out, something I'm sure is a cry for attention, and you're trying to save her because that's what you do.

"In fact, you might not know it, but I've been watching you three girls for months because your teachers are concerned that you're co-dependent and don't get along with others," he continued. "At first I didn't think there was anything wrong with your relationship. After today, though, well ... I'm starting to think your teachers were right to worry."

My temper flashed before I could bank it. "I see you're not worried about Lila's temper. She was the one, after all, who pulled my hair and threw a soda on Thistle. But she's not in here. Why is that?"

"Because I found her crying on the floor."

"After she attacked us," Thistle argued.

"Actually, from what I understand, she went after Bay," Jordan argued. "Now, I'm not saying what Lila did is right. In fact, I've been watching her closely the last few months. She seems to have a problem with Bay ... and that's concerning. Whatever reason she's focused on Bay, I plan to get to the bottom of it."

"Oh, well, hallelujah," Clove drawled. "If you plan to get to the bottom of it, surely Lila will stop being the school jerk and leave Bay alone. I mean ... Bay graduates in three months. All should be right with the world by then and Lila will get the punishment she's been earning since elementary school."

Jordan cocked an eyebrow and fixed his full attention on Clove for the first time. "Did you say something?"

"You heard her," Thistle shot back, her tone acidic. "Lila started this. Lila always starts it. You let Lila do whatever she wants, yet we're called into the office at least once a week because we've made Lila cry. Well, guess what? Lila has it coming and we're not sorry."

I lowered my forehead to my hand and attempted to rub away the building stress. "I think what Thistle means is that we're sick of getting in trouble for protecting ourselves," I offered.

"No, what Thistle means is that Lila is getting exactly what she deserves and we don't care if you think we're mean," Thistle shot back, her narrowed eyes pinning Jordan, as if daring him to contradict her. "Bay didn't do anything to earn Lila's wrath today. In fact, Bay never does anything to earn Lila's wrath. Lila attacks first, we retaliate, and we're always the ones who get in trouble. How is that fair?"

"I doubt this is the first time you've heard the statement, but life isn't fair, Thistle," Jordan said. "As for Lila ... ."

"As for Lila, we're not sorry," Thistle repeated. "I don't care what you say ... or do ... or how you look at us. I don't care if you use the puppy dog eyes or that disappointed noise you make with your tongue. We're not sorry."

"I see." Jordan tilted his head to the side. "Is that true, Clove? Is Thistle correct when she says that you're not sorry?"

Instead of immediately responding, Clove swiped at tears that had magically appeared and sniffled. "I'm sorry that you're hurting my feelings the way you are," she said, her voice low. "I think my heart might be breaking."

Instead of reacting out of sympathy, Thistle smacked Clove's arm and glared. "Stop that. We're not sorry, so you don't have to fake cry."

Clove balked. "I'm not fake crying. These are real tears."

Clove could muster real tears no matter the circumstance, so I had my doubts. Still, I was agitated enough with the school's response to Lila's most recent attack that I was officially out of patience for anyone's shenanigans ... including my cousin's latest attempt at manipulation.

"What do you want from us, Mr. Jordan?" I asked. "We didn't start the fight today."

"We finished it," Thistle growled, folding her arms over her chest. "That's why we're in trouble ... again. We always finish the fights."

"You did finish the fight," Jordan agreed, although he didn't look nearly as proud as Thistle clearly felt. "Lila is in the principal's office filing a complaint. She has a black eye, her backpack is ripped and one of her shoes somehow ended up in a toilet even though witnesses swear up and down you three never left the hallway, so I'm not sure what to make about that."

I knew exactly how the shoe ended up in the toilet. Thistle magicked it there in a moment of fury. I could hardly admit that — we were real witches trying to hide our identities, after all — so I was forced to change the subject.

"That doesn't change the fact that she attacked us first," I argued.

"She also ripped that backpack herself when she swung it at me," Thistle pointed out. "We're not to blame for the backpack. She was going for my head and ripped the seams on that cheap thing herself."

"Fine." Jordan held up his hands. "Lila did this to herself. I get it. You still ganged up on her. It was three against one."

"To be fair, when she first came after me she had four people with her, so it was five against one," I countered. "When Clove and Thistle joined the fight, the other girls got scared and ran. That's not our fault."

"And I will be talking to those girls later in the day," Jordan said. "Right now, though, I'm talking to you. I want to know how you feel, what you think should be done to solve this situation."

"I have no idea how to solve this situation," I said dully, my earlier indignation fading. "Do what you think is right. What Thistle said earlier is true. We're not sorry."

"Definitely not sorry," Clove agreed, all traces of her earlier tears absent. "In fact, if Lila is lucky she'll take the long way home to avoid the fight we plan on finishing after school."

Jordan widened his eyes to saucer-like proportions. "Do you think it's wise to threaten another student in front of me?"

Clove either didn't understand the question or simply didn't care about her answer. "We're not going to attack her on school grounds. You don't have to worry about that."

"I *am* worried," Jordan supplied. "I'm worried that you girls are starting to lose yourselves in an unhealthy vendetta. I'm sure your mothers would agree with me. For the record, I've placed a call to the house and one of them is on her way to discuss this situation. You'll sit here until she arrives and we come up with a solution."

My heart dropped to my stomach. "You called our mothers?"

"Oh, that was a narc move," Thistle complained, making a face. "How could you call our mothers?"

"Now I really do want to cry," Clove lamented.

"We had no choice but to call your mothers," Jordan replied. "You got into a brawl in the hallway. We can't allow fights on school property. Someone could get hurt."

"Did you call Lila's mother?" I asked, something occurring to me.

"We ... ." The way Jordan broke off and licked his lips told me everything I needed to know.

"So you only called our mothers," I finished.

"You attacked Lila," Jordan stressed. "She's going to end up with a black eye and a pair of ruined shoes. I didn't think I could let this particular fight go without warning."

"You never let us go without warning," Thistle said. "We're always warned. Lila is never warned."

"I'm sure it feels that way, but ... ." Jordan broke off, frowning when his door handle started turning. "That's odd. I thought I would get an announcement before your mothers arrived." He placed the palms of his hands on the desk and pushed himself to a standing position. "I'm sure you won't get into too much trouble. A good talking to is in order, though."

"I'm sure we won't either," Thistle said, her lips curving as the individual on the other side of the door began making noises. "In fact, I wouldn't be surprised if our day ended with ice cream after all."

Jordan was legitimately puzzled. "What do you mean by that?" Before he could reach for the handle the door popped open, revealing our great-aunt Tillie. It was getting toward the tail end of winter, so she wore snow pants and a football helmet (she was a big proponent of plowing snow into her enemies' driveways and that involved a lot of jostling and potential head injuries), and her cheeks were red from the bitter wind blowing outside. "Ms. Winchester? I ... um ... was under the impression your nieces were coming." Jordan didn't look thrilled with the turn of events.

"My nieces are busy running a business and don't have time for your trivial games," Aunt Tillie said as she stalked into the room. She took a moment to study us in turn, taking in Thistle's defiant glare, Clove's drying eyes and my weary head rub before focusing her full attention on Jordan. "Why are they in jail this time?"

"I hardly think this is jail, Ms. Winchester," Jordan replied, gesturing toward the open chair on my left. "Would you like to have a seat?"

Aunt Tillie immediately started shaking her head. "Nope. We won't be staying long."

"We need to talk about your nieces' behavior," Jordan pressed. "They beat up the Stevens girl, made her cry and ruined her shoes. I'm still not sure how they did the shoe thing. It's all very confusing."

"I don't care if they chopped her head off and hid the body in the school pool," Aunt Tillie shot back. "Lila Stevens is a menace and I guarantee that she attacked first."

"That's neither here nor there," Jordan said. "They ganged up on her. Violence is never the proper solution."

"That's where you're wrong. I've been telling them for years to hit Lila harder. That little brat has it coming."

"Your nieces really should've made the time to come in for this discussion," Jordan groused. "You refuse to see the dangerous situation your great-nieces have created. Until you do, we can't fix what's been broken."

"There's nothing to fix." Aunt Tillie was firm. "I told these girls to protect themselves when an enemy attacks. Lila is an enemy. She always has been. She's still alive. I don't know what you're whining about."

"So ... you don't see anything wrong with how your great-nieces responded to this situation?" Jordan countered. "You think they're correct in their reactions."

"Obviously not. They got caught. If they were perfect, Lila would have two black eyes and they would already be on their way home. I'll sit them down later and we'll come up with a plan so they won't get caught next time. How does that sound?"

"Like you're compounding the problem."

"That's exactly what I'm going for." Aunt Tillie flashed an evil smile and then snapped her fingers. "Come on, girls. We're done here. I'll give you a ride home. We'll even stop for ice cream on the way back."

"Ms. Winchester, I didn't say you could leave." Jordan was on his feet, his eyes wild. "This is a serious situation and we need to discuss it."

"You're not the boss of me." Aunt Tillie was blasé. "I don't like all this shrink stuff you do. I don't like that you go after Bay, Thistle and Clove while allowing Lila to do whatever she wants. I think your whole profession is a bunch of bunk, and I don't care what you have to say.

"As for Lila, as long as she continues to go after Bay she's going to get what's coming to her," she continued. "The girls aren't at fault for what's happening here. Also, before you give me crap, I don't think the girls are without fault. I'm sure they can hone their attack so it's quicker and more efficient. We'll work on that.

"Also, the girls screw up all the time and I have no problem yelling at them when they do," she said. "I'm not blind to their faults. But in this instance they're not at fault."

"So ... you'll do nothing?" Jordan challenged. "That won't make them healthy adults who turn to words instead of fists when it comes to solving their problems."

"Who said words were better than fists?"

"Everyone."

"Well, I've never been one to follow the crowd." Aunt Tillie offered a sweet smile that I knew meant she had plans for Mr. Jordan should he continue harping on her. "We're Winchesters. We set our own rules."

"That's not how things work in the real world," Jordan persisted. "You have to follow rules or the world chews you up and spits you out."

"Oh, you're cute." Aunt Tillie winked. "That's only true for people like you. For people like us, we can rule the world ... and rule it well. That's not going to happen while the girls are trapped in this place. Lucky for you, Bay and Lila are almost done. They'll be out of here soon."

"And what will happen then?" Jordan pressed. "How will Bay fight when she's not stymied by rules?"

Aunt Tillie shrugged. "I don't know, but I'm looking forward to finding out. It's going to be an interesting ride. I, for one, am looking forward to seeing where things end up. As for you, your part of this story ends soon. I would say I'll miss you but that would be a lie." She offered him a mocking salute. "Because I'm not a liar I'll tell you the truth. If we never see you again it will be too soon. Have a nice life.

"Now, come on girls," she said, pointing toward the door. "If you want ice cream, we should get it now. I need to be at the end of Margaret Little's driveway in forty minutes because that's when she's due to come home and notice the present I left for her."

"Is it yellow snow?" Thistle asked.

"More like brown snow."

"Even better."

"I thought so."

ONE

PRESENT DAY

"So ... you want the ad to say 'I love everything about you, especially your butt'?"

I pursed my lips as I tapped the tip of my pen against a pad of paper and regarded Felix Worthington with a hard look. The middle-aged and newly-divorced real estate developer didn't appear to share the same worries rolling through my busy brain.

"That's what I want it to say," Felix confirmed. "It's for Debbie Winslow, but I don't think you should put her name on it. She'll know I'm directing it to her, so there's no need to make it public or anything."

"Well, I don't think her husband would like it if you tagged his wife in a personal ad, so I happen to believe you're making the right decision," I offered. "It's still going to cost you fifty bucks without the name."

"I'm fine with that." Felix dug in his wallet and came out with a credit card. "Can you put a heart on it or something, to make it stand out?"

I nodded as I took the credit card and slid it through the reader. "Sure. I think a heart will class the ad right up."

"I think you're right."

I waited until he disappeared from the office to let loose a weary sigh and lean back in my chair. This was the fortieth personal ad I'd taken in three days. I had the bright idea to do a "Lost in Love" section of The Whistler, the newspaper I'd purchased several weeks ago, in honor of the upcoming Hearts and Crones Festival to mark the start of the spring tourist season. That's right. I, Bay Winchester, was no longer simply a reporter. I was an entrepreneur ... and I was still getting used to it.

The venture was a moneymaker — the newspaper was solid even though it was more of an advertorial at times — but I had ideas to increase profit margins, and the first I'd implemented was the special ads section to coincide with the upcoming festival. Unfortunately for me, I had no idea how quickly the messages could turn from sweet to perverted.

When the front door of the newspaper office opened I slapped my hand over my eyes before I could see who was entering. "Go away," I whined, peeking through my fingers when I heard a familiar chuckle.

"And here I thought you were enjoying being a titan of industry," my boyfriend Landon Michaels laughed as he strode toward the front desk. He had a small bakery bag in one hand and a cup of coffee in the other. "I brought you gifts and everything. I expected a better welcome."

I eagerly reached toward the bag. "What is it? Is it a doughnut?"

Landon teasingly pulled back the bag before I could get my hands on it. "I want a reward first."

I met his gaze. "What kind of reward? I can't get freaky in the newspaper office during business hours."

"You could, but you're too much of a prude for that."

"I am not a prude."

"You're kind of a prude." Landon tilted his head down and presented his cheek. "Lay it on me."

I might've fought the demand out of pride, but I wanted whatever he had in that bakery bag, so I smacked a loud kiss against his cheek. "Gimme!"

"Here." He handed over both items before grabbing the notepad I'd been writing on. "Who especially likes whose butt?"

"Ugh." I rolled my eyes as I dug in the bag, my irritation turning to ecstasy when I caught sight of the cake doughnut he'd lovingly selected with me in mind. It had chocolate frosting and sprinkles. "It's still warm."

"I know. That's why I decided to surprise you with sugar despite seeing you two hours ago."

Even though the road hadn't been bump-free, Landon and I had managed to settle into a state of domestic calm since moving in together several weeks ago. Sharing the same space with each other wasn't the issue. However, our proximity to my family was occasional cause for concern. Most everything else was a breeze, especially the fact that he was spending more time in town working — even doing paperwork at the local police station — and popping in to surprise me with food whenever the mood struck.

"Thank you. You have no idea how much this means to me." I bit into the doughnut, a moan of delight easing past my lips. "Oh, man. If I didn't already love you this would tip you over into 'forever my love monkey' territory with one bite. Do you want some?"

"Oh, now that's true love," Landon teased, his eyes flashing as he smoothed his shoulder-length black hair. "I already ate two. The only reason I knew they were warm is because Chief Terry and I stopped for a mid-morning snack."

"Two, huh?" I took another bite and thoughtfully chewed. "You're going to get fat if you keep eating like that."

"I know." Landon's smile disappeared. "When we first started dating I didn't worry too much. At most I ate here three or four days a week. Then, when I headed back to Traverse City to work, I ate healthily and worked out hard for three days. It was a balancing act, but it worked.

"Now I eat with your family almost every meal and there's no gym," he continued. "I need to come up with a workout plan."

"Maybe we should get an elliptical or something."

"I prefer getting my workouts another way." He lifted a suggestive eyebrow and poked my side, grinning when my cheeks began burning. "I love how easily embarrassed you are, my little prude."

"I'm not a prude." I tapped the notepad he held by way of proof. "I mean ... seriously. I took all those ads and some of them are rather risqué."

"So I noticed." Landon's eyes scanned the paper. "Who placed the one about loving the light of someone's soul until the end of time? That's kind of sweet."

"Father Markham."

Landon stilled. "A priest placed a lusty personal ad for the spring love festival?"

"It's for God."

"Oh, well, that's okay." His smile was back. "Who is Tommy Rivers and who does he want to love until his dying day?"

"Tommy Rivers is a senior at the high school."

"Ah. Young love. Is Jenna Barkley a senior, too?"

"She's the high school librarian."

Landon's mouth dropped open. "Are you serious?"

"Yes."

"Well ... crap." Landon dug in his pocket until he found a small notebook and jotted down some notes. "I'm just going to ask a few questions at the high school. I'm sure the kid has a crush on her and she's not encouraging him, but I want to check."

"That's probably wise," I agreed, snatching my notebook from him before he could continue reading. "You're done looking through my notes. I don't want you arresting all my customers."

"Fair enough." He tilted his head to take in the office. "You still haven't decorated."

"No. I don't know how I want to decorate."

"It's not life-or-death stuff, Sweetie. Just pick a few paintings you like. Although ... why are you working out here today? I expected to find you in your office."

"I've been busy with ads. It's easier to take them out here because this is where we keep the credit card reader."

"Ah. I see."

"Also, it seems too weird to take sexy ads in my office. I'm worried about a random pervert coming in off the street. Other than you, I mean."

"Ha, ha." He flicked my ear. "Now that you mention it, I think it's smart to take the ads in the front like this. Do you have your pepper spray for protection in case one of these guys attacks?"

As an FBI agent, Landon had certain ideas when it came to my safety. He needn't have worried. I had other ideas ... and they were far more diabolical than his.

"I don't need pepper spray," I reminded him. "I'm a witch."

"You are. But it doesn't hurt to have more than one weapon in your arsenal."

"I'm a witch who can call ghosts to attack people," I reminded him. "I can control ghosts."

Even though he would've heard if someone had entered the office through the front door, Landon glanced over his shoulder to make sure no one was listening before continuing the conversation. "I know you can."

"I used them to kill someone." I was still flustered by that development. I was used to being a witch. I was born that way. Only recently, though, I experienced a power boost that allowed me to order several dead girls to attack their killer. He was trying to kill me at the time, so I didn't feel all that guilty, but I'd muddled through a few sleepless nights since. I had no idea what to make of the new development.

"You used your new power to protect yourself," Landon clarified. "As for the little rodent in question ... I can't feel sorry that he's dead, Bay. He killed four girls. He wanted to kill you. You're the one still standing. I'm thankful for that."

He was so calm, so rational, it relieved some of the anxiety coursing through me. "I know. It's just ... I keep waiting for something else to happen. I know that controlling the spirits of four dead girls isn't the first and last time this is going to come up."

"No."

"Doesn't that worry you?"

"No." Landon's lips curved. "I get that you're still worked up about this. It's a big deal. You're a good person, Sweetie. We'll figure this out."

I couldn't understand why he wasn't more worried. "What if I accidentally raise an army of dead spirits and bring about the end of the world?"

Landon shrugged. "At least I'll be with you when the end comes."

I narrowed my eyes. "You're trying to be charming."

"Is it working?"

I nodded. "Yeah."

"Good." He leaned over and pressed a soft kiss to my mouth. "We'll figure it out, Bay. Nothing has happened since that day. Well, you've been a little tense — which is another reason I brought you the doughnut — but it's been quiet. We have time to test your new power and figure out how it works."

I hated how pragmatic he sounded. "You know, two years ago you didn't even know witches were real. Now you're all, like, 'You can control ghosts and it's totally fine' about everything and I think it's a little weird."

Landon's grin was quick and charming. "Is that your imitation of me? The way you deepened your voice, I mean."

"Maybe."

"It's cute." He tapped the end of my nose. "You don't need to worry, Bay. I'm not nearly as worked up about this as you are."

"Maybe that's because you don't understand the ramifications."

"Fair enough. What are the ramifications?"

I absolutely hated when he used that rational tone with me. I mean ... hated. "I can make ghosts do my bidding."

"I've noticed. Although, technically, you've only done it with the girls who were killed and dumped in the snow on the highway. I have a theory about why your new power kicked in when it did, if you're interested."

Oh, well, this should be good. "Lay it on me."

"I think you were upset about being the one who found those girls in the snow," Landon supplied without hesitation. "You were outraged on their behalf, which is understandable. You essentially tethered those girls to you because you were fighting on their behalf.

"Now, I get that you didn't realize you were doing it and you want to learn to control the ability," he continued. "I think that's a good idea and I'll be at your side as you figure things out. But this is not the end of the world. In fact, I think it might be useful."

"How?"

"You've helped me solve cases before. You talked to the dead and they led you to answers. Now you're even more powerful. That means the answers will come faster and we'll be able to get more killers off the streets."

He would see things that way. "And what if I accidentally set ghosts to other tasks?" I challenged. "I mean ... what if I send ghosts to haunt someone without realizing I'm doing it?"

"We'll figure it out."

"We'll figure it out?" I hated how shrill I sounded, but I couldn't contain my worry. "Tell that to the poor soul I haunt until he or she loses their mind."

"That's a little dramatic."

"I'm a Winchester. We idle at dramatic."

"True. The fact remains that you're the best person I know and I love you. You're stuck with me. We'll figure this out together. Getting worked up about it doesn't help anyone."

"Fine." I rubbed my forehead. "Do you think I was crazy to do these personal ads?"

"How many have you taken?"

"Forty-five, I think. At this rate, I expect another forty-five before we go to press. I hired Stella from the diner to come in and take over for me this afternoon because I have other things to do."

"How much are you charging for the ads?"

"Fifty bucks each."

"So that's, like, forty-five hundred bucks, right?"

"Essentially."

"I think it was a genius idea, like all your ideas."

My expression turned rueful. "I think you're just saying that because you want to romance my socks off later."

"I honestly don't care if you wear socks when I romance you." He gave me another kiss. "I simply want you to relax."

"That's why you brought me the doughnut; you're checking up on me."

"That doughnut was warm and I knew you would love it. And it did allow me to check on you."

"So it was a multi-pronged doughnut excursion."

"Basically."

I heaved a sigh. "You don't have to worry about me. I know I'm a little nervous, but this is hardly the first time a new power has popped up out of nowhere. I'll figure it out."

"I believe that's what I've been telling you for weeks."

"Yes, well ... I wouldn't be a Winchester if I didn't blow things out of proportion before listening to reason."

"I've yet to meet a Winchester who listens to reason." Landon's grin was mischievous as he pushed himself away from the desk. "Text me at lunchtime. If I'm around we can eat together."

"Okay, I ... ." I forgot whatever I was going to say when a ghost popped into existence to Landon's right. I didn't immediately recognize the man's features — they were twisted, contorted — but I knew he was a ghost because I could see through him. "Oh, great!"

"What?" Landon shifted his eyes to the place I stared and jolted, taking a wild step away from the visitor and crashing into the desk.

I reacted out of instinct, flying around the counter and racing to Landon's side. For some reason I thought perhaps the ghost hurt him. Landon was human and couldn't see ghosts. The only rational reason for his reaction was that I empowered the ghost to hurt him ... a notion that terrified me.

"Are you okay? Do I need to call 911?" I patted his torso looking for wounds as Landon stared at a spot behind me.

"Knock that off, Bay," he said finally, grabbing my wrist before I could start patting lower. "I'm not hurt."

"Then why did you react like that?"

"Because of me," the ghost answered automatically, annoyance rolling off him in waves. "He's looking at me."

"Oh, don't be ridiculous," I scoffed. "He can't see ghosts. I'm the only one who can."

"I don't think that's true," the man argued. "He's looking at me ... and gaping, with his mouth so big a bat could fly in there and disappear."

I shifted my eyes to Landon's handsome face and saw the ghost was right. "Can you see him?"

Landon nodded. "And hear him."

"But ... how?"

With what looked to be great difficulty, Landon dragged his eyes from the ghost and focused on me. "I think you did it, Bay."

"But ... ?" Frustration bubbled up as I glared at the ghost. "Why are you here? Why did you come to me?"

"I have no idea. As for why I'm here, I'm pretty sure I'm dead."

"How did you die?"

He shrugged. "I don't know. It probably had something to do with the knife I saw in my chest before I was compelled to find you. That's just a wild guess"

"That sounds like a good guess." Landon calmly stroked his hand down the back of my head. "So ... are you local?"

"Yup. At least I was." For a ghost, the man was remarkably calm. "My name is Mike Hopper. I'm pretty sure I was murdered."

Ah, well, the day looked to be taking a turn. It was bound to happen eventually.

TWO

"Who are you?"

It was the obvious question. I could've been kind and offered him a mountain of sympathy due to his death, but I was too frazzled to waste time with niceties.

"Mike Hopper."

"Right." Had he already mentioned his name? I couldn't remember. "Why does that sound familiar?"

"I'm famous in these parts."

I didn't believe that. "Why are you famous?"

"He's the guy on the radio," Landon said after a beat. "The Dr. Lovelorn guy. He has that radio show on the weekends. I remember listening to him a few times when I was commuting between Traverse City and Hemlock Cove."

That's when things clicked into place. "Oh, I know who you're talking about. You're the relationship guru. I never listened to your show, but Aunt Tillie did. She said you were a moron."

Landon squeezed my wrist tighter and shook his head. "I don't think Aunt Tillie should be giving relationship advice."

He had a point. "I just meant that ... it doesn't matter what I meant." I shook my head to dislodge my earlier train of thought. "You

AMANDA M. LEE

live over on Peach Street, in that nice ranch house with the ginger-bread trim. You're a licensed therapist, right?"

The ghost nodded. "That's correct."

"You hold sessions in your house for couples. They call you Dr. Lovelorn."

"You can call me Mike."

"Okay, Mike." I did my best to organize my thoughts. "So ... you're saying you were killed in your house?"

"I guess." Hopper's expression turned cloudy. "I can't quite remember what happened. I just know that when I woke up my body was on the floor. I'm guessing that means I was dead."

"That would definitely be my guess," I agreed. "You said you saw a knife sticking out of your chest. I don't think that's naturally occurring."

"No, but I don't remember what happened. You would think I would. I mean ... death by knife in the chest has to be traumatizing. I keep drawing a big blank, though. I can't remember any of it. I feel calm about the situation. I don't understand."

That made two of us. "You are pretty calm for a new ghost," I agreed. "Most ghosts are upset when they first appear. They have to be convinced they're dead before they can settle. You're the exact opposite."

"Maybe it's because I understand that acceptance is key for emotional health."

Oh, geez! A ghost who happened to be a therapist on the side. That wouldn't be irritating or anything. "Well, yeah. I'm sure acceptance is important. It's just ... why did you come to me? How did you know I'd be able to help you?"

"I'm not sure. I mean ... we've all heard rumors about the Winchesters. I believe there was a time when you were a child that the town was considering banding together to have you locked up because you were seen talking to thin air around town. I know because people tell me stories about your family all the time. They want me to diagnose all of you."

Ugh. "I wasn't talking to thin air," I groused.

20

"No. Apparently you were talking to ghosts. That's it, right?"

"Technically," I hedged.

"It's not as if he can spread it around town, Bay," Landon noted. "You can admit what you are to him."

"I know. It's just ... I don't usually do that. It's a secret."

"Well, it's a secret that this guy can't spread," Landon supplied. "I am curious, though. If you didn't realize Bay could talk to ghosts until right now, how did you end up here? This seems a random place to visit if you're not looking for something specific."

"I was compelled to come here."

"By whom?"

Hopper shrugged. "I don't know. I woke up, saw my body and lamented how young I was to die such a tragic death. I briefly wondered what kind of memorial service I would have, wondered if I should stick around long enough to see it and instead decided I wanted to move on. A voice told me to move on, you see, and it seemed like a fairly rational choice.

"Then a stronger voice started calling to me," he continued. "It was a female voice and it was yelling my name, drowning out the other voice, so I followed it on a whim. It led me here. I'm pretty sure it was your voice, Bay."

My heart skipped a beat. "What? You heard my voice? I didn't call out to you."

"And yet here I am."

"Oh, geez." I slapped my hand to my forehead. "This can't be good."

"Calm down." Over his initial fright, Landon seemed intrigued more than anything else. "This guy has answers. We should see what he can tell us. There's no need to get worked up."

That was easy for him to say. "He heard a disembodied voice talking to him. It sounded like me. I was talking to you at the time. If that's not something to get worked up about, what is?"

"I don't know. We need to hear his story and move on from there."

Ugh. I hate it when he sounds like Mr. Rational. It's beyond annoying. "Whatever."

Landon ignored my tone and went into investigator mode. "Tell us exactly what you remember."

Hopper didn't appear bothered by Landon's need to take over the conversation. "I woke up in my living room and I was dead. There was a knife sticking out of my chest. I had a choice to move on or come here. I decided to come here. The other choice felt more permanent for some reason."

Landon leaned forward, intrigued. "Like ... was it the voice of God?"

"It wasn't a voice as much as a feeling inside of my head, if that makes sense."

"It makes no sense at all."

"Yes, well, I don't know how else to explain it. I heard words, but they weren't spoken. The same when I got called here. I knew a female was calling to me and she sounded relatively nice, although commanding, so I decided to postpone one trip in favor of the other."

"This is unbelievable." I rubbed the back of my neck and shifted from one foot to the other. "I didn't call him. I swear I didn't."

"No, but you're powerful," Landon noted. "Obviously your magic called to him."

"Wait ... are you guys really magic?" Hopper looked tickled at the prospect. "There have been rumors about that for a very long time, but I always thought that was Margaret Little being ... well, you know how she is."

I knew exactly how she was. As well as a business owner in Hemlock Cove, the small tourist hamlet in northern Lower Michigan where I grew up and chose to make my future, Mrs. Little was also the town busybody. She had an opinion about how everyone should live their lives ... and if you didn't happen to agree with that opinion she gave you nothing but grief. She was also Aunt Tillie's arch nemesis, but that's a story for another day.

"What's your beef with Mrs. Little?" Landon's curiosity was obviously piqued. "I know why I dislike her. Why do you?"

"She's a pain. She tried to get my business shut down because she said I shouldn't be running a doctor's office in a residential area. I explained that I'm not that kind of doctor and couples prefer a homey setting when they sit down to try to save their relationships. But she took me before the town council to fight it."

"Oh, wait ... I remember some of this." I tapped my chin as my memory kicked in. "It was a few years ago, right? She said you didn't have the proper license to run a business out of your home."

"Pretty much." Hopper nodded his head in confirmation. "I had just moved from Traverse City. I wanted a quieter environment and I'd always been a fan of Hemlock Cove. I had to go before the town council and swear I wasn't performing illegal plastic surgery techniques — and had no plan to throw Botox parties — and ultimately they sided with me despite Margaret's screeching. She is a complete and total freak, by the way. She never let it go."

"What do you mean?" Landon asked.

"She stalked me after that for five straight months. She hung around my house, spied through the windows when I had clients. I think she was convinced she was going to catch me doing something nefarious."

I snorted, some of my anxiety lifting. "That sounds just like her. She did the same to us, hid on the property and tried to catch us dancing naked out by the bluffs."

Landon cocked an eyebrow. "You guys dance naked in that area all the time."

"Yes, but that's none of her business."

"Wait ... there's really naked dancing going on out there?" Hopper's eyes sparked. "I can't believe I missed that. I thought all the people who claimed that were crazy ... or perverts."

"There are plenty of perverts in this town," Landon said, sobering. "I happen to like a good pervert." He winked and it was somehow soothing. "For now, we need to focus on you. We need to confirm your death and then call Chief Terry. He's technically in charge."

"How do we confirm his death without owning up to how we found out?" I asked.

"We'll figure that out once we confirm things. For now, our first order of business is confirmation. After that, we'll figure out what we'll put in the reports."

"Okay, but I want you to know I'm going to freak out about a disembodied voice sounding like me later."

"I expect nothing less."

"THIS PLACE IS CUTE."

Landon was unusually chipper when he parked on the street in front of Hopper's house. For his part, the ghost didn't seem to think it was abnormal to ride with us. He climbed in the back, forcing Landon to open the door for him because he was uncomfortable moving through doors yet, and he kept up a steady stream of chatter during the ride.

"I thought it was a lovely home," Hopper agreed as he hovered on the sidewalk next to me. Landon shut the rear door and moved closer. "I loved the gingerbread accents."

"Yeah, they're great," I drawled. "I can't tell you how cute the house is. By the way, there's a dead body inside."

"Sweetie, you need to calm down," Landon, firm, instructed. "You've seen dead bodies before. If you don't want to see this one, you don't have to. Stay here."

I bristled. "It's not the dead body that bothers me."

"I know. It's the disembodied voice. We'll talk about that later."

I was of the mind that we should talk about the disembodied voice now, but as an FBI agent, Landon was in charge. I couldn't exactly argue with his decision to focus on a potential murder rather than my freak-out. "How do you want to confirm it?"

"Where is the living room, Mike?" Landon asked. He was surprisingly comfortable talking to a ghost. Technically, it wasn't the first time he'd held a conversation with a spirit. A year ago the ghost of a little girl appeared to him when I was in trouble and warned him to come after me. He never questioned it. He hadn't seen a ghost since, but he was handling our current circumstances extremely well.

"The bay window looks into the living room," Hopper answered.

"Bay window. Bay Winchester. Oh, that's funny. Did your mother name you after her favorite window?"

I found the question ludicrous. "Of course not."

"She was named after the herb," Landon volunteered. "The same with Clove and Thistle."

"Oh, that makes sense. Your mothers must have been full of whimsy."

They were full of something. Usually it was complaints and guilt trips, but that was hardly the thing to focus on now. "Let's just look through the window, shall we?"

"Come on." Landon linked his fingers with mine, perhaps offering me support. I didn't need the support but I was happy for the contact. He led the way up the steps, taking me by surprise when he knocked on the front door before looking through the small window at the top of the door.

"He's dead," I reminded him. "He can't answer."

"No, but the neighbors are watching," Landon explained. "See that curtain moving over there?" he gestured to the house on the left with his chin. "Whoever is inside has been watching since we parked."

"Esther MacReady," I said automatically. "She's in her eighties. She's a regular at the senior center. I'm sure she spends all of her time watching the street. I think that's normal for older people."

"Well, we don't want to appear as if we already know he's dead," Landon said. "She might find that weird." He knocked again and called out. "Mr. Hopper? It's Landon Michaels and Bay Winchester. We need to talk to you."

No one answered. Of course, I didn't expect anyone to. "Now what?"

"Now we do the normal thing." He released my hand and moved to the window, raising his fingers to shield his eyes from the glare of the sun. I remained rooted to my spot and watched as his body demeanor stiffened.

"Do you see him?"

"Yeah." Landon was grim as he turned back to me. "It's just as Mike said. He's dead on the floor."

I didn't need to look, yet I couldn't stop myself. I shuffled closer to the window and mimicked Landon's earlier movements to peer inside.

Mike Hopper was indeed dead on the floor. He looked to be wearing a robe, although it was open. His chest was a mess of blood and a knife remained firmly planted to the hilt in a spot close to his heart.

"He would've died quickly," Landon said quietly, sparing a glance for Esther's moving curtain. "There's a lot of blood, but he would've bled out fast given the location of the wound. Even if someone had called 911 immediately it's doubtful that he would've lived."

"How can you be so sure?"

"It's a chest wound, Bay, and it's deep."

"Okay." I sucked in a breath and tore my gaze from the garish tableau on the other side of the window. "He looks as if he was either going to bed or getting up when it happened. He clearly wasn't dressed for meeting people."

"Definitely not," Landon agreed. "That means someone either snuck in or Mike was expecting a guest and didn't mention it." He shifted his gaze over his shoulder and focused on the ghost, who didn't appear upset to see himself dead a second time. "Were you expecting anyone last night?"

"Not that I can remember." Hopper turned thoughtful. "Things are a blur. I remember finishing up with my clients yesterday, a young married couple from Traverse City. They were having difficulties agreeing on children. He wanted them. She didn't. They decided to give it a year and then talk about the issue again, when it wasn't so soon after the wedding.

"They left in relatively good spirits, and I closed my office for the day," he continued. "I was going to cook dinner but decided I didn't want to deal with it and headed to the diner instead."

"Did you make it to the diner?" I asked.

He bobbed his head. "Yes. I had meatloaf. That seems a bit mundane for a final meal. I kind of wish I'd splurged on the prime rib."

"Always splurge on the prime rib," Landon suggested. "And bacon. Always add bacon to everything."

"That's a given." Hopper smiled. "I finished dinner. I walked home."

"You walked?" Landon queried. "It was cold last night."

"It's only four blocks and I try to get exercise in whenever I can," Mike supplied. "Hemlock Cove really needs a gym."

"That's what I've been saying," Landon agreed.

"A gym doesn't fit in with the touristy nature of the town," I argued.

"Tourists like to exercise," Landon persisted. "I'm going to talk to your mother about adding a gym to The Overlook. I bet it would be a draw for the guests."

"The guests come for the food and dinner theater."

"That doesn't mean a gym won't be welcome. That's not important now. You walked home, Mike. Obviously you arrived. Did you go to bed?"

"I can't remember."

"Well, I guess we'll find out when the medical examiner gets here. We can't start questioning people until we get a time of death. To do that, we need to call Chief Terry and get him over here."

"How are you going to explain us finding the body? You know he gets squirrelly when talk of ghosts pops up."

"I've already got a plan. Everything is under control. Trust me."

THREE

"So ... you were visiting Dr. Lovelorn so he could help you with your relationship?"

Chief Terry looked far from convinced when he arrived and Landon spun his yarn.

Landon nodded without hesitation. "We're committed to having a healthy relationship, and we thought Dr. Hopper could help us with our issues."

"Uh-huh." Chief Terry slowly tracked his eyes to me. "Why were you really here, Bay?"

"I just told you," Landon snapped.

"Bay?" Chief Terry prodded.

I hated the way he looked at me, as though he was disappointed I would dare lie to him. He was something of a father figure — he'd spent endless hours with Clove, Thistle and me after our fathers moved out of town following contentious divorces with our mothers — so I could do nothing but stare at my shoes. I muttered something unintelligible.

"Try again, Bay," he insisted.

"Dr. Hopper's ghost found me at the newspaper office, and we came here to make sure he was really dead," I admitted.

Landon slid me a sidelong look. "You're the worst liar ever."

"She shouldn't lie to me," Chief Terry argued. "Although, we're definitely lying on the report. Stick with the relationship counseling thing. It's much more believable than the witch thing."

I pursed my lips. "I didn't want to lie."

"Of course you didn't." Chief Terry smiled indulgently. "You're my little sweetheart. I know Landon made you lie. He's the one I'm angry with."

I brightened considerably as Landon's smile dipped. "Yay! Punish him. I'm the good one."

"You're always the good one," Chief Terry agreed, planting his hands on his hips as he returned to business and stared at the house. "The medical examiner is on his way. I'd guess Hopper died sometime during the night, but we'll need a firmer estimate to go on. I don't suppose this ghost gave you somewhere to start, did he, Bay?"

I shook my head but Landon answered before I could.

"No. He doesn't remember what happened after he returned home from dinner," Landon volunteered. "He's tried to home in on the details, but it's all a blur."

"I see you already tasked Bay with ferreting out the information."

"No, I asked him myself."

Chief Terry stilled. "I'm sorry ... what?"

Landon realized immediately why Chief Terry was so surprised. "Oh, right. You don't know the big news yet." He plastered a wide smile on his handsome face. "Bay can make random people see ghosts now. I saw and talked to Hopper myself. It's going to make questioning the ghosts so much easier going forward."

Landon's voice was laced with false bravado, but the look on Chief Terry's face told me that he didn't agree in the least with the FBI agent's assertion.

"Are you kidding?"

"No."

Chief Terry looked pained as he glanced at me. "You can make people see ghosts? Bay, that's not good. What happens if you cause the wrong person to see a ghost?"

"Who is the right person?" I was genuinely curious.

"I don't know, but there are definitely wrong people, though. Like Margaret Little. It would be great if she couldn't see any ghosts."

Hmm. That hadn't even occurred to me. Still, I felt the need to defend myself. "It's not as if I'm doing it on purpose," I protested, waving my hands for emphasis. "It just happened. I can't control it."

"Well, you'll have to learn." Chief Terry was firm. "I'll help you if need be, but until then if a ghost pops up in front of someone, pretend you don't see it. Don't look at the ghost. Don't make eye contact. That way the other person will assume they're crazy and you'll be fine."

My mouth dropped open. "You want me to encourage people to think they're insane?"

"It's better than putting yourself at risk." Chief Terry was unruffled as he turned to Landon. "So, what do we have?"

Landon winked at me before answering, as if to say "I told you it would be fine, now stop whining." I wasn't a fan of the expression, although he was kind of cute while delivering it. "Not much. We know he went to the diner for dinner, had meatloaf, walked home and was killed sometime after that."

"When did he wake up?"

"This morning. He was going to cross over but instead heard Bay's disembodied voice calling him."

I slouched my shoulders when I felt Chief Terry's eyes barreling into my soul.

"Bay's disembodied voice?" Chief Terry's voice was unnaturally squeaky.

"I like it," Landon enthused. "I'm going to have her use it on Aunt Tillie one of these days so we can finally win a battle."

I recognized he was trying to make me feel better, but I wasn't sure that was possible. "Let's focus on Hopper," I suggested. "He was a relationship therapist. I think that means he didn't have a perfect rate when it came to saving marriages. That's a motive right there."

"Good thinking, sweetheart." Chief Terry beamed. "We need to go through his client records."

Before Chief Terry could make a move toward the house, Hopper popped back into existence and planted himself directly in front of Chief Terry. He seemed anxious, as if he was about to blow, and unfortunately he chose to blow all over Chief Terry.

"You cannot go through my client records," Hopper barked. "That's private. I promised my clients complete secrecy. You'll ruin that if you go through their files."

I expected Chief Terry to ignore the ghost — I wasn't used to the new reality, after all — but instead he reared back and stumbled to the left to get away from the apparition. "Son of a ... ghost!"

"Geez!" Landon shot out his hands and grabbed Chief Terry's arm before he could fall over. "Are you okay?"

Chief Terry briefly pressed his eyes shut and shook his head, reminding me of when I was a kid and I said something goofy and he had to force himself to calm down before responding. "There's a ghost staring at me, isn't there?"

My stomach twisted. "Yeah."

"Well, great." He rubbed his forehead. "This is not good, Bay."

I looked to Landon for help and found him watching me with overt curiosity. "What do we do?" I didn't want to panic but I was beyond acting calm. "The medical examiner will be here any minute. If he sees a ghost I'll be exposed."

"You're not going to be exposed." Landon blew out a sigh and glanced around the yard. "I won't let it happen, Bay. You've got to get your emotions under control. That's the reason you can't keep a lid on this. You're making all of it happen. You simply need to figure out how and then you'll be able to control your new ability."

"Oh, well, great," I deadpanned, my temper flashing. "Do you have any tips for how I can make that happen in the next five minutes? Because that's when the medical examiner is going to arrive."

"No." Landon grabbed my arm and directed me toward his Ford Explorer. "That's why you're getting in here with Chief Terry and the doctor. Mike, you can't just appear in front of others when Bay is around. You could get her in trouble. You don't want that, do you?"

"I don't see how I would get her in trouble," Hopper protested as Landon opened the door and eased me into the passenger seat. "I'm a big proponent of people being who they are and not kowtowing to the expectations of others. I don't foresee my opinion on that matter changing simply because I'm dead."

"Yes, well, Bay is alive." Landon smoothed my hair and smiled. "She's going to stay that way ... and safe. That's why I'm going to show the medical examiner where he needs to go and Chief Terry is going to stay in the Explorer with you guys and ask questions."

"Why do I have to hang out with the ghost?" Chief Terry huffed as he climbed into the driver's seat. "Why can't you hang out with him?"

"Because it makes more sense for you to be interviewing Bay in private when they arrive because we discovered the body together," Landon answered without hesitation. "We wouldn't necessarily be together for questioning, even though you're tight with both of us. We need to be practical given how the discovery was made."

"That's actually smart thinking," Chief Terry said. "We can say I'm doing it in the Explorer because it's cold out."

"And Mike can duck down when the medical examiner arrives," Landon added. "That way no one will see him."

Hopper made a face. "I'm already dead. Haven't I been through enough?"

"We're going to solve your murder, but we can't do it if people start talking about Bay dragging ghosts around town with her," Landon snapped. "I'm not joking. I will not help you unless you help me. I'll let your murder go unsolved for all eternity."

For the first time since Hopper had reappeared I cracked a genuine smile ... that turned into a hearty laugh.

"What?" Landon asked, confused.

"You're even more worked up than I am." I grabbed his hand and gave it a hard squeeze. "It's going to be okay. I'll figure it out."

"I know you will." Landon was sincere. "But until you do, Mike needs to hide. Use your disembodied voice to order him around if you have to. I'll handle the medical examiner."

I nodded. "Consider it done."

CHIEF TERRY SPENT a full twenty minutes interrogating Hopper. The initial surprise gave way to curiosity, and by the time the medical examiner arrived and Hopper followed Landon's instructions and ducked to the floor, Chief Terry was in his groove.

"You've dealt with ghosts before, Bay," he said. "Do you think it's possible that Dr. Hopper will remember more about his death going forward?"

I wasn't sure how to answer. "There's no hard and fast rule when it comes to ghosts," I replied. "Some remember. Some don't. Some take time to remember. Mike is trying hard to access his memories but coming up against a wall. I think the more he relaxes the more likely he is to access those memories. It probably won't happen today, though."

"That means we're going to have to go about this the old-fashioned way," Chief Terry said. "We have to go through the client files to see if we can find someone who would have motive to kill the doctor. We need warrants for that."

Hopper's head popped up. "I've already told you those files are private."

"And I've already told you that we don't have a choice," Chief Terry fired back. "Odds are one of your clients killed you. Can you think of anyone who was especially angry with you over the past couple months? It might not be a current patient. It could've been someone who dropped your services a while back and let the anger grow and fester."

"I would be lying if I said all my clients left in great spirits and went on to live happily ever after," Hopper said. "I don't take on killers for clients, so I don't think it was a patient."

"How would you know clients were killers if they were good at hiding it?" I asked.

"I'm good at reading people."

"So am I, and I've almost been murdered a good ten times or so."

"You do have a knack," Chief Terry agreed, leaning his head against the seatback and offering a wan smile. "You're upset about all of this, aren't you?"

I immediately started shaking my head. "I'm not. I'm being strong."

"I didn't say you weren't strong. I said you were upset."

"I just ... don't know what to do about it," I admitted, giving in to my childish urges to confide in him so he could fix things like he did when I was a kid. "I didn't know I was doing it. If I don't know what I'm doing, how can I fix it? What if I screw up in front of the wrong person and end up exposing my family? What if I explode and ruin things for you and Landon?"

"We'll figure it out." Chief Terry patted my hand as he tsked. "Honey, you'll make things worse if you dwell on it. Take a deep breath. You think better when you're calm. I know that's easy for me to say and you're doing the best you can, but I really do think things will start looking up when you get a handle on your emotions."

He wasn't wrong. "Fine." I blew out a heavy sigh. "Let's talk about something else. Maybe that will calm me."

"Good idea. What do you want to talk about?"

"Um ... ." I pressed my lips together and tilted my head to the side, considering. "Thistle has a naked statue she made and Marcus doesn't want it in the house. They're having a battle of sorts about it."

"That sounds ... very freaky."

"Thistle won't let us see the statue."

"It must be a doozy." Chief Terry smirked. "I don't want to see the statue, but I wouldn't mind getting a gander at your mother's face when she sees it. Somehow I just know that statue is going to land at The Overlook before it's all said and done."

I had a feeling he was right. "Tell me something about you," I suggested, changing the subject. "The big spring festival is coming up. That early thaw we had is a memory, so it's cool again. Spring is around the corner. Do you have any vacation plans?"

"I don't really take vacations. When I do, I stick close to home."

"Yeah, but ... the festival is coming up," I prodded. "It's all about love and romance. Are you going to do anything special?"

I expected him to answer with a resounding "no." Instead, he turned his head to stare out the window. "What are you and Landon doing for the festival? You can leave out all the gross stuff that will make me want to break his legs."

Realization dawned and excitement began building in my chest. "You have a date for the festival!"

Chief Terry balked. "I do not," he protested, jerking his eyes to me. "Why would you think that?"

"Because I'm not the only one who is a bad liar," I replied. "You have a date. I ... who ... when ... ." My mind was moving at a fantastic rate. A few months ago, I sat Chief Terry down and told him that it was okay to build a life for himself. He'd spent years as the center of my mother and aunts' attention. He didn't choose because he didn't want to hurt anyone. He was the one hurt in the process. On Christmas Day I told him it was okay to choose ... no matter who he settled on. The fact that he took my advice to heart was exciting.

"Her name is Melanie Adams," Chief Terry volunteered, causing the oxygen to flee from my lungs. "She's a yoga instructor at that place that just opened on the highway. I met her a few weeks ago and we've been seeing each other for a bit."

I forgot how to breathe at his words, spots forming in front of my eyes. When I finally remembered, I let loose a long gasp that sounded unbelievably dramatic. "What?"

"She's a lovely woman," Chief Terry said hurriedly. "I think you're really going to like her. She has a great personality and she loves going out to restaurants and trying different sorts of food. I planned to introduce you to her when things calmed down a bit. With you taking over the newspaper and everything, it's been a very busy time."

"But ... ." I had no idea what to say. I was far too old to start whining, even though my first inclination was to scream "You were supposed to date my mother." I didn't get a chance to say more because Landon picked that moment to return to the Explorer and pull open the passenger door.

"Hey, the medical examiner is packing up the body and preparing to leave," Landon announced. "Mike, that means you need to hide. After the medical examiner leaves, you can all get out again. How does that sound?"

Chief Terry seemed thrilled at the interruption. "That sounds great."

"How are you doing, Sweetie?" Landon asked me. "Are you okay?"

I wanted to bury my head under a pillow and go to bed until the world was normal again. "I'm fine." I placed my hands on my lap and stared at them. "I'm absolutely fine. Nothing weird going on here."

Landon cocked an eyebrow but didn't press. "Okay. I'll be back in a few minutes. Mike, make yourself scarce."

"Sure," Hopper responded absently. "I'm much more interested in what's going on in here anyway. It's a fascinating psychological experiment."

"Well, great." Landon made a face. "We'll talk about that later. For now ... we're almost there, kids." He flashed an enthusiastic thumbs-up. "I told you this would all work out."

"Yes, everything is perfect," I said dryly. "I can't tell you how perfect things are. You were definitely right." Actually, he was so completely wrong I wanted to shake him. That would have to wait for later. "We'll wait for your signal to get out of the Explorer."

"It won't be long."

FOUR

"*M*elanie Adams."

I was still moping about the turn of events when Landon picked me up at the newspaper office shortly before seven.

"Hello, Sweetie." His smile was wide as he swooped in to kiss me. "How was the rest of your day?"

That had to be a loaded question.

Once the medical examiner had finished up at Hopper's house, Landon decided the safest plan was to drop me at The Whistler while he and Chief Terry focused on the investigation. He stated over and over that he didn't like cutting me out of the action, but he thought it was best for the time being until I could control my new necromancy abilities. I didn't put up a fight because I had other things on my mind.

"I don't like Melanie Adams," I announced, handing Landon my computer bag so I could shrug into my coat. "I don't like her one bit."

Landon heaved out a sigh. I had filled him in on Chief Terry's announcement during the drive back to the newspaper, and it was obvious he was already annoyed with the topic. "Have you met her?"

"Yes."

"Really?"

"I met her when she came to place an ad for the yoga studio," I replied, haughty. "She was picky and annoying. The ad had to be perfect."

"She was putting something in the newspaper that reflected her business. I can understand the inclination."

I absolutely hated it when he was reasonable, especially when the situation called for a dramatic reaction. "Listen ... ."

"No, you listen," Landon shot back. "I know you're upset because you assumed Chief Terry would date your mother — or maybe an aunt — once you gave him the go-ahead, but that's obviously not what happened. He's allowed to have a life that's not of your choosing. You're being ridiculous."

"I am not being ridiculous."

"Uh-huh."

"I'm not," I persisted, fury oozing from my pores. "I'm simply trying to explain why I think Chief Terry dating Melanie Adams is a bad idea."

"Fine." Landon held open the door so I could exit ahead of him. "Tell me why this woman you've met once is so very bad for the man you wanted to date your mother."

His tone was grating. "I didn't want him to date my mother."

"I don't believe you."

"I don't really care what you believe," I shot back, my infamous Winchester temper on full display. "I didn't say I wanted him to date my mother. I didn't say he had to date someone in my family. It's just ... ."

"That's what you expected him to do," Landon finished.

"I didn't expect him to do it." I recognized my petulance when I realized my arms were crossed over my chest and my lower lip was jutting out. I adjusted my stance immediately. "I thought he wanted to do it."

Landon's expression softened. "You wanted him to date your mother so he would always be your second father. I get it."

"What's wrong with that?"

"Nothing, from your perspective. From his perspective, it's possible that he wanted something else. He's obviously attracted to this Melanie Adams. I can't comment on her because I've never met her."

"She's evil." I drew my eyebrows together. "I bet he's dating her because she can bend like a pretzel. He probably thinks that means she can do freaky stuff in bed."

Landon was clearly caught off guard by the remark because he choked on his own laughter. "Oh, is it any wonder that I love you?" He grabbed my hand and squeezed. "Bay, you're being ridiculous. Chief Terry is a grown man and he's allowed to date who he wants."

"Have I said otherwise?"

"Yes."

"Well, he's not supposed to date Melanie Adams." The rational part of my brain understood that Landon was right. I *was* being ridiculous. I had been so convinced that Chief Terry would start dating my mother that I didn't allow myself to consider anything to the contrary. "I don't like her."

"You don't know her."

"I still don't like her."

"You'll change your mind."

"How can you be so sure?"

"Because you love Chief Terry," Landon answered simply. "You want him to be happy. If he got up the gumption to tell you he was dating this woman that means he's willing to take the relationship public. That means he's already been dating her, and probably for a bit because he wouldn't risk introducing you to her unless he was serious."

"Do you think that makes things better?" Something occurred to me. "Wait ... you didn't know he was dating someone else, did you? You guys are all buddy-buddy. You bump fists and do that 'women are crazy' eye roll thing when you think no one is looking. Did you know he was dating the pretzel chick?"

Landon snickered. "I didn't know ... and you've got to stop calling her the pretzel chick. If you're not careful, that'll catch on."

"I don't care."

"You care." Landon tested the lock to make sure it held and then gestured toward the Explorer. "You cannot live Chief Terry's life for him. You can't make decisions about what he should do, who he should care for. You're not the queen of his world."

"I should be."

"You can be the queen of my world. Every queen only has one kingdom, so ... you need to let it go."

"What if I can't?"

"You have to." Landon refused to back down. He only dug his heels in when he was convinced he was right. That made me wonder if perhaps I was wrong ... although it was something I didn't want to consider.

"I didn't expect him to pick someone outside my family," I admitted after a beat. "I thought, even if he didn't pick Mom that he would pick Marnie. I didn't think he would pick Twila because she's too scattered. I thought for sure we would be seeing more of him."

"And now you're worried that you'll see less of him," Landon said. "I get it. The thing is, you might find that you like Melanie Adams if you give her a chance. Instead of losing a member of your family — which won't happen no matter how you fret — you might gain someone you like. Have you considered that?"

"Not for a second."

"That's what I figured." Landon opened the passenger door of his Explorer so I could climb inside. He placed my computer bag by my feet and watched as I fastened my seatbelt. "You've got to get control of your feelings, Bay. Getting all worked up over Chief Terry won't help the ghost situation."

"I'm not worked up," I protested. "I don't know why you think I am."

"Because I've met you." He pressed a quick kiss to the corner of my mouth. "I'm taking you to the diner for dinner. Before you start arguing, there are two reasons I think it's a good idea.

"The first is that I want you to calm down before getting the rest of your family riled up about Chief Terry's dating situation," he continued. "It seems like a good idea given how you guys fly off the handle. The second is because I want you to focus on controlling your new ability in a public setting. The diner is as good a place to start as any."

I immediately started shaking my head. "What if Mike shows up?"

"Then you'll know you're not exerting enough control."

"But ... ."

"No." Landon cut off further argument with a headshake. "I don't want to put you at risk, but you have to start working on this. Putting it off won't help anybody, least of all you."

And he had another point. Drat!

"Fine." I exhaled and narrowed my eyes. "If this goes badly I'm blaming you."

"I can live with that."

"YUP. I'M DEFINITELY blaming you."

The annoyance I thought I'd put to rest upon leaving The Whistler roared back full force when I walked through the door of the diner ten minutes later and the first thing I saw was Chief Terry sitting at a table with the pretzel chick.

Landon, who should've been quaking in his boots, merely smirked. "I have the worst timing ever. Sometimes even I'm baffled about how things backfire on me."

"We should go to the inn."

"No." Landon pressed his hand to the small of my back and directed me toward a cozy booth in the corner. "This will be a good test for you."

The only thing he was testing was my patience. "I don't like this," I hissed as we drew closer to Chief Terry's table. "I don't want to talk to her."

"Well, you're going to." Landon pasted a bright smile on his face as he slowed. "Wow. This is a happy meeting of the minds."

Melanie's expression was quizzical as she flicked her eyes to us. I took a bit of satisfaction in the fact that Chief Terry's cheeks flooded with color as he cleared his throat — he clearly wasn't expecting us — but he was all smiles when he met my gaze.

"I didn't realize you guys were going to be here," Chief Terry said. "I thought you would head out to the inn for dinner."

"Four nights a week with Aunt Tillie is my limit," Landon supplied. "We're catching a quick dinner here and then heading home."

"Yes, well ... ." Chief Terry cleared his throat. "Sorry, I've forgotten my manners. Melanie, this is Landon Michaels. He's an FBI agent stationed out of Hemlock Cove. And, of course, I believe you've met Bay. She owns The Whistler."

"Of course." Melanie, her strawberry blond hair smooth and in place, beamed at me. "You were a reporter when we met. I came into the office to place an ad. You had to help me because the normal girl wasn't there. This was right before you purchased the business, so you were busy. You probably don't remember."

It was a struggle, but I found my voice. "I remember you." Landon's insistent hand on my back reminded me that I should smile, even if I didn't mean it. "It's nice to see you again. I wasn't aware that you spent much time in Hemlock Cove."

"I split my time between here and Traverse City," Melanie explained. "The yoga studio is halfway between both, so I usually end up in Traverse because it's bigger and easier to get the things I need. I find Hemlock Cove charming, though."

"Yes, it's all kinds of charming," I said dryly.

We lapsed into uncomfortable silence. Melanie was the first to break it.

"Terry tells me that he's extremely close with your family," she said. "I understand that he spent a lot of time with you and your cousins when you were children. I'm glad we finally got a chance to meet in a social setting."

"He did spend a lot of time with us," I agreed, fighting the urge to show my teeth. I had no right to be territorial, but I couldn't seem to stop myself. "He took us fishing ... and for hikes in the woods ... and he got us a dog for Christmas one year ... and a fairy house ... and he made us a tree house ... and a bunch of other stuff."

"Wow! That sounds great for you guys."

"It was." I pressed my lips together to keep from exploding. "He was the best."

As if reading the change in my demeanor, Landon slipped his arm around my waist. "We should probably sit. We've had a long day. Bay needs sugar and carbs if she's going to keep going."

"You could join us," Melanie offered.

"No, we don't want that," Landon said hurriedly. "You're on a date. We're on a date. That could get awkward."

Definitely awkward, I internally agreed.

"Then we'll have to get to know each other later," Melanie insisted, her eyes snagging with mine. "Terry talks about you all the time. I feel as if I already know you."

That was funny, because she was a virtual stranger to me. "Sure. I'm always at the newspaper office. You can find me there."

Landon kept me pinned to his side as he led me toward the booth, lowering his voice so only I could hear. "That was pretty good. You didn't explode and choke her or anything, so I'm considering that a win."

"She seems nice." It wasn't exactly a lie, but it didn't feel like the truth either.

"She does seem nice," Landon agreed. "I think, if you allow yourself, you'll like her. Just give yourself a few days to get used to the idea."

"Yeah. Sure. In three days all those things I imagined happening for years will completely disappear. Three days will fix everything."

Landon sighed. "Bay."

I held up my hands in capitulation. "No, you're right. I'm being a total baby." I didn't say the words merely to placate him. I felt them deep down, and I wasn't proud of myself. "Tell me about what you found at Mike's house this afternoon. That seems like a safe subject."

Landon snorted. "Yes, talking about a murder victim seems so much safer than talking about Chief Terry's date." He winked as he sat across from me and grabbed the specials menu from the center of the table. "They have prime rib."

I'd always wished I was the sort of person who couldn't be

comforted by food. But my mother and aunts were kitchen witches, so there was no chance of that. I knew better than drowning my sorrows in food.

"They have chocolate cake, too," I noted, perking up a bit. "I know what I'm getting."

"That makes two of us."

"SO, HOW LONG DO you think it will take to go through all of Mike's files?" I asked an hour later as I cut into my mountainous slice of cake.

"I don't know," Landon replied, an equally large slice sitting in front of him. "He had quite a few clients. Some were former clients. I'm not even sure where to start. We need to wait for a warrant before we're officially cleared to go through the files, and I'm not sure when it will come through because the regular judge is on vacation and the sitting judge has a full plate."

"Do you have a time of death?"

"Between midnight and two."

"Hmm." I ran the information through my mind as I shoved a heaping forkful of cake into my mouth. I swallowed before continuing. "That's late, but not too late if he had an overnight guest."

"Did he mention having a girlfriend?" Landon asked. "I didn't see signs that he had a regular overnight friend."

"What are the signs?"

"An extra toothbrush in the bathroom. Space carved out in the closet and drawers. Chick stuff in the bathroom."

"Like tampons?"

Landon smirked. "Like lotion ... and frilly body spray ... and makeup. You know, all that stuff you have in our bathroom that takes up seventy-five percent of the space."

"I think it's sexist to call it chick stuff."

"You can flog me later."

"I just might do that." I stretched out my legs until my feet found his under the table, pressing the soles of my boots against his and causing him to smile. "You're right about Chief Terry." I'd made a point not to stare at the police chief and his date throughout the meal. I couldn't completely refrain from staring, but I managed to cut it down to the point I looked only once every sixty seconds. "I wanted him to do things my way. That's not fair. I just thought he wanted things to go my way, too."

"He may have at one time, Bay." Landon's face filled with sympathy. "Years ago, he might have wanted to try with your mother, but he changed his mind because he realized he was really in love with you, Clove and Thistle. I'm sure he'll tell you the truth if you ask him."

"I don't want to ask him."

"Because it's too much right now on top of everything else," he surmised. "I get it. Once you've calmed yourself, I think you might like her. She seems desperate to like you."

"Yeah. That's not normal."

"No?" Landon cocked an eyebrow. "For all intents and purposes, he's your father. That means you're his daughter. Of course Melanie wants you to like her. If you don't, she'll get the heave-ho."

His words bolstered my spirits. "Do you really think so?"

"I didn't say that to make you turn evil."

"I know. I was simply wondering if you think that's true."

"I do. I also think you should put Chief Terry's needs ahead of your own on this one. He's done the same for you for decades. I think you owe him one."

Ugh. I hated it when Landon was rational. Just once, I wanted him to channel my family and fly off the handle for no good reason. "Fine. I'll be nice to her."

"Good."

"That doesn't mean I'll be best friends with her," I warned. "I mean ... she's my age. Chief Terry is dating a woman my age. That's creepy."

Landon made a face. "She's in her forties."

"Close enough."

"She's closer to your mother's age."

"Are you trying to tick me off?"

He snickered. "I can see now is not the time to push this further. I think we've hit the end of the road as far as conversation this evening. Do you want to go home and do something else?"

"Something other than talk?"

"Yes."

My cheeks warmed at his suggestion. "You have a dirty mind."

"I was talking about watching Netflix."

My mouth dropped open. "You were not."

Landon's smile was mischievous. "I guess we'll have to go home and find out, huh?"

I looked away from him.

"Come on." He held out his hand. "I'll get the check. Let's put this day behind us and focus on tomorrow. It's a new day ... and we're both going to have a lot of work to do."

"That sounds like a plan."

FIVE

To prove a point, Landon turned on Netflix the second we got home. I changed into comfortable knit pants and a T-shirt and found him on the couch rather than in bed.

"Are we seriously watching television?"

Landon shifted his eyes to me. He was dressed in boxer shorts and a T-shirt, clearly opting for comfort. He lifted the blanket so I could snuggle next to him. "It's not even nine yet. We'll see where the night takes us."

"This is kind of domestic," I noted as I rolled onto the couch next to him.

Landon tucked the blanket around us as we got comfortable. "That's the whole point of living together, isn't it?"

"I thought it was so we could be wild and crazy."

"Do you want to be wild and crazy?"

I shrugged. "I don't know. I thought you wanted to be wild and crazy."

"What I want is for you to take a breath," Landon countered. "You've had a long day. I thought maybe we could talk about a few things."

Instantly my antenna went up. "What things? Oh, man. Are you going to lecture me about my reaction to Melanie Adams? If so, I don't want to hear it. I already know I'm being a baby. We don't have to talk about it."

"Melanie Adams is the least of my worries. You'll do the right thing where she's concerned."

"What makes you say that?"

"You're a good person. That means you want to be good to Chief Terry. You love him. You'll get over it."

"Maybe I don't want to get over it," I grumbled as I pressed my face into the hollow between his chin and neck. "Maybe, just this once, I want to pull an Aunt Tillie and get my way no matter what."

"You're not Aunt Tillie."

"I could be."

"You're not."

"Now I think you're arguing just to argue."

"I was going to say the same about you." He pressed a firm kiss to my forehead. "Either way, I want to talk about the necromancy stuff." He muted the television, although he left *Santa Clarita Diet* running in the background. "What do you know about what you can do?"

"What do you mean?"

"I mean, what do you know about what you can do?" he repeated. "When we met, you could talk to ghosts. You could see them. No one else could see them, but when Clove and Thistle spent enough time around you they could hear them. I got used to that."

"You know as much as I do."

"Yeah. I've been giving it some thought."

That didn't sound good. "You're worried."

"I'm ... trying to be cautious," he clarified, choosing his words carefully. "The most important thing to me is keeping you safe. I don't have a problem with what you can do. I think it's going to be helpful with investigations, and because you're always knee-deep in stuff you shouldn't stick your nose in, that's another layer of protection.

"The thing is, you were good at hiding what you could do before things shifted," he continued. "I knew your secret, but that's because we couldn't have a strong relationship otherwise. Chief Terry knows, but he's trustworthy. You had to develop the perfect way to protect yourself. There was a lot of trial and error. You had a system. We need a new system."

He was so earnest, so serious, I couldn't disregard his feelings. Instead, I propped myself on my elbow and stared hard into his eyes. "What do you think I should do?"

"Well, for starters, I think you're going to get a handle on this and control it in such a way that exposure won't happen," he said. "I think you're strong ... and smart ... and powerful."

"Oh, geez!"

"Don't roll your eyes. I mean that."

"What aren't you saying?"

"Your emotions are at the surface because you're afraid you can't control this," Landon replied without hesitation. "You're doubting yourself."

"I can't help it," I admitted. "I'm afraid. It's not just me I could hurt if this comes out. I could hurt my family ... and you ... and Chief Terry."

"You won't. I have faith."

"Fine." I growled as I pressed my cheek against his chest. "I'm going to control everything. I'm going to turn myself into a super witch and everything will be perfect."

"You *are* a super witch."

"I don't feel super."

"Well, that's why we're going to work on this together." He ran his hand over my hair. "Starting now. We haven't seen Hopper since this afternoon. I'm guessing that means you haven't called him. I want you to try now."

"Try what?"

"Calling him."

"Why?"

"Because I want to see if you can do it on purpose. After that, I want to see if you can make it so I can't see him when you're talking. I think it's neat to talk to him, but the most important thing to worry about right now is control. So, one step at a time. Call him."

I shook my head as I considered his request. "Fine. If he never leaves again once I call him, I'll blame you."

"I'm fine with that."

"You might feel differently if he watches us in the bedroom."

"I'm fine performing in front of others."

He didn't mean it, but that was hardly fueling his worry. "Okay." I forced myself to a sitting position and rubbed my forehead. "Here we go."

Landon rubbed soothing circles on my back as I screwed my eyes shut and tapped into the magic bubbling under the surface. It was there, coiled and ready. In recent weeks I'd felt it growing ... and was terrified at the power I touched whenever I gathered the courage to engage.

"Mike, it's time to have a conversation."

Nothing sizzled, so I knew it didn't work.

"Mike, we need to speak to you."

Still nothing. My irritation ratcheted up a notch.

"Mike!"

This time the magic fired and something of a flash moved through me — I was certain Landon couldn't see it, but I felt it — and when I opened my eyes I found Hopper's ghostly countenance staring at me.

"You bellowed?" he asked dryly.

When I risked a glance at Landon I found him staring. "Can you see him?"

He nodded. "I can. I also ... felt something. I don't know how to explain it."

"You felt something?"

"When you focused. I felt it. It was like my body was reacting to a loud noise, except I didn't hear a loud noise."

Huh. "I felt a flash."

"That's a good way to describe it."

"I guess I'm going to have to make sure other people can't feel the flash."

"That's probably a good idea, but it's not the most important thing right now," Landon countered. "I was watching you, waiting for something to happen. Most others wouldn't be in the same situation."

"Good point." I licked my lips as I regarded Hopper. "Where did you go? You disappeared once we left your house. Did you go somewhere specific?"

"Actually, I sort of faded away," Mike replied, making a big show of settling his lanky frame in one of the chairs across the way. He was a ghost who didn't need to sit, but he seemed big on retaining his mannerisms from life. I'd seen similar ghostly responses before, but his control was interesting. "I didn't go anywhere."

"Did you wake up on your own?" Landon asked.

"No. I was gone and then suddenly back when I heard Bay calling."

"Well, that's interesting." Landon rolled his neck as he stared at the ghost. "How does it usually work with ghosts, Bay? I mean ... do they fade in and out of existence like Mike did?"

"Yeah. It's harder for new ghosts to control their surroundings. In fact, when they first wake up, they're weak. They grow stronger with time. It's different for every ghost, but Mike is stronger than most new ghosts I've run across. He managed to hang out a lot longer than any other new ghost I've come into contact with."

"Did you do that voluntarily, Mike?"

Hopper shrugged. "I don't feel as if I have control over much of anything, if you want to know the truth."

"Which means Bay kept you here," Landon mused. "She called you, even though she's not sure how. She kept you here. She's the one providing the power."

"I think I would know if I was providing power," I argued.

"I think you're too freaked to focus on that part of it yet." Landon shifted so he was sitting. "Okay, so we've ascertained that Bay can call you to her when she wants. Now I want to see if she can hide you."

"Hide me?" Hopper made a face. "What fun is that? That means I'll only be able to talk to her."

"And Aunt Tillie," I added. "She can see and talk to ghosts, too."

"Ah, that's interesting." Hopper brightened considerably. "I've only talked to her once or twice, and she was always eager to get away from me. She said she thought psychiatrists were quacks. I explained I was a therapist, not a psychiatrist, but she didn't see a difference. I think she would make a fascinating case study."

"And if I can't get rid of you later I'm going to suggest that you spend the evening haunting her," I said. "For now, Landon merely wants to see if I can control who sees you. That will come in handy if I need to see a ghost in front of the wrong person."

"Like Margaret Little?"

I bobbed my head. "Exactly. She would crap kittens if she realized I was calling ghosts."

"You have such a wonderful way with vivid language, Sweetie," Landon teased. "Crapping kittens is really the most sought-after crapping ability."

I shot him a look. "You're feeling full of yourself tonight."

"Merely trying to lighten the mood." He kept his hand on my back. "See if you can make Mike disappear for me but stay for you."

I pursed my lips and nodded. "Okay." I closed my eyes again, sucked in a breath and searched for the flash I knew was hidden inside me. It took me a few seconds to find it, but when I did I seemed to instinctively know what to do. I tugged on one of the strings trailing behind the flash, focused hard on the outcome I wanted, and when I opened my eyes I found the chair where Hopper had been sitting empty. "Huh."

"He's gone," Landon noted.

"Yeah. I can't see him either."

"Well, that's not exactly a bad thing. That means that in a pinch you can send a ghost away to avoid detection. It would be easier if you could make it so only you can see the ghost, but small steps. I ... ." He didn't get a chance to finish because the front door of the guesthouse burst open.

Landon's instincts kicked into gear and he moved to shove me behind him so he could serve as a sort of shield, but it wasn't necessary. The intruders were family ... but that didn't mean I was happy to see them.

"Clove." I shot her a dirty look. "You don't live here any longer. You're supposed to knock when entering."

My cousin Clove, her long dark hair wild and flowing around her shoulders, pulled up short at my greeting. "Oh, right." She turned on her heel and marched out the door, dragging her fiancé Sam Cornell with her. "I'll be right back."

"Oh, you don't have to knock now," I called after her.

"No, no. Etiquette demands I knock." She shut the door and applied three hard raps. "It's Clove. I have news. Can I come in?"

I exchanged a look with Landon and found him amused. "This isn't funny."

"It's kind of funny," he countered, clearing his throat. "Come in."

Clove's smile was so wide it almost swallowed her entire face when she crossed the threshold a second time. "Hello, Landon. Bay! I'm so happy to see you this fine evening."

I rolled my eyes. "And we're thrilled to see you. It's a pip of an evening, isn't it?"

"It definitely is," Clove agreed. This time the smile she offered was legitimate. "So ... I have some news."

Given the buildup, only one thing popped into my head. "Are you pregnant?"

She scowled. "No, but I'm not going to wear these pants again if you think that's a possibility."

I had no idea what else she could be so excited about. "Then ... what is it?"

"We've set a date."

"For what?"

"The wedding. Duh!"

"Oh." I caught up quickly. "That's great." I meant it. Clove was so excited for her wedding she practically floated around in a bubble most of the time. "When is the big day?"

"June eleventh."

I stilled. "That's so soon."

"Not that soon," Clove countered. "It's four months away. That gives us plenty of time to plan."

"Right." For some reason, I thought she would wait a bit longer. That seemed ridiculous in hindsight. Clove and Sam had been engaged for months. Clove was excited to get married, more excited than anyone I'd ever met. Of course she wanted it to be sooner rather than later. "Why'd you pick the eleventh?"

"It's a Saturday and we wanted to get married in the summer. I thought about waiting until August, but it's always so humid then."

"Well, June eleventh." I rolled my neck. "I think that's a good day. We'll have to start making plans, having regular meetings with everyone. Four months seems like a long time, but it's really not that far out."

"No. It's soon, and it will come faster than you think. I'm so excited." Clove clapped her hands as she hopped up and down. "I can't believe I'm going to be a married lady in a few months. It's unbelievable."

I returned her smile. "It is unbelievable."

"And clearly a cause for concern for your cousin," Hopper announced, popping into existence behind Clove and causing her to squeal as she scrambled to get away from him. "This is very interesting. Why aren't you excited about your cousin's big day, Bay?"

"What is that?" Sam asked, shoving Clove behind him as he worked to protect her. His face had gone ashen. "Is that a ... ghost?" That seemed a strange question from him because he'd been known to see a spirit or two since joining us in Hemlock Cove. His mother was a witch, and she passed the ability on to him. Of course, he wasn't expecting a ghost. The idea of seeing one could jar anybody.

I nodded as I pursed my lips. "It's Dr. Hopper. He was murdered last night."

"The radio guy?" Clove peered out from behind Sam, her curiosity overruling her fear. "He has a lot of insight into relationships and stuff, right?"

"So he says."

"I'm a professional," Hopper agreed, beaming at Clove. "You'll make a lovely bride."

"I know." Clove, over her fear, planted herself on the arm of the chair in which Hopper sat. "Why do you think Bay isn't happy for me?"

"I didn't say she wasn't happy for you," Hopper clarified. "I said she seemed concerned. She's a bit conflicted. I think that's the best word to describe her feelings. I'm not sure why, but I look forward to getting to the bottom of the mystery."

I ran my tongue over my lips as I spared a glance for Landon. "I definitely need to figure a way to make him invisible to others."

Landon smirked. "You'll figure it out."

Clove ignored our conversation. "So, do you do pre-marital work-shops? I think it might do Sam and me some good to go over a few things before the big day. I mean, we already live together and every-thing, so there are no surprises. I was reading in Bride magazine that you should always have pre-marital counseling."

"Oh, good grief!" Sam wrinkled his nose. "You want us to get counseling from a ghost?"

"He's Dr. Lovelorn," Clove argued. "They wouldn't let him on the radio if he didn't know what he was talking about."

Sam pinned me with a dark look. "Did you hear that? I'm going to get counseling from a ghost."

"Don't blame me." I was defiant. "I'm suddenly doubly magical and have no idea how to fix anything. You're on your own."

"Well, great." He rubbed the back of his neck. "This is going to go badly. I can just feel it."

He wasn't the only one.

SIX

I slept hard.

Despite the excitement of the previous evening — and Clove's insistence on Dr. Lovelorn (she preferred referring to him by his radio name) examining her relationship with Sam — we managed to turn in before midnight. Landon had to force Clove out of the guesthouse, ultimately suggesting they take Hopper with them. Sam wasn't happy about the turn of events, but we were free, so I considered it a win.

We tumbled into bed, curled together, and I was out minutes after my head hit the pillow. When I woke, it was with clear eyes and a new resolve.

"What are you thinking?" Landon asked, running his fingers through my hair to order the chaos.

"I'm thinking that you were right."

"I'm always right."

I smirked. "About my new powers."

"I was definitely right about that. We'll work together to get things under control. You got a good start last night."

"Yeah." I shifted so I could stare into his deep blue eyes. "Why are you so calm about this?"

"Because you're magical and I've known that almost from the start. Sure, that very first day I thought you were simply a cute woman with a big mouth. But I knew you were different even then. There was something otherworldly about you, which is why I couldn't stay away."

"That's kind of schmaltzy."

"I'm a schmaltzy guy."

I chuckled when he tickled my ribs before giving me a long hug. "I think I'll be able to figure things out."

"I know you'll figure it out. You might not believe this, but you're a pretty good witch."

"Yeah, well, I think I need to talk to the big witch if I expect to work things out sooner rather than later."

Landon's fingers, which were moving in a lazy circular pattern over the back of my neck, stilled. "You want to talk to Aunt Tillie about this?" He seemed surprised. "I thought you turned her down when she offered to help you before."

"I turned her down because she wanted me to practice my new abilities on Mrs. Little. She thought that would be a safe place to start, to say nothing about the possibility of Mrs. Little being locked up when people accused her of being crazy because she was seeing ghosts."

"Ah."

"This time I'm going to tell her how things are going to be. I'm going to be the boss." When Landon didn't immediately comment, I lifted my chin to study his face. He appeared calm, but his lips were pressed together, and I didn't miss the hint of mirth in his eyes. "What?"

"While I admire your attitude this morning, I think you'll be disappointed if you walk into the inn and start ordering Aunt Tillie around. She won't do what you want if you bark orders."

That was rich coming from the king of barking orders. "I'm not going to bark orders. I'm going to ask nicely."

"I think you should try bribing her."

My eyebrows flew up my forehead. "What?"

"I'm serious. Aunt Tillie seems to work best when there's something in it for her."

"There *is* something in it for her. She'll be helping a family member."

"She'll want more than that."

Sadly, he was probably right. "It can't hurt to ask nicely," I hedged.

"No. But when that doesn't work we'll put our heads together and bribe her."

"That sounds like a plan."

IT WAS EARLY IN the week, which meant The Overlook was mostly devoid of guests. Still, the dining room buzzed with energy when we finally found everyone grouped together. The family living quarters and kitchen were empty — making me wonder if the apocalypse had finally begun — but the voices on the other side of the swinging door told me something else was going on.

"I was thinking we could get married in the garden here," Clove supplied, a magazine open on the table in front of her. Mom, Marnie and Twila grouped around and stared over her shoulder as she tapped a page in the periodical. "Wouldn't something like this be perfect?"

"That is lovely," Marnie agreed, her hand on Clove's shoulder. She looked thrilled about her only daughter's upcoming nuptials. "You can even put flowers in your hair. It will be beautiful."

Aunt Tillie snorted from her spot at the head of the table. "If she wears flowers in her hair she'll end up with bees up her nose."

"She will not," Marnie fired back, her eyes flashing. "Stop being a pain."

Hmm. That was interesting. "Why are you being a pain?" I asked as I crossed behind Aunt Tillie and took my usual spot at the table, allowing Landon to sit at my left and Aunt Tillie's right. "Why aren't you looking at the magazine with everybody else?"

"Why aren't you?" Aunt Tillie shot back.

"We just got here," Landon reminded her. "I'm more interested in breakfast ... where is the food?" He looked lost when he realized there was no bacon to munch on.

"Once Clove got here food preparations ceased," Aunt Tillie replied. "It's been an hour of 'look at those flowers' and 'I think you should wear a tiara and go sleeveless.'" Aunt Tillie's wrinkled nose told me exactly what she thought of those suggestions. "No one cares that I'm old and starving to death."

Aunt Tillie only referred to herself as "old" when she was feeling whiny.

"So, your nose is out of joint because everyone has forgotten about you this morning." I surmised.

"Of course not."

"That's exactly what's wrong with her," Mom snapped. "That's why we're ignoring her."

"I get ignoring her," Landon interjected. "Why are you ignoring me? Where is the bacon?"

Mom let loose a long-suffering sigh, one she'd perfected to the point it caused a shiver to run down my spine. "I will get your bacon, Landon. I would hate for you to have to wait."

Landon smiled. "I'm willing to get my own bacon. Tell me where it is."

Mom studied him for a moment. "It's warming in the oven. Don't eat the entire pan."

"I'm on it." Landon happily hopped to his feet. He pressed a hand to my shoulder when I moved to follow. "Stay here and talk to Aunt Tillie. I'll be back in a minute."

I knew exactly what he wanted me to talk to Aunt Tillie about, and suddenly I was nervous. "Okay." I forced a smile for his benefit and waited until he was out of the room to focus on my great-aunt. "So ... how's life?"

"It sucks," Aunt Tillie replied. "I want to buy a pet pig, but your mother and her sisters have vetoed it. Can you believe that?"

There was very little about life at The Overlook that I couldn't believe. "Why do you want a pig?"

"They make fabulous sidekicks and they're cleaner than dogs."

"And why won't you let her have a pig?" I asked Mom.

"Because she won't take care of it and they need room to move around. We have the room, but no one to watch it."

"Yeah, but ... with a pig you might eliminate the inn's food waste," I pointed out. "They're garbage disposals. They're also supposed to be smart. I don't necessarily think a pig is that big a deal."

"Are you going to help her take care of it?" Mom challenged.

Ugh. I should've expected that question. "Maybe," I hedged, sliding my eyes to Aunt Tillie. "Let me think about it."

"Well, then think about it." Mom promptly turned back to Clove's wedding plans and forgot I was in the room.

"You seem agitated," Aunt Tillie said after a beat, tilting her head to the side. "You don't have to be worked up about the pig. I'm getting that pig whether they say I can or not. I'm an adult. I have rights."

I wasn't worried about the pig in the least. "I need your help," I admitted, tamping down my worry and forcing myself to do the unthinkable and ask for a favor. "I'm having trouble with the necromancer stuff. It's not as easy as I thought it would be."

Aunt Tillie snorted. "You never thought it would be easy," she countered. "You simply wanted to pretend it wasn't happening for a bit. You were overwhelmed, and like you always do when things get too hard, you took a step back and pretended nothing had changed. That's your normal way of dealing with things."

I wasn't a fan of her tone ... or words ... or the fact that she had a point. "I used ghosts to kill a guy. Actually, he was more of a kid than a man. I needed time to settle."

"He was a murderer who couldn't be helped," Aunt Tillie corrected. "But I get what you're saying. The truth is, this isn't a big change. It's not a shift in powers. It's an addition."

"Does that make it better?"

Aunt Tillie shrugged. "I think it's better. In fact, I think it's kind of cool. Do you think you can raise the ghost of a really annoying person — think those big booty girls on television who are only famous for being in sex videos and having bad taste in men — and send her over to haunt Margaret Little? I think that would be a great way to test your powers."

When Aunt Tillie found a topic she enjoyed, she rarely let it go.

"I think I'll pass on that right now. I'm dealing with another ghost." I told her about Mike Hopper, and what had happened in the hours surrounding his death. "So, apparently I'm calling to ghosts without realizing it," I finished. "That can't be normal, right?"

Aunt Tillie pursed her lips. "I don't know about it being normal. It is cool. Do you think you can do that haunted voice thing to scare Margaret?"

"No! Forget about Mrs. Little!"

"Don't take that tone with me." Aunt Tillie extended a warning finger. "I'm trying to help."

"You're trying to drive me crazy."

"Actually, that's only a side benefit." She cocked her head as she absently scratched at her cheek. "The truth is, I don't know how to help you." Her tone was low, serious. "To my knowledge, we've never had a necromancer in the family. Do you know how rare necromancers are?"

"No." I shifted on my chair, uncomfortable. "If we've never had a necromancer in the family before, why is this happening to me?"

"You're special."

"That's just a lame way of saying that you have no idea why this happened."

"I believe I already said that ... and I'm never lame." Aunt Tillie fixed me with a pointed look. "We'll figure it out. You can't turn into a spaz if you expect us to solve your little problem. That's not how this works. We need to be calm and regal. That's how Winchesters roll."

I gestured toward her shirt, which sported huge alien heads where her boobs would be if they hadn't sagged over the years. "That's regal?"

"I want the aliens to know I'm open to suggestions when they land," she said. "I know you think the government really did crash a drone in that field a few weeks ago, but I know otherwise. It was aliens."

Oh, geez. "I can't talk about the aliens. It gives me a headache."

"Fine. We'll talk about something else. You're clearly worked up this morning, and it's not entirely about the necromancy thing. Something else is going on. Why are you so out of sorts?"

The question caught me off guard. "Isn't controlling the dead enough to worry about for one day?"

"You would think, but I'm a great multi-tasker," she drawled. "Your nose is out of joint. I don't like it."

Landon picked that moment to swing back into the room, his arms laden with platters of food. "I've got bacon ... hash browns ... eggs ... and sausage links."

Mom spared him a glance. "You forgot the toast."

"I only have two arms."

"Fine. I'll get the toast." Mom winked at him before disappearing into the kitchen. "I would hate for you to do without for five minutes. You might die of starvation or something."

"How did your talk go?" Landon asked as he returned to his chair. He'd conveniently placed the bacon platter directly in front of us, so I knew his mind would be otherwise engaged in exactly thirty seconds. "Is Aunt Tillie going to help you?"

"She doesn't think there's anything to worry about," I replied. "She thinks I should send annoying ghosts to haunt Mrs. Little."

"That could be fun." He patted my knee under the table. "I've been telling you for weeks that there's nothing to get worked up about."

That was easy for him to say. He hadn't killed a man by wielding the souls of tormented dead girls as a heavy sword. "Yeah, well ... ."

"She's upset about more than her growing powers," Aunt Tillie noted, refusing to let it go. "She's all ... flustered. There's something else on her mind."

"Oh, that." Landon scooped eggs onto his plate, seemingly oblivious to the silent warning I was trying to send his way with my eyes. "She's angry because Chief Terry has a new girlfriend and it's not Winnie. Bay had big plans to control his dating life around Christmas, but it didn't work out in her favor."

My eyes flew to the swinging door, where my mother stood with a platter of toast in her hand. The look on her face told me she'd heard what Landon said ... and she wasn't any happier about the development than me.

"What?" The single-word question came out as a strangled cry.

"Oh, man." Landon realized far too late that he'd stuck his foot in his mouth. It wasn't unheard of for him to stay something stupid. In this family, those with Winchester genes usually jumped to the front of the line when it came to saying insensitive things. "I'm sorry. I ... ." He looked to me for help and found me scowling. "I'll be the one paying for having a big mouth tonight, won't I?"

I nodded without hesitation. "You have no idea."

"Wait ... Terry is dating?" Marnie abandoned interest in her daughter's wedding and straightened her shoulders. "Is this a joke?"

I felt sick to my stomach. My mother and aunts had been vying for Chief Terry's affection for so long I couldn't remember another way of life. For them to find out this way seemed cruel. "He's dating the woman who owns that yoga studio out on the highway."

"Melanie Adams?" Clove leaned forward, curious. "She's come into the store a few times. She seems nice. I didn't know Chief Terry was dating her."

"I just found out yesterday," I muttered, staring at my empty plate.

Landon, uncomfortable with the heavy silence that slid over the room, cleared his throat. "She seems pleasant, engaging. I'm sure everybody will like her."

Aunt Tillie made a derisive sound in the back of her throat. "You're not very smart, are you, Sparky?"

Landon glared at her. "You're not helping."

"I don't want to help you. You're the one who stuck your big foot in your big mouth. I think you should have to clean up your mess for a change."

"I didn't mean to do this," Landon groused. "You brought up Bay being pouty. I was merely explaining why she was in a bad mood."

"I'm not in a bad mood!" I snapped.

Aunt Tillie ignored my outburst. "Honestly? I didn't know about the Terry situation, but that's clearly part of the reason she's moping. I simply thought she was upset about Clove getting married."

"Why would she be upset about Clove getting married?" Landon challenged. "Clove has been engaged for months. This is hardly news."

"No, but when they were engaged without a wedding date there was still a chance for Bay to be first."

"First to do what?" Landon queried, grabbing a slice of bacon.

"First to get married," Aunt Tillie replied matter-of-factly, causing my stomach to twist. "She's the oldest. She should marry first. Clove is going to make sure that doesn't happen. It's no wonder Bay is embarrassed. She's turning into a spinster."

I slapped my hand to my forehead and sank lower in my chair, refusing to look at Landon because I knew what expression I would find waiting for me on his chiseled face. "I can't believe you just said that," I muttered. "I am not jealous."

"Of course not." Aunt Tillie pretended I wasn't close to melting down and grabbed a handful of bacon, refusing to use the provided tongs. "You want Clove to be happy. You're simply sad that you're being left behind."

"I'm not being left behind."

"Of course you're not. But you feel that way. Between Clove setting a date, Terry moving on with someone you don't approve of and you being able to control the dead, you're having quite the month."

I wanted to crawl into a hole and die. Or at least run back to the guesthouse so I could go to bed and pretend this morning had never happened. "I've had better months," I admitted finally. "But I'm not jealous of Clove." Finally, I summoned the courage to look at Landon and found him watching me with narrow-eyed speculation. "She's making that up. Chief Terry dating the pretzel chick and controlling the dead are more than enough for me to worry about right now."

"Sure." Landon didn't look convinced. "Have some breakfast." He tipped half the bacon pile from his plate to mine. "We have a lot to do today. You'll need some energy."

He sounded odd, as if lost in thought. "Okay. Energy sounds good."

"Energy sounds great," Aunt Tillie agreed, smiling. "So ... given the fact that everyone is stunned into silence and no longer wants to talk, I think now is the time to make plans for my pig. I'm going to name it Peg. Peg the pig. Get it? Plus, Peg is short for Margaret. It's an insult wrapped in a cute package. Oh, and I'm going to buy it a hat."

SEVEN

I'd left my car at The Whistler the previous night, so Landon dropped me at the office before heading to the police station. He said he would be working with Chief Terry all day and to call if Hopper showed up with any insight about his murder. He conveniently ignored Aunt Tillie's statement about my jealousy regarding Clove's wedding. I was thankful for that.

I wasn't jealous Clove was marrying before me. That was ludicrous. When she'd first announced her engagement, I figured they would wait to get married. Apparently I was wrong. Sam and Clove had been on an accelerated timetable since they started dating. I shouldn't have been surprised that she was in a hurry to marry. Still, her announcement the previous evening had been unexpected. I wasn't sure why.

I spent two hours working in the office, waiting until Stella showed up to take over the spring festival edition ads for the first time without supervision. I told her to use her best judgment, and if anything was over-sexualized or seemed stalkerish to hold off booking until she checked with me. Stella was happy for extra money, however she earned it, so she merely nodded and waved as I left the building. Even though the ads were a moneymaking endeavor, I had other things to focus on ... like Mike Hopper and his murder. That clearly took priority.

I headed toward Hopper's house. I walked because the sun was out and it felt like a nice day. It wasn't exactly warm, but it wasn't frigid. It felt as if spring was just around the corner, and I couldn't wait. As much as I loved three of Michigan's seasons, winter was always a bummer, thanks to longer nights and endless snow.

It took me ten minutes to walk to the house. The front door was closed off with police tape, although there were no official vehicles on the premises. That was a relief because I was in no mood to run into Chief Terry — I just knew he would want to talk about his date — and giving Landon an opening to ask if Aunt Tillie was right about my jealousy issues seemed a poor way to start the day.

Instead, I marched straight to Esther's house and knocked on the door. She was retired, which meant she spent an inordinate amount of time at home. Given the way she watched the action the previous day, I knew she was interested in the investigation and I was hopeful that meant she could provide gossip for me to move on.

It took Esther almost two minutes to open the door. She wore a housecoat and plaid slippers, and her short gray hair was wrapped around plastic curlers that had to date to the eighties. "What do you want?"

I plastered a fake smile on my face. "Good morning, Esther. I don't know if you remember me, but ... ."

"You're Tillie Winchester's great-niece," Esther supplied. "You're the one who owns the newspaper. Not the ones who own the magic shop. That means I like you better than the devil worshippers."

I cocked an eyebrow. "I hardly think Clove and Thistle are devil worshippers."

"That one with the purple hair looks like a devil worshipper. I watch television. I know what they look like."

"Her hair is more of a deep red than purple."

"Red is the color of the devil."

I pursed my lips as I changed tactics. "You're right. She could totally be a devil worshipper. I'll have a serious discussion about her allegiance to the Dark One the very next time I see her. That's not really why I'm here, though."

"I know why you're here." To my utter surprise, Esther pushed open the door and turned on her heel. I remained rooted to my spot, confused about whether she wanted me to follow. "Come on, girl. You're letting all the warm air out. I can't afford to heat the neighborhood."

"Right." I hurried inside, making sure to shut the door tightly before following the woman toward the kitchen. She was already at the counter pouring tea when I caught up to her. "I wasn't sure if you would be willing to talk to me."

"Why wouldn't I? You provide an important service. Newspapers are necessary for a healthy society. People don't realize that. They won't until most of the newspapers are gone. I want to help if I can. And, as far as I can tell, you're not a devil worshipper. That gives you a leg up on that cousin of yours."

"Thistle isn't so bad."

"She's not good either. But you're not here to talk about her." Esther carried two mugs of tea to the table and sat across from me. "You want to know about the doctor."

I bobbed my head in confirmation. "I do. What can you tell me about him?"

"He was a sick man."

"Like ... dying?"

"Like perverted."

"Huh." I sipped my tea, which was unsweetened and strong, as I debated the statement. "How was he a pervert?" I asked finally.

"He was talking to people about sex."

Of course. I should've seen that coming. "I believe he was talking to them about relationship issues," I clarified. "I'm sure that sex came up because that's a natural and healthy part of relationships, but I don't believe he was talking about sex simply to talk about sex."

Esther's expression was withering. "Sex is for procreation, not recreation."

"Good point." The conversation was making me uncomfortable.

There was very little chance Esther was going to come around to my way of thinking, and I knew for a fact I would never cross over to her narrow view of the world. I had to turn the conversation in another direction. "What can you tell me about the man, though? I mean ... I understand he had clients visiting. He also produced his radio show in the basement. He must have had frequent visitors."

"He had visitors all hours of the night," Esther confirmed. "It started in the morning. He had people show up at his door — mostly couples — and they would disappear inside for an hour. Most of the time, when they came back out, they were shouting and screaming at one another. It seems to me that he wasn't a very good doctor."

That was interesting. "So, you're saying that Dr. Hopper made things worse?"

"He wasn't making things better. In fact, I think more of his couples broke up than stayed together."

"What makes you say that?"

"I have eyes and ears."

"What else makes you say that?"

"Most of the couples who visited came only a few times and never returned. That says to me that he was failing."

"Or succeeding," I pointed out. I wasn't looking for a fight but it seemed unfair not to mention the other possible conclusion. "Maybe he managed to help these couples so they didn't need to return."

"I doubt very much that's the case."

"Fair enough. Do you know who he was seeing recently? My understanding is that he only took on a handful of clients at a time so he could do intensive workshops with them over multiple sessions. That means the turnover must've been pretty high."

"I don't know who he was seeing. It's not my business to spy on my neighbors and gossip."

"Of course not."

"I did see Brad and Helen Dickens here two weeks ago," she volunteered. "They came out of the house sniping at one another. Helen was angry because Brad preferred ice fishing to spending time with her, and Brad thinks Helen has a shopping addiction and that's why she buys all of those crazy-looking dolls."

I had to bite the inside of my cheek to keep from laughing at Esther's version of not gossiping. "That doesn't exactly sound like the stuff of murder."

"No," Esther agreed. "If you're looking for someone who might've had murder on the mind, I suggest you consider Maxine and Jonathan Wheeler. They've been seeing the doc for about four weeks, and every single time they visited they left hating each other more than when they arrived.

"I mean, last week, for example," she continued, warming to her story. "They were relatively quiet when they entered. I was watching through the window because I thought I heard a rapist in my garden, not because I'm a busybody or anything. I want you to know that."

"I would never think you're a busybody," I lied. "You're just looking out for the neighborhood."

"Exactly," she nodded. "Anyway, they were quiet going in and absolutely screaming at each other on their way out. Jonathan yelled that he hoped she died a painful death ... and then he threatened the doctor that if he ever saw him again he would rip his nuts off and feed them to him."

Alarm bells dinged in the back of my mind. "He threatened to kill Dr. Hopper?"

"I don't know that ripping a guy's nuts off would kill him, but it would hurt something fierce."

My mind was busy. "Did Jonathan and Maxine ever return for more counseling?"

"I don't spy."

"I know. While you were watching the neighborhood for evildoers, though, did you see them come back?"

"Maxine did."

"When?"

"She's been back multiple times. I haven't seen Jonathan again."

That didn't necessarily mean anything, I reminded myself, but it was a place to start. "Thanks for your time, Esther. I'll be in touch if I need more information."

THE WHEELERS LIVED in a colonial on the east side of town. The homes there were nice, well taken care of, with beautiful landscaping when it was warm enough to bloom. Given the bare trees, there was something stark about the neighborhood now.

I parked in the driveway and knocked on the door. I wasn't sure exactly how I intended to approach the couple, who I only knew sparingly from festivals and meetings, but all thoughts of a soft approach fled when Maxine opened the door and I heard Jonathan screaming from another room.

"Stop telling me what to do!"

Maxine's expression was bright when she focused on me. "Hello, Bay. What a nice surprise."

She seemed normal. That should've calmed my nerves. Instead, Jonathan's bellowing from inside the house only set my teeth on edge.

"I hope you die, Maxine! I hope it hurts, too. I hope you fall off a bridge, get eaten by crocodiles, thrown up and then set on fire."

That was a level of vitriol I'd never witnessed. "If this is a bad time ... ," I hedged.

"It's not a bad time." Maxine's voice was smooth as she held open the door. "I love visitors."

Jonathan appeared in the hallway, poking his head around the corner to see who dared darken his doorstep and interrupt his fit. When he saw it was me, he lost interest quickly. "She loves visitors of the male persuasion," he countered. "She loves visitors when she can get on her back and open her ... ."

I held up my hand to stop him. "This is obviously a bad time."

"It's a bad marriage," Maxine corrected, her hand going to my elbow as she tugged me toward the kitchen. "Ignore him. He's packing to move out. Apparently he can't do it with his mouth shut."

"He's moving out?" I was interested despite myself. "Why?"

"Because he's a jerk."

"Because she's a whore," Jonathan corrected, proving he was listening to the conversation even though he was in a different room. "I'm leaving because she's a whore and she broke our marriage vows."

This was a toxic situation. "I'm sorry to hear that." I didn't know what else to say. "That's terrible."

"It's not so bad," Maxine countered, heading for the coffee pot on the counter. "It's better to have loved and lost than ... however the rest of that saying goes."

"I've got a saying for you," Jonathan said, appearing in the open doorway. "Once a whore, always a whore. My mother told me I shouldn't have married you after she caught us in the car that one night. I never told you that, but she was adamant that I would live to regret it. I guess she was right."

"Your mother is a narcoleptic dipsomaniac. Like I care what she says."

"My mother is a saint!"

"Your mother gets drunk and talks to the house plants," Maxine shot back. "She thinks they talk back to her."

"They could talk back to her."

"Ugh. I'm done talking to you." She held up a hand to quiet her husband and focused on me. "Let's talk about you, Bay. Are you here for a specific reason?"

I swallowed hard and nodded. "I'm here about Dr. Hopper."

Jonathan was back, whatever he was doing in the other room abandoned, his eyes keen as they locked with mine. "How dare you mention that man's name in my house?"

"It's not your house for much longer," Maxine snapped. "As for Mike, I'm always happy to talk about his therapy skills. Are you and that boyfriend of yours having trouble?"

I shook my head. "No. I'm here to talk to you about his death."

"Whose death?"

"Dr. Hopper's death."

Maxine's face crumbled as she absorbed my words, her hands clasping together. "What?"

"I'm so sorry," I said hurriedly, horrified. "I thought you knew. It happened yesterday. News spreads faster around this town than jam on toast. I simply assumed you knew about his death."

"Wait ... Dr. Lovelorn is dead?" Jonathan's scowl flipped upside down. "You're not messing with us, are you?"

I shook my head. "No. He was stabbed in his house."

Suddenly serene, Jonathan grinned. "Did you hear that, Maxine? Your boyfriend is dead. All that whoring you did with him was for nothing. You ruined our marriage and now he's gone. I would like to say I'm too good of a person to crow, but ... ." He made a strangled sound that I figured was supposed to mimic a rooster crowing.

"Mike can't be dead," Maxine argued, her lower lip quivering. "It's not possible. I ... he ... we ... he can't be dead."

"I'm sorry to be the one to tell you this, but he's definitely dead," I offered. "I assumed you knew. I wish I hadn't blurted it out the way I did. It's just ... I was at the house and one of the neighbors said you guys had been seeing him. I thought maybe you might have some information about his enemies."

"I'm sure that guy had more enemies than a video game hero," Jonathan said. "You should get his patient rolls and go through every name because I'm sure most of the male clients wanted him dead as much as I did."

"You probably shouldn't say that so loudly," I offered. "People might think you had something to do with it."

"I didn't kill him. That doesn't mean I'm not happy he's dead."

A sob bubbled up in Maxine's throat as she buried her face in her arms and began to cry.

"I don't think I'm following the story correctly," I said. "Why do you hate Mike so much? I mean ... I get that your marriage has fallen apart. You and Maxine clearly have issues. Why do you blame Mike?"

"Because he's the root of it. We went to him because we were fighting about whether or not we should have kids. We're divorcing because he had an affair with my wife."

Oxygen whooshed out of my lungs as I absorbed the statement. "W-what?"

"You heard me. Maxine and Dr. Lovelorn had an affair. She wasn't supposed to tell me about it — supposedly it was some sort of therapy technique — but I found out because I came home from a business trip early. Guess what I found."

I didn't have to guess. I could imagine. "So Mike told Maxine that she should have sex with him to save your marriage?"

Jonathan shook his head. "Yeah. Can you believe that? I confronted him in his office about a week ago and he didn't deny it. He claims it's a valid technique … the snake."

"I can't believe that."

"Well, Maxine believed it. She did it. Now our marriage is over and he's dead. I think the therapy worked perfectly. I'm free!"

"Wow!" I spared a glance for Maxine and found her shaking with sobs. "I don't suppose you can tell me the story from the beginning, can you? I need the full picture."

"What does it matter?' Maxine sniffed. "He's gone and the world is a poorer place for it."

"I'll tell you," Jonathan volunteered. "The guy was a jerk and I want everybody to know it. You'll put it in the newspaper. I can't think of a better revenge plan. Let me grab a beer. This might take a while."

EIGHT

J stopped at the police station on my way back to town to inform Landon and Chief Terry about my discovery.

"Are you saying that the good doctor was sleeping with his patients?" Chief Terry asked, disgust obvious.

"I'm saying that he was sleeping with Maxine," I corrected. "She didn't deny it, and Jonathan is not a happy camper. In fact, you might want to go over there and help him finish moving his stuff. I don't think he would hurt her, but that's not a healthy situation."

"Did he threaten her?" Landon asked.

I held my hands up. "Kind of."

"Did he threaten you?"

"No. He gave me all the information I needed ... and some that I didn't want because it was gross. I mean, he went into great detail about how he discovered the affair and let's just say there were furry love cuffs involved and leave it at that."

Landon's lips twitched. "That's probably smart."

"There's a lot of screaming, and Maxine is a mess. She didn't know that Hopper was dead."

"Did they have plans to be together?" Chief Terry asked. "Were they going to be a couple?"

"I don't know. I didn't ask. Maxine was too far gone to ask questions, so I focused on Jonathan. He was more interested in dancing on Hopper's grave than worrying about Maxine's future plans."

"Maxine is in her thirties, right?" Chief Terry turned thoughtful. "Hopper was in his early forties. That's not too much of an age difference. Still, according to what you've told us, it sounds like Hopper suggested the affair as a therapeutic tool. How does that even work?"

"I think he wanted to use his tool for therapy," I answered automatically, earning a stern look from Chief Terry.

"That's not funny, young lady. You know I don't like when you make bawdy jokes."

"And I don't like when you use the word 'bawdy.'"

"I happen to like it when Bay makes bawdy jokes, but we can talk about that later," Landon interjected. "I want to talk more about this Jonathan guy. Do you think he killed Hopper?"

"He seemed surprised by the news."

"That could've been an act."

I thought hard about the time I'd spent in the Wheeler house. "I guess he could've been acting," I said finally. "My gut instinct is that he wasn't. He was far too happy to hear about Hopper's death. He didn't hide his glee. If he killed Hopper and then wanted to act surprised when told about the murder, he would've feigned being upset. He was pretty far from upset."

"You can never tell how people will react in situations like this, but that's a fair point," Landon said. "I guess we'll have to question him ourselves."

"That's why I stopped by."

"Thanks for the tip." He followed me out of the office and to the lobby, ignoring Chief Terry's surly secretary and keeping a firm grip on my arm so I couldn't bolt through the door before he was ready to release me. "Are you okay?"

"I'm fine." The question caught me off guard. "Why wouldn't I be okay?"

"Just checking." He released my arm and moved his fingers to my hair so he could brush it behind my ear. "I've been thinking about you all morning. I went to the newspaper office to check on you, but the girl at the front desk said you were out. I thought about calling, but that seemed like a needy chick move, so I decided to wait.

"Then, an hour later, I talked myself into waiting a little longer," he continued. "I'm glad you were brave enough to come to me."

"Why wouldn't I? I figured that was important information you needed."

"Yes, but you're clearly embarrassed about what Aunt Tillie said at breakfast this morning."

Heat rushed to my cheeks. "I'm not jealous of Clove."

"I know. Still, if you want to talk about what Aunt Tillie said I don't think it's necessarily the worst idea in the world."

"I don't want to talk about it. I'm not jealous."

"Fair enough." He held up his hands in capitulation. "I didn't mean to upset you. There's so much going on right now I can't help but worry. You're dealing with a lot. I want you to remember that I'm here to help you no matter what has your mind churning. You're not alone."

I was ashamed to admit that my heart melted just a little bit. "I know I'm not alone. I'm dealing with everything to the best of my ability. Would it be easier for me if everyone else would stop living their lives and allow me to focus on this necromancer thing for a bit? Yes. That's not the way the world works, though. I've got to suck it up and multitask."

Landon grinned. "That's an interesting way to put it."

"Part of me is angry," I admitted. "Things were going well. They were perfect. Then I started controlling ghosts out of nowhere. Who knew that would throw our lives into upheaval the way it has?"

"Sweetie, I don't feel as if my life has been upended. To me, it's just another cool witchy thing you can do. You're the one feeling the pressure, and I get that. I want to help. I simply don't know what I can do to make things better."

"What you did last night was pretty good."

"Watch Netflix and cuddle with you? It's a tough job, but somebody has to do it. I'm willing to take one for the team."

I barked out a laugh. "I meant the exercise we did calling Mike."

"That kind of died when Clove showed up. We didn't get a chance to experiment after that. You could always call Hopper and ask him about his affair with Maxine. We could practice again."

I shifted my eyes to the busy downtown street. Even though the weather wasn't warm, the area bustled with activity. "I'd rather wait until we're alone. I'm not ready to risk doing something in public. At least not yet."

"That's a very mature decision."

"That's me. Mrs. Maturity."

Landon grinned as he planted a firm kiss on my mouth and drew me in for a long hug. "You're awesome no matter how you approach things, Bay," he whispered before kissing my cheek. "You're doing remarkably well under difficult circumstances."

"I feel a bit overwhelmed." It was hard to admit. "I'll get through it. Maybe the key is to focus on one thing at a time."

"That's a solid plan." He gave me another kiss before releasing me. "We'll head over to the Wheeler house and check on them so you don't have to worry about that situation. Keep in contact and we'll get dinner together later, okay?"

I nodded. "I already feel better. Although ... I'm grossed out about Mike sleeping with his clients. Do you think he slept with more than one of them?"

"I think that's a likely possibility."

The ick factor doubled. "Keep me updated."

"Always."

I was feeling better, light even, when I slid through the door and headed down the sidewalk. I was lost in my own little world, plans for a romantic evening that involved nothing but relaxation and maybe a bath flitting through my head, when I smacked into an unsuspecting figure that I didn't see until I was already upon it.

"I am so sorry," I sputtered as I attempted to stay on my feet. "I didn't see you."

"It's okay. I wasn't looking either."

The voice was female, and when I righted myself, the feelings from seconds before evaporated as I came face to face with Melanie Adams.

"Oh, hi." I felt like an idiot as I blinked and stared.

"Hello, Bay." Melanie's smile was warm as she looked me up and down. "It's nice to see you."

I could think of a few other words to describe our interaction. Awkward. Uncomfortable. Tense. "It's nice to see you, too," I offered, although I didn't mean it. "I'm so sorry for smacking into you that way. I didn't hurt you, did I? I was lost in my own little world and not paying attention. It's on me."

"I wasn't paying attention either," Melanie argued. "You're not the only one at fault. In fact, since neither of us is hurt there's no reason to blame anyone. No harm, no foul, right?"

I nodded. "Right."

"Good."

We lapsed into uncomfortable silence, something I was desperate to escape. "So, I should be heading back to the newspaper office," I said lamely. "I only stopped by to share information with Landon and Chief Terry."

"Do you have to go right now?"

"Well ... ."

"It's just that I was hoping we could get some coffee." She gestured toward the bakery down the street. "I've been hoping to get a chance to talk to you and this seems as good a time as any."

I had other ideas, but since she put me on the spot I figured only one answer was acceptable. "Coffee sounds great."

MRS. GUNDERSON WAS WORKING behind the counter when we entered. She waved when she saw me and gestured toward a clean table. I slid into a chair and nervously ran my hands over my knees as Melanie sat across from me.

"So, this is weird, huh?" Melanie appeared as nervous as I felt as she slipped out of her jacket. "You don't like me, do you?"

I wasn't expecting the question. "I don't know you."

"That wasn't really an answer."

"I just meant that I can't dislike someone I don't know," I said hurriedly. "I don't know you, so it's impossible to dislike you."

"Anything is possible. Also, 'like' is probably the wrong word. You're right about not knowing me. Still, I want us to be friends."

It was a simple statement, yet it irked all the same. "Why?" I blurted out. "Why do you care if I like you? I mean ... I don't dislike you. There's no reason to worry about that. You seem invested in me liking you, though, and I don't understand the reasoning."

"Really?" Melanie arched an eyebrow and shifted her hair over her shoulder. "Terry loves you."

"We're close."

"He thinks of you as a surrogate daughter," Melanie pressed. "He told me that himself, in case you're wondering. He talks about you all the time. He tells stories about when you and your cousins were little, the adventures you went on. He tells other stories about when you were teenagers and the trouble you found.

"For every three stories he tells, you're the lead in at least one of them," she continued. "Sometimes it's you and your cousins. Sometimes it's your mother and her sisters and how they reacted to something you did. Sometimes it's you and Landon. You're always there and close to the surface."

I swallowed hard. "My father left when I was a kid," I explained. "All our fathers left. They claimed it was because of Aunt Tillie ... but that's not really important. They were gone."

"My understanding is that they're back now."

"They are, and we see them."

"You're still close with Terry, though."

"He'll always be part of my life." I decided to put everything out there. There was no point in holding back. "He took care of me when I was a kid and going through some things. He was always there when we needed him.

"He got us a dog for Christmas one year, He was dressed as Santa when he did it," I continued. "He spent a lot of time with us. Aunt Tillie is a piece of work and she always dragged us with her when she was looking for trouble. Chief Terry was always there to get us out of it, make sure we knew the difference between right and wrong."

"Yes, I believe I've heard some of those stories." Melanie's smile was soft. "Something about torturing Margaret Little and having to carry all three of you through waist-high snow at the same time. He laughs when he tells the story."

"I laugh whenever I think of that story," I admitted. "Anyone else would've made us wade through the snow on our own because we were technically breaking the law."

"He's not just anyone."

"No, he's not."

Melanie sucked in a breath. "I like him a great deal, Bay. We've only been dating for a few weeks, but he's a lovely man. Did he tell you how we met?"

"He hasn't told me anything about you."

I didn't miss the quick burst of disappointment that flashed across Melanie's face. "Nothing?"

"I haven't seen much of him the past two weeks," I offered quickly. "I thought it was weird that he hadn't been around. I've been dealing with some stuff, though — Landon and I are painting and arranging offices — and I didn't think much about it. I guess he was with you."

"We met at my yoga studio," she offered. "I came into work one morning and the back door had been kicked in. There was nothing worth stealing inside. The only things missing were two yoga mats. Still, for insurance purposes, I had to file a report. He was the one who took the call.

"I thought it was odd that the police chief came out for a simple breaking and entering," she continued. "At first I thought it was because the department was so small, but then I realized he's simply the sort of man who would never ask others to complete a task he wasn't willing to take on himself."

"No," I agreed. "He wouldn't do that."

"We got to talking and he made me laugh. He's very funny, but I'm sure you already know that."

"I know."

"He didn't ask me out," Melanie continued. "I asked him. He seemed surprised when I extended the invitation. His first inclination was to say no, but something inside told me I didn't want to pass up this opportunity so I asked a second time and he said yes.

"We had coffee at the little place down the road from my studio," she said. "We talked for hours. We had a great time. He didn't ask for a second date. I did. I asked him to dinner. We went and had a wonderful time. It was only when he was dropping me off at my house after that date that he finally asked me out."

It was a sweet story, but it made me uncomfortable. "I'm not sure he would want you telling me this."

"I have every intention of telling him about our conversation," Melanie said. "He knows I want to get close to you, form a bond of sorts. He told me not to push you, but when I saw you in front of the police station I figured this was my chance. He probably won't be happy when he hears, but I'm not sorry I pushed the issue."

"I don't understand why you're so keen to get me on your side," I admitted. "Why is that important to you?"

"Because Terry loves you. I hope that one day he and I will be able to get to that point ourselves, but it'll never happen if you're throwing up roadblocks."

"Why would I do that?"

"I don't know. I could tell that seeing me with Terry last night upset you."

"It surprised me," I corrected. "I don't do well with change. It's not that I dislike you." It's that I wanted him for my family, I silently added. I couldn't tell her that. I would look petulant ... and infuriate my mother in the process if she ever found out. "I'm fine getting to know you. I want Chief Terry to be happy. He smiled all through dinner last night. You're obviously a welcome presence in his life."

"I don't want to remove him from your life, Bay," Melanie said gently. "He wouldn't allow that even if I tried. I'm not an adversary. I simply want to find a way to share him."

She sounded reasonable, which only served to bother me more. I wasn't used to reasonable people, so I stole a line from Landon's repertoire to hold her off. "We'll figure it out. I'm sure everything will be fine."

"I certainly hope so."

"We should start by getting to know one another," I suggested as Mrs. Gunderson signaled that she was bringing coffee. "Tell me about yourself. I'm dying to hear ... everything."

NINE

I wasn't exactly unsettled after coffee with Melanie. I wasn't thrilled with the turn of events either.

She was a perfectly nice woman who wanted to make Chief Terry happy. I loved him, so I wanted him happy. I simply failed to see why he couldn't be happy with someone in my family, or why I had to share.

After realizing that I was being absolutely ridiculous, I closed The Whistler office and left for the day to wallow in shame at home. I knew I was being something of a jerk, but I couldn't shake the feeling that Chief Terry had made the worst possible choice.

I texted Landon and told him I would be home early. He asked if I was sick — something I denied — and then promised to join me as soon as his schedule cleared. I had every intention of looking inward to quell my childish leanings when I hit the guesthouse. That should've involved meditating, but I was thinking of watching Netflix instead. I didn't get a chance, because a stack of photo albums on the shelf caught my attention and I couldn't stop myself from grabbing them.

I flipped through the books until I found the one I was looking for. I was barely a teenager, fourteen and still figuring out the world. I was almost thirty now and I was still figuring out the world. Fourteen-year-old Bay was a mess. She was sick of being looked at as different and terribly afraid she would go through life with people pointing, laughing and ultimately screaming "witch."

I was over most of that. Sure, the necromancer thing threw me for a loop, but in hindsight I wondered if I shouldn't have seen it coming. There were signs that I was growing more powerful. I simply didn't see them for what they were. And now, looking back, I felt like an idiot for not recognizing what was happening.

"What are you doing?"

I jolted when Hopper materialized, clutching the photo album to my chest and glancing up from the floor where I sat cross-legged. "You need to learn to knock."

"I have no corporeal hands." As if to prove it, he mimed smacking me across the face. Thankfully I didn't flinch. "I can't knock."

"Then you need to make a doorbell sound when you're coming in," I countered, frustrated.

"I can do that." Hopper smiled as he lowered himself to the floor and sat across from me. "What are you looking at?"

"Photos from when I was a kid." I turned back to my task, something occurring to me. "You had to go to school to be a therapist, right?"

"I did."

"Why did you focus on couples?"

"I'm a fool for love."

I made a face. "Did you have sex with Maxine Wheeler as therapy?"

Instead of reacting with embarrassment — or lying, which is what I would've done in his position — Hopper nodded. "I did. She was bored with her marriage and believed there were thrills to be found elsewhere. She said Jonathan had lost sight of her, was no longer in love with her, and they were simply two people sharing the same roof. She felt she was missing something. I wanted to show her what she was missing."

"And you thought she was missing your penis?"

"You're looking at this in a simplistic manner when you should be looking at it as one of those panoramic photos that moves when you turn your camera." His tone was reasonable, which only served to irritate me more. "If you're standing still, you can't possibly see everything."

"Yeah, you can dress it up however you want, but you took advantage of Maxine," I argued. "I'm not saying she was right — it's never okay to cheat on your significant other — but you're supposed to be the expert and you purposely led her astray."

"It's a legitimate treatment."

"You just wanted to get your rocks off. Admit it."

"I did nothing of the sort."

I didn't believe him. "How many other couples did you 'treat'?"

"Only those who needed a boost of their excitement factor."

"So ... all of them?"

Hopper's eyes momentarily flashed with something I couldn't quite identify. He shuttered it quickly, but I saw a glint of something dark before he managed to blank his face, and I couldn't help but wonder if we were somehow missing something when it came to his death.

"I don't have to put up with this," Hopper snapped, mimicking brushing off his clothing as he stood. He had a lot of fussy mannerisms he was holding onto from life. It was both intriguing and annoying. "I worked hard for my clients and I don't need you casting judgment on me. You have no idea how many couples I've helped."

Landon picked that moment to arrive, his eyebrows winging up when he saw Mike. I wasn't sure how much of the conversation he'd heard, but Landon didn't look happy with our visitor. "Oh, look," he drawled. "It's the pervy psychiatrist."

"I prefer the term therapist," Hopper snapped. "And, as I was just explaining to your girlfriend, I don't have to take this. I'm dead. I can go wherever I want."

"Not if I force you to stay," I challenged, taking control of my new power and glaring. "We both know I can make you stay."

Hopper frowned. "I see someone is getting a bit too big for her britches. I understand you've had a rough couple of days and you're feeling out of sorts because you don't like your father figure's new girlfriend and you're upset that your younger cousin is getting married before you. Perhaps we should focus on those issues instead of your need to take out your aggression on me."

My mouth dropped open. "I am not jealous of Clove. I wish people would stop saying that."

"They're saying it because it's obvious."

"Whatever." I dragged a hand through my hair and glanced at Landon, who was watching me with unveiled interest. "What? Do you think I'm jealous of Clove, too?"

"I think jealous is one of those words middle-school girls whip out to win a fight," Landon replied as he stripped out of his coat and kicked off his shoes. "I do think you might be slightly out of sorts because they've set a date. We'll talk about that tonight."

Oh, well, great. He had his stern face on. That meant he was going to dig his heels in and fight if I didn't agree to spill my guts. "I'm not jealous."

"I didn't say you were."

I glowered at Hopper. "He's a pervert, by the way. He won't admit it, but I'm pretty sure he had sex with most of his clients."

"And on that note ... ." Hopper absently brushed at his ethereal arms. "I have someplace to be. I'll be around when you stop taking out your misery on others and want to talk about your issues."

"I don't have any issues other than you being a pervert."

"You have so many issues we'd need a year of therapy to get through them," he shot back. "I have other things to worry about. Next time you call, make sure you have something substantial to discuss."

"I didn't call you this time."

"You certainly did."

"I did not!"

"Then why did I hear your disembodied voice calling to me?"

"Because you're a tool."

"Okay, I think this conversation has gone on long enough." Landon stepped between us. "Dr. Hopper, I think you should take a breather and do ... whatever it is you do when you're not driving Bay batty. I will take over her therapy session from here."

Hopper shot Landon a withering look. "Good luck."

"Yeah, yeah." Landon waited until the ghost disappeared to fix his full attention on me. "Do you want to tell me what's going on?"

"What makes you think anything is going on?" I challenged, suddenly defensive. "I'm sitting here minding my own business."

"Right." Landon lowered himself to the floor and rested his back against the couch, pressing his thigh against mine as he got comfortable. "What are you looking at?"

"Photos of when I was a kid."

"That sounds fun ... and kind of weird for the middle of the day. But I'm game." He snagged the book from me and opened to the first page, grinning at the huge photo my mother had blown up of Clove, Thistle and me. "How old were you here?"

I leaned my head against his shoulder. "Fourteen."

"You're cute."

"I didn't feel cute. I felt ungainly and awkward."

"That's the age, Bay. I felt the same way. That's not a girl thing. That's an early-teenager thing."

"Maybe."

He flipped the page. "Is that Chief Terry?"

I nodded. "We were having a bonfire and s'mores."

"Here?"

"Yeah. He came out a lot in the summers because he said we couldn't be trusted with fire."

"I can see that." Landon slid his gaze to me. "Is that why you came home early? To look at photos of Chief Terry?"

"Melanie ambushed me outside the police station and insisted we have coffee."

"I know. She stopped at Chief Terry's office after. She was excited, and said the meeting went really well. I could tell he wasn't thrilled with the development, but Melanie was so excited he didn't say anything to her. You weren't mean, were you?"

"No."

"Were you nice?"

"As nice as I could be. She's a bit intense."

"She wants you to like her." Landon flipped another page, his eyes moving to a photo of me standing next to Aunt Tillie. "Where was this? It doesn't look like the property around the inn."

I smirked at the photo. "Summer camp. It was a full week. Mom ran the girls' camp and Chief Terry ran the boys' camp. We were separated by water to make sure there weren't any late-night shenanigans. You know, hormones and stuff."

"I'm well aware of teenage hormones." Landon grinned at the photo. "Look how tan you were."

"We spent a lot of time outdoors that summer. Aunt Tillie was in teaching mode. She wanted us to learn spells, a few random curses, which our mothers weren't happy about."

"You know, I went to one of those camps when I was a kid, too," he mused, adopting a far-off expression. "I wasn't sure what to expect when my parents informed me that I was going. They sent my brothers, too. They said they wanted a week of peace."

"Oh, yeah? Where was the camp?"

"I don't remember. Everything south of where I lived as a kid was Detroit and everything north was the woods."

"That's kind of funny. Do you remember much about the camp?"

"Just that we had cabins and the guy who served as the counselor was always yelling at us not to stare at the girls. I remember there was this girl I saw — she was blond and had big blue eyes — and my hormones totally kicked into overdrive."

"Ah, to be young and fifteen," I teased.

"Yeah. I fell head over heels, but I barely talked to her. The counselor told me to stop staring at her, and then he cuffed the back of my head. He was absolutely no fun." Landon flipped another page. "Is this still from camp?"

I nodded as he looked over the collage, which featured photos of a second-cousin I absolutely despised. "Mom took a lot of photos that week. I remember because Rosemary was there. That was one of the few times Aunt Willa tried to integrate her with us. It didn't go well —

she bonded with Lila and tried to torture me — but I think that was one of the last times we saw her until she returned a few months ago."

"I don't think you were missing much."

"Definitely not," I agreed.

"Look at you guys." Landon tapped a photo. "You look as if you're about to get into trouble."

"We were probably trying to spy on the boys. I had hormones back then, too."

"Yeah? Tell me about them." Landon's smile was mischievous as he scanned another photo, his smile dipping as he leaned closer and stared at the snapshot.

"What's wrong?" I was confused at the way his merriment shifted.

"I ... don't know," Landon replied after a beat. "Are there more photos from that camp?" He flipped the page without waiting for an answer and focused on a campfire photo. "Is this from the same camp, Bay?"

"Yeah. It's the same year. We only went to one camp that year. What's wrong?"

Landon pressed the heel of his hand to his forehead. "Okay, this is going to sound weird, but ... that's me."

"What's you?"

"That." Landon pointed toward the dark-haired boy standing about three feet behind me in the photo. "That kid with the black hair, Bay, that's me."

I was dumbfounded. "Are you sure?" I leaned forward. "Maybe it's just a kid who looks like you."

"No, it's me." Landon shook his head as he flipped another page. "And that's my brother Denny. Right there."

I had no idea what to make of the turn of events. "So ... we went to the same summer camp. That's weird. Do you think we met?"

"I do, Bay. I know we met because you're the girl who sent my hormones revving."

"Get out."

"You're the girl I had a crush on." Landon flipped back two pages.

"You were wearing the same outfit. I remember two girls being mean to you and I stepped in. That was Rosemary and Lila, wasn't it?"

I opened my mouth to answer but couldn't find the appropriate words. "I ... ."

"It was. I know it was you." Landon transferred the photo album to my lap and hopped to his feet and began pacing the living room. "How is it possible I met you when I was a kid and didn't remember?"

"Because you were a kid," I automatically answered, opening to the photograph that featured him. I remembered him. Now that it was right in front of me I couldn't forget. "You did stand up for me with Lila and Rosemary. I had a crush on you, too, but I was way too embarrassed to admit it."

"Your mother. I talked to your mother."

"What did you say?"

"I don't know. That I was going to marry you or something. I was gone for you because you were so sweet and cute and you made my heart do funny things."

"Are you sure it was your heart doing funny things?"

"Hey, I was a teenager. My hormones were out of control. I'm not going to deny that."

"That's probably wise."

"That doesn't change the fact that there was something about you that touched me ... and not in a gross way. I remember you. I remember staring at you during that bonfire. You had your head bent together with two other girls ... who I'm just realizing were Clove and Thistle. Wow!"

"I'm more interested in the fact that Chief Terry was your counselor and you didn't remember him. How could you forget Chief Terry?"

"Oh, geez!" Landon slapped his hand to his forehead. "At the time he was a nice guy who kept warning me about getting ideas about a certain girl. You were the girl. He was acting as your father even then."

I snickered, genuinely amused. "Oh, that's kind of sweet. That was one of the things Melanie brought up during coffee today. She said that she wanted me to like her because Chief Terry thought of me as a daughter. That's why I got out the photo albums in the first place."

"Yeah, yeah." He offered a dismissive wave as he went back to his pacing. "We'll talk about your irrational dislike of Melanie later. I want to talk about us right now."

"What do you want to talk about?"

"That!" Landon waved at the photo album. "We knew each other as kids."

"So? Thistle and Marcus knew each other as kids. He visited during the summers."

"Yeah, but ... this is different. Don't you think there's something magical going on here?"

"Like what?"

"Like ... I don't know ... destiny?"

"You think we were destined to meet at summer camp, fall into puppy love and then meet again as adults?"

"I think it's possible."

I wanted to argue, but the words died on my lips.

"Oh, I can see your mind finally working," Landon noted. "You're starting to wonder, too. I never believed in that goddess you always pray to before casting a spell, but now I'm not so sure. I mean ... think about it."

He moved closer and knelt directly in front of me.

"Maybe someone was leading us the whole time," he said quietly. "Maybe this was always going to happen."

He was so serious I instinctively gripped his hand. "I've always kind of believed that. You came into my life at the perfect time."

"You came into my life at the perfect time, too." He linked our fingers. "It's weird to think about, isn't it?"

"I think it's kind of neat."

"I think it's kind of neat, too."

That made me absurdly happy. "Maybe other things are meant to be besides us," I mused, my eyes traveling back to the photo. I could see Mom and Chief Terry standing next to each other in the background. They were laughing and having what appeared to be a good time. "Maybe it's all about timing ... and other things will work out once the timing is right."

Landon followed my gaze. "Oh, geez. I thought you were going to let that go."

"You just said things happen for a reason and some things are destined."

"I meant us."

"We're not the only people in the universe."

"No, but you're going to stick your nose into Chief Terry's private business and cause trouble. I just know it."

"I'm going to make sure things end the way they're supposed to end."

"I can't even ... ."

I squeezed his hand tightly. "You said it yourself. Some things are meant to be." I flipped another page in the photo book with my free hand, turning to a photo that featured young Landon and me looking at one another next to the river as the sun rose. It was a beautiful photo that meant very little to me before I realized the true implications. "Maybe more than one thing is meant to be."

Landon smirked at the photo. "You're turning into a schmaltzy woman, Bay."

"Yeah."

"Yank out that photo. I want to frame it."

"Now who's schmaltzy?"

"Oh, sweetie, I'm the king of schmaltz. I can't wait to show you later."

TEN

"I want to go through Hopper's house," I announced as Landon and I walked the back path that led to The Overlook.

Initially we were going to get takeout and stay home, but my mother texted that they were having pot roast — one of Landon's favorites — so our plans quickly changed.

"Why?" Landon asked, his fingers linked with mine. He was in a relatively good mood after our discovery. Once his emotions settled, he grew to like the idea that we'd met as kids. In fact, he was obsessed with talking about it. This was the first time we'd chatted about something else in almost two hours.

"Because I figure that the good doctor probably broke up more than one marriage. I want to get a look at his patient records."

"I can get those tomorrow if we can get the judge to agree. It shouldn't take much to get him to sign off."

"I want to do it tonight."

"What's the rush?"

"I don't know. I don't like the way he was acting when I questioned him about his treatment methods. He acted as if he didn't do anything wrong. While he technically didn't break the law, he definitely crossed an ethical line. I doubt very much he did it only once."

"That's a fair point. I need to get authorization to go through his patient files. That shouldn't take long, two days at most."

"If we follow the letter of the law," I agreed.

Landon slowed his pace. "Wait ... you want to break into his house and illegally go through his files?"

"I want to magically slip inside and look at the files without taking them," I clarified.

"How is that different from what I said?"

"Perspective."

Landon pursed his lips. "Fine. We'll break into Hopper's house and go through his files. We have to be sneaky about it, though, so you can't tell anyone what we're going to do."

"Why would I tell anyone?"

"You have a big mouth."

"I do not."

"You have a huge mouth."

I rolled my eyes. "I'm like the wind, buddy. I can get in and out without anyone knowing, and I'm so good at keeping a secret that I could be a spy."

Instead of agreeing, he snorted. "Oh, you're so cute I just want to kiss you."

"You're still feeling schmaltzy, I see."

"That won't fade anytime soon."

"Good to know."

AUNT TILLIE SAT ON the couch, her gaze focused on *Jeopardy*, when we entered through the back door of the family living quarters. She didn't bother looking in our direction as she yelled at the screen.

"What is the Great Barrier Reef," she barked at the television.

"What is the Taj Mahal," Alex Trebek corrected.

"Oh, he's full of it," Aunt Tillie muttered as she flicked her eyes to me. "I didn't know you guys were coming for dinner tonight. I thought it was just going to be Clove and her big book of marriage stuff."

I snickered at her annoyance. "Mom texted to say there was pot roast."

"And your Fed can't live without pot roast," Aunt Tillie surmised. "I should've seen that coming."

"He's a slave to his stomach," I agreed.

"And, on that note ... ." Landon slid me a sly look and planted a quick kiss on the corner of my mouth. "I'm going to see what's cooking in the kitchen. I'll leave you two to ... I have no idea. I'm sure you have things to discuss, though."

I knew exactly what he wanted to discuss, but I had no idea how to broach the subject. Aunt Tillie eyed Landon speculatively until he disappeared from the room, and then she shifted her eyes to me. "What was that about?"

"Something weird happened," I admitted as I sank to the couch next to her. Now seemed the perfect time to bring it up. "Do you remember that summer camp we went to the year I was fourteen?"

"You went to a lot of summer camps."

"It was the one Mom and Chief Terry ran. The one Rosemary attended because Aunt Willa got a bug up her butt that we needed to act like a family."

"Ah, yes." Aunt Tillie made a face. "The summer camp of annoying little girls. I remember it well."

"There were boys there, too," I reminded her. "They were across the lake. Chief Terry was in control on that side."

"I vaguely remember that."

"Well, I happened to be looking through the photos with Landon and he noticed something."

"What?"

"He was in them."

Aunt Tillie slowly shifted her eyes to me, her expression unreadable. "What do you mean?"

"He attended the same camp. He remembered going to camp as a kid, but not the specifics. We met there. I found photographs of us together."

"Huh."

"That's all you have to say?"

"I'm sorry, what was the appropriate response?"

I wanted to throttle her. "You don't find it weird that we met as kids, developed crushes on one another for a few days and then reconnected as adults?"

"No."

"But ... it's so weird. He didn't grow up here."

"You're such a putz sometimes," Aunt Tillie lamented. "It was summer camp, Bay. It's not as if you guys fell in love and carried a torch for each other for fourteen years. You flirted — which is what you do when you're teenagers — and then you went on your merry way."

I deflated a bit. "So ... you don't think it was destiny? I know that sounds ridiculous, but I was kind of wondering about it."

"I didn't say it wasn't destiny," Aunt Tillie countered. "I said it wasn't some miraculous thing. Destiny plays a part in our lives every moment of every day. Do I think you and Landon were destined to find each other? Yes. I'm a big believer in karma and you guys deserve each other. You're both bossy whiners when you want to be."

I bit back a sigh. "Thank you for that."

"You're welcome."

"I was being sarcastic."

"You should practice because your skills are fading. You used to be much better at it."

"Being sarcastic?"

"No, being a clown. See, that was sarcasm."

I flicked her ear, earning a dark look. "I'm serious. Do you think Landon and I were always meant to end up together?"

"Yes." Her answer was quick and simple. "I knew that the moment I saw you together for the first time. There's more than one type of magic in the world, Bay, and what you and Landon found together is magical."

"That might be the sweetest thing you ever said to me."

"You're still a putz."

"That's less sweet."

"It's the truth."

"It kind of is," I agreed, getting to my feet. "By the way, do you want to break into a dead guy's house with me later? I wouldn't ask under normal circumstances, but something weird is going on with his ghost and I want you to help me control him should the need arise."

"What makes you think I can control a ghost?"

"You frighten people. That probably extends to ghosts."

"Fair enough. There's nothing good on television tonight, so yes, I'd love to break the law with you."

MOST OF THE FAMILY was already settled around the table when Aunt Tillie and I made our way into the dining room. Landon had three slices of fresh bread in one hand and the pot roast gravy ladle in the other when he caught sight of me.

"I see you waited," I said dryly.

"That was better sarcasm," Aunt Tillie offered as she took her seat at the head of the table. "I expect that to be on display when we go on our adventure tonight."

Landon slid me a sidelong look. "What adventure?"

Uh-oh. "Well ... ."

"She wants me to help her with Dr. Lovelorn's ghost," Aunt Tillie supplied. "She thinks he's a liar and she wants to control him. She's going to break into his house to do it."

I pressed the tip of my tongue to the back of my teeth and steadfastly avoided Landon's gaze.

"I see my spy has been hard at work," Landon teased, shaking his head. "No one can crack you, Sweetie."

"Do I even want to know what you're talking about?" Mom asked, her tone laced with annoyance. "You're not going to get arrested, are you?"

"I won't let her get arrested," Landon replied. "I might punish her myself, but I don't want anyone else to do it."

"If that's some sexual reference ... don't say it at the dinner table," Mom ordered.

"Fair enough."

Desperate to change the subject, I focused on Thistle and Clove at the end of the table. "So ... how are the wedding plans coming?"

"They're endless," Thistle replied, her hair standing up in short spikes, making me think she had swiped it so many times during the day it had taken on a life of its own. "That's all I've talked about the entire day. Veils. Trains. Flowers. I'm pretty sure I'll have to kill myself if the conversation doesn't turn to something more entertaining."

"I happen to think my wedding is very entertaining," Clove sniffed. "It's the biggest day of my life, after all."

Aunt Tillie made a derisive sound in the back of her throat. "It's a party, Clove. The biggest days of your life are yet to come."

"I don't want to be a downer, but that's kind of true," Marnie hedged. "Wait until you have children. Then you'll be able to say that every day is a new biggest day and mean it."

"Well, that's a bit down the line," Clove snapped. "Right now I want to talk about my wedding. I'm sorry that you're all bored with the topic, but it's a big deal to me."

"And here we go," Thistle muttered.

"We want you to talk about your wedding, Clove," I said hurriedly, pity for my sensitive cousin washing over me. To her, a wedding wasn't simply a big deal. It was the only game in town and would be until the actual day. "You said you were thinking about having an outdoor wedding, right?"

"I am ... but Mom thinks that's a bad idea because it might rain."

"I thought Aunt Tillie could control the weather," Landon noted, half his dinner already devoured. He was a food-oriented guy on a normal day but even I was impressed by his dedication to joining the clean plate club this evening. "Why can't she just make it sunny the day of the wedding?"

Clove brightened considerably. "I didn't even think of that. Good idea."

"What if I don't want to control the weather that day?" Aunt Tillie challenged. "Or what if I happen to be out of town that day?"

"Where are you going?" Mom challenged. "You haven't been out of town in twenty years."

"I could be out of town."

"You're going to be here and we all know it, so stop being you," Mom instructed, shaking her head. "The weather is the least of our worries for the big day. I'm more interested in the guest list. You know you have to invite all the coven members from around the state, right?"

Clove's smile faltered. "I was hoping to break from that tradition."

Mom balked. "You can't. The other witches will take it as an insult if you snub them."

"I find all those other witches insulting," Aunt Tillie muttered as she doled pot roast onto her plate. "They're not real witches. Half of them are wannabes and the other half can float a pencil if they're lucky. I say we cut ties with them."

"You've wanted to cut ties with them since we were kids," I said. "I've never understood why. It's not as if we see them more than once a year."

"What's the deal with these other witches?" Landon asked as he sopped up gravy with his bread. "Are they like you guys?"

"No one is like us," Aunt Tillie replied. "We're special. Heck, we have a necromancer in our midst. That makes us triply special because necromancers are rare. I can't wait to tell those idiots about Bay's new power."

Now it was my turn to balk. "I'm not sure that's a good idea. I mean ... we shouldn't be spreading it around."

"Especially because Bay can't control it yet," Thistle noted. "The last thing we need is word getting out at a solstice celebration. Can you imagine? Bay will lose her temper and witches from centuries past will descend on us. That sounds like the absolute worst thing."

"Things could be worse," Aunt Tillie countered pointedly.

Thistle snorted. "I don't see how."

"Things can always get worse, Mouth."

"Only when you're around."

Aunt Tillie extended a warning finger. "You're going to end up on my list if you're not careful."

"Whatever."

Aunt Tillie watched her for a moment before shifting her eyes to me. "I don't understand why you don't want people to know about your new ability. It's a good one. People will drool because they'll be so jealous. That's the only reason to keep in touch with those other witches, if you ask me."

"Yes, well, I prefer we keep it within the family for the time being," I said. "I'm not ready to go public."

"That's because you're a prude when you want to be," Aunt Tillie offered. "You've always been that way. If I was a necromancer, everyone would know it."

"You're a pain in the butt and everyone definitely knows that," Thistle interjected.

"That's it. You're definitely on my list."

"Stop," Thistle drawled. "You're scaring me."

"I'm going to scare you."

Landon held up a hand to still Aunt Tillie. It wasn't so much that he didn't want a family argument — he was used to those — but he was in the middle of enjoying his pot roast and I realized he wanted to hold off on family fisticuffs until he was done eating. "Bay is in charge of decisions when it comes to her magic. If she doesn't want people to know, then you should respect that."

"She's being a baby," Aunt Tillie protested. "That's a cool power. I've heard more about the fact that you guys met at summer camp than her being a necromancer. What does that tell you?"

"You met at summer camp?" Thistle wrinkled her nose. "Which summer camp?"

"The one Rosemary visited." I launched into the tale, keeping it succinct. When I was done, everyone — with the exception of Aunt

Tillie, who was beyond caring because she had potatoes and wine — was flabbergasted.

"Holy crap!" Thistle moved to stand and then sat again. "I remember that camp. I can't believe Landon was there."

"He's in the photos," I said. "That's how we figured it out. He saw himself."

"Why were you looking at the photos?" Mom asked, her eyes piercing as she watched Landon. "Now that you mention it, I think I do remember you. It's so odd that I didn't remember before. You said something sweet about Bay."

"I was hot for her even back then," Landon agreed, sliding his arm around my back. "You need to eat, Bay. You're going to need your strength if we're breaking the law tonight."

He had a point. I scooped a huge slice of pot roast onto my plate, my stomach growling in appreciation at the scent. "I think it's kind of fun. I was weirded out at first, but now I like the idea that we were always meant to find each other."

"It's definitely romantic," Clove agreed, her eyes going dreamy as she slid them to Sam. "Why aren't you romantic like that?"

"Oh, man." Sam scorched me with a glare. "Thanks for that."

I pressed my lips together to keep from laughing.

"I think it's freaky that you guys met as kids and didn't remember each other," Thistle argued. "Marcus and I met as kids and we never forgot each other. Maybe that simply means that you're both forgettable."

"You and Marcus spent entire summers running around with the same group," Mom added. "Bay and Landon met once and spent five days together. It wasn't even full days. Bay was too busy looking for the body of the former camp counselor to focus on much else."

"Holy crap!" Landon leaned forward, tilting his head. "I forgot about the dead counselor. Bay disappeared. There was a search for her. I just remembered."

"She went to find the body," Mom supplied. "Terry and I went into the woods to find her. He was very supportive while I was freaking out." She looked bitter about the memory. "He helped me find her. He was good that way."

My stomach rolled at her expression and a sharp pang of dislike for Melanie reared its ugly head. There was no way I could accept her, not as long as my mother was this unhappy.

"He did help find me," I agreed, exchanging a quick look with Landon. "You guys brought me back. There was a bonfire that night. Everyone made s'mores."

"And you stared at me over the fire," Landon added.

"I think we stared at each other."

"I choose to remember it as you staring … and drooling."

"That's kind of obnoxious."

"So is inviting Aunt Tillie on our evening crime spree."

Crap. He had a point. "There's cake for dessert," I said quickly. "It's chocolate. That should make things better."

Landon smirked. "Smooth."

"I thought so."

ELEVEN

histle decided she wanted to break the law with us, which wasn't a surprise. Clove begged off, opting to remain behind and talk over wedding plans with Mom, Marnie and Twila. That also wasn't a surprise.

By the time we'd parked around the corner from Hopper's house, our small foursome was ready for mischief.

"Okay, here are the rules," Landon said from the driver's seat of his Explorer. "Everyone has to be quiet and you can't steal anything from the house. Understood?"

From her spot in the back seat next to Thistle, Aunt Tillie made a face that was almost grotesque thanks to the limited light afforded by the moon. "Why are you in charge?"

"Because I'm an FBI agent."

"Yes, but you're breaking the law with us. That means you're just one of the motley crew. Given that, I think I should be in charge. I'm the oldest."

"I think it should go by IQ," Thistle argued. "That puts me in charge."

"Your IQ isn't higher than mine," I shot back.

"It is so."

"It is not."

"We got tested in high school," I argued. "My IQ was a full ten points higher than yours."

"Actually, I seem to remember that," Aunt Tillie mused. "You were furious when the results came back, Thistle. You were ahead of Clove by ten points and behind Bay by ten points. You didn't take it well."

"Hey! I still maintain that guy who tested us gave Bay an extra ten points simply because she was blond," Thistle snapped. "He thought she was cute, so he rewarded her smile. She was flirting with him."

I balked. "He was, like, eighty."

"Eighty is the new thirty," Aunt Tillie supplied. "Don't discount him because he was eighty."

"I can't believe we're even having this discussion," Landon muttered. "It doesn't matter who is smarter ... ."

"Because you know I'm smarter," Thistle grumbled.

"No, Bay is definitely smarter," Landon said. "She picked me. That means she's a genius."

"Oh, I think we know who has the lowest IQ in the car," Thistle drawled. "That was some weak arguing there."

"I have to agree." Aunt Tillie shoved open her door. "I'm the smartest one here. That means I'm in charge."

"Don't make me cuff you," Landon warned.

"As if you could catch me, Sparky."

THE PROCESSION TO HOPPER'S house was slow. We stuck to the sidewalk until we hit his hedges and then ducked into the yard and pressed close to the bushes, forming a single line of bodies. No one spoke. Even though the argument about who was in charge was far from finished, we were all accomplished lawbreakers (even Landon) and we knew better than to argue when Esther was close enough to spy on us.

Once we reached the front door, Thistle took up watch to make sure we didn't garner attention from the people across the street, and Landon fumbled in his pocket for his lock pick.

"Just a second," he whispered.

Annoyed, Aunt Tillie brushed him aside and extended her fingers so they were even with the lock. She muttered a quick spell under her breath and the lock tumbled open. "Never let a man do a job designed for a woman," she said triumphantly.

"You cheat when you use magic," Landon groused as he grabbed the handle and twisted. "I know you're fine with cheating, but I'm not."

"Wah, wah, wah."

Once we were all inside, Landon closed the drapes before turning on the lights. If someone was interested enough to move closer to the house it would be obvious that people were moving around inside. Hopefully that wouldn't be the case, because explaining our presence was bound to be tricky.

"Where should we start?" Thistle asked, glancing around the living room. "Wait ... where did he die? I don't want to step on death cooties."

"There's no such thing as death cooties," Aunt Tillie scoffed.

"That's not what you told us when I was ten and you found that body in the woods," I reminded her.

"You found a body in the woods?" Landon's eyebrows winged up. "How?"

"It wasn't a body," Aunt Tillie replied. "It was my wine stash. I put it under a blanket and the girls discovered it. I told them it was a body to make sure they wouldn't squeal to their mothers."

I was horrified. "I thought we really discovered a body. I had nightmares."

Aunt Tillie snorted. "Yeah. That was funny."

"It wasn't funny!"

"I knew that wasn't a body," Thistle countered. "You said it was Mrs. Little's boyfriend, the hairy hose beast without a name, but I knew you were lying. There's no such thing as a hose beast. Unless ... what kind of hose were you talking about?"

"And we're done with this conversation," Landon said. "I can't believe I've let it go on this long."

"I've let it go on," Aunt Tillie corrected. "I'm in charge."

"You're definitely on my list," Landon shot back.

"Oh, I'm shaking in my leggings."

"Speaking of those leggings, I thought you were warned about wearing them," I interjected. "Mom said she burned them all."

"She burned the dragon ones, but I'm ordering more. Also, what your mother doesn't know can't hurt her."

"Fair enough."

Landon, Thistle and I moved into the office, leaving Aunt Tillie to search the living room. I doubted very much that Hopper was the type to leave files out for anybody to read, which meant he probably had them correctly labeled and filed in a cabinet. Once we hit the office, we realized the cabinet was large enough that it took up an entire wall. It was also locked.

"We need to get this open," Thistle said as she fruitlessly tugged on a drawer. "We could use magic."

"Or you could let me handle this one." Landon's lock pick was already in his hand as he focused on the small lock. "Just give me a second. I'm magical when I want to be, too."

Thistle and I exchanged amused looks but wisely took a step back to watch him work.

"So, word on the street is that you had coffee with Melanie Adams today," Thistle said. "How did that go?"

"How did you hear about that?"

"I saw you when I walked past the bakery."

"That's not really word on the street then, is it?"

"I was on the street and I speak words so ... how was it?"

I wasn't keen to talk about Melanie, especially in front of Landon. He was under the impression that I was going to be nice and do the right thing. In this particular situation, I knew Thistle would side with me and want to direct Chief Terry back to our family. That made her an ally ... something I couldn't admit in front of my boyfriend.

"It was fine," I said evasively after a beat. "She's a very nice woman."

Thistle drew her eyebrows together. "That was a generic response."

"It's the truth."

"Yeah, I'm not buying it."

"She doesn't want to tell you what she really thinks in front of me," Landon said as he yanked open the file drawer. "Hah! And you guys thought I couldn't do it."

"I don't believe we said anything of the sort," I countered. "I knew you could do it. You're brave, strong and ... whatever skill goes with breaking into someone's file cabinet."

"Industrious," Landon suggested.

"Sure."

"Also, you can't change the subject," he added. "I know you're plotting something to get Chief Terry to look away from Melanie and toward your mother. I would just like to point out that you're a little old to be starring in a modern version of *The Parent Trap* and that Chief Terry seems happy."

I blinked several times. "I'll take that under advisement."

"You're still going to try to get rid of her, aren't you?"

"Oh, I definitely think we should do that," Thistle enthused. "I want Chief Terry to date Winnie."

"You do?" I was surprised. "What about your mother?"

"Listen, I love my mother — no, really — but she's a pain in the rear end. I don't know how anyone puts up with her, and that includes people who share genes with us. Chief Terry would kill himself inside of a week if he tried to date my mother. Your mother is a different story. I always thought they had something going even though neither of them would admit it."

Intrigued, I accepted the stack of files Landon handed me and lowered myself to the floor. "You did? I always wondered that, too. Not when I was little, of course, but when I was a teenager and I often caught them with their heads bent together. There were a lot of secret smiles."

Thistle bobbed her head. "Definitely."

"Are you sure you guys aren't imagining things?" Landon challenged as he handed over another stack of files to Thistle. "Maybe you're only seeing what you want to see."

"And maybe you weren't there," I fired back.

Landon made a face. "Geez. Fine. Blow up his life. I won't say another word about it."

"I don't plan to blow up his life. I plan to make him see what he's apparently forgotten ... that my mother is perfect for him."

"You just want him to be your father."

"I have a father." Guilt rolled into a ball in my stomach. "He even lives in town ... although I haven't seen him in two weeks. We should probably make a stop out there."

Almost a year ago, my father and uncles returned to Hemlock Cove after more than two decades in exile. They'd opened a competing inn — The Overlook was essentially the premiere Hemlock Cove vacation destination thanks to the food and dinner theater, which was provided by our family on a nightly basis — and were keen to forge new bonds with us. So far, it had been a long process. We'd made some headway, but the sailing was hardly smooth.

"I think that's a good idea." Landon settled on the floor next to me with his own stack of files. "Tell me what we're looking for here, Bay. I don't mind breaking the law — at least in this particular case — but I don't even know what you expect to find."

"I told you. If Hopper was sleeping with Maxine, he was probably sleeping with other patients. That's motive for murder in my book."

"Wait ... Dr. Lovelorn was sleeping with his patients?" Thistle made a face. "That's gross."

"You haven't seen him," I argued. "He's not bad looking. He's kind of handsome, in a clinical way."

"Don't tell me you have a crush on the dead doctor," Landon said. "I'm ending this right now if that's the case."

"I only have a crush on you."

"And apparently since she was fourteen," Thistle added. "That's kind of neat. I can't say I remember Landon from that week, but I had other things on my mind."

"Like terrorizing Lila and Rosemary."

"I'm always at my best when it comes to terrorizing people," she agreed. "I still think it's neat. It feels somehow kismet."

However schmaltzy, I agreed. "I kind of like it. There's a cute photo of us by the water. We're going to frame it."

"Oh, that's adorable," Aunt Tillie drawled from the open doorway. "It's like you're fourteen all over again. Are you going to buy a note-book and doodle his name and draw little hearts everywhere?"

"She sees hearts whenever she looks at me," Landon supplied. "If you're going to be in here, you should grab some files and go through them."

"I didn't come to look through files," Aunt Tillie argued. "I came to watch Bay in action with this ghost. If she really did force him to stay behind, I think that means she can control him."

"I think she proved with those other ghosts that she's in control," Landon said. "As for Hopper, he's not here."

"Not yet." Aunt Tillie focused on me. "Call him. I want to meet his guy."

I shifted on the floor, suddenly uncomfortable. "I don't know if that's a good idea. What if I can't get rid of him?"

"You're the boss of him. You can get rid of him. Have you tried?"

"Not really."

"Then you're not a failure."

I balked. "I wasn't worried about being a failure."

Aunt Tillie arched a dubious eyebrow. "Really?"

"I'm worried about being a failure now."

"Just call him. I want to meet this guy. He sounds like a real tool."

"He definitely sounds like a tool," Thistle agreed. "Clove thinks he's a relationship genius because he was giving her advice on her engage-ment. I don't understand why she needs advice. She's the one getting married — even though I've been dating Marcus longer than her — but she's one of those idiots who buys self-help books, so it fits she would take advantage of this situation."

I narrowed my eyes. "Wait ... are you jealous that Clove is getting married before you?"

"Of course not."

She answered a little too fast. "You are. You're jealous."

"You're jealous," Thistle fired back. "You're the oldest. If anyone should be jealous, it's you. She's basically turning you into a spinster."

I wasn't a fan of that word. "That is ridiculous," I shot back. "I'm not a spinster."

"You've been dating Landon longer than she's been dating Sam." Thistle refused to back down. "In fact, she moved in with Sam before Landon decided to move in with you. She's been ahead of us this entire time ... even though she started out behind us."

"You're the one who sounds jealous."

"You both sound jealous," Aunt Tillie countered. "It feels as if you're fourteen again and I'm stuck babysitting while you fight over the Hill boys. Do you remember them? Hoodlums each and every one. Two of them were handsome, and one looked as if he'd been run over by his father's truck eight times in a row. You spent an entire summer squabbling about who was going to win their affections."

"I won," I pointed out. "Sebastian Hill totally fell for me."

"He was only the second cutest," Thistle argued. "Dickie Hill was cuter, and he fell for me."

I snorted. "In your dreams."

"I'm going to just assume that I'm cuter than both of them combined," Landon interjected.

We ignored him and remained focused on each other.

"Dickie Hill had a bad name," I reminded her. "Plus, I believe he's bald now. Sebastian still has all his hair."

"And a gut so big you can balance a pizza box and a case of beer on top of it."

"Wait ... these guys are still in town?" Landon asked. "I want to meet them. I'm positive I'm better looking."

"Yes, you're a prince amongst men," Aunt Tillie drawled. "That's not the point."

"I lost track of the point twenty minutes ago," Landon complained.

"The point is that Thistle and Bay, while happy for Clove, both have their noses out of joint because Clove is winning this particular game," she explained. "Thistle started dating Marcus first. She knew him from childhood. He should've proposed by now. I'm not sure why he hasn't ... except for her attitude."

"Hey!" Thistle glared. "I have a great attitude."

"Yes, you're sunshine and kittens every day of the week," I agreed.

"You're not innocent in this either, Bay," Aunt Tillie charged. "You've been dating Landon longer than Clove and Sam have been together, too. You don't seem stressed out regarding marriage — we all know it's going to happen — but you're still being a bit of a baby. It was easier before Clove set a date. Now she's going to be married while you're just living with your boyfriend. You can't help being a little jealous."

I didn't like that she was right. I was a giving person. At least that's the way I saw myself. I wanted Clove to be happy, and Sam made her happy. "You're imagining things," I groused.

"And you're annoyed that I'm right." Aunt Tillie puffed out her chest in triumph. "Ha! I won the argument. That proves I should've been in charge from the start."

"I'm in charge and I want you to sit down and help us," Landon instructed. "Getting Thistle and Bay worked up isn't helping."

"You just want me to stop talking about marriage because it gets your mind working," Aunt Tillie countered. "You're wondering if you're behind, if you should've proposed already and if you're somehow lacking in the romantic partner department. I can put your mind at ease. No one should work on anybody else's timetable. You're fine.

"Besides that, you and Bay have more to deal with than the others given her new powers and your job," she continued. "You're not behind. You're right where you should be. Stop worrying about inconsequential stuff. That drives me crazy. You guys witch and moan about the stupidest things. There are more important things to worry about in this world."

"Like what?" Thistle asked, genuinely curious.

"Like where that ghost is. I want to talk to him. I happen to love a good pervert ... especially if he's dead."

I risked a glance at Landon and found him watching me with speculative eyes. "I'm not jealous ... just so you know."

"Okay."

"We should probably look at these files," I suggested lamely.

"I agree. Focus on the files. We'll talk about the rest of it later."

Oh, well, that was something to look forward to ... or not.

TWELVE

e sorted the files. It took time to figure out Hopper's system, but when we finally did we managed to weed out twenty that looked as if he took the low road when offering his services.

"I think that's it." Thistle stood and dusted off the seat of her jeans. "None of the rest have that notation for 'special treatment' like he has in Maxine's file."

"He's only been in town a few years," I noted. "That's quite the number of special clients for that amount of time."

Aunt Tillie, who finally got involved in the files when she recognized one of the names, was positively apoplectic by the time we'd finished. "I hate this guy!"

"You're not the only one." I glanced around the room. "We need to put the files back."

"What about the ones we pulled out?" Thistle asked. "We can't put those back. It will take forever to find them a second time."

I risked a glance at Landon, whose nose was buried in Maxine's file, and shook my head. "We can't take them. That's breaking the law."

"We broke the law when we entered the house," Aunt Tillie pointed out. "Why not continue our streak?"

"Because ... it's not right." Technically, I agreed with Aunt Tillie. I didn't see the harm in taking the files. Plus, there was probably more to glean from each one. But Landon wouldn't like that. "Tell them, Landon."

Instead of answering straightaway, he closed the file and added it to the smaller stack. He groaned as he stood and stretched his arms over his head. When he finally spoke, I was flabbergasted by his response. "We're taking them. We have to keep them at the guesthouse because I don't want Chief Terry knowing what we did. We can't explain it. If we have to sneak the files back into the house, we'll do it later. If I have to admit what we've done, that will be on me down the line."

My mouth dropped open. "Are you serious?"

"Yes."

"But ... that's stealing."

"We're already breaking and entering. We might as well add stealing to the list."

"That's what I said," Aunt Tillie supplied, beaming. "I think we've been a good influence on you."

Landon snickered as he bent over and scooped up the files. "I was thinking the opposite, but we'll go with that."

WE DROPPED AUNT TILLIE and Thistle at the inn before heading to the guesthouse. It was well after midnight by the time we slid into bed. My body ached from sitting on the floor so long.

"What do you think?" I murmured as Landon slipped his arm under my waist and drew me to him. "Do you think one of Hopper's clients killed him?"

"I think that's a good place to start."

"How are you going to broach the subject with Chief Terry without letting him know what we did?"

"I haven't decided yet." He brushed a kiss against my forehead. "Go to sleep, Bay. We'll strategize in the morning."

"Okay. I love you."

"I love you, too."

I was out within seconds and slipped into an odd dream minutes later. I recognized the location. It was the campground from when I was a kid. The area was a hive of activity, young Clove racing past me with a doughnut in her hand, black hair streaming behind her. She didn't so much as look in my direction.

"What the ... ?" I jolted when a figure moved in at my right, pulling back sharply until I realized I recognized the individual invading my space. "Landon?"

"What are we doing here?" Landon glanced around the spacious campsite, obviously confused. "Where is this?"

"It's the campground."

"Which campground?" His eyebrows migrated north as he figured out the answer before I could help. "The campground where we met?"

I nodded. "Yeah. Mom is over there with Marnie making doughnuts." I pointed for emphasis. "Aunt Tillie is over by the cabins with Thistle and Clove, which probably means I'm not far away." I craned my neck to search. "I don't know where I am, though."

"Wait ... we're in the same dream together?"

"Yeah. I think it's my dream and I created a likeness of you to bring along for the ride."

"Why can't it be my dream?"

"Because I'm fully aware of what's happening. That means it's my dream."

"I'm aware, too."

"Yeah, but ... huh." I rubbed my cheek and shifted so I could see the large picnic tables to the right of the cooking area. "There's Chief Terry."

Landon followed my gaze and smiled. "He had a bit more hair then, huh? I bet helping you guys through your teen years caused him to lose it."

"He still has a full head of hair."

"He's getting a bald spot." Landon twirled his finger around his crown. "I'm worried I'm going to lose my hair one day because you guys might make it fall out with your antics."

"You were with us for our antics tonight. It was voluntary. I would've snuck out of the house without you if it came to it. You insisted on participating."

"That's because I prefer being part of the group."

"Even when we break the law?"

"Always." Landon linked his fingers with mine as he watched the show. "There's my brother." He smiled when a young boy let loose a loud bellow and mimed smacking his chest like King Kong. "He always was an embarrassment in public."

I snickered and came to attention when I caught sight of a blond head out of the corner of my eye. When I tilted in that direction, I found what I was looking for. "I'm over there."

Landon walked with me so we could have a better view, his expression softening when he saw the younger version of me sitting under a tree. "What are you doing?"

I shrugged. "I have no idea. I might have been pouting. I seem to remember Mom being down on me because I was overwrought about the ghost I was seeing."

"Is the ghost here now?"

I shook my head. "I don't see her. She was haunting me. She wanted to be found."

"You found her. I remember. You found a body. That's all my brothers could talk about when we got home."

"I went off to find the body myself," I clarified. "I was angry that Mom wouldn't allow it, so I took off. Chief Terry and Mom followed, and he gave me one of his patented 'You'll understand when you get older' speeches. I remember being furious at the time, but he was right. I understand why they didn't want me wandering around without supervision."

"You obviously survived."

"Yeah. I ... ." I trailed off when a dark-haired boy with familiar blue eyes broke away from the male pack and headed in young Bay's direction. "That's you."

"It is." Landon's grin widened. "I was an operator even then. Look at that. I bet I'm smooth talking you."

We weren't close enough to hear the conversation, which was fine. I doubted that we said anything all that illuminating. Simply watching the interaction was entertaining enough, especially when Landon's younger self sat on the ground next to teenaged me and launched into a long tale about ... something.

"What do you think you were saying?" I asked.

"I think I was laying the groundwork for when we would meet again. That's why you practically melted at my feet when we met in that cornfield fourteen years later. Part of you remembered me and you were warm for my form all those years."

I made a face. "I did not like you the day we met. I thought you were a tool."

"Don't cover up your feelings."

"I'm not covering up my feelings. I thought you were a tool."

"You liked me and you know it." He poked my side, his eyes alive with memories and magic. "This is really cool. I can't believe you managed to do it."

I balked. "I didn't do this. You're not even really here."

"Oh, I'm here. If you didn't do it, how did it happen?"

"I made it happen, Skippy," Aunt Tillie announced, appearing beside us. She looked the same as she had when we broke into Hopper's house, including the same clothes and jacket. "I thought you might enjoy it."

"You did this?" I didn't understand. "Why?"

"Because I wanted to remember, too," she admitted. "I don't know that I particularly remember Landon at this age — he looks like a goof, doesn't he? — but it's nice to see you guys together."

"I do not look like a goof," Landon argued. "I look young and strapping."

"Oh, please." Aunt Tillie rolled her eyes. "You look like you weigh a hundred pounds soaking wet. You clearly hadn't come into your own yet."

"I was always a smooth operator."

"No, you weren't." Aunt Tillie was matter-of-fact. "If you were a smooth operator, Bay wouldn't have trusted you ... and she clearly trusts you. That means you were sweet and probably dorky, because that's how she was before she grew up to be cynical."

"I was always cynical," I argued. "You taught me to be cynical."

"I taught you to be a survivor ... and maybe cynical," she conceded. "I wanted to make sure no one took advantage of you. The same with Clove. I never worried about that with Thistle. I had to watch her for other things."

"Like what?"

"Taking advantage of those weaker than her," she replied. "There are all types of kids, Bay. You and Landon were clearly sweet and basically nerds. Clove was sweet with a hint of manipulation running through her. And Thistle, well, she was something else entirely."

Aunt Tillie had a nostalgic streak. It survived despite her hard demeanor, and it was one of my favorite things about her. "Why did you give us this?"

"I already told you. I thought it would be fun ... for me, too."

"You did it for us."

"I did it because you need to calm yourself, Bay," Aunt Tillie corrected. "You're dealing with a lot. I get that. The simpler things in life are still there for the taking. Nothing that's happened uproots your life. It merely enhances it."

"I've been telling her that from the start," Landon grumbled. "She doesn't listen."

"She listens. It just takes time for the truth to infiltrate that hard head of hers." For emphasis, Aunt Tillie rapped the side of my head and smiled. "I'm heading off. You guys can hang out here a bit longer if you want, but it's probably best to let it go.

"The past is fun to reminisce about, but the present is more impor-tant," she continued. "Focus on the present and let the rest float away. Everything will come together the way it's supposed to."

I WAS ENERGIZED when I woke, a good night's sleep easing the aches and pains I'd felt when I dropped off. I shifted my eyes to

Landon and watched as he greeted the day, enjoying the way he stretched his lanky body and smiled.

"Good morning, Sweetie." He gave me a soft kiss. "How did you sleep?"

"Great. I feel good."

"Me, too."

I doubted that Landon would remember the dream. The odds of him being there were slim, no matter what Aunt Tillie said. Still, when he smiled at me, my heart pinged. "Did you dream?"

"Yes."

"About what?"

"You should know. You were in the dream with me."

I stilled. "Seriously? You remember that?"

"Did you think I wouldn't?"

"I didn't know if it was real," I admitted. "I thought maybe I dreamed all of it."

"We dreamed it together, and it was nice. Aunt Tillie was right, though. We need to reminisce about it and then move on. We're exactly where we're supposed to be."

"Yeah." I fluttered my fingers over his cheek. "I'm kind of hungry. I bet they have bacon up at the inn."

Landon's smile turned wolfish as he graced me with a lavish kiss. "You had me at bacon."

WE WERE GIGGLY by the time we reached The Overlook. The family living quarters were empty, which was to be expected, and when we hit the main dining room we found everyone already eating.

"We weren't sure you were coming," Mom said as she eyed us with overt curiosity. "Aunt Tillie made it sound as if you guys would be doing something else."

I rolled my eyes and shot Aunt Tillie a warning look. "We're not animals."

As if to prove me wrong, Landon reached for the meat platter before sitting. "Yum. Bacon." He shoved two slices in his mouth and proceeded to chew as he poured himself coffee and juice.

"Fine. I'm not an animal," I corrected, shaking my head.

"Do you want juice, Sweetie?" Landon was oblivious to the show he was putting on.

"That would be great." I sat across from my mother and snagged her gaze. "What?"

"Nothing. You just look ... happy. I see finding out you knew each other years ago has invigorated the two of you."

"I think that's the breaking and entering they did last night," Marnie corrected. "Did you guys find anything useful?"

"We think we did," I replied. "It seems the good doctor was having sex with at least twenty of his patients, including Maxine Wheeler."

Mom, Marnie and Twila wrinkled their noses in identical looks of disgust.

"That's horrible. That has to be illegal."

"Technically it's not illegal," Landon countered as he heaped pancakes onto his plate. "It's definitely unethical. I'm sure he could've been brought up on any number of charges with the medical board and had his license revoked."

"That's if he even has a license," I pointed out.

Landon's hand paused next to the syrup bottle. "What do you mean?"

"I mean that he might not have a license. He was a radio personality who happened to treat people out of his home. Does he need a license for that?"

"I'm not sure." Puzzlement washed over Landon's features. "That's a good point. You're smart and pretty."

"Oh, geez!" Mom rolled her eyes. "I can always tell when you guys are feeling all fluttery around each other. I'm guessing the dream your aunt sent you caused romance to shoot out of your noses when you woke up."

"Now that is a lovely visual," Landon deadpanned, earning a small smile for his efforts.

"I'm just saying that you're acting a little ridiculous," Mom sniffed. "We're trying to eat breakfast and your antics make me want to gag."

"I'm sorry," I offered quickly. "We don't want to make anyone gag."

"Ignore her," Marnie supplied. "She's still upset about the Terry situation and she's taking it out on you."

"I am most certainly not upset about the Terry situation," Mom barked. "There's nothing to be upset about. Quite frankly, I'm glad he's finally found someone to make him happy. Terry is my friend. I want him to live a fulfilled life. If that's with this woman ... then more power to him."

It was a good try, but no one was buying it. "You could tell him how you feel," I suggested. "I bet if he knew you were interested he would drop the pretzel chick in a heartbeat."

Mom made a face. "Pretzel chick?"

"She teaches yoga, which means she can bend herself like a pretzel. Men like flexible chicks, but you have history with Chief Terry. I think you could still win."

Mom's face shifted through a myriad of emotions as she absorbed what I'd said. "Wait ... flexible?"

"Nice one, Bay." Landon tapped my plate. "Eat your breakfast and stay out of Chief Terry's love life. We've had this discussion ... multiple times."

"We have," I agreed. "I've decided I'm not staying out of it. He doesn't belong with Melanie. She's evil."

"You barely know her," Landon protested. "She seems perfectly nice. She brought us doughnuts yesterday and everything."

"Oh, well, if she brought you doughnuts," Aunt Tillie drawled.

Landon extended a warning finger. "You stay out of this, too."

"I certainly will not." Aunt Tillie didn't even pretend to play the game. She had no interest in doing Landon's bidding. "I agree with Bay. This pretzel chick is evil and we need to get her out of Terry's life."

Uh-oh. When Aunt Tillie agreed with me, I knew I'd taken it a step too far. "Well, I didn't mean it exactly like that," I hedged. "I just meant that Mom should tell Chief Terry how she feels so he'll drop the pretzel chick and we won't have to see her anymore."

"That's not what I heard," Aunt Tillie countered. "I heard we should come up with a plan to scare her off so we can save Terry from his hormones."

Double uh-oh. "Aunt Tillie ... ." I trailed off, uncertain what to say.

"You've done it now," Landon noted. "You've got Aunt Tillie riled up. She'll keep you riled up. You'll get Clove and Thistle involved. I pity that poor pretzel chick. She seems like a nice woman."

I found my voice. "I don't want to hurt her."

"Yeah, we don't want to hurt her," Aunt Tillie echoed. "We simply want her gone."

"That a healthy and mature attitude," Landon deadpanned. "I'm always excited when Bay's opinion of a situation coincides with yours. That never terrifies me."

He had a point. "I'll give it some more thought," I said finally. "I'm not saying that I think she's good for him no matter how much you guilt me, though."

"I don't expect miracles. She's a perfectly decent woman, and I want you to think long and hard before you do something you'll regret."

I nodded, solemn. "That seems fair."

Aunt Tillie made a derisive sound, halfway between a snort and a guffaw. "I'm not going to think about it. I'm simply going to act on it."

"Somehow I knew that," Landon muttered. "You're going to be trouble, aren't you?"

Eyes twinkling, Aunt Tillie grinned. "I'm always trouble, Sparky. Get used to that."

THIRTEEN

J took the pilfered files to Hypnotic. I figured it wouldn't hurt to have more than one set of eyes on them. Clove and Thistle were busy conducting inventory when I entered. They barely looked up when I let loose an exaggerated sigh and dropped the files on the coffee table in the center of the store.

"That won't work on us," Thistle offered. "We have our own work to do. We can't help you today."

"Why not?"

"It's inventory day."

"You guys do inventory every month," I pointed out. "I don't see why it's even necessary."

"That's because you don't work in retail."

A fact for which I was continuously thankful whenever Clove and Thistle had a big sale and worked twelve hours to empty their shelves. "Yes, well, I would think having a murderer on the loose is more important than inventory."

"That was low," Clove complained.

"I can go lower. In fact, I'm thinking of going really low and spying on Chief Terry's new girlfriend so we can dig up dirt on her."

I didn't immediately look to Clove and Thistle to see if I had their attention, but I felt their eyes on me.

"That's a great idea," Thistle enthused. "I bet she's got all sorts of skeletons in her closet."

"It's a bad idea," Clove countered, her internal Mary Sue on full display. "Chief Terry has been good to us. We shouldn't ruin his life simply because we don't like his choice in girlfriends. Besides, Melanie is a nice woman. I don't want to see her hurt."

I narrowed my eyes. "Wait ... you know her?"

Clove, realizing her mistake too late to take it back, averted her eyes. "Of course I don't know her. Don't be ridiculous."

When it came to manipulating strangers, Clove was a fabulous liar. When it came to fooling us, she was downright terrible. "You're hiding something." The files forgotten, I moved closer to Clove. "How do you know her?"

"I didn't say I knew her." Clove turned shrill. "Why do you naturally assume I know her?"

"Because you said she was a nice lady."

"That's what I heard around town."

"You're full of it." I looked to Thistle for help. "What is she hiding?"

Intrigued, Thistle abandoned her inventory list and joined me in crowding Clove. "I have no idea," she admitted. "Now that we don't live together, we're not all up in each other's business. It's easier to hide things."

"Like the naked statue you're hiding in the barn?" Clove challenged.

"I'm not hiding that statue," Thistle shot back. "I'm proud of that statue. Marcus is the prude. He doesn't want it in the house, and when I suggested putting it in the big barn so tourists can see it he said no because he's afraid it will warp the minds of children when they visit the petting zoo."

On general principle, I was on Thistle's side, but Marcus had a point. "It's a naked witch," I reminded her. "You can't traumatize kids with a naked witch statue. Marcus will get in trouble."

"It's tasteful."

"She's still naked."

Thistle turned pouty. "Maybe I can talk Mom into putting the statue in front of The Overlook."

While I had no doubt Thistle could manipulate Twila into doing her bidding, I was equally convinced that Marnie and Mom would have a thing or two to say about that possibility. "Yeah, that won't fly."

"What am I supposed to do with it? I spent weeks working on it."

"You could put it here," I suggested, earning a scathing look from Clove.

"Absolutely not. We'll get trouble from Mrs. Little. And we might scare away customers," Clove snapped. "It can't be on display here."

Thistle turned a set of hopeful eyes to me. "What about at The Whistler?"

"Um ... yeah, no."

Her scowl back, Thistle shot me the finger. "I see that you're volunteering everyone else's space but your own. Nice."

"You made the statue," I argued. "That makes it your responsibility."

"Whatever." Thistle rolled her eyes as she returned to her inventory list. "That still doesn't change the fact that Clove knows Melanie Adams and doesn't want us to know how."

Now it was Clove's turn to frown. "I should've known you wouldn't let that go."

"She has a point." I returned to my original topic. "How do you know her?"

"I may have stopped by her studio yesterday to get a list of classes," Clove replied, bitterness evident. "I want to get in shape before the wedding, and it's not as if we have a lot of options. This town really needs a gym."

"Landon mentioned the same thing. He's afraid he's going to get fat eating at the inn constantly."

"A gym isn't a bad idea," Thistle noted. "Maybe I will bring it up with Marcus. He's always looking for ways to expand his business. That might not be a bad idea."

"Maybe he and Landon can go into business together," I suggested.

"That way Landon will have something to focus on besides FBI work when he's old enough to retire."

"That's actually not a bad idea."

"Wait a minute." Clove straightened her shoulders. "What if Sam wants to be involved, too? Why are Landon and Marcus always considered a solid twosome but you cut Sam out?"

I bit back a sigh. "Nobody is cutting Sam out. It's not even really a thing. It's just something we were talking about."

"Well, it sounded like you were cutting Sam out."

"It sounds like you're being a ninny," Thistle fired back. "Let's talk about Melanie Adams. Why didn't you tell us you met with her?"

"Because Bay and Landon were all worked up at dinner about meeting as kids and then you made plans to break the law together. There wasn't time."

I knew better than that. "She didn't bring it up because she was afraid to upset my mother. She's as worried as I am that things are about to get rough around The Overlook."

"Your mother isn't the only one with feelings for Chief Terry," Thistle argued. "My mother and Marnie are hot for him, too."

"Not really. They simply want to drive my mother batty. I mean ... they care about Terry. They don't care the same way my mother does."

"I still don't understand why they never hooked up," Clove said. "The attraction was there for a long time. They were always flirting. But neither took the next step, and I don't understand why."

"I don't either. It's frustrating. Now Chief Terry is dating a human pretzel and someone is going to end up hurt. The thing is, I'm not about to let it be my mother. Landon is on me about minding my own business, but I think we need to delicately lead Melanie in another direction.

"I mean ... I don't think we should terrorize her or anything," I continued. "I simply think we should find a different man for her to wrap her tentacles around."

"Tentacles, huh?" Thistle arched an amused eyebrow. "The more you talk about this woman, the meaner you get. I'm not used to you acting this way."

"Do you have a problem with it?"

"Problem? No. In fact, I approve. I've always thought you would make a fabulous sidekick for me when I launch my plan for world domination. You'll need to be mean to accomplish it, and this is a fantastic first step."

That didn't make me feel better. "Maybe I should think about it some more."

"That's a good idea," Clove said. "Melanie is nice. I don't want to see her get hurt. Of course, I don't want to see Aunt Winnie get hurt either. It's all very *Dynasty*."

Confusion won out over indifference. *"Dynasty?"*

"You know ... hair pulling and screaming. That's what I imagine will happen if your mother ever gets it together and stakes a claim on Chief Terry."

"Ah." I considered the statement for a long beat and then shook my head to dislodge the image of my mother and Melanie yanking each other's hair. "I think we should talk about something else. This conversation is giving me a stomachache, and I promised Landon I wouldn't do anything without giving it proper thought."

"That's a good idea," Thistle agreed. "Let's talk about where I should move my statue."

"We've talked about that for weeks."

"And we're sick of it," Clove added. "I think we should talk about which one of you is going to be my maid of honor."

The change in topic threw me for a loop. "I ... you ... oh."

"That's right." Clove turned prim and proper. "I need a maid of honor and there's three of us so ... that could get tricky. I don't want you guys fighting over the title."

I exchanged a quick look with Thistle. The only thing we would fight over is the opportunity to stick the other with the job. "Oh, well ... ."

"Why does that have to be decided right now?" Thistle interjected, her mind clearly working overtime. "We have a lot going on right now, between Bay's new power and Chief Terry dating the pretzel chick. That's on top of a murder. We should wait until things die down to make that decision."

"Thistle is right," I said quickly. "We should definitely wait until we have more time to really dig into the issue."

Whether she understood what we were doing or not, Clove vehemently shook her head. "I want to decide now. I've been giving it some thought, and I think the only fair way to make the decision is to have a competition."

I furrowed my brow. "Like a game of horse on the basketball court?"

"Like a trivia game in which you guys can compete over who knows me best."

That sounded absolutely tragic. "Um ... ."

"Maybe we could just draw straws," Thistle suggested. "That might be easier."

And less time-consuming, I silently added. Knowing Clove, she would create the world's longest trivia game so Thistle and I would have no choice but to compete for days over a job neither of us wanted.

"Drawing straws is boring," Clove argued. "I think the trivia game is better. That way, whichever of you wins, we can arrange the lineup for the other weddings."

"What other weddings?" I blurted out before I could grasp what she was getting at.

"Your wedding to Landon and Thistle's wedding to Marcus. We all know they'll happen eventually, so we have to get a rotation going."

"A rotation?"

"You know ... if you're my maid of honor that means I'll be Thistle's matron of honor and she'll be your maid of honor. Or we'll switch it around if it goes the other way."

"Oh, well, that makes sense ... I guess."

"That way no one will be left out," Clove added.

The look Thistle shot me said she was more than willing to be left out. I recognized Clove would melt down if Thistle suggested anything of the sort, so I lobbed a quelling glare in her direction and shook my head in warning.

"I guess we can do the trivia thing," I said. "It'll have to wait a few days. You guys have inventory and I need to go through these files. We have to find a murderer before we can focus on the wedding."

"Okay." Clove brightened considerably. "I'll come up with questions and we can have the competition the second this case is solved. How does that sound?"

Like the worst thing ever. I forced a smile for her benefit all the same. "Sounds great."

I LOST MYSELF IN HOPPER'S files while Thistle and Clove finished up their inventory. Before I realized what was happening, they'd joined me on the furniture in the middle of the store and started delving into client backgrounds.

"This whole thing is sick," Thistle said after an hour of reading one file. "This guy kept copious notes about what his clients were doing with each other and intermingled it with the things he was talking the women into doing with him. It was ... freaky."

I'd come to the same conclusion. "He wrote everything down," I agreed. "He was obviously getting off on convincing these women to have sex with him, but he was treating it as something of a clinical trial.

"I mean, in this one, the husband was complaining that the wife was frigid," I continued. "This is Sarah and Buck Bishop, by the way, so you can now picture her withholding sex from him the same way I'm forced to."

"Hey, I've seen Buck shirtless at the lake in the summer," Thistle drawled. "I would withhold sex from him, too. He looks like a mid-sized bear. If that's not an advertisement for back waxing, I don't know what is."

"Yes, well, Sarah lost interest in sex after their third kid and Buck was threatening to get a girlfriend if she didn't get with the program."

"That was nice of him," Clove countered sarcastically. "She birthed three babies for him – probably big, hairy babies – and he threatened to get a girlfriend."

"A girlfriend he would have to pick up at a fuzzy convention," Thistle muttered.

"Dr. Lovelorn gave them some exercises to do at home — they were intimacy exercises that involved sitting across from each other and talking about their feelings — while he held separate sessions with Sarah," I explained. "During those sessions, he suggested that she absolutely needed to get over her aversion to sex if she hoped to save her marriage ... and the only way to do that was to have sex with him."

"Oh, that is just low." Thistle made a face. "Sarah Bishop is fairly religious, if I remember correctly. He must've had to push hard to get her to agree."

"He did." I read further. "It says it took him three months to convince her. After they did it, he gathered a list of her reactions to his various attempts at stimulating her and came up with the conclusion that she was frigid but willing to allow a man to do what he wanted to get it over with. He deemed that an acceptable outcome."

"Oh, if this guy wasn't already dead I would kill him myself," Thistle complained. "That is disgusting."

"It's definitely disgusting," I agreed. "The thing is, I'm not sure that Buck ever found out what was happening. As the file progresses, Sarah starts having sex with Buck again, and he thinks the therapy is working. He clearly has no idea how Hopper fanned the flames of Sarah's fire."

"I so want to punch him," Clove groused. "I have Maxine's file and it's even worse. He's making fun of her in here because he knows she's falling in love with him and he doesn't care about her other than the sex. He thinks it might make a good paper to follow the progress of Maxine's obsession with him after the fact. He mentions this isn't the first time a woman has fallen in love with him, and he always finds it amusing."

"What a turd." Thistle furrowed her brow as she flipped the file she was holding to the table and focused on the one beneath it. "I think we took this file by mistake."

"Why do you say that?" I asked, leaning closer to see what she was looking at.

"Because the file tag with the identity is missing and there's only one sheet of paper inside. It was kind of stuck to the other file, and there's nothing in here about Hopper having sex with ... whoever this is. I'm assuming it's a woman, but there's nothing in here to indicate that."

"What is in there?" Curiosity got the better of me and I shifted closer to Thistle's chair. "What's the paper say?"

"It's a copy of a diagnosis from what looks to be a medical book."

"Meaning?"

"Just that. It's a basic breakdown of a medical condition."

"What medical condition? I mean ... what kind of person?"

"A psychopath."

My heart skipped a beat. "A psychopath?"

"That's what it says."

"And there's nothing else in the file?"

Thistle shook her head. "The file looks worn, as if it was looked at quite often. But it's empty."

"I wonder how that happened," Clove said. "Maybe the contents fell out."

"Or maybe someone removed the rest of the file," I suggested, my mind busy. "Like perhaps the person who killed Dr. Hopper."

"That's a little freaky."

It was indeed.

FOURTEEN

I Googled "psychopath" and looked at the results.

"A person who exhibits abnormal or violent social behavior," Thistle read over my shoulder. "Well, at least we know how to describe Aunt Tillie now."

I shot her a look. "This is serious."

"I know it's serious, Bay. We have a dead body. We don't have a name to go with the file, though. What do you want me to do?"

"I think we should go back to Esther's house. She's been watching Hopper for a long time. She'll be able to tell us who's been in and out of that house."

"Sure, but we're looking for one person and Hopper had a bunch of clients. We'll need a list to check Esther's memory against. I'm guessing she can't remember everyone who visited."

I wasn't so sure. "She denies being a busybody, but she knows who has been in that house. It can't hurt to question her."

"And I suppose you want us to go with you when you question her?" Thistle clearly wasn't thrilled with the prospect. "Okay, but if that woman makes me drink tea I'm going to dump it over your head."

"Yeah, yeah."

ESTHER LOOKED ANYTHING but happy when she found us standing on her front porch.

"Oh, geez! What do you three want?"

"It's lovely to see you, too," Clove crooned. She was better with people than Thistle and me, especially when it came to digging for information. "We wanted to check on you after all the excitement the other day. With your neighbor being murdered and all, you're probably afraid."

Esther scorched her with a withering look. "Why would someone want to kill me?"

"Perhaps they've met you," Thistle suggested.

"You've got a mouth on you." Esther looked Thistle up and down, distaste evident. "You may not look like Tillie, but you've certainly got her attitude."

"On any other day I would take that as an insult," Thistle said. "But we're trying to track down a murderer and we need to go through you to do it, so I'll let it slide."

"Yup. That's definitely something Tillie would say." Esther left the door open and turned on her heel. "Come on. If you're going to ruin my afternoon with questions we might as well have some tea to get through it."

Thistle's gaze was heated when it snagged with mine. "You'd better start running now."

"You'll survive. There are worse things in life than tea."

"Like what?"

"Like those little stale cookies that are often served with tea."

"Fair enough."

Esther had four mugs on the kitchen table by the time we caught up with her. She was fast for her age. In addition to the tea, there was a package of cookies resting on the center of the table. They looked to be shortbread ... and well past their "good by" date.

"You were saying?" Thistle drawled.

I forced her disdain out of my head and plastered a smile on my face as I sat. "So, Esther, how well did you know Dr. Hopper?"

"I already told you. I hardly ever talked to him. He would make a big show of waving when he saw me out in the yard ... or with my binoculars ... but it's not as if we hung out."

"What binoculars?" Thistle asked.

"The ones I keep by the window so I could do my part to keep the neighborhood safe," Esther replied. "I'm the founding president of the Hemlock Cove Neighborhood Watch."

"How many other people are members?" Clove queried.

"Enough that we keep the town safe."

"Your neighbor was just murdered," Thistle pointed out. "That doesn't seem very safe."

"Just like Tillie," Esther muttered.

"Stop saying that."

Clearly agitated, the concerned neighbor turned her full attention to me. "You still haven't told me what you want. I don't have all day."

"What else are you going to do?" Thistle challenged. "Do you have a hot date tonight?"

"I could have a hot date."

"Do you?"

"I'm done talking to you." She held up her hand to quiet Thistle. "I can't tell you how annoyed I am by the sound of your voice. Tillie taught you well, I'll give her that. But she didn't do you any favors in the popularity department."

Thistle focused on me. "Was that supposed to be an insult?"

I was rapidly getting annoyed with the direction of the conversation. "We've found out some rather disturbing things about Dr. Hopper's practice," I started. "We were hoping you might be able to fill in some holes for us."

"You mean about him sleeping with all those women?"

I couldn't swallow my surprise. "You know about that?"

"You'd have to be blind not to notice."

"But ... why didn't you mention this when I was here yesterday?" I worked hard to bank my fury. "We had to find out through other means. You could've saved us some time."

"It's not my job to do your job."

"There's a killer on the loose."

"And whoever did it had motive to kill that kinky creep next door," Esther pointed out. "I'm not kinky. There's no reason to kill me."

"I notice you've refrained from denying you're a creep," Thistle noted.

"Do you want me to thump you?" Esther threatened.

I tapped the table to break up the bickering and get Esther's attention back on me. "I'm not trying to be a pain ... ."

"Then you're failing miserably."

I bit the inside of my cheek and glanced away from Clove and Thistle, who looked as if they were about to break out in riotous guffaws.

"I'm not trying to be a pain," I repeated. "This is important information. These couples visited Dr. Hopper because they were trying to save their marriages. He took advantage of his position and manipulated those women into doing his bidding. That's a motive for murder if I ever heard one."

"Manipulated?" Esther arched a drawn-on eyebrow. "He didn't force himself on those women. He might have smooth-talked them — he looks the type, all handsome and full of himself — but they had a choice and they opted to implode their own marriages."

"Except he was running everything as a science experiment," Thistle interjected. "He was trying to see what he could get away with ... and it seems he got away with a lot. The women who agreed to his terms were convinced he was helping save their marriages. That's pretty oily if you ask me."

"Oh, he was a total snake oil salesman," Esther agreed. "I could tell the minute he moved in that he was a jerk of the perverted variety. That doesn't mean he's entirely to blame for what happened. Those women agreed to his terms and encouraged him."

"I think we'll have to agree to disagree on that point," I said. "It doesn't really matter. We're trying to track down a murderer, not change the course of thinking for an entire generation."

"Fair enough." Esther rested her wrinkled hands on the table and met my gaze head on. "What is it you want from me?"

"We need to know who went in and out of that house."

"That's a lot of couples. I'm not sure I can remember them all."

"Then focus on the couples who visited recently," Clove suggested. "Whoever did this probably found out about Dr. Hopper's hidden ways within the past few weeks. Can you think of anyone who might have wanted him dead?"

"I think any of those men would've wanted him dead if they heard about what their wives were doing."

"Okay, let's take it from there," I said. "What couples have you seen visiting the past three weeks or so?"

"What business is it of yours? I've already told you I'm not a busybody. I can't possibly keep up on all the comings and goings in that house."

"Yes, but ... there has to be someone."

"You're not the police," Esther reminded me. "You don't have jurisdiction to be asking these questions."

"Yes, but I own The Whistler. I'm asking these questions because I plan to write an article." That sounded totally reasonable. "The public has a right to know what was going on under their noses."

"That sounded a little Big Brother," Thistle chided.

"I heard it the second I said it," I admitted. "Move on."

"I don't want to talk to the press," Esther argued. "I'm not a fan of fake news ... or whatever it is you're trying to do here. By the way, I don't buy your story that you're simply doing this because you own the newspaper. Something else is going on."

I wanted to throttle her. She obviously disliked Aunt Tillie a great deal, but they shared some of the same mannerisms. "I don't understand how you can just ignore the fact that a murderer is running free. You said you're part of the Neighborhood Watch. Don't you want to make sure that the killer is caught?"

"Sure."

"So?"

"The police solve crimes. Not you."

"But ... ."

"Bay, you're not going to get anywhere with her," Thistle interjected, catching me off guard. "She's set in her ways ... just like Aunt Tillie. You have to treat her how you would Aunt Tillie."

"You want me to lock her out of the house and withhold food?"

Thistle snickered. "No, you have to talk to her on a level she understands." She flexed her fingers, as if gearing up. "What's your price, old lady? Do you want wine? Money? What will it take to loosen those lips of yours? You're not fooling anybody with that 'I'm not a busybody' shtick. You were obviously up in everybody's business, and we need to know who has been visiting that house."

Instead of reacting with anger or outrage, Esther merely snickered. "You're kind of funny."

"I can be mean, too."

"Oh, I have no doubt about that. I can't tell you what you want to hear. I don't feel right spreading people's private business around. If the police come by asking questions, that's a different story. You guys aren't the police."

"Oh, well, great."

WE TRIED TO GET ESTHER to talk for another thirty minutes. The conversation went nowhere — and the cookies were as gross as they looked — so we excused ourselves once we tired of banging our heads against Esther's impenetrable brick wall.

"If you change your mind, give me a call." I handed her a business card as we walked to the front door. "I really do think you're making the wrong decision here. The faster we find the killer, the better."

"I'll keep that in mind." Esther opened the door, revealing two familiar figures on the front porch.

Chief Terry, his hand raised as if he was about to knock, looked furious. When I risked a glance behind him and caught sight of Landon's sheepish smile my heart gave an uneasy jolt.

"What's going on?" I asked, innocence on full display. "Are you here for the tea and cookies? They're divine."

"I'm here for you," Chief Terry growled, his hand shooting out to grab my wrist. His expression said he expected me to bolt. "We need to have a long talk."

Uh-oh. That didn't sound good. I kept my eyes on Landon as I licked my lips. "As much as I love spending time with you — and I really do — I have a full slate of activities this afternoon."

"Oh, really?" He rolled his eyes. "What activities?"

"Um ... ."

"Clove is hosting a trivia contest to see which one of us knows her better," Thistle answered for me. "The winner gets to be her maid of honor ... and we're really excited to find out which of us is going to win."

Landon pressed his lips together. I could tell he was battling the inclination to laugh.

"Why are you here?" Chief Terry challenged.

"Can you have this discussion away from my front door?" Esther asked. "It's time for my nap and I don't care for the noise."

"I need to talk to you," Chief Terry argued.

"I'm sure by the time you're finished with these three I'll be up and about. I'm too old to miss my nap. You'll have to wait."

Fury flashed over Chief Terry's face, but he offered her a curt nod. "Fine. We'll take it outside."

"Marvelous."

Chief Terry was in such a hurry to drag me down the porch steps that I almost tripped and pitched forward. He caught me before my face could meet the pavement, and when I raised my eyes to meet his the disappointment waiting for me there was enough to crush my heart.

"I didn't do anything," I volunteered automatically.

"I know that's not true." He released my wrist and shoved his hands in his pockets as he glared. "Do you want to tell me about it, apologize and take your licks? Or do you want me to start yelling now?"

That was a loaded question. "I ... ."

"We would like to know what you're accusing us of first," Thistle said smoothly, her expression unreadable. "We're not admitting to anything without a hint of what you think you've got on us. If we don't like what you say, we'll need to wait for lawyers to answer any questions."

"That's probably not the way to go," Landon warned.

Thistle ignored him. "What is it you think we've done?"

I wasn't sure how he would answer. I could've made it on his witch list for myriad actions. The worst was my plan to figure out a way to get him and my mother together by erasing Melanie from his life. There were several other options, but I wasn't about to start admitting to any of them until I knew which way to go.

"I'm talking about breaking into Dr. Hopper's house last night," Chief Terry barked.

I jerked my eyes to Landon and found him pursing his lips. "What makes you think we broke into the house last night?"

"I have a witness."

I narrowed my eyes. "I see."

"Don't look at him," Chief Terry ordered. "He hasn't said a thing. In fact, when I asked him if he was with you, he requested his own lawyer."

"Smooth."

Landon shrugged. "I wasn't expecting the question. I'm not good at the lying thing."

"We definitely need a lawyer," Thistle lamented.

"Speak for yourself," Clove countered. "I wasn't with you last night, so I'm not in trouble."

"I decide who's in trouble," Chief Terry snapped.

True to form, Clove's lower lip started to tremble and her eyes glistened. "Why are you being so mean to me?"

"Oh, geez." Chief Terry paced away from her. "Don't start that nonsense. You're not a teenager any longer. That won't work on me."

He said the words, but it was obvious he didn't believe them because he couldn't meet her gaze.

"I don't know what you want us to say," I started. "We weren't in the house. If someone told you otherwise, well, he or she was mistaken."

"So you want me to go back to Margaret Little and tell her she was mistaken? She has video of you guys. Thankfully for your boyfriend here, the video is too grainy to make a positive identification. Otherwise he would be out of a job right now. I know your voices, though."

I stilled, dumbfounded. "Wait ... Mrs. Little claims we broke into Dr. Hopper's house last night?"

Chief Terry nodded. "She does. She expects me to arrest you."

"How does she even know we were there?" Thistle asked.

"She saw you."

"Why was she at Dr. Hopper's house in the middle of the night?"

"I ... don't know." Realization dawned on Chief Terry. "She said you left with what looked like files ... or maybe a box of something ... and she seemed agitated that you might've taken sensitive case information."

"Maybe because she was a client of Dr. Hopper's, too," Thistle suggested. "But ... she's single, and I don't want to imagine them getting freaky together."

That made two of us. "What was she doing out in the middle of the night?"

"I ... ." Chief Terry looked conflicted.

"And why is she worrying we took important files?" Thistle added. "It seems to me you should be asking her questions instead of us. We're the wronged parties here. We were minding our own business when she decided to spy on us. That has to be against the law."

Chief Terry's eyes filled with fire. "Don't push it, Thistle. You're walking a tightrope here, kid."

Thistle shrugged as she shifted her eyes to me. "I had to try."

"Definitely."

FIFTEEN

$\mathcal{T}$he idea that Mrs. Little could be a murderer was intriguing.

Sure, Clove and Thistle were only interested in the idea for twenty minutes and then made their getaways, but it was a notion I couldn't shake.

Why would Mrs. Little make time to see Dr. Lovelorn? Last time I checked, she wasn't dating. She hadn't shown interest in a man since her husband died years before. He turned out to be a murderer because she was having an affair with Mrs. Gunderson's husband (a violent jerk who had death coming to him) and he ended the man in something of a murder mystery for the ages, but I always heard good things about Mrs. Little's husband. Er, well, mostly. In truth, compared to her, almost anyone would've been preferable.

After Clove and Thistle abandoned me to return to Hypnotic, I planted myself on the bench in front of Mrs. Little's Unicorn Emporium and watched her through the window. This was the worst time of year for tourists in Hemlock Cove — the weather called to absolutely no one — and her kitschy corner of the universe was empty. That didn't stop her from pretending to look busy.

She buzzed from one shelf to the next, a feather duster in her hand, and arranged her displays so that they were exactly as she liked them. Not a single unicorn was out of place.

At one point she lifted her head and looked out the window, immediately snagging my gaze. She didn't say anything, nor move to meet me on the sidewalk for a showdown of epic proportions. Instead, she merely held my gaze for several seconds before turning back to her task. A lot was said in that silent moment, but the answers I was looking for weren't forthcoming.

"What are you doing out here?"

I glanced over my shoulder at the sound of Landon's voice. "What are you doing out here?" I challenged. "I thought you were off telling tall tales to Chief Terry."

"I saw that coming." Landon didn't appear especially bothered as he lowered himself to the bench. He let out a low hiss when his legs made contact with the cool metal. "Couldn't you have picked a warmer place to spy from?"

"Like where?"

Landon shrugged. "How about the coffee shop across the way?" He gestured toward Mrs. Gunderson's bakery. "There's a clear view of the unicorn store, and they have hot coffee and doughnuts. In fact, that's where I assumed you would be, so I headed there first."

I made a noncommittal noise in the back of my throat. "I don't see any coffee in your hands."

"When I couldn't find you I decided you were my highest priority, and I was willing to give up comfort to find you."

Part of me was angry, but I couldn't stop myself from laughing at his earnest expression. "That was weak."

"I know."

"Really weak."

"It worked, didn't it?" He linked his gloved hands with mine and stared at the shop. "You don't really think that Mrs. Little is a killer, do you?"

"We didn't find a file on her."

"So? Maybe she didn't warrant a file because she only went once. If I was Hopper, I would've sent her in a different direction the second ɛ walked through the door. There's no check in the world big ɛnough to encourage most men to spend time with Mrs. Little."

"Yeah, but ... we found something in the stack of files this morning. That's what propelled us to question Esther in the first place."

"I figured."

"There was an extra file. The name was ripped off the corner and there was only one diagnosis sheet inside. Everything else was gone."

"Diagnosis sheet?"

"It was a photocopied page of the definition of a psychopath."

Landon shifted on his seat, clearly uncomfortable. "Wait ... what?"

"I just told you."

"I know but that's unbelievable. What are the odds we would accidentally grab that?"

I wasn't sure what he was insinuating. "What do you mean?"

"We somehow grabbed that file even though we didn't see it. That has to mean something ... or be a form of destiny."

I tilted my head, considering. "You're big on the notion of destiny now, aren't you?"

Landon nodded without hesitation. "Things happen for a reason. Aunt Tillie has been saying it since the day I met her. Although ... I think I probably met her way before I realized I met her. I wonder what she said to me that day?"

He was losing it. Thankfully it was in a cute way. Otherwise I would be worried. "So, you think we found the psychopath file by destiny?"

"Yup. It's going to lead us to a murderer."

"How?"

"I don't know yet. We'll figure it out."

I flicked my eyes back to Mrs. Little. "Did you ask Esther if Mrs. Little was one of the people visiting Dr. Hopper?"

"You know I can't answer that question. It's against the rules to share information with a civilian."

I frowned. "You broke the law with me last night. I wasn't a civilian then."

"Technically, you were."

"But not really."

"Well ... ." He trailed off and focused on Mrs. Little. "Truthfully, I think you would have to be a psychopath to be that obsessed with unicorns. Maybe she is our suspect."

He didn't sound convinced. "Landon ... ."

He barreled forward before I could get up a full head of steam. "Chief Terry knows we did something. He even knows we looked at files, although I didn't confirm that for him. He doesn't know we took files."

I wasn't sure how to respond. "Okay."

"He wants to go through the patient files, but we need a special warrant for that. We expect to get it today. Things are moving glacially slow on that front."

My heart rate picked up a notch. "That means we need to get the files back in Hopper's house before he notices. If you get the warrant today then we have to do it right now."

Landon squeezed my hand before I could scurry to Hypnotic to collect the files. "Chief Terry has stationed one of his officers at the house. We can't get back inside without being noticed."

He was unnaturally calm given what he was telling me. "Landon, you could lose your job over this."

"I could," he agreed.

"Why aren't you freaking out?"

He shrugged. "Because I made the decision to break the law with you last night. I didn't think anything of it. I don't know when that even happened. I used to be very law and order, totally by the book. You changed that for me."

"I'm guessing not in a good way."

"No, I think everything that's happened since we met has made my life better. Sure, there were a few times where you almost died or I wanted to pull my hair out because you did something stupid, but on the whole, things are better."

"You could lose your job." I kept my voice low. "We have to come up with a plan to make sure that doesn't happen. I can take the files back, admit what I did. Chief Terry will yell and have a meltdown, but he won't arrest me. He'll find a way to protect me."

Landon's eyebrows rose speculatively as he cast me a sidelong look. "That might change if you keep going after his girlfriend."

I wrenched my hand free from his grip and flapped my arms. "And here we go. I told you I'm going to think about what I want to do before acting. You don't have to accuse me of doing something before it's actually happened."

"Hey, don't yell at me." Landon turned serious. "I'm simply trying to make you see reason before you hurt someone you love. I know you want Chief Terry to be with your mother, but it's not about you. It's about him."

I wanted to argue the point, but now wasn't the time. We were far too exposed on the street. Anyone could hear us. "Let's talk about something else," I growled.

"Fine." Landon's eyes fired and I knew the argument would be coming around for a second showing when we got home tonight. "Let's talk about the files. We can't return them. That means we'll have to own up to how we got them."

I didn't like that idea one bit. "I'll own up to it and leave you out of it. He'll take it better from me."

"No. I'm the one who should admit what happened."

"You'll lose your job." I was starting to sound like a broken record.

"Maybe. Maybe not."

I pictured Chief Terry's furious face if he found out exactly what our late-night excursion entailed. "No, I'll tell him. He'll be angry but he'll get over it. He never stays angry at me very long."

The sound of a throat clearing caught my attention and caused my spine to stiffen. When I swiveled slowly to look at the sidewalk behind us, I found Chief Terry listening to the conversation with his hands on his hips.

"Oh, crap," I muttered, my cheeks burning despite the cold air.

"Why do I feel as if we're about to be sent to the principal's office?" Landon complained as he shifted on the bench. "I'm an adult and I feel like a kid."

"Maybe it's destiny," I remarked.

"No one needs your sarcasm."

"No one needs sarcasm from either of you," Chief Terry countered, his eyes busy as they bounced between us. "Is there something you want to say to me?"

That had to be a trick question. "You look very handsome. Have you been working out? We've been talking about the fact that Hemlock Cove doesn't have a gym. I think it's something we should definitely consider because the town needs one."

"He's probably been working out at the yoga studio with Melanie," Landon pointed out, causing me to scowl. "I bet he's ten times more flexible now than he was two months ago."

I fought the urge to snap at him. "Right."

"Don't say things like that." Chief Terry flicked Landon's ear and shook his head. "It's uncomfortable for all of us."

"I'm not uncomfortable discussing your sex life," Landon countered. "I'm fine with it."

"I can't believe we're having this conversation." Clearly mortified, Chief Terry shifted from one foot to the other. "Wait a second ... I know what you're trying to do. You want to embarrass me so I'll leave, giving you guys a window to escape and put back the files you stole."

My heart sank. "I figured you heard that."

"Of course I heard that." Chief Terry's eyes fired. "I knew you guys were up to something. You were acting squirrelly at Esther's house — and that's saying something because you always act a little nuts — and I could tell you were sticking your noses into the investigation.

"I figured you broke into the house last night so you could go through the files, but I couldn't very well accuse you of that in front of Esther because it would make the rounds through town in five minutes flat," he continued. "You shouldn't be involved in this. It's police business."

I pressed my lips together and glanced at Landon, my guilt growing to mammoth proportions. "Here's the thing ... ." My voice cracked as I tried to gain control of my emotions.

"I stole several files from Hopper's house last night," Landon interjected quickly as I tried to find my courage. "He's been sleeping with women as a therapeutic tool and I figured he did it with more than just Maxine, so I wanted to see if I could get a jump on things and figure out which women he focused on."

I was dumbfounded. "Wait a second."

Landon ignored me. "I know it's against the law, but I thought I could go through the files there and no one would be the wiser. I needed a place to start looking if I expected the investigation to move forward. Once I did, I made a rash decision to take the files. It was wrong and I'm sorry. It's done, so we need to figure a way to move on."

Chief Terry's eyes filled with something I couldn't quite identify. It was an emotion I recognized from my childhood, but he only whipped it out a few times when he was so angry he couldn't find words and had to refrain from throttling someone ... usually Aunt Tillie. "You personally stole files?"

Apparently he could find words this time. I didn't take that as a good sign.

Landon nodded. "I did."

His simple confession snapped me back to reality. "I stole the files," I said hurriedly, earning a furious glare from Landon. "It was my idea to break into the house. I'm the one who talked to Maxine. I knew she couldn't be the only one he manipulated. I wanted to see who else was involved."

"So Margaret was right?" Chief Terry stroked his chin as he regarded me. "She really did see you guys breaking into Hopper's house last night. She said Tillie and Thistle were with you. I didn't want to believe her because that was a ridiculous combination, but she was right."

I wasn't sure what to say to make things better. "If it's any consolation, Aunt Tillie made us miserable the entire time," I offered finally.

Now it was Landon's turn to make a face. "Smooth, Bay." He exhaled heavily and collected his patience. "We just wanted to look at the files. We didn't intend to take them. That was a whim. I really don't regret it because Bay found something else in the stack this morning and it might lead to a suspect."

Chief Terry was apoplectic. "How can we arrest a suspect with information we gleaned illegally?"

"I'm sure we'll figure something out."

"Oh, well, if you're sure." Chief Terry paced behind the bench. "This is unbelievable. You know, I expect this sort of crap with Bay, Clove and Thistle. They were partially raised by Tillie and they never met a rule they didn't want to break. Tillie encouraged it because of who she is and what she believed the girls would grow up to become. You know better, Landon. You're a duly sworn agent, for crying out loud. What happens if someone other than me finds out?"

Landon held out his hands and shrugged. "I don't know."

"You could at least be a little sorry about it!"

"I'm not." Landon refused to back down. "I broke the law last night, and I'm not sorry. Do you want to know why?"

"No."

"I'll tell you anyway," he persisted. "I know we did the right thing because Bay found something in the files today, something only she could find because she's ...magical."

"Oh, geez." Chief Terry slapped his hand to his forehead. "Here we go. You are the schmaltziest piece of work I've ever met."

"I'll take that as a compliment."

"It wasn't meant as one."

"It doesn't matter." Landon refused to back down. "I think Bay was meant to find that other file. I think she was meant to go to Esther's house. I think she was meant to cross paths with Mrs. Little. I think it was all destiny."

Chief Terry turned to me, incredulous. "What is he even talking about?"

"He's been a little whimsical since he found out we went to summer camp together," I admitted. "Do you remember the year I discovered the former camp counselor's body? Landon was at that camp. He was one of your campers."

"Yes, I've heard." Chief Terry didn't look nearly as thrilled by the development as Landon clearly felt. "So what?"

"He thinks that means we're meant to be together. Apparently that also means he's embracing the idea of bigger forces controlling our lives."

"Great. Basically you're saying he's having an existential crisis and we have to cover for him."

My expression turned pleading. "I don't want him to lose his job. His job is important to him."

Chief Terry rolled his eyes as he tapped his foot on the cold concrete. "You're trying to kill me, aren't you?"

"No. I'm trying to protect him."

"I don't need protection." Landon was firm. "I'll take whatever punishment is coming my way."

"Oh, you need protection," Chief Terry growled. "You need all kinds of protection."

"I did the crime. I'll do the time."

"Whatever." Chief Terry looked so morose when he met my gaze I wanted to throw my arms around him and offer a gentle hug.

"We need to get the files back in Hopper's house before you get the warrant," I suggested.

"No, we'll simply keep the files out and then claim we took them from his property after the fact," Chief Terry corrected. "If you break into the house a second time you'll compound matters. As it is, I'm going to have to park an officer outside the house tonight to make sure Margaret doesn't try to break in. She adamant that something fishy is going on at the house."

"Because she was there in the middle of the night."

"I noticed."

"Why was she there in the middle of the night?" I pressed. "Could it be she's looking for her file in his house?"

"You're suggesting Margaret killed him," Chief Terry surmised. "I know you dislike her, Bay, but do you really think she's capable of doing what you're suggesting?"

I rapidly searched my memories of the woman in question and

nodded. "Yes. I think she's capable of doing whatever it takes to protect her image. That's all she cares about."

Chief Terry stared for a beat without saying anything. Finally, he merely sighed and dragged a restless hand through his hair. "Keep those files safe and under wraps. Don't get caught carrying them around."

I nodded perfunctorily. "Okay."

"Watch your delusional boyfriend, too. His newfound destiny kick could get him into trouble."

"That's the plan."

"Well ... I guess that's it then."

I called out to him before he could storm away. "You're not angry with me, are you?"

The exasperation etched on his face when he turned back was profound. "Yeah. I'm angry, Bay."

"You're not going to stay angry, are you?"

"For now."

I rubbed my forehead and tried to keep from whining. Anger seemed totally justified in this situation, even though I didn't like it. "Okay, well, when you're done being angry ... I'll still be here."

Chief Terry looked down at the ground and then back at me. "I'm guessing I won't be angry very long."

Landon snorted. "I'm guessing that, too."

Chief Terry ignored him. "Try to stay out of trouble the rest of the day, Bay. I can't promise I won't blow up if you make matters worse."

I saluted. "No trouble from me, sir. I'll be an absolute angel."

"That's what I'm afraid of. Your version of an angel rides around on a broom."

He wasn't wrong. Still, he clearly needed reassurance. "I'll be good."

"See that you are."

SIXTEEN

*L*andon walked me to the newspaper office after Chief Terry departed. He was quiet, clearly lost in thought. Once we cleared the front door, though, he let me have it.

"I was trying to protect you."

I blew out a sigh. "I know."

"Why didn't you let me?"

That was a complicated question. "I was trying to protect you."

"That's not really an answer."

"No?" I cocked an eyebrow as I shrugged out of my coat. "I really wish spring would get here. This is the time we should be looking forward to flowers and seasonal festivals. It still feels as if we're going to get another snow this year."

Landon's angry expression didn't waver. "Bay, why did you try to take the blame?"

"Because you have more to lose."

"I wouldn't have lost my job. No matter how angry he was, Chief Terry wouldn't have turned me in. You know that."

"I do know that." I nodded in confirmation. "But you're just as important to me as I am to you. You don't get to be the great protector simply because you have a penis, no matter what pop culture has taught you."

Landon moved his jaw but didn't speak, giving me an opening to continue.

"It was my idea. That was the truth. Chief Terry will be angry for a bit and then get over it. That's how he is. You're still in the doghouse because he thinks you should know better and you went along with us all the same. He'll get over that, too. We have a plan."

Landon's sigh was long and drawn out. "I don't like that you have a point."

"I had multiple points."

"The one about me feeling like I need to be the protector because I'm the man," he supplied. "I don't mean to be sexist — I really don't — but I want to protect you. I can't help myself."

"I know." This seemed like a weird time to talk about sexism, but I opted to play along. "You're an FBI agent. It's your job to save as many people as possible. Of course you get even more determined when it comes to someone you know and love. I think that's human nature."

"So ... you're not angry?"

I shook my head. "Not as long as you realize I want to protect you, too. I'm capable of taking care of myself, but it's a nice feeling to know that you care enough to risk your entire career for me. However, this particular time, there is no need for you to fall on your sword. Chief Terry will get over it."

"I know he will." Landon took two steps forward and rubbed his hands up and down my arms. "Thank you for volunteering to fall on your sword. It meant a lot."

"I don't have a sword." I shot him a wicked grin.

"Ha, ha." He tweaked my nose and gave me a quick kiss. "Now I can't go back to the office for at least an hour because Chief Terry needs time to decompress. I can guarantee he's over there kicking his desk and calling us idiots. That means I need to steer clear of him."

"What did you have in mind?" I was picturing something flirty and fun.

"I thought you could call Dr. Hopper so we could have a talk with him."

His answer caught me off guard. "Seriously?"

"Did you think I was going to suggest something else?"

I had no idea how to answer without making myself look stupid, so I decided to change course. "That's a fabulous idea." I shifted to move away from him but he caught me. "What?"

"We can do the other thing you were thinking about when it's warmer. That should be a spring adventure."

My cheeks burned. "I wasn't thinking anything."

"You're a terrible liar."

"I'll have you know that I aced Aunt Tillie's class on lying when I was a kid."

"Fine. You're a terrible liar when it comes to me."

That was probably true. Still, I didn't want to dwell on it. "So, you want me to call Dr. Hopper? Do you think that's a good idea? It's been quiet for a bit. He's loud."

"I'm surprised he hasn't been buzzing around," Landon admitted. "I thought for sure he would show up last night and cause a scene."

"Ugh. I was hoping he wouldn't. In fact, I worried about that right before we left the inn. I was relieved when he didn't show."

"That's why I want you to call him now." Landon's tone turned reasonable. "I want to know what he has to say — if anything — about Mrs. Little."

"I think Chief Terry wants to wait until the warrant comes through for patient files."

"Then we won't tell him about this conversation unless it yields something important."

That sounded like a good idea. "Okay."

Landon moved to the front door to lock it while I swung my arms and geared up to call a ghost. He smirked when he saw me stretching — an expression I chose to ignore — and positioned himself so he was close when I called out with my mind.

I thought I would have to try two or three times to get Hopper to appear. Instead, he burst into being four steps in front of me before I even let loose his name.

"It's about time!" Hopper looked furious.

I exchanged a quick look with Landon. "Um ... ."

"You've had me locked away for what feels like forever," Hopper snapped. "I don't appreciate that, by the way. I've been nothing but helpful. You're the reason I'm here in the first place and for you to do what you did ... well, it's not nice. No wonder people call you a witch with a 'b' all the time."

"Hey, don't give her attitude," Landon warned, extending a finger. "She's had a rough day."

"Oh, whatever." Hopper made a face. "You're not the boss of me. I hope you realize that. I understand you have bossy tendencies — that's normal for people who choose careers in law enforcement, by the way — but you're not in charge."

Landon's expression twisted. "I am not bossy." He looked to me for confirmation. "Tell him I'm not bossy."

I absently patted his arm. "I happen to like bossy people. Heck, I grew up with Aunt Tillie and my mother. I only know how to deal with bossy people. If someone isn't bossy I assume there's something wrong with them."

Landon's expression was withering. "I'm not bossy."

"I know. I'm not bossy either."

"You're totally bossy."

"Right back at you." I fixed what I hoped was a pleasant smile on my face and focused my full attention on Hopper. "So ... how are things?"

"How are things? How are things?" With each word, Hopper became shriller. "Things are not great. They're not good at all. They're ... terrible."

"Do you want to talk about it?"

"Oh, that's lovely," he sneered, shaking his head. "You're using what you think are standard psychological responses to act as my therapist. I know what you're doing."

"I wasn't doing that." I opted for the truth. "It just slipped out. I don't want to shrink you."

"That's a derogatory term. How would you like it if people walked around calling you a witch all the time?"

"I self-identify as a witch, so I would be fine with it. Plus, well, the whole town is full of witches."

"You're a real witch."

"Fair enough." I rubbed my palms against my jeans to wipe away the sweat. For some reason, I was nervous. "So ... we have a few things to discuss."

"Like the reason you locked me in that dark box for ten years?" Hopper barked, his eyes on fire.

"Dark box? I didn't lock you in a box."

"You most certainly did." Hopper was clearly in no mood to back down. "I was out and about and enjoying myself — Pippa Martin held her monthly book club meeting yesterday and they were serving wine, so the gossip was flying fast and furious — when all of a sudden I found myself trapped in a dark box. I couldn't move, and the only thing I could hear was your voice."

That sounded downright terrifying. "But ... I didn't put you in a box."

"Hold on." Landon rested his fingers on my forearm as he focused on Hopper. "About what time did this happen?"

"How should I know? I don't need to check the clock anymore because I'm dead. I don't have to be anywhere at a specific time, so I can mosey about as I choose. That's the only good thing about being dead."

"You said you were at a book club," Landon pressed. "What time were you there?"

"I don't know. It was after dinner. That's all I can tell you."

Landon slid his eyes to me. "I think you did put him in a box."

I balked. "I did not! That's a horrible thing to say. I would never put someone in a box. That's something a serial killer would do."

Instead of yelling back, Landon remained calm. "Sweetie, you said it yourself. You were nervous last night when we broke into Hopper's house and went through his files. You didn't want him to show up. I think you accidentally made it so he couldn't possibly catch us in the act."

Hopper's face filled with fury. "Excuse me?"

"She didn't mean to do it," Landon repeated. "She's still learning to control her powers. There's no reason to get worked up. You're obviously not suffering any lingering effects from your incarceration."

"I'm mentally spent!"

"I think you were mentally spent before this." Landon was grim as he rubbed a hand over my back and regarded Hopper with outright disgust. "How many of your patients were you treating with sexual therapy that involved your participation?"

Hopper sputtered. "I don't have to listen to this, to your accusations. I'm an adult. Also, I'm a doctor. There's such a thing as doctor-patient confidentiality. You're not allowed to dig into that information."

"We found the files," I offered, my anger bubbling. "We know about Robin Daughtry ... and Beth Hamilton ... and Sarah Rothschild. We found the special notation you made in your files for the women you had sex with. I couldn't help but notice it was all the young and pretty ones. That doesn't seem like a coincidence."

"Well, I never!" Hopper turned haughty. "I don't have to answer your questions. This is ... completely undignified!" He couldn't show color in his pallid face. I knew if he could his cheeks would be red with fury rather than embarrassment.

"You're not going anywhere." I was firm as I folded my arms over my chest. "If you try, I'll just bring you back. If you try again, I'll purposely put you in a box and this time you won't be alone. I'll put a clown in there if you're not careful."

Hopper furrowed his brow. "A clown?"

"They're totally freaky," Landon muttered as he involuntarily shivered. "That's quite the threat."

"I learned from the best." I leaned my hip against the desk. "We know about all the women. We have their names. The question is, which husbands found out? They're the ones most likely to kill you or have you killed."

"I'm not answering that."

"I could make you."

"I'm still not answering." I had to respect Hopper's refusal to back down. He really was trying to protect his patients. At least it appeared that way. "I'm a professional."

"You're trying to protect your own legacy," Landon corrected. "You don't want to be known as the doctor who slept with his patients. You don't want the town to still be whispering about the doctor who was stabbed by an angry husband.

"I heard you on the radio," he continued. "I commuted between Traverse City and Hemlock Cove for years. You were the only one talking some nights, and I listened. Your fans thought you knew a lot about healthy relationships, but it's clear the only thing you cared about was your own gratification."

"I don't have to listen to this." Hopper's fury was on full display. "You're not in charge here. I don't have to answer your invasive questions. I refuse to put my patients at risk."

"You do have to answer me," I pointed out, momentarily relishing the surge of power that flowed through me. Landon was right; I was in control. I could make Hopper answer me whether he wanted to or not. "I want to know if any husbands found out what you were doing. I also want to know why Margaret Little was booking sessions with you. She doesn't have a boyfriend or husband, so what relationship was she trying to save?"

Hopper's expression twisted into something dark and dangerous. "You've been going through my files!"

"I believe we already told you that," Landon said. "That's how we found the names of the women you were sleeping with."

"You had no right!" Hopper was spitting mad. "Those files are private!"

Landon remained calm despite the ghost's growing fury. "We're trying to keep a community safe," he argued. "Whoever killed you is still out there. He or she might not be stable. Our need to keep the residents of Hemlock Cove out of the line of fire supersedes your need to pretend you were a good doctor."

"That ship has already sailed," I added. "We know what you were doing with your patients. Jonathan Wheeler is already telling anyone who will listen that you were banging his wife. That news is going to spread ... and cause the other husbands to question their wives. It's only a matter of time."

"It was a genuine therapeutic tool," Hopper persisted, although some of the energy had gone out of his voice. "I wasn't hurting anyone."

"I'm sure some of the women you took advantage of would beg to differ," Landon argued. "We need information. I don't care how safe you were. Other husbands had to find out."

"Two did, but I denied the charges when confronted and they backed off."

"Who?"

"Lance Hamilton and David Strawser."

I ran the names through my head. "I saw both their files last night. Did they confront you in a public or private setting?"

"Private. They both drove to my house and accused me of all manner of terrible things."

"Things you were doing with their wives," Landon pointed out. "Don't act like a martyr. You were taking advantage of the situation. Instead of helping those marriages, you were hurting them."

"A little sexual therapy never hurts anyone as long as the information is kept private. It's the wives' fault for telling their husbands what was going on."

"They probably felt guilty."

"Yes, well, guilt is a needless emotion."

I ran my tongue over my teeth as I regarded him with steely eyes. "Let's talk about Margaret Little. Why was she seeing you?"

"I can't talk about that."

"You have to. Were you sleeping with her, too?"

The question was enough to get a reaction out of him. "Absolutely not!" He snapped his head up and glared. "How can you even suggest such a thing? That woman is in her eighties."

"Hey, I have no idea how you roll," I said. "I was simply asking a question. You focus on relationships. That's your shtick. I don't understand why you were seeing Mrs. Little when she's not in a relationship."

"I can't talk about a client's private business. It's unethical."

"You were sleeping with your patients," Landon pointed out. "That doesn't put you in the best light when it comes to ethics."

"Oh, get off your pedestal," Hopper snapped. "You look at me with disdain. I get it. You don't hate me for the reason you think you do, though."

"Oh, yeah? Why do I hate you?"

"Because you're jealous. No man wants to stick to one woman. He wants to jump around. Society frowns on that, but it wasn't always that way. I think we were better off when monogamy was something women participated in and men occasionally considered."

I felt sick to my stomach. "You're disgusting."

"And you're worried that he really feels that way," Hopper shot back. "You're afraid that you're not enough for him. I can see the insecurity whenever it washes over you. I can feel it when you call for me. You're afraid of what's happening, that things will get out of control and someone you love will end up hurt.

"The thing is, you have the power but you're afraid to use it," he continued. "You could crush your boyfriend like a bug on a windshield to ensure he does what you want, but you're too afraid. That makes you weak."

My mouth dropped open. "I can't believe you just said that."

"Ignore him, Bay," Landon admonished. "He's trying to get you worked up because he wants you to forget the questions you were asking. He doesn't want to talk about his misdeeds. He wants to distract you and this is how he's chosen to do it."

It was an effective attack. I was feeling a bit out of sorts, especially since finding out I could lock a ghost in an invisible box for long stretches of time. That seemed mean ... and a little frightening. Still,

Landon had a point. Hopper was on the offensive because he didn't want to answer questions about Mrs. Little. That much was obvious.

"I want to know why Mrs. Little was visiting you," I pressed. "If it wasn't for sexual therapy — which I'm absurdly happy to hear because that would've given me nightmares — it had to be something else. What was it?"

"I'm not answering your questions."

My temper flared as power washed through me. "We'll just see about that."

SEVENTEEN

O o matter how I cajoled and pleaded, Hopper refused to divulge the reason for Mrs. Little's visits to his house. The tighter he clammed up, the more I was convinced he was doing something nefarious with Hemlock Cove's self-proclaimed queen of the hill.

Landon suggested I get more aggressive with my questioning – and I considered it – but, ultimately I wasn't comfortable with the notion. Sticking Hopper in an invisible box without realizing it was one thing. Purposely torturing him was another.

"Was Mrs. Little the only person outside of a relationship you were seeing?" I asked after a full hour of back-and-forth with the belligerent ghost. "Were you seeing other single people?"

"I can't answer that." Hopper sounded weary. "You know I can't. Why do you keep pressing on issues I've told you are off the table?"

"Because we're trying to figure out who killed you," Landon answered automatically. At some point he'd given up standing and was sprawled in one of the large chairs in the lobby, his feet resting on the coffee table. "Someone entered your home and stabbed you. We're trying to figure out if you were expecting this person or it came as a surprise."

"I can guarantee that I wasn't expecting to die."

"That doesn't mean you weren't expecting your guest," I pointed out. "If you were making time with these women, maybe you were doing it at your house. You would need privacy. They were married, so I doubt you could do it at their homes."

"He did it with Maxine Wheeler at her house," Landon interjected. "That's how Jonathan found out what was going on."

"But Jonathan was supposed to be out of town," I said. "That's what he said anyway."

"Still, it was a risk." Landon linked his fingers and rested them on his flat stomach. "Were you expecting someone at your house the night you died? You said you went to dinner alone and came home. Was someone supposed to meet you there when you returned?"

"I don't remember." Hopper practically spat the words. "How many times do I have to tell you that? I honestly don't remember anything after leaving the restaurant. I'm not making it up."

"You're not exactly forthcoming with the information," I reminded him. "Of course, your answers are suspect. You won't tell us the truth."

"I've told you everything I can."

"Except the truth." I refused to let it go. "You won't tell us why Mrs. Little was seeing you. You've barely spoken of the two husbands who found out what was going on, but Landon and Chief Terry will definitely be questioning them. You had a file in there with the name ripped off the label and one sheet of paper inside. I mean ... who was the psychopath you were treating?"

Hopper blanched at the question. "What are you talking about?"

Something niggled the back of my brain. "There was a file. We stumbled across it by accident. The name was ripped off so we have no idea who it belonged to. All that was inside was a printed-out sheet of paper with information about psychopaths on it. Are you saying you didn't do that?"

"Why would I file something that way? It makes no sense."

It really didn't. "I didn't see a file in there for Mrs. Little." This time I spoke to Landon more than Hopper. "You didn't see one, did you?"

"If I'd seen a file on Mrs. Little I would've shared with the group," Landon replied. "You know that."

"Thistle would've shared, too." I chewed my bottom lip. "How closely were you watching Aunt Tillie?"

"I try to refrain from watching her as much as possible. She takes it as a challenge."

"I wasn't watching her either. I simply assumed that she was going through the files the same way we were."

"So?"

"So, she disappeared for a few minutes." I attempted to organize the timeline from the previous evening in my busy brain. "She excused herself to go to the bathroom."

"And you think she stole the information from Mrs. Little's file when that happened?"

I shrugged. "It's a possibility. The other possibility is that Mrs. Little didn't arrive after us. Maybe she was there before us and stole her own file. Then she saw us on the sidewalk and decided to spy, maybe even plotted a way to blame her stolen file on us if it became necessary."

Landon angled his head, considering. "I guess that's possible, but I think we would've noticed if she was parked on the street."

"We parked around the block. Maybe she parked around a different block."

"I guess that's possible. Still, I think it's unlikely. If you're going to break into someone's house, especially if it's still a crime scene, the later the better."

"Except Mrs. Little is old and goes to bed at nine o'clock every night."

"She stayed long enough to know we were there for hours last night," Landon countered. "If she'd already found what she was looking for, why wait?"

That was a good question. "We're back to Aunt Tillie."

"Do you really think she would steal the file?"

"You've met her."

Landon sighed. "She stole it."

"Yeah." I groaned as I got to my feet and slid a dark look in Hopper's direction. "It would be helpful if you would simply tell us what we need to know."

The pouty therapist jutted out his lower lip. "I have no intention of doing that."

"Fine. We'll find out on our own. Just remember, I can make you do stuff. I don't want to be the sort of person who forces ghosts to do her bidding, but I will if I have to. I don't feel much sympathy for you because of the things you were doing."

"Allegedly doing," Hopper corrected, prim. "You have no proof."

"You admitted it."

"I don't remember that."

Now he was just being a pain. "Well, you think long and hard about what I said. I have to go fight with Aunt Tillie. If she doesn't give me what I want, I'll be coming for you. I have a lot fewer qualms about bossing you around."

"I stand by my previous statement. It's unethical to divulge patient secrets."

"Yeah, yeah." I waved my hand. "I'll be back ... and you'd better be prepared."

"I knew I should've crossed to the other side and not followed orders from a disembodied voice," Hopper grumbled. "No good ever comes from listening to the voices in your head."

"You've got that right."

INSTEAD OF HEADING straight to the inn, Landon suggested a strategy session during dinner at the diner. At first I couldn't figure out why he wanted to eat in town when there was perfectly good meatloaf waiting at The Overlook. I understood when we walked through the door and caught sight of Chief Terry and Melanie sitting together in a corner booth.

"You're trying to ascertain if he's still angry with you," I surmised when my gaze linked with Melanie's. She enthusiastically waved before leaning forward to say something to Chief Terry. When he turned to look in our direction his gaze was dark ... and he certainly didn't wave. Instead, he narrowed his eyes and glared before turning back to the bread basket he shared with Melanie.

"Well, that wasn't very welcoming," Landon complained as he pressed his hand to the small of my back and pointed me toward a booth about three tables away from where Chief Terry sat with his date. "I guess he's going to be angry longer than we expected."

The simple truth of his words was enough to cause the small ball of guilt sitting in the pit of my stomach to double in size. "Maybe we should force the issue," I suggested. "If we invite ourselves to sit with them, he'll have no choice but to forgive me."

I was hopeful it was a sound suggestion until Landon shook his head. "Sweetie, how would you feel if Chief Terry interrupted one of our dates?"

"We don't date."

"We used to date."

"And he interrupted us several times. I remember a few breakfasts where he took over the entire conversation to talk about dead people."

"I don't think he'll be happy if you invite yourself on his date."

"Probably not. Things can't get worse, though."

"Fine." He threw his hands in the air, resigned. "Do what you want."

"Thank you." I plastered a smile on my face as I changed direction and headed toward Chief Terry's booth. He sensed when I'd closed the distance, his shoulders going stiff, and I had to force myself to remain cheery even though I wanted to burst into tears and beg for forgiveness. "It's nice to see you guys here tonight. It's a surprise." I glanced at Landon for help. "It's a surprise, right?"

Landon's forehead wrinkled, his disdain for being dragged into the conversation evident. "Yes, it's a complete surprise."

"It probably wouldn't have been a surprise if you'd returned to the station this afternoon," Chief Terry said stiffly. "Where were you?"

"Oh, um ... I figured you needed some time alone to go through the notes from the case and Bay has that big newspaper office to herself, so I worked there. She doesn't like being alone when there's a killer on the loose so I was doing my duty as her boyfriend."

I scorched him with an annoyed look. "I'm fine being alone."

"No, you cried. I can't leave your side when you cry. That's simply the way I'm wired."

"I did not cry!"

Landon wasn't the type to give in, and this conversation was no different. "You don't need to be embarrassed. It's okay to cry. I'm sure Melanie cries occasionally, don't you?"

"I do." Melanie enthusiastically nodded her head. "I find that crying alleviates tension. Sometimes I put on a sad television show or movie simply so I can sob out my toxins."

"I prefer drinking wine when I'm feeling tense," I admitted.

"That sounds fun." Melanie beamed. "Um ... would you like to join us?" She looked confused and focused on Chief Terry when my eyes automatically went to him.

"We would love to join you," I said automatically. "That will give us a chance to get to know each other better."

"Sure."

Chief Terry cleared his throat, and when he finally pinned me with a dark look I felt an involuntary shudder go down my spine. "I don't think that's a good idea."

"You don't?" My voice sounded squeaky. "You don't want to have dinner with us?"

"I had lunch with Landon. One meal a day is enough."

"You didn't eat with me, though."

"No. You're on a date, Bay. We're on a date, too. I don't think anyone wants to make it a double date." He was cold, remote, as he focused on Melanie. The smile he offered her was warm, but his reaction to me was the exact opposite. "I'm sure we can find another day to have dinner. Maybe in a few weeks or so."

Weeks? He was really angry. "But ... ."

"Bay, they want to be alone." Landon wrapped his fingers around my wrist and gave me a gentle tug. "You remember what it was like when we first started dating. We were in our own little world and no one else could visit."

I remembered plenty of people inviting themselves to visit our private little world. "Right." My stomach felt hollow and my appetite vanished. "I guess we'll leave you to it."

"That would be best," Chief Terry agreed.

The look Melanie shot me was confused. "I ... if you think we should be separate for dinner, Terry, that's fine. As long as I get to spend time with you, I'm happy."

What a suck-up. I was back to wanting to punch her.

"We'll just grab our own booth." Landon was insistent as he pulled me away from Chief Terry's table. "Try the turtle cheesecake if you get dessert. It's amazing."

Melanie nodded. "That sounds great."

"Yes, everyone is happy with their separate dates," Chief Terry agreed, refusing to as much as look at me as Landon forced me away from the booth. "Now, what were we talking about before we were so rudely interrupted?"

Chief Terry was angry, and I hated it when that happened. I always cried as a kid until he agreed to forgive me. That left me feeling morose and unsure of myself. For a brief second, when Landon gave me a particularly insistent tug and my chin shot up so I was looking directly at Melanie, I saw what could only be described as smug satisfaction wafting over her features. The expression was gone practically the second I registered it and she was back to looking sympathetic, but I was sure it was there.

I felt defeated and annoyed, and there was nothing I could do about it. This day was not going how I envisioned.

"DO YOU WANT TO share a piece of cheesecake?"

Landon turned his plate so the caramel-covered triangle of creamy goodness was basically staring me in the face.

"No thanks."

"Are you sure?"

"I'm sure."

"Okay." He sliced into the cake and shoved a heaping forkful into his mouth with moaning designed to cajole a smile out of me as I stared at Chief Terry's back.

Dinner had been a depressing affair. I ate fried chicken but didn't really taste it. Instead, I stared at the booth where Chief Terry ate and laughed with the pretzel chick ... and all the while plotted her bloody demise.

"Hey! Look at me." Landon tapped his fork against my temple, causing me to frown.

"Did you just get cheesecake on my forehead?" Annoyance ran roughshod over my patience. "That's disgusting."

"Don't worry. I licked the fork clean before touching you."

"Is that supposed to make things better?"

Landon sobered, all attempts at lightening my mood evaporating. "He's angry with both of us. It's not just you."

"He never stays angry at me. He always forgives me right away."

"You're no longer tiny and ten."

"He forgave me when I was sixteen and getting in loads of trouble."

"Yes, well, you're an adult now. You're supposed to know better."

"You were right there with me, pal!"

Instead of engaging in the fight, Landon merely chuckled. "Wow. You're wound tight tonight, aren't you? I almost wish it was a full moon so we could go to the bluff and you could get your drink on. You need something to unwind."

He wasn't wrong. "Maybe I'll have a chocolate martini when we get home. We have to stop at the inn and talk to Aunt Tillie first."

"I know." He rested his hand on top of mine and met my gaze across the table. "He'll forgive you. That's what he does. Part of the anger fueling him right now is directed toward me."

"I think she has something to do with it."

"Who?"

"You know who."

AMANDA M. LEE

"Oh, man." Landon's expression was almost comical. If I was in a better mood, I would've laughed. "She was perfectly nice to you. In fact, she looked confused. That means Chief Terry didn't tell her what was going on. She didn't even know he was ticked at us. That means, even though he's furious, he's still protecting us."

I brightened considerably. "You have a point."

"I always have a point."

"I still don't trust her. You didn't see what I saw. She made a face."

"I would've made a face, too. He pretty much shut us down and you almost turned into a puddle of goo you were so upset. That is not normal behavior."

"That's not the sort of face she made. It was more as if she was ... winning."

"Winning what?"

"A game I didn't even know we were playing."

Landon rolled his eyes to the sky. "I can't even ... ."

I ignored his theatrics and grabbed the fork out of his hand to slice off a big piece of cheesecake for myself. "She's up to something."

"Why is it that you only find your appetite when it comes time to plot? I mean ... I thought you weren't hungry."

"Things change."

"Obviously so."

"As for plotting, I'm going to do nothing of the sort. I'm simply going to look out for my friend ... who is so blind to that woman's machinations that he's actually going to try to stay angry with me."

"No offense, Sweetie, but we've earned his ire. We broke the law."

"Barely."

"He doesn't really look at it the same way you do."

"He'll get over it ... as soon as I figure out what that woman has been doing to poison his mind against me."

"Oh, this will end well. Give me back my fork."

I did as he ordered. "That cheesecake is really good. I want another bite."

Landon made a big show of cutting into the dessert and pointing his fork toward his mouth before he detoured it to mine. "Fine. I'm just warning you now, if you make things worse with Chief Terry it's every lawbreaker for him or herself."

"I can live with that. He'll forgive me. He always does."

"I have no doubt."

EIGHTEEN

*E*ven though I didn't want to admit it, I was frustrated after dinner.

Melanie offered what I'm sure she thought was a friendly wave as Landon and I packed up to leave, but Chief Terry refused to look in our direction. It wasn't until we were at the front door that I risked a final glance and found his eyes on me.

I wanted to apologize, promise it would never happen again, but that was a lie. We both knew I wasn't above breaking rules here and there when the need struck. I always promised him I wouldn't break the rules a second time when caught as a kid, but I always did. It would be an empty promise, and I felt too old to be making empty promises.

Landon headed straight for The Overlook. He knew I wanted to question Aunt Tillie about Margaret Little's file. I was in a foul mood, so now was as good a time as any.

The dinner dishes were finished and my mother and aunts had spread out around the inn for some quiet time. Mom had a book open on her lap in the library when she caught sight of us, her eyes filling with curiosity.

"I thought you guys ate elsewhere tonight."

"We did."

"If you're looking for dessert it's in the kitchen."

"We had dessert, too. We're looking for Aunt Tillie."

"Now ... hold up." Landon lifted his hand to still us. "What kind of dessert are we talking about here?"

I rolled my eyes. "You just ate a huge slice of cheesecake."

"You ate half that slice."

"I ate, like, two bites."

"Um ... you ate half."

I didn't like his tone. "One-third."

"Half."

"Fine. Be a pig. See if I care."

Mom's sigh was heavy. I could tell listening to our antics was the last thing she wanted. "Why do you want Aunt Tillie? She's been pretty quiet all day, good even. I would really prefer you not rile her up so late in the evening. She'll be up all night."

"We think she stole a file from Dr. Hopper's office last night and we need to see it."

Mom's eyebrows nudged together. "Why would she steal a file and not tell you? That doesn't sound like her. Are you sure you're on the right track?"

"It's Mrs. Little's file."

"Oh, well, that explains that." Mom turned rueful. "She's in the family living quarters. If she attacks, you're on your own. I'm too tired to deal with her." Mom returned to the book. I didn't miss the shadows under her eyes, as if she hadn't been sleeping. It stirred something inside of me.

"You're upset about Chief Terry, aren't you?"

"Of course not." Mom kept her eyes on the book. "Terry and I are just friends."

I didn't believe her. "Why didn't you get together when I was a kid? I always thought you would."

"The timing was never right."

What was that supposed to mean? What timing? I opened my mouth to ask just that when Mom admonished me. "You should get going, Bay. Aunt Tillie might already know you're in the house, and she's an expert at hiding when she thinks it will keep her from getting into trouble."

She had a point. "Fine. We're not done talking about this, though."

"I can't wait."

True to form, we found Aunt Tillie watching television in the living room. She had her feet propped on the table and was wearing some sort of freaky housecoat. It almost looked as if it had an anime design, although I'd never known Aunt Tillie to be a fan of the medium. Stranger things had happened.

"I want to talk to you." I moved in front of my great-aunt and planted my hands on my hips. "I know what you did."

"I know what you did, too." Aunt Tillie was blasé. "You and your boyfriend are absolutely filthy and he's a bit of a pervert."

She was trying to derail the argument. She was good at that. I had no intention of letting her.

"You stole Mrs. Little's file, didn't you?"

Aunt Tillie furrowed her brow as she finally lifted her chin and met my gaze. "Oh, that? I thought you were talking about something else. Yes, I stole Margaret's file."

I wasn't used to Aunt Tillie admitting the truth so readily. I expected her to lie ... or at least distract me with some outrageous story nobody could possibly believe. Instead, she merely shrugged and smiled.

"Why did you take the file?" Landon asked, his tone even. He wasn't nearly as worked up about the theft as me. "Why not read it out loud and share it with the class? It seems to me that's something you would enjoy."

"I wanted to read it for myself first," Aunt Tillie replied simply.

"And?"

"And it's exactly as you would expect. She has narcissistic tendencies and she's manipulative. She also feels that she's under-appreciated and suffers from a victim mentality."

"That's it?"

Aunt Tillie nodded. "For the most part. There were some funny anecdotes in there ... like she has a reoccurring dream about being buried in an avalanche of yellow snow. I'm going to play with that and see if I can drive her insane. Other than that, it was fairly boring."

"So ... she wasn't listed as a psychopath?"

Aunt Tillie's brow turned into one big wrinkle. "What? No. Why would you think that?"

I briefly told her about the file we'd discovered hidden between two others at Hypnotic.

"Oh, no, I didn't do that. I took the whole file because it was easier. That psychopath thing must refer to someone else ... although now I'm curious to find out who."

She wasn't the only one. "We need that file," I supplied. "We have to keep everything together and return it to Chief Terry as soon as he secures a warrant."

"I figured." Aunt Tillie was calm as she got to her feet. "I made a copy, so it's fine."

"You made a copy?" That sounded frightening ... for Mrs. Little. "Why?"

"Why do you think?"

"You really are the devil when you want to be," I complained. "Thistle is right about that. You're mean."

"Just be glad I'm not focused on being mean to you."

"I feel that way every day."

LANDON AND I WAITED until we were back at the guesthouse to open Mrs. Little's file. Perhaps it was by tacit agreement — or maybe simply instinct — but we sat on the couch together and flipped through the pages.

"This feels somehow invasive," I admitted.

"Yeah, well, we're looking for a murderer," Landon noted. "Mrs. Little has shown a few undesirable tendencies in the short time I've known her. We know she kept secrets for years, including the fact that she was well aware that her husband killed Floyd Gunderson. That's only the tip of the iceberg. She's been up to her neck in other scandals.

There's always the possibility that there's something in there strong enough to propel her to murder."

He had a point, still ... . "I think Mrs. Little is more likely to keep the secret rather than spread it and have to kill someone."

"Maybe she couldn't keep the secret any longer," Landon suggested. "Everyone needs to confide in someone. Mrs. Little went years hiding her darkest secret from everyone. That had to be difficult."

"I guess."

"You and I have each other to confide in. Even if angry words are spoken, it's still a relief to unburden ourselves. I think that's why our relationship is so strong. We tell each other *almost* everything — I mean ... even we can't share everything — and then we work out our issues together."

"That's been a work in progress, though," I pointed out. "We didn't start out that way. I was keeping the witch secret from you back then ... and you were an undercover FBI agent and didn't tell me."

"We weren't technically involved then. We were circling each other. I had a job to do, but I was still worried about keeping you safe. I couldn't understand why you kept showing up to visit a cornfield where a kid had died in a horrible way. Not only did you keep visiting, it was happening in the middle of the night. None of it made sense."

"I was trying to be covert."

"I get that. It was still weird."

I chuckled as Landon slid his arm around my shoulders and tugged me close. "I thought you were weird, too. I considered that maybe you were a murderer and you were stalking me."

"I was trying to figure out where my biker friends were hiding their drugs. After I stumbled across you the first time, I started paying more attention. I wouldn't say I was stalking you as much as keeping an eye on you. I knew you were up to something. I was hoping it wasn't drugs, because I didn't want to arrest you."

The notion was absurd. "When did you realize that I wasn't running drugs?"

"When you brought your mother and aunts to a cornfield in matching tracksuits in the middle of the night."

"Yeah. That was a fun night ... other than you being shot."

As if reading my mood, Landon steered the conversation away from a potentially dark turn. "Let's not dwell on that." He pressed a kiss to my temple. "I'm here. We've come a long way. Let's focus on Mrs. Little and put that particular story behind us."

"Fair enough." I snuggled close to Landon as we perused the documents. "There are some interesting notes in here. Like this one: Mrs. Little was complaining that Aunt Tillie was following her around town and trying to kill her."

"Hopper wrote that she was paranoid and possibly needed medication," Landon said.

"Yeah, except Aunt Tillie spent an entire week this past winter following Mrs. Little around. She wasn't trying to kill her or anything, but we had a bet how far she could push things before Mrs. Little flipped her lid."

"Yeah, well, there are two sides to every story." Landon flipped a page. "Oh, here's something. It's about us."

"Us?" My eyebrows migrated higher on my forehead. "What does she say?"

"That she's convinced you've infiltrated the FBI in an attempt to cover for your family. Apparently I'm just some poor, unsuspecting moron who has been dazzled by sex and possible witchcraft to cover for you guys."

Even though I knew Mrs. Little had probably said ten times worse about me over the years, I was agitated all the same. "She's a horrible old biddy."

Landon snorted. "I think it's kind of funny."

"You think it's funny that she believes I got you through curses and spells?"

"Kind of. I'm guessing you don't think it's funny."

"Not even a little." I was stiff when I went back to reading the file. "She's horrible."

"And your nose is out of joint," Landon mused. "I didn't see that coming."

"It's a manifestation of the guilt she feels," Hopper volunteered as he popped into existence on the chair across from us. He looked relaxed, as if he was explaining something clinical to a reporter for one of those medical journals and he was almost bored by the task. "You've fallen in love with a woman who metabolizes guilt the same way others do water. It's going to be a part of your life going forward if the relationship survives — which isn't a given — so you should get used to it."

My mouth dropped open as annoyance and worry warred for supremacy in my brain. "What?"

"Ignore him," Landon instructed, disgust on full display. "He's trying to distract us because he's upset about you shoving him in an invisible box. This is how he's decided to get payback."

"I'm a little bit upset about putting him that box, too," I admitted. "Maybe that's some of the guilt he's talking about."

Hopper bobbed his head. "Exactly!"

"Oh, geez." Landon rolled his eyes. "Bay, he's trying to lead you off on a tangent. This isn't going to help."

"I know what he's doing." That was true. Hopper was a user. I recognized that within hours of meeting him. That didn't mean he didn't have insight into my relationship with Landon. "Why do you think I'm riddled with guilt?"

"I don't know all the specifics obviously — we would need full sessions to work through all that — but from what I've observed you're afraid of losing yourself to this new magic you've discovered and you're afraid of putting Landon into a position where he will have to risk his career to protect you."

He wasn't far off. "I can't quite seem to stop worrying," I admitted. "If Landon gets in trouble because of me ... ." I left it hanging.

"What happens if I get in trouble with my superiors?" Landon asked, honestly curious. "I mean ... what do you think is going to happen?"

I held my hands palms out and shrugged. "You'll lose your job and never forgive me."

"Um ... no. Neither of those things will happen."

I balked. "You helped me steal files."

"That is illegal," Hopper agreed. "You should stop going through them to prove you're remorseful."

"Nobody is that remorseful about stealing the files," I shot back.

"I did help you steal those files," Landon agreed. "But I won't lose my job over that. Anything that I would lose my job over, I wouldn't do."

"Even to protect my family?"

"No." Landon was firm. "I will do what it takes to protect you, but there are always ways to do that without breaking the law. Er, well, breaking the big laws. If you were in mortal peril and I had to break the law to save you I would because I wouldn't be able to stop myself. That would be justifiable.

"You're the one worried about things that won't happen, Bay," he continued. "I get it. This whole necromancer thing threw you for a loop. What happened with Danny in the snow was ... traumatic ... for you. It was traumatic for me, too, because I couldn't get to you in time. But you saved yourself. You always do."

"Still, you didn't even hesitate when it came time to stealing files last night," I pointed out. "That's against the law, too."

"Only a little bit."

"I didn't think law enforcement officials were allowed to see shades of gray when it comes to the breaking the rules."

"Actually, you'd be surprised. I'm an FBI agent, but I'm a human being, too. I have feelings and impulses. While stealing the files might not have been the best idea, I'm not sorry. We'll be ahead of the curve when it comes to tracking down a murderer. How can I be sorry about that?"

"That was a good answer." I gave him a warm grin and quick kiss. "I'm still kind of sorry for getting you into this mess."

"You'll get over it. The more time you spend with your new ability, the more comfortable you'll be. I don't expect it to happen overnight."

"Yeah." I flicked my eyes to Hopper and found him watching us with overt curiosity. "What?"

"I find it interesting that you can talk each other into breaking the rules and that somehow alleviates the guilt you originally felt. You would make a fascinating case study."

"Yeah, well, you're not going to participate in any case studies unless they have a big nuthouse in the sky for you to work at," I pointed out. "Also, given the fact that you were sleeping with your patients, you have no right to judge us for being a bit co-dependent. What you were doing was far worse."

Hopper rolled his eyes. "And here we go. You just can't accept that I was trying to help and move on. Why is that? Why do you hold a grudge the way you do?"

"Because you're disgusting."

"I'm trying to help. Most of those couples will have a stronger relationship because of my intervention. Just you wait and see."

"What about the couples who won't? Like Maxine and Jonathan. Are they stronger?"

"You have to break a few eggs."

"That is a really tired saying."

"That doesn't mean it's not true."

I stared at him for a long beat. "I really don't like you. I've tried. I thought at first you might be a good guy and capable of offering insight into people. Now I realize you're nothing but a randy tool and my only hope is that you'll see the error of your ways before this is all said and done."

"I've made no errors."

"You actually believe that, which worries me." I shook my head. "Either way, we're getting ready for bed. We don't want an audience."

"So?"

"So ... go." I flashed a weary smile. "Go and do whatever it is you do. I promise not to put you in a box this time."

"Shall I get down on my knees and thank you for that?"

"I don't care what you do. Just don't come back until I call you. Oh, and ... think hard about the file in your cabinet. The psychopath one.

Odds are that's who killed you. You've already broken every rule in the doctor-patient handbook. By breaking this one you might lead us to a killer. That's a good thing ... and you could use the karma."

He sighed. "I'll consider it."

"That's all I ask."

NINETEEN

*R*eading Mrs. Little's file was enlightening. Hopper diagnosed her with three personality disorders, but I remained unsure of why she went to him in the first place. Nothing in the file explained it. I was also confused about why he agreed to see her since he generally dealt with couples. I wasn't curious enough to summon him — mostly because I found him unbelievably arrogant and annoying — but I made a mental note to question him about it the next time we crossed paths.

Landon was awake and watching me when I opened my eyes the next morning. He seemed relaxed, a small smile playing at the corners of his lips. It took me longer to wake up than him, so I merely rolled and buried my face in his shoulder.

"Why do you always wake up in a good mood?" I complained. "I don't think that's normal."

"I don't always wake up in a good mood. Sometimes I'm crabby. You're just not a morning person." He poked my side to elicit a giggle. "As for this morning, I haven't been up long."

"Why are you smiling?"

"Because you look like an angel when you're asleep."

I snorted. "You're laying it on a bit thick."

"Maybe. There's something about the way that blond hair fans out that reminds me of angels, though. I don't know how to explain it."

I opened an eye and focused. "If you're looking to play games this morning, I don't think we have time. We need to head up to the inn. I want to talk to my mother."

"About Chief Terry?"

"Yes."

"What do you think she's going to say?"

That was a difficult question to answer. "I don't know," I said after a beat. "She's upset. She won't admit it, but I see it."

"I see it, too. The thing is, I think maybe she's upset because she believes her chance has passed and it's time to let Chief Terry move on and be happy."

I sensed a stern admonishment in my future if I didn't gain control of the conversation. "I think she's upset because she's going to have to put forth some effort to snag Chief Terry. Before, it was easy for her. He always showed up and threw out nonstop compliments about her pie. Wait ... that came out dirtier than I meant for it to."

Landon's chuckle was warm as he tightened his arms around my back. "I understand what you're saying. I also understand that you could make things worse if you get involved in this. It's not your business."

"I didn't say it was my business."

"But you're plotting something. I know you."

"I'm not plotting against Chief Terry." That was true. I would never plot against him. He was part of the family and rarely did anything that deserved plotting.

"You're plotting against Melanie," Landon argued. "Don't bother denying it. I see it whenever you look at her. You're working hard to come up with a plan to knock her out of the running."

"See, I think you're looking at this the wrong way. She shouldn't even be in the running. Somehow — and I'm still not certain how it happened — but somehow she was allowed into the game even though she didn't meet the team requirements."

"Oh, I love it when you use sports metaphors. You think I'll simply agree with you because I'm a dude, but that's not the case this time."

"You think I'm going to purposely hurt Chief Terry."

"I think you're going to hurt yourself," Landon clarified. "I saw the look on your face last night when Chief Terry froze you out. He was angry — and he had a right to be angry — but you didn't take it well because you're used to him doting on you. How do you think things are going to be if you manage to get rid of Melanie and he finds out what you've done?"

It was a fair question. That didn't mean I wanted to answer it. "I think they're going to have bacon at the inn for breakfast this morning. We should get cleaned up." I moved to slip out of bed but Landon kept a firm grip on me so I couldn't escape.

"Don't even think about it. You might believe you're being smooth, but I know better."

"I'm hungry."

"The bacon will wait. Wow. That's something I never thought I would say."

That made two of us. "Landon ... ."

"No, you listen to me." He was firm. "I know that you want Chief Terry to be part of this family. He already is.. He'll always your father figure. He doesn't have to date your mother to make that happen. Why can't you just let this go?"

"Because ... it's not right."

"What's not right?"

"All of it. He was always supposed to be part of the family. An official part, not just a ceremonial part. I recognized that when I was a kid, even though I'd let the notion fall by the wayside at some point. Now things are different and it's the perfect time for all those forgotten dreams to come together. They're not supposed to come together this way."

"Because you want him with your mother."

"I want him to be happy."

"Bay, he is happy." Landon's eyes filled with sadness. "He won't stop loving you because he's with Melanie. That's not how he operates. He's angry right now because he doesn't understand why we did what we did, but he'll get over it. I promise you that."

"You're missing the bigger picture."

"Then tell me what the bigger picture is."

"He's supposed to be here, with us. Not here in the guesthouse or anything, because that would be weird. He's supposed to be at the inn. He's supposed to be happy ... but here."

"That's what you want." Landon's temper came out to play. "Sweetie, let me ask you something. If your mother had tried to get rid of me back in the day and managed to accomplish it, would you have been satisfied with her explanation that she wanted you to be happy with someone other than me?"

He was making things too personal. "She wouldn't have done that."

"Why?"

"You said it yourself: We were meant to be."

"I'm glad you see that, because I'm hopeful it will cause you to relax, but that's not the point. Maybe Chief Terry believes he and Melanie are supposed to be."

"No."

"He seems happy, lighter than he has since I met him," Landon persisted. "Why can't you give that to him?"

"Because he'll be happier here."

"No, you'll be happier here."

"We'll all be happier here."

"I can't even ... ." Landon rolled to his back and brushed the hair from his eyes. "You're going to do this even though you know things will blow up in your pretty face. There's no stopping you, is there?"

"I'm going to do this because it's best for everybody."

"I don't want to hear you whining when things go sideways. I'm putting my foot down. I warned you about this and you refuse to listen."

"She's not the right person for him." I believed that with my whole heart. "There's something off about her."

"You're making that up to justify your actions, but ... whatever." He smacked a loud kiss against the corner of my mouth. "You're going to do what you want. That's how you are and I don't expect things to change. I love you for who you are ... even when you're going to do something stupid. So ... have at it."

"I don't need your permission."

"You don't have it."

"Things will work out. Just wait and see."

"I'm terrified of seeing how they'll work out. You have no idea."

WE'D PUT THE MINI-ARGUMENT behind us by the time we hit The Overlook. Guests were due to arrive later in the afternoon, although the expected number was small. Things wouldn't start heating up for another two weeks. Once the weather turned, the bus traffic would increase and we'd be slammed all summer. I was always eager for the break when winter hit, but by the time spring rolled around, I was also ready for the busy period.

Despite the fact that Landon was agitated with my plan to insert myself into Chief Terry's relationship, he shoved the disagreement aside and was all smiles when we entered the kitchen. Marnie and Twila, seemingly lost in their own little world, happily carried platters of pancakes and bacon to the dining room as Landon sprung into action to help. That left Mom, Aunt Tillie and me in the kitchen ... and the unhappiness hanging over the room was pronounced.

"How did your evening with Mrs. Little's file go?" Mom asked, her attention on the fruit she was chopping.

"It was interesting, but nothing we didn't suspect. She's paranoid about Aunt Tillie and she's a rampant narcissist."

"She's been that way as long as I've known her," Mom agreed. "She's always believed Aunt Tillie was out to get her. One time, she swore up and down her soda tasted funny and accused Aunt Tillie of slipping cyanide in it."

Aunt Tillie snorted from her recliner in the corner. She didn't appear to be in a hurry to join the rest of the crew around the dining room table. "She should've been worried about that wine she bought at the store. It was in a box, which means it was easy to tamper with. I didn't drop any cyanide in there, but I did experiment with happy pills one time."

"I believe that was the week Mrs. Little danced in the town square and blessed all the residents with a plastic magic wand if I remember correctly," Mom noted.

"That would be the week."

I snickered, genuinely amused. "That must have been when I was living in Detroit. I don't remember that ... and I surely would if I'd been here to witness it."

"I believe Aunt Tillie took video of the phenomenon," Mom offered. "Ask her to let you see it. She overlapped the footage with a Bon Jovi song. It's delightful."

"I can't wait." I rested my palms on the counter and knit my eyebrows as I studied my mother. She was pale and quiet, two things that didn't fit her personality, and she seemed withdrawn. I knew why. I also knew she didn't want to talk about it. That wasn't going to stop me from pressing the issue.

"Have you talked to Chief Terry?"

Mom's sigh was more exasperated than resigned. "And why would I do that?"

"Because you're upset."

"I'm not upset. I'm simply not feeling myself. I think a bug must be going around. It's that time of year."

"Except no one in our family ever gets sick," I countered, my patience wearing thin. "That's why we take all those witch herbs Aunt Tillie foists on us. They boost our immune systems. We never get anything worse than a few stray sniffles in the winter. In fact, Landon was so impressed with my immune system this year he's started taking the herbs."

"I'm glad to hear that," Aunt Tillie offered, her eyes thoughtful as they roamed my mother's drawn face. "He's a real baby when he gets sick. When he had that sore throat in January you would've thought the world was ending. He made your mother make him chicken noodle soup and you waited on him hand and foot. It was pathetic."

"He wasn't that bad," Mom countered. "In fact, I liked taking care of him."

"He was kind of whiny," I hedged. "I think it's a man thing."

"I'll definitely agree with you there," Aunt Tillie supplied. "Men are not as strong as women when it comes to colds and the flu. I think it's something in their genetic makeup. In fact ... do you remember that time when the girls were teenagers and Terry came down with strep throat?"

Mom's shoulders stiffened. "I don't think we need to discuss that story."

Aunt Tillie ignored the change in Mom's demeanor. "He was hacking up a lung and his throat was on fire. Bay was worried that he was going to die because she saw some program on the news that said flu patients were passing at an alarming rate."

"They shouldn't put that sort of thing on television if they don't want people to overreact," I complained.

Aunt Tillie snickered. "The girls insisted on making him soup. His favorite was navy bean and ham. You worked with them in the kitchen until they came up with the perfect recipe. Then they took fresh juice, tissues, magazines, cake and that soup to his house and proceeded to wait on him the entire day. You let them skip school to do it. Do you remember that?"

Mom's sigh was weary. "I remember. Bay refused to go to school because she was convinced he wouldn't die if she was with him."

"So the four of you sat over there all day," Aunt Tillie continued. "Clove read articles from a gossip magazine. Thistle read short stories from a science fiction magazine. Bay read newspaper articles, although she cleaned them up so Terry wouldn't be upset by bad news.

"All the while, you sat next to his bed and monitored his temperature and doled out medicine," she continued. "Eventually, the girls fell asleep and you sat with Terry and made sure he got the rest he needed. He bounced back quickly, and the girls were convinced it was the soup that did it. We know better, though, don't we?"

I wasn't sure where she was going with the story, but I was intrigued. "What happened?"

"Your mother mixed a special herb blend and added it to the soup," Aunt Tillie replied. "She chanted over Terry for a full hour as he slept to bolster his immune system. Your mother, who is a big believer in getting over ailments yourself, broke the rules because she didn't like seeing Terry in discomfort. Even more, she didn't like watching you girls worry about him. She was trying to make everybody feel better, which is her way."

Tears pricked the back of my eyes as I fought to keep from crying. "Why didn't you get together when I was a kid? I want to know the truth."

"It was never the right time," Mom answered stubbornly. "I had you ... and Thistle ... and Clove. I had Aunt Tillie."

"You weren't responsible for all of us," I argued. "Aunt Tillie was an adult."

"Who often acted like a child."

"That doesn't mean you were responsible for watching me," Aunt Tillie countered. "I was never your responsibility. You were mine. I took you in when your mother died and I never regretted it. I think you believed it was your responsibility to take over as the adult in the family at a certain point, but it was never necessary."

"That ultimately doesn't matter," Mom argued. "I would be lying if I said I didn't believe Terry and I would eventually find a way to work things out. That didn't happen. There was always something going on. When the girls were younger he was afraid that they would get too attached to him and he would somehow let them down. He gave them most of his focus. I'm not sorry about that. The girls thrived thanks to him."

"But you were shoved to the side," I pointed out. "You didn't get what you wanted because we were the focus. We're adults now. You can get what you want."

"That's what I've been telling her," Aunt Tillie said. "She doesn't want to listen."

"All you have to do is tell him how you feel," I pressed. "Things will work out if you do."

"Well, I'm not doing that." Mom was firm as she grabbed the bowl of fruit she'd finished chopping. "He's moving on. That's his right. I won't insert myself into his life." She moved toward the door, pulling up short when she caught Landon standing in the threshold. He looked sympathetic, something that caused Mom to sneer. "Why aren't you eating your bacon?"

"I was just checking on you guys," Landon replied.

"We're all set here."

"Okay." Landon stepped to the side so Mom could breeze past him, and met my gaze head on. Something in his demeanor had changed. "Fine. If you want to get rid of Melanie, I'm all for it. Clearly things haven't worked out as they were supposed to."

My lips curved, unbidden. He'd been listening on the other side of the door. "I thought you wanted me to mind my own business."

"I changed my mind. Go get her."

That was the best thing I'd heard all day. "You really are the perfect man."

"I know. I'm getting a T-shirt made up and everything."

TWENTY

$\mathcal{L}$andon lamented the fact that I'd turned him into a busybody for most of breakfast. Aunt Tillie found his change of heart amusing. When it came time to depart for the day, I took Aunt Tillie with me so we could collect Clove and Thistle at Hypnotic and left Landon to what was sure to be a long slog.

"He'll forgive you eventually," I offered, mimicking his earlier words.

"Ha, ha." He lightly flicked the spot between my eyebrows before giving me a quick kiss. "I'm a big boy. I can handle it."

"You just spent an hour complaining that we've turned you into a girl," Aunt Tillie pointed out. "Which one is it?"

"I said you've turned me into a busybody, not a girl."

"You say tomato."

"Whatever." Landon's sigh was full of weariness. "You guys need to behave yourselves. Whatever you have planned for Melanie, make sure it can't be traced back to you."

"We're not going after Melanie today," I countered, matter-of-fact. "We need to come up with a plan for that."

Puzzled, Landon furrowed his brow. "Then what are you doing?"

"We're going to cast a spell to figure out who has been at Hopper's house."

"We are?" Aunt Tillie made a face. "I thought we were going to cast a spell to get rid of the pretzel chick."

"I'm still hoping if we give Mom another day she'll handle that problem herself," I admitted. "If she doesn't, we'll handle it for her, but I haven't come up with an acceptable plan for that yet. That means, for today, we need to focus on something productive."

"If you ask me, whoever offed that guy did the world a favor," Aunt Tillie said. "He was a blight on Hemlock Cove, a boil on the butt of humanity, if you will."

"You have such a way with words," Landon muttered, shaking his head. "What is this spell you're casting at Hopper's house supposed to do? If you can create a trail to a killer, that would be great. I don't want you guys investigating on your own, though."

"If it was as simple as creating a trail to a killer, we would've done it that first day. That's not what we're doing."

"So ... what are you doing?"

"Creating trails to and from everyone who visited the house."

"That's bound to be a lot of trails."

"Yes, but it will give us a better idea of who we should look at. We're trying to find who was there the day he died. We can narrow the scope of the spell and see what we come up with. It can't hurt."

"I guess not." Landon slid his hand over the back of my head and leaned over so I had nowhere to look but his eyes. "If you find answers, I want you to call me. Don't confront whoever you find on your own. We need to come up with a reason to question the person the spell points at."

"I know the rules."

"Good."

One more kiss and Landon headed toward his Explorer. "Be careful ... and try to be smart if you move on Melanie. Don't bother denying you've got something brewing. I can tell."

"We haven't decided on a plan of action yet."

"You will. When you do, cover your butts. Even if Chief Terry eventually thanks you for sticking your big noses into his business, he won't do it right away. He'll be angry if he finds out ... and you don't do well when he's angry with you."

That was a fair point.

THISTLE AND CLOVE WERE keen to get out of the shop, so they didn't put up a fight when we dragged them to Hopper's house. Even though Clove had grand plans that didn't include getting in trouble, she thought an outing was a great idea because it would give her the chance to start her trivia game.

"I thought we were waiting until this case was solved before getting tangled in that web," Thistle groused.

"What web?" Aunt Tillie was focused on the sidewalk, her mouth moving as she counted paces. Her hearing was as good as ever.

"Clove wants us to compete to see who will be her maid of honor," I supplied. "She's come up with a game, and whoever wins gets the honor."

Aunt Tillie snorted. "Oh, that sounds just like her."

Annoyed, Clove planted her hands on her hips. "I'm right here and I can hear you."

"Yeah, yeah." Aunt Tillie waved off Clove's agitation. "Why can't you simply put names in a hat and pick that way?"

Clove balked. "What's the fun in that?"

"What's the fun in a trivia game?"

"It's fun for me."

"I guess that's fair." Aunt Tillie reached into her pocket and grabbed a package of herbs. "Okay, I'm going to drop the first mixture. Then we have to wait ten minutes before dropping the second. If this goes as planned, the sidewalk should light up with trails. There will be more than one so it's going to take some time to follow them."

I expected that. "Will anyone else be able to see the trails?"

"Only if they've got a bit of witch in them. I think that rules out pretty much everybody in town."

"That you know of," Thistle clarified. "You're hardly the all-knowing Tillie when it comes to that stuff. You hide in your own little world and only allow visitors when it suits you."

"You say that like it's a bad thing."

"Either way, it doesn't matter," I interjected, hoping to head off an argument. "If someone does see the trail it's doubtful anyone else will, and the original person will simply assume she's seeing things, so it shouldn't be a problem."

"Good point." Aunt Tillie sprinkled the herbs across the pavement. "While we're waiting, I think we should play a rousing game of maid of honor trivia." Her eyes gleamed as Thistle scowled. "I think Thistle should be first."

"You are a demon in old lady's clothing," Thistle muttered.

"That's a great idea." Clove enthusiastically clapped her hands. "I can't tell you how excited I am for this."

"That makes two of us." I faked as much enthusiasm as I could muster. "Right, Thistle? You're excited, too, aren't you?"

"I'm so excited I might burst," Thistle deadpanned.

"Great." Clove either didn't notice the sarcasm rolling off our cousin in waves or purposely ignored it. I was leaning toward the latter. Clove was better at reading people than she was often given credit for. "We'll start with Thistle because she clearly has an advantage over Bay because we work together."

"Oh, you've got an advantage over me," I drawled, enjoying the evil glare Thistle pinned me with. "I bet that means you'll win."

"Oh, we'll just see about that."

WE BOTH MADE AN EFFORT to lose the game. The idea of being Clove's maid of honor and having to wait on her for months as she prepared for the big day was daunting, to say the least. Because we were Winchesters, though, our true competitive spirit came out to play. By the time Aunt Tillie dropped the second bag of herbs and we hopped in my car to follow the trails, we were at each other's throats for trivia superiority.

"She was not fourteen when she had her first kiss," I argued, my eyes on the red trail that led down Plum Street. "She was thirteen. It was at the lake and she got tongue action on her first try. I remember because she wouldn't stop talking about it for weeks."

"I remember that, too," Aunt Tillie interjected from the passenger seat. "She was so proud that she announced it over dinner. I thought Marnie was going to melt down when Clove said it in front of Terry."

"I remember that." I smiled at the memory. "Chief Terry offered to track down every boy at the lake because Clove refused to admit who kissed her."

"That's because I knew Chief Terry would threaten him," Clove said, grinning. "If that happened, I wouldn't get another kiss all summer."

"You were weird," Thistle supplied. "You were excited because you said that was the next step to becoming a woman. Of course, you were also excited when you got your first period."

"That's because it meant I would stop getting dolls for Christmas."

"You didn't stop getting dolls," I pointed out, making a right and frowning when the trail stopped in front of Gregory Lapinski's house. "Huh. He's not married. I wonder what he was doing at Hopper's house."

"He's been picking up shifts at the grocery store," Aunt Tillie offered. "People call in orders for groceries and he delivers them. That's probably what he was doing at Hopper's house. I don't remember seeing his name in the files."

I arched an eyebrow, surprised. "How do you know he's been delivering groceries?"

"Because your mother ran out of brown sugar the other day and paid him to pick some up for her. She was knee-deep in molasses cookies and he showed up, like, ten minutes later. She said it was well worth the money."

"Huh. I didn't know that. Maybe I'll put a notice in the newspaper for him. I bet a lot of people would like to take advantage of that service."

"That's a good idea," Thistle said as I rolled around the block and headed back to Hopper's house. "We only have two trails left to follow," she noted. "We've managed to cut down the suspect list drastically. Unless these final two trails lead to something fantastic, I think we're dealing with the Walkers. They were the only ones on Hopper's list for special sex therapy."

Once back at Hopper's house, I picked the purple trail to follow. It led us toward town, which I found interesting.

"Bay gets a point for remembering my first kiss," Clove offered, a notebook in hand as she tallied the score. "She's ahead of you by two, Thistle."

"The day is young," Thistle muttered. "Ask your next question."

"What did I want to do for a living when I was a kid?" Clove asked.

"Oh, that's not fair." Thistle wrinkled her nose. "You wanted to be, like, ten different things. You have to be more specific than that."

"Fine. What did I want to be when I was eight?"

Thistle's disgusted expression didn't slip. "I can't remember that either. You jumped around from thing to thing. When you were really little you wanted to be a baker because you liked cookies. Then you spent a year wanting to be a princess. When your mother told you we don't have princesses in the United States, you insisted on moving to the UK."

"She also wanted to own a flower shop at one time," I added, smiling as a particularly funny memory from our childhood pushed to the forefront of my brain. "She cut all of Mom's roses from the garden and arranged them in a big bucket. She was so proud of herself she didn't even get in trouble for ravaging those rose bushes."

"She wanted to be a foot model, too," Aunt Tillie said. "When she found out she had tiny feet — especially compared to you two — she was thrilled at the idea of standing out. She loved shoes, so she thought being a foot model was the way to go."

"Oh, you guys really do know me." Clove beamed. "I'm giving all of you credit for that answer."

"I'm not playing the game," Aunt Tillie pointed out, straightening her neck when she saw where the purple trail was leading. "You've got to be kidding me."

Everyone sobered when the ramifications of our latest discovery hit hard.

"The Unicorn Emporium." Clove sounded a little dazed. "Do you think Mrs. Little is really a murderer? I mean ... I know she's unpleasant and everything, but I never thought she was capable of murder."

"I think Mrs. Little is capable of more than we give her credit for," I said as I parked my car in front of the police station and killed the engine.

"What are you doing?" Thistle asked, genuinely curious. "I thought you promised Landon you wouldn't investigate if you found answers."

"I'm not investigating. I'm simply ... shopping for a unicorn. Clove will need something to give away as prizes at her bachelorette party."

"Oh, that is a lame reason for going in there."

"I'm fine with that."

Aunt Tillie was already out of the car and waiting for me on the sidewalk when I exited the vehicle. She seemed excited at the prospect of Mrs. Little being a murderer. I wasn't sure that was a good sign.

"We're just going over there to take a look around," I cautioned, sober. "We don't want to tip her off that we suspect she's a killer."

Aunt Tillie's expression was withering. "I know how this works. I'm not an idiot."

"No, but you do get excitable when it's time to mess with Mrs. Little. You can't help yourself."

"Yeah, yeah." Aunt Tillie wasn't in the mood to be admonished. "I've got everything under control. She's a murderer and we're going to take her down. You have nothing to worry about."

I sighed as Aunt Tillie zipped across the street. Thankfully, traffic wasn't heavy, so she didn't risk an accident when she refused to look both ways. By the time Thistle, Clove and I caught up with her, she was standing on the other side of the store window peering inside.

"You're a marvelous spy," Thistle deadpanned, shaking her head. "No one would ever notice you standing out here with your face pressed against the window. Very covert."

"Stuff it." Aunt Tillie's eyes flashed with anger. "One more word and you're on my list."

"You can't use that as a threat any longer. You've whipped it out too many times. You're like the girl who cried list. I no longer fear being on your list. That makes you impotent."

The annoyance washing over Aunt Tillie was palpable. "Oh, really?"

"Now isn't the time for this," I admonished, slipping between them. I was hopeful Aunt Tillie's zest to mess with Mrs. Little was greater than her need to keep control over Thistle. If I was lucky, she would simply forget her anger and move on. "We need to focus on Mrs. Little. I ... ." I trailed off when I saw the group of laughing women in the store. It seemed Mrs. Little wasn't alone despite the lack of tourists in the area. "Huh."

"That's a loaded 'huh,'" Clove said. "What do you mean with that huh?"

"Well ... ." I rolled my neck as I considered the rather obvious problem. "The spell was supposed to point toward the people who visited Hopper's house the day he died. We were specific in the language ... the people, not the house. The reason those other trails led to houses is because the suspects were home at the time. We confirmed that."

"So?" Clove clearly hadn't caught up.

"So ... there are six people in Mrs. Little's store right now," I replied. "Mrs. Little, Maxine Wheeler, Esther MacReady, Tori Corbin, Janet Hall."

"And Melanie Adams," Aunt Tillie finished ticking off the names, her expression turning grim. "Basically the spell is saying that one of the people in the store was at Hopper's house that day. We don't know which one."

"It has to be Mrs. Little," Clove persisted. "She was seeing him."

"So was Maxine," I pointed out.

"Janet Hall was on the list, too," Thistle added. "She's in the files we separated. She was having sex with Hopper."

And Esther lived next door to him," I added. "Basically, everybody but Tori and Melanie has ties to Hopper. We didn't cut down our list all that much."

"So ... what does this mean?" Clove asked.

I shrugged, unsure how to answer. "We have fewer people to focus on, but we can't rule out very many in that group because more than half of them had ties to Hopper. We need to figure out who wanted him dead most."

"Is there a way to do that?"

"I have no idea."

TWENTY-ONE

*I*f we were good spies, we would've quietly slipped away from the window and found an isolated spot to discuss the next phase of our plan.

That's simply not how we work.

"Where are you going?" Thistle hissed as Aunt Tillie pushed through the weak wall of Winchesters and headed toward the front door.

"What's she doing?" Clove asked, jerking her eyes to me. "Is she going inside?"

That was a very good question, but I had no idea why I was the one expected to answer. "Who knows what she's doing?" I barked as I began following. "But we need to stop her."

"Oh, sure," Thistle drawled behind me, in no hurry to follow. "We'll just stop her. It's as easy as saying it. We'll say 'stop' and she'll agree out of the goodness of her heart."

"No one needs your sarcasm," I shot back.

"If I didn't have sarcasm, I'd have absolutely nothing to say," Thistle complained as Aunt Tillie wrapped her fingers around the front door handle. "And if Aunt Tillie didn't have an inherent need to poke and prod like she's Dr. Frankenstein and Mrs. Little is her monster we wouldn't be here right now."

I desperately fixed my attention on Aunt Tillie. "I don't know what you're planning to do ... but this is a terrible idea."

"I don't have terrible ideas." Aunt Tillie was matter-of-fact. "Every idea I have is gold. This will be the same. Trust me."

"You once told me that we were going to get rich by taking a metal detector to the lake every summer and collecting all the jewelry people lost," Clove pointed out, a last-ditch effort to rein Aunt Tillie in. "That wasn't a good idea, was it?"

Aunt Tillie made a face. "I still haven't been proved wrong on that."

"No, but what do we usually find?"

"Beer cans," Aunt Tillie admitted sheepishly.

"Wait a second ... ." Something occurred to me. "Since when do you two sneak off to spend time together at the lake?"

"Oh, well ... ." Clove's cheeks colored.

"Who cares?" Thistle challenged. "If that old biddy wants to search for someone's missing ring at the lake, I say let her. That's one afternoon we don't have to worry that she's going to do something stupid."

Aunt Tillie's eyes lit with fury. "Hey, mouth, I never do stupid things."

"I've got a whole childhood spent with you that begs to differ," Thistle shot back.

"Oh, we'll just see about that." Aunt Tillie was clearly spoiling for a fight because she narrowed her eyes and glared. "This is going to be the best idea I've ever had. Given that I've had some of the best ideas anyone has ever had, that's saying something. You need to trust me." She flicked her eyes to me. "You trust me, right, Bay?"

Oh, well, geez. There was nothing I liked better than being put on the spot. "Well ... ."

"See!" Aunt Tillie jabbed an emphatic finger into the air. "Bay trusts me. Why must you always be the difficult one, Thistle?"

"I don't believe Bay said that she trusts you," Thistle argued.

"Then clean your ears. Bay totally trusts me." Aunt Tillie was done waiting. This time when she grabbed the door handle she pushed the door open and strolled into the Unicorn Emporium as if she owned it. "Hello, Margaret. I think we have something to discuss ... and for once it's not your need to fill your life with phallic symbols. I mean ... what's that about?"

Thistle, Clove and I could've run. Most people wouldn't have blamed us. That's not the Winchester way, though, so instead we hurried into the store behind Aunt Tillie. We would offer her solidarity and support ... even if we all agreed that she was crazier than a Kardashian without access to a mirror.

"Excuse me, Tillie," Mrs. Little drawled, taking up position at the center of her small circle and planting her hands on her hips. "This is a private establishment."

"Technically it's not," I reminded her, cringing when she bored her eyes into me. "It's a business. This is a tourist town, so business doors are always open. I believe that was your suggestion. You even wanted to make it the town motto, if I remember correctly."

"Businesses are only open until seven," Thistle corrected, her eyes gleaming with something I remembered well from childhood. She was excited for the hunt, even if she wasn't quite sure who she was hunting. "Mrs. Little believes doors should always be open ... but only until seven because people out after that are clearly up to no good. She actually put that in those little brochures she carries around."

"And I stand by that," Mrs. Little sneered. "Only people looking for trouble are out after seven. I bet you guys are always out after seven."

"It depends on if there's cake at the inn," Clove countered. "If there's cake, we like to stick close to it."

"Yes, well ... ." Mrs. Little trailed off as she defiantly squared her shoulders and stared into Aunt Tillie's eyes. They were mortal enemies who enjoyed making scenes. They were also diminutive, barely five feet tall, although they packed a wallop of attitude.

"What do you think you're doing here, Tillie?" Mrs. Little asked as she settled on her plan of attack. "You're not welcome. I'm going to have to ask you to leave."

"The sign says 'open,'" Aunt Tillie pointed out. "That means that you're open for business ... just like you used to be when you slept your way around town."

I bit the inside of my cheek to keep from laughing. Leave it to Aunt Tillie to throw out her version of a skank insult one minute into the argument. She was clearly loaded for bear.

"I'm not open for business with you," Mrs. Little snapped. "That sign on the front window says that I can refuse service to anyone. I'm refusing it to you, so ... get out. I don't even know what you're doing here."

"We're here because we want to know if you were sleeping with Dr. Hopper like Maxine there ... and a few others ... or if you might have killed him for a different reason," Aunt Tillie countered without hesitation, causing my stomach to sink. "I think you're too old to be one of Hopper's conquests — he wasn't blind, after all — but Bay here isn't so sure. I'm leaning toward you guys having a different arrangement. I'm dying to know what it was."

Mrs. Little's mouth dropped open. "Excuse me?"

Maxine furrowed her brow as she caught up to the conversation and spoke for the first time. "Wait ... I'm confused."

"You weren't the only one sleeping with Dr. Hopper," Thistle offered helpfully. "He was doing it with at least twenty of his patients, including Janet. You weren't special."

Her cheeks flooding red, Janet took a step back when Maxine's eyes landed on her. "She doesn't know what she's talking about," Janet offered lamely.

"Oh, we know all about the people who were sleeping with Hopper," Thistle said. "He kept copious notes ... and was a total sleazeball. By the way, there is no such thing as therapeutic sex with your doctor to save your marriage. He was using you."

"He was not!" Maxine was beside herself. "We were in love."

"You're deluding yourself," Thistle argued. "Tell her, Bay."

The last thing I wanted to do was insert myself in this conversation. "He was a total tool," I said finally. "He used a lot of women. Don't take it personally."

"Ugh!" Instead of thanking Thistle for telling her the truth, Maxine stormed in her direction. "You take that back! I'm not going to stand for you sullying the name of the man I love."

"Oh, this is getting out of hand," Clove complained, skirting behind Thistle so she wouldn't end up with a fist in the face. "I can't be a part of this if it turns violent. I'm getting married in a few months. My face needs to look perfect for the big day."

"Your face won't look so perfect when I rub dirt all over it," Thistle warned.

"I always look perfect."

"Or when I go after your dress because you simply won't shut up," Thistle hissed.

That did it. Those were fighting words for Clove. "You're dead to me, Thistle!"

"Oh, how will I ever get over the heartbreak?" Thistle drawled, pressing her hand to her chest. "The sadness will never end and I will walk the Earth a lonely and broken woman."

I was trying to figure out a way to stop the inevitable fight between Thistle and Clove (and possibly Maxine, who looked to be considering a physical attack) when I realized there was more than one fight brewing.

"If you don't leave right now, I'll make you leave," Mrs. Little warned Aunt Tillie, closing the distance between them and planting her feet directly in front of my glowering great-aunt. "We both know I'm stronger than you."

Aunt Tillie's snort was derisive. "In what alternate universe?"

"In every universe."

"You're dreaming."

"Oh, yeah?" Mrs. Little launched herself at Aunt Tillie. She was surprisingly quick for a woman in her eighties. That didn't mean she wasn't breakable. If a healthy Mrs. Little was insufferable, I couldn't imagine what she'd be like if she actually had something to complain about … like a broken hip because of a fight.

With that in mind, I took two long strides forward in an effort to intercept her, shooting out both hands to grab her by the shoulders.

"Mrs. Little, think about this. You don't want to fight. It's beneath you."

Unfortunately for me, my hands missed their intended targets because of her size and I inadvertently gave her a hard shove rather than catching her. Mrs. Little's furious eyes caught fire as they locked with mine.

"If you want to play that way," she sneered.

"Wait a second ... !"

The brawl was on.

BY THE TIME LANDON AND Chief Terry arrived, the fight had been raging for five minutes and at least five porcelain unicorns had paid the ultimate price and hit the ground during the melee. Most of the women involved gave up after a few scratches. They weren't used to fighting, and we had stamina on our side. Mrs. Little and Maxine refused to back down, though, and they looked a little worse for wear when law enforcement arrived.

Of course, we didn't exactly look put-together ourselves.

"What happened?" Chief Terry, bewildered, planted his hands on his hips as he looked around the store. "I don't understand what's going on here."

"Ask them," Melanie offered, pointing a shaking finger in our direction. She'd wisely stayed out of the fight. That didn't mean she wasn't injured. Janet accidentally caught her with a wild punch when she tried to sidestep the action. She went down hard ... and was barely back on her feet before Chief Terry put an end to the brawl.

Chief Terry looked anxious when his eyes tracked to me. "Bay?"

I shifted from one foot to the other, uncomfortable under his scrutiny. "Well ... ."

"Don't give her grief," Aunt Tillie ordered, her temper on full display as she thumped her chest and silently challenged Mrs. Little to go again. "She didn't start this."

"Who did?" Landon asked as he leaned over to study my face. His finger was gentle as he traced it over my bruised lip. "Are you okay?"

"Why are you asking her that?" Melanie challenged, her voice turning shrill. "She came in here and attacked without provocation."

"Um ... wait a second." Thistle, her hair standing on end thanks to Maxine's insistence on trying to pull it, held up a hand to quiet the gathering. "You might not be happy about what happened — the Goddess knows it's not one of our finer moments — but you can hardly blame this on Bay. She was trying to stop the fight."

"She kicked me!" Janet yelled.

"Only because you bit me," I fired back, holding up my arm for emphasis. "Who bites someone? I mean ... come on!"

Landon snagged my arm and studied what were clearly teeth indentations on my forearm. "Did she break the skin?"

I shook my head.

"Well, then you probably won't get an infection. But it might not hurt to have it looked at."

"I don't think my dignity can take that hit," I admitted. "I'm fine."

Landon sighed and stroked my hair away from my face so he could look deep into my eyes. He must have seen something there that told him I meant business, because he merely shook his head. "Fine. We'll revisit it later if I feel it's necessary."

"Whatever."

"I still don't know what happened here," Chief Terry noted as he paced the small open space separating their group from ours. "You're all grown women. What were you doing brawling?"

"I blame them," Melanie announced. "We were minding our own business and having a good time when they stormed in and ... well, quite frankly, said some rather ridiculous things."

"I have trouble believing Bay said anything ridiculous," Chief Terry countered, his loyalty rising to the surface.

"She said thirty ridiculous things!"

"To be fair, Bay didn't say anything ridiculous," Thistle argued. "She was on her best behavior. She didn't even throw a single punch until she got bit ... and then it was on. I forgot how good she was in a fight."

Worried, I risked a glance at Landon out of the corner of my eye and found his shoulders shaking with silent laughter. It wasn't what I was expecting.

"You guys were all spouting ridiculous nonsense when you walked through the door," Melanie argued. "I heard it."

"Bay didn't say anything." Thistle was obstinate. "She just stood there. Aunt Tillie said the ridiculous stuff. That's why we brought her. But I don't think Aunt Tillie said anything ridiculous. Everything she said today was true."

"Um ... she did say that Mrs. Little's hair turns into snakes at night and eat the souls of the young and innocent," Clove interjected. "That was a little ridiculous."

"She hasn't been proved wrong on that," Thistle argued.

"Right on!" Aunt Tillie gave Thistle an enthusiastic high-five, causing me to smile. They fought with each other so often that I'd forgotten how amusing — and strong — they were when they joined forces.

"Okay, I need to hear this story again from the beginning," Chief Terry said after a beat, pulling a pad and pencil from his shirt pocket. "We're going to separate everyone and take statements. We'll start with ... um." His eyes tracked over the room and briefly touched on me before landing on Melanie. "We'll start with you, Ms. Adams. Please come over here and give me your statement. We'll get to the rest of you in a few minutes."

I was flabbergasted ... and a little hurt. He always took my statement first. He always used my statement as a measuring stick against all others. When I focused on Landon, I realized he was equally surprised.

"What just happened?"

Landon shrugged. "I guess it makes sense."

Now he was simply making excuses for his buddy. "How does that make sense?"

"I always take your statement first," he reminded me. "That's the normal thing to do ... give your girlfriend preferential treatment. He's not doing anything out of the ordinary."

"Yeah, but he always gives me preferential treatment."

"I guess you're not so special any longer, are you?" Mirth flitted across Mrs. Little's face. "How does it feel to be replaced?"

I didn't like the idea one bit. "Hey, Aunt Tillie, did I ever tell you about the time that Mrs. Little said your wine tasted like sour grapes on strike? She wanted to have your operation shut down and even called the ATF to see if she could get you locked up in a federal facility."

Aunt Tillie clutched her hands into fists at her sides as Mrs. Little blanched. "No, but I'm on it. There will be no place you can hide this time, Margaret. You'd better start running now."

TWENTY-TWO

*C*hief Terry questioned me second, which was something, but the damage was already done. I was cool and clipped when delivering my responses to his questions. Landon's distaste for my attitude was evident, but I refused to back down. I obviously didn't mention the real reason we were at the store — that would've opened us up for challenges nobody wanted to face — and when Chief Terry ordered all sides to disperse without arresting anyone, he left a lot of women unhappy. The most obvious was Melanie.

"So ... they're not even getting a reprimand?" She challenged Chief Terry as he directed us through the front door. "There's no punishment for what they did? I see how things work."

"I haven't decided who will be punished for what," he clarified, his tone grave. "I need to go through all the reports."

"They were the aggressors."

"Except everyone says that Mrs. Little and Maxine attacked first."

"They came into the store when they weren't invited."

"It's a place of business."

"Right." Melanie's anger was palpable as she shook her head. "I guess I should've seen this coming. All the signs were there."

"What signs?" Frustration bubbled up as Chief Terry gave Aunt Tillie a small push to get her moving. "I'm making them leave. What more do you want from me?"

"You'll always be more loyal to them," Melanie pressed. "They'll always be the priority."

I wasn't sure why I missed the signs before, but I recognized them now. She was trying to force Chief Terry's hand, make him declare her top of the relationship heap, and she wanted him to do it in front of other people. It was beyond disgusting.

"We're not his priority," I forced out, wiping the palms of my hands on my jeans. "He questioned you first. Don't give him crap for doing his job."

Chief Terry's eyes widened with surprise. "Aren't you going to give me crap for doing my job?"

"No." Weariness momentarily swamped me as I fought to gather my emotions. Landon was right. When I lost control, bad things were more likely to happen. This was the worst time for Hopper to show up, and the way the magic crackled in the back of my head reminded me that it was a distinct possibility. I had to get out of the store and regroup in private. It wasn't a luxury, but a necessity. "I'm going to head back to The Whistler to do my job. If you want to arrest me later, that's where you'll find me."

I was stiff as I pushed past Aunt Tillie, refusing to glance over my shoulder and meet Chief Terry's conflicted gaze. I felt it resting on my shoulders, but I was emotionally wrung out and I didn't want to risk something terrible happening if I lost control.

"I'll walk you back to The Whistler," Landon offered, falling into step with me when I reached the sidewalk.

"You don't have to."

"I want to." He linked his fingers with mine, his lips curving as we put distance between us and the gaggle of women inside the Unicorn Emporium. "So ... how many people did you smack around?"

"Nowhere near as many as I wanted."

"Did you win?"

"What do you think?"

LANDON WAS WORRIED. Perhaps "worried" was the wrong word. He was definitely concerned by my silence, but he didn't press me. He left me to my imaginary work at the newspaper office and promised to check on me in a few hours, after I had time to calm down.

I watched from the front lobby window as he trudged across the parking lot, crossing paths with Chief Terry close to the sidewalk and slowing his pace so they could talk. Whatever words passed between them, Landon wasn't happy. He gestured wildly at one point and jabbed a finger toward the newspaper building. I had no doubt who he was talking about. He was taking up my cause with Chief Terry, something that had never been necessary before.

It seemed I had been supplanted, and it wasn't a good feeling. Melanie was Chief Terry's priority now, and even though I understood it, that didn't mean I could accept it. She definitely had to go.

With nothing better to do, I headed to my office. Earlier in the day we'd moved the pilfered files from Hypnotic because we were worried someone might discover them. Even though the newspaper building was also open to the public, the odds of someone wandering into Hypnotic were much greater.

I was fired up, the aches and pains I incurred during the brief skirmish in the Unicorn Emporium serving as fuel. I decided to use the burst of energy to my advantage and go through the files again, to find a key tidbit I might have missed.

It was mostly a losing endeavor. I went through all of Hopper's sex partners and found nothing out of the ordinary. Er, well, nothing other than the obvious. He was still a perverted jerk who took advantage of troubled marriages so he could get what he wanted without caring about what these couples needed. If he were still alive I would've reported him to the medical board and had his license stripped.

The last file in the stack was Mrs. Little's. It was thick, a lot of notations in the margins. While I found her ruminations on the state of her life enlightening, it was nothing I hadn't already heard or suspected.

Mrs. Little went to high school with Aunt Tillie. They were rivals of sorts — just like Lila and me, although I didn't discover my true strength until I was much older, so the fights were largely one-sided — and they apparently hated each other with a fiery passion. Mrs. Little claimed that Aunt Tillie was jealous of her upon first meeting. I didn't believe that. Aunt Tillie always taught us that jealousy was a useless emotion.

"It doesn't matter what others have or how they achieved it," she once told us. "It matters what you can do, the limitations you set upon yourself. Don't worry about others. You do you. Everything else will fall into place."

At the time, I thought she was full of crap. Aunt Tillie was in our lives from the moment we were born, a larger-than-life character who had spent loads of time with us. She was funny and entertaining. She enjoyed getting us in trouble. Because of that, I very rarely took her teachings to heart. She was more of a distraction than anything else. With age, I'd learned that she was more than the sum of her parts. Sometimes — and sure, the occasions were rare — but sometimes she knew exactly what she was talking about and was unbelievably wise.

"What are you doing?"

I jerked my eyes to the office doorway and let out a relieved breath when I saw Clove and Thistle. I'd forgotten to lock the front door, something Landon frowned upon when I was working alone in the building. I felt lucky that the women from Mrs. Little's shop hadn't been the ones to track me down.

"Reading Mrs. Little's file," I admitted, offering them a slight smile. "What are you guys doing?"

"Checking on you," Thistle replied, neatly sidestepping the piles of folders on the floor and settling to my right. "We thought maybe you'd want some company."

Did I? I wasn't so sure. "I'm fine."

"Landon thought you might like some company, too," Clove admitted, sheepish. "He stopped by Hypnotic a few minutes ago. He wanted us to check on you."

I wasn't surprised. "He doesn't need to worry."

"I think he's worried about the Chief Terry thing," Thistle offered as she plucked a file from the floor and opened it. "He thinks you're upset about how things went down."

"I'm fine."

"I think you're upset, too."

I gritted my teeth and bit back a hot retort. "I'm fine."

"You can keep saying that, but we don't believe it," Clove offered. "We know how you feel. We love Chief Terry, and while we might not have the same relationship with him as you do, he was like a father to us, too."

"I'm not feeling anything." I refused to crumble in front of my cousins. It was undignified and I was better than that. "I'm simply trying to find a clue in these files. Someone must've had a reason to kill Hopper. We need to find out who."

"You can't hide what you're really feeling from us," Thistle challenged. "We know you too well. I saw the look on your face when Chief Terry chose to interview Melanie first. It was as if he'd smacked you across the face, something he would never do. The thing is, I don't believe he did it to purposely hurt you. He was simply trying to get a read on the situation."

"Then he should've asked."

"We were part of the fight," Clove supplied. "It was us against Mrs. Little ... and Maxine ... and Janet. Sure, the other women might've thrown a slap or two, but the real fight was between us. I think Chief Terry was trying to get an unbiased explanation about the fight."

"I would've given him an unbiased explanation."

"Really?" Clove cocked a dubious eyebrow. "You would've said we were equally at fault for what happened?"

"No. We weren't equally at fault. Mrs. Little was to blame."

"And that's why he asked for Melanie's take on the situation first."

It made sense. I still didn't like it. "We have to get rid of her. I was only half-serious before. I thought for sure my mother would come through and put her foot down, launch a claim on Chief Terry and put things right. But I don't think that's going to happen."

"She's too upset and hurt," Thistle offered. "She thought there was always going to be time to move forward with him. The reality that she was out of time was akin to being run over by Aunt Tillie's plow. She's still regrouping. By the time she gets herself together it might be too late. We have to do it for her."

"I don't know," Clove hedged, chewing her bottom lip. "Doesn't fiddling with Chief Terry's personal life make us the bad guys? I don't want to be the bad guys. We're supposed to be the heroes."

"Oh, please!" Thistle rolled her eyes. "I can't believe we're even related sometimes. I definitely can't believe I'm going to be your maid of honor and have to listen to this stuff nonstop for the next few months. What did I do to deserve this?"

The statement caught me off guard. "Wait ... you're her maid of honor?"

Clove bobbed her head, her chocolate eyes filling with instant apology. "I didn't choose her because I love her more than you," she said hurriedly. "We've been talking about it. You're going through a lot.

"It's not just Chief Terry," she continued, resting her hand on my knee as I absorbed the reality that I hadn't won the competition. Surprisingly, it was a bitter pill to swallow. "You're a necromancer now. I don't know everything that entails, but I gather it's a big deal. I know Aunt Tillie has been contacting witches from other covens trying to get information. That's how big it is."

"It's huge," Thistle agreed. "Aunt Tillie would rather set those other covens on fire than accept their help. She's looking, though. For you. We all want answers to make this transition as easy as possible."

"That's the main reason we decided it would be best if Thistle stepped in this go-around," Clove added. "You need to focus on figuring out how to make this work. The Goddess wouldn't have given you this power if you couldn't handle it. You simply need to figure out how to control it. Once you do, it will be easier."

I wanted to believe her. "You're afraid that I'll accidentally call ghosts to your wedding and ruin everything. I get it."

"I'm not afraid of that." Clove was dismissive. "Sure, that would be weird. But it would be memorable. I'm more worried about you. Being my maid of honor is going to be labor intensive. I have lists and things I need done."

Thistle let loose a groan. "Oh, geez!"

I pressed my lips together to keep from laughing.

"You have enough on your plate right now," Clove said. "Thistle will be my maid of honor. I'll stand up for you when it's time. You'll stand up for Thistle, which is kind of a punishment, but there's only three of us, so that's how it worked out."

I bit back a sigh. "That's a good plan. I'm sad that I didn't win the competition, but this is probably for the best. I can control some aspects of the necromancy thing, but I'm far from a master."

"And you need to focus on that," Thistle said. "I remember when we were kids, I heard my mom talking to your mothers in the kitchen one day. I eavesdropped because ... well, I like knowing other people's business. I was intrigued because they were talking about Bay.

"It was right after you saw Chief Terry's mother in the cemetery and she told you where to find that watch thing for him," she continued. "Everyone was finally convinced you could actually see and talk to ghosts. They were worried because it's a rare gift and it's driven more than a few witches crazy.

"Aunt Winnie was terrified you weren't strong enough to carry the burden, but Aunt Tillie stepped in and told her to stop being a ninny," she said. "Aunt Tillie said right from the beginning that you would handle it and be fine. She also said that you were young for the gift to manifest, but there had to be a reason behind it.

"You've always been stronger than us when it comes to the magic, Bay," she said. "We're dabblers of the highest order because we don't like being bossed around. It comes naturally to you when you follow your instincts. That's what you should do this time. You excel when you listen to your heart instead of your head. You get that from Aunt Tillie."

I made a face. "Do you really think now is the time to kick me when I'm down?"

"Believe it or not, that was a compliment. She's an instinctive witch, too. Don't get me wrong, I think Clove and I could be stronger if we put effort into it, but for you it comes naturally. It's time to embrace that."

I swallowed hard. "I killed a man, though."

"You've fought off attackers before."

"This was different. I used the souls of those dead girls to kill. That makes me feel guilty."

"Because they were innocent before being killed?" Thistle's smile was knowing. "I thought about that, and I get it. You can't take it back. You have to move forward."

"Besides, I think those girls would be happy to know that they essentially avenged their own deaths," Clove added. "Sure, what happened surprised us all. You stepped up to the plate and you protected yourself. That's the most important thing."

"The rest of it will come with time," Thistle added. "You'll figure it out."

"How can you be so sure?"

"You always figure everything out. That's your strength. It drove me crazy when we were kids. It always appeared to me that things came easier for you. I didn't understand what was really happening, that you simply thought things out longer and harder than the rest of us. It seemed easier, but it was actually harder."

"This won't be solved overnight," Clove said. "You'll get a handle on it. We'll help while you go through the process. We'll serve as back-up ... and we'll gladly get in another fight at the Unicorn Emporium if need be to prove our loyalty."

I laughed despite myself. "That was pretty funny. I had no idea Mrs. Little could move that fast."

"And I had no idea the pretzel chick was such a manipulator," Thistle said. "Did you see what she did with Chief Terry? She's trying to turn him against us. It's probably jealousy, but we have to stop that."

"Definitely." My spine stiffened as defiance rushed through my veins. "She's not the right person for Chief Terry."

"Of course not. Your mother is the right person. She'll win in the end. She just needs a little help."

"It's a good thing we're such good helpers."

Thistle smirked. "I think you mean diabolical helpers."

"Oh, yeah. We're definitely diabolical."

"So, let's figure things out."

TWENTY-THREE

*L*andon was waiting for me in front of The Overlook when I arrived for dinner. He sat on the front porch bench, his long legs stretched out in front of him, and he appeared at ease. I knew him better than anyone, so I recognized he was putting on a front, essentially waiting to see how I reacted before tackling the big issues of the day.

"It's cold out. Why are you waiting here?" I asked as I climbed the steps.

"I didn't want an audience in case you needed to melt down."

"I'm not going to melt down."

He didn't look convinced. "That sounds very unlike you."

"I'm a calm and chill person."

"Right." He snorted and held out a hand. "It's not that cold. It's not warm, but it's not cold. Spring is right around the corner. You can feel it." ·

I linked my fingers with his and sat, taking a moment to absorb the cold wood before shifting closer to share some of his warmth. "I love spring, but autumn is my favorite season."

"I like summer." He ran his hand over the back of my head. "So ... I talked to Chief Terry."

I expected the conversational shift. "Yeah? Is he going to arrest us?"

"You know he's not."

"I know that before Melanie Adams entered his life he wouldn't have arrested us. Now, I'm not so sure. She's pushing hard for it."

"Yeah. I noticed that." He looked caught. "She came into the station about an hour after the fight broke up. She headed into his office and closed the door. I heard raised voices."

Intrigued, I tipped up my chin. "What did they say?"

Now that he had easier access, Landon pressed a soft kiss to my mouth. "I don't know. I didn't listen outside the door. I know you would have, but I try to refrain from eavesdropping if I can help it."

I patted his knee. "I'll break you of that."

"I have no doubt."

"How were things when she left?"

"Better, but I don't think she got the outcome she was looking for. They weren't fighting and things still seemed tense."

"Yeah, well, I don't trust her." Landon was already aware of my feelings regarding Melanie, but I decided to double down all the same. "She's manipulative ... and probably evil."

"Bay, I think you're reading too much into the situation." He sounded exasperated. "I don't even understand what you were doing at Mrs. Little's shop. I thought you were following trails from Hopper's house."

"We were. One of them led to the shop."

Landon straightened. "Really? Does that mean Mrs. Little was at Hopper's house the day he died?"

As much as I wanted to confirm that, all I could do was shrug. "The spell was set up to lead us to individuals rather than homes or places of business. Someone inside that store was at Hopper's house the day he died. It could've been Maxine — we know they were doing the mattress rumba — or it could've been Janet. She was in his files as a bed buddy. It also could've been Mrs. Little."

"Hmm."

"I spent the afternoon going through the files again," I offered. "Nothing stood out. I even went through Mrs. Little's file from front to back. There were a few things in there I found enlightening."

"Such as?"

"I think she was treating Hopper as a normal therapist," I replied. "You know, spilling her guts and talking about all the wrongs she'd incurred through life. I'm not sure why."

"You could ask him."

"That would require talking to him."

"Fair enough."

"Hopper made extensive notes in her file, even more than he did with his other patients," I said. "There was a lot of paranoia in there. She thinks everyone is out to get her, not just Aunt Tillie. I think she was seeing Hopper a long time before his death."

"Who does she think is out to get her?"

"Half the people at the senior center. She's determined Esther is out to get her, although Esther was at her store today. I'm not sure what's up with that. Oh, she had a run-in with Melanie right after she opened the yoga shop and Mrs. Little was convinced she was trying to move in on her turf even though unicorns and yoga don't overlap."

"So ... Mrs. Little thought Melanie was out to get her yet she invited her to her store today?" Landon rolled his neck as he absorbed the new information. "That doesn't make much sense."

"Maybe Mrs. Little was calling her enemies to her for a meeting of the Hemlock Cove Supervillain Society."

Landon chuckled. "Maybe. What did the file say about Melanie?"

"It was a single notation. Melanie came into the store and acted nice. Mrs. Little was convinced she was spying. Mrs. Little thinks everyone in town is spying on her. She has an overblown sense of ego. The only other mention was after Mrs. Little discovered Melanie was dating Chief Terry. It was the last notation in the file. Mrs. Little was convinced Melanie wanted Chief Terry to help steal her status in town."

"That's out there, even for Mrs. Little."

"That's what I thought. It bothered me that Mrs. Little knew about their relationship before I did. I know it's petty, but ... it's annoying."

"I think you're hurt more than anything." Landon kissed my forehead and sobered. "I'm not going to lie, Bay. I understand why you're upset, but I think you're taking things too far. The more you dig your heels in, the more likely Melanie will follow suit. That could create problems for Chief Terry, which I don't want to see."

"That's why I'm going to get rid of her." I was determined. "As soon as we solve Hopper's murder, she's my primary focus."

"I love how you say that without a hint of guilt."

"She's all wrong for him."

"Well, she's in his life for the time being and he's under a lot of stress. I don't think it's fair to him ... so I decided to take matters into my own hands."

I was instantly alert. "What did you do?" The sound of crunching gravel in the driveway assailed my ears, and when I turned to stare at the approaching vehicle I recognized Chief Terry's truck. He wasn't alone. A familiar face sat in the passenger seat ... and it belonged to someone I didn't want to see. "You invited them to dinner?" I was furious and my fingers itched to pinch Landon's flank.

"I thought it would be best for everyone." Landon was unruffled as he stood, grabbing my hand before I could beat a hasty retreat inside to gather reinforcements. "I think that you need to spend time with Melanie in a social setting. The same goes for your mother. Maybe you all can work things out together."

"But you said you were on my side earlier today," I hissed, temper as hot as lava burning through my chest. "You said that we should get rid of her."

"That was before I saw how miserable Chief Terry was after the incident at the unicorn store. He's in a terrible position, Bay. He desperately wants you and Melanie to get along. It's important to him."

Landon was earnest, but that didn't mean I was going to play the game his way. "This is going to backfire. You realize that, don't you?"

"I'm hopeful you'll make sure that doesn't happen."

"You're putting far too much faith in me."

"Try. I would ask you to try for me, but that's not fair. I want you to try for him." He inclined his chin toward Chief Terry. "That man is essentially your father. Do what's right for him, not for you."

Oh, well, now he was hitting below the belt. "I'll make you pay for this later."

"I have no doubt."

IF I THOUGHT MY REACTION to seeing Melanie at The Overlook was outrage, the look on my mother's face when she realized we had guests for dinner was outright heartbreaking. She put on a brave face, introduced herself to Melanie, and then disappeared into the kitchen.

Marnie and Twila, realizing who was responsible for our dinner nightmare, glared so hard at Landon I figured he was hoping a hole would open up under his feet and swallow him whole. He held it together until they followed my mother into the kitchen, but just barely.

"It's nice when I'm not the most hated one in the house," Thistle drawled as she placed a martini in front of me before moving to the opposite end of the table.

"Where's my drink?" Landon asked, annoyed.

"You know where the drink cart is."

For her part, Melanie made a big show of stripping out of her coat and handing it to Chief Terry so he could hang it on the rack. She was clearly unhappy about the turn of events, even though she forced a smile for Chief Terry's benefit when he mixed her a drink and delivered it to the table.

"This is a lovely room," Melanie said after a drawn-out silence. "Who was your decorator?"

"They didn't have a professional decorator," Clove answered as she sipped a martini, Sam beside her. "They put it together themselves."

"Well, they did a marvelous job."

"I was technically their decorator," Aunt Tillie announced. Mischief swirled around her like a tiny tornado as her eyes gleamed. She looked like a bird of prey about to swoop in and gobble up her squawking dinner. Unfortunately for Melanie, she was very clearly going to end up as nothing but a picked-over carcass. "I think I have a certain pizazz when it comes to picking accents for a room."

Melanie rolled her eyes. "Right."

"You didn't decorate this room," Thistle argued as Marcus delivered a drink to her. The men present could clearly sense that the evening was about to veer off the rails. They would try to keep things in check ... and fail miserably. That was the norm in this house. "I remember when they were decorating this room. You wanted to hang shrunken heads from the chandelier."

"I still maintain that was a viable decorating choice," Aunt Tillie challenged.

"You wanted them to talk, too," I remembered, smirking. "You had a plan for allowing them to have conversations to entertain the guests."

"Yeah." Clove involuntarily shuddered. "Our mothers put the kibosh on that."

"Mostly because they thought you would have nightmares," Thistle supplied. "Bay and I were fine with it ... but we don't freak out over stupid stuff."

That was a gross exaggeration. I didn't remember being fine with it. Of course, during the construction period when the old bed and breakfast was upgraded to the new inn I was in Detroit doing other things. I fancied myself as a big-time reporter who would tackle important stories. After a few years, I realized living the big life was nowhere near as fun as being close to my family and I returned home.

"I actually remember the great shrunken heads debate," Chief Terry offered. "I believe Tillie was outvoted by a sound number that day."

"Yes, you didn't take my side either, Terry." Aunt Tillie's eyes darkened. "I haven't forgotten."

Melanie swallowed hard as her gaze bounced between faces. "I gather you guys are especially close. When Terry mentioned that you eat together four or five nights a week I thought he was exaggerating."

"Oh, it's no exaggeration," Landon said as he returned to the table with a bourbon and soda. He sat in his usual chair between Aunt Tillie and me and immediately started rubbing my back, a soothing habit he'd picked up not long after we started dating. He had magic hands and knew it. "Everyone in this family is tragically co-dependent."

"Does that include you?" Melanie asked pointedly.

"I'm the worst of all," Landon answered without hesitation. "My life revolves around Bay. Everything she does is a maddening joy."

Oh, geez. I didn't bother to hide my eye roll. "That's a lot of manure you're shoveling," I offered. "It won't get you out of the doghouse."

"Why is he in the doghouse?" Chief Terry asked.

"Because he's got it coming." I shifted on my chair and focused on Aunt Tillie. Anything was better than talking to Melanie. I didn't care what Landon said, or how he pleaded with those big eyes of his, I was never going to accept Melanie. We were way beyond that. "I know you're going to be getting your greenhouse going in the next few weeks, Aunt Tillie. I can carve out some time if you need help."

Instead of reacting with gratitude, Aunt Tillie blinked several times in rapid succession. "You're volunteering to help me garden?"

"I figure with Annie and Belinda moving to their new house you won't have Annie as a sidekick until the school year is over with. I'd like to help."

"Who are Annie and Belinda?" Melanie asked.

When none of us answered, Chief Terry filled the silence. "Belinda was involved in a car accident months ago. She almost died. Thistle and Bay found Annie wandering around dazed, and took care of her while Belinda recovered.

"After that, Belinda needed a job," he continued. "She's been living in the attic room with Annie and working here, but she's saved up enough for her own place. She'll still be working here while going to school, but they're moving out. I think that's soon, right?"

"They already moved out," Thistle replied. "They're spending this week setting up their new place."

"I miss Annie," Marcus noted. "She's always so happy to see me."

"I'm happy to see you," Thistle shot back.

"Yes, but you don't screech my name and throw your arms around me."

"I could do that."

"Maybe we'll play that game later," Marcus teased.

"Oh, man." Chief Terry stared into his drink. "I remember when you guys were ten and hated boys. I think we should go back to that."

"I never hated boys," Clove announced. "I was always a fan of love."

"You were," Chief Terry agreed. "But Bay and Thistle weren't, and they managed to keep you from going on and on about whatever boy you happened to have a crush on at any particular time. I miss those days."

"It sounds like you spent a lot of time with them," Melanie said. "You built forts for them ... and took them fishing."

"They never liked the fishing. They did hunt for frogs for Tillie, so the outings were still fun."

"I think you spoiled them." Melanie's gaze was pointed when it landed on me. "That's probably why they think they can enter another woman's place of business and order her around."

"That's not what happened," I snapped, my temper coming out to play. "If you think your little games are going to work on Chief Terry, you've got another think coming. He's too smart for that. He can see right through you."

Chief Terry looked shocked. "Listen ... I don't think now is the time for this conversation."

"Then you shouldn't have brought me here." Melanie shoved back her chair and stood, her voice climbing as she glanced around the room. "I understand that Landon was simply trying to ease some of the tension from earlier, but that's not going to work. You girls were out of line and I think I — along with Margaret and the others — deserve an apology.

"Now, I've heard enough stories about Ms. Winchester to know that she's not the type to apologize no matter what," she continued. "That's probably dementia given her age, so I'm willing to let it slide. You girls are another story.

"I'm not going to sit by and watch you run roughshod over Terry," she said. "He's a good man and you're obnoxious girls. You might've gotten away with murder in the past, but those days are over. I demand respect."

She moved away from the table and fixed Chief Terry with an expectant look. "Well?"

Chief Terry's face flushed with color. "Well, what?"

"She wants you to demand an apology," I supplied. "She expects you to force us to do her bidding."

"I don't believe that's what I said," Melanie said dryly. "I do demand respect, though. If you're not going to give it, I'm not staying."

Chief Terry shot me a pleading look, but I hardened my heart. I had no intention of letting this woman come into my mother's home and dictate terms. Sure, my mother was hiding in the kitchen like a great big coward, but it was far too late to back down.

"I'm not apologizing to you." I was firm. "You attacked us. We were minding our own business."

"Your crazy aunt came in and accused Margaret of being a killer!"

"Did she just call me crazy?" Aunt Tillie sipped her wine as I nodded.

"She also said you probably have dementia," Thistle offered helpfully. "You might have missed that."

"Well, bless you!" Aunt Tillie shoved her middle finger in the air, causing Clove and Thistle to duck their heads as they burst into hearty guffaws.

Disappointment rolled across Melanie's features. "Well, I can see you girls never had a chance if this was your role model."

"You'd be surprised the things she taught us," Thistle said, sobering. "We're more well-rounded than we seem."

"Well, at least you believe it." Melanie tapped her foot. "Come on, Terry. I'm not staying here to be insulted."

Even though he was clearly torn, Chief Terry did as instructed. He didn't have a lot of choice. He was her ride, after all, and we'd been less than hospitable. His eyes briefly locked with mine and I felt his sadness. "I'm disappointed, Bay."

I blinked back tears. "So am I."

"We'll need to talk about this."

"I can't wait."

"Come on, Terry!" Melanie was furious as she tugged on his arm. "I want out of this freak show."

Chief Terry and Melanie were barely out of the room when Mom appeared on the other side of the swinging door with a platter of bread in her hand. The first thing she heard was Melanie screeching before the front door slammed.

Confused, Mom tilted her head to the side. "What did I miss?"

TWENTY-FOUR

*L*andon was quiet for most of the walk back to the guesthouse. We'd left our vehicles at The Overlook, where we could claim them the following morning, and opted to enjoy the pleasant evening.

"You can smell spring," I noted, my nose lifted. "It's almost here."

"Yeah." His fingers were intertwined with mine, but Landon seemed distracted. "Can I ask you something, Bay?"

Bay, not Sweetie. That meant he was about to ask a serious question. "I feel guilty about what happened," I announced. I knew exactly what he was going to ask. "I don't feel guilty because of her. I maintain she's not a good person. I feel guilty about him."

Instead of chastising me, Landon sighed. "Bay, you have too good of a heart to not feel anything. I feel bad for him. I think he had grand plans for introducing Melanie to your family."

"Like ... you think he sat around imagining how things would go?"

"Pretty much."

"I didn't realize Chief Terry was a middle-school girl."

"It's not just teenagers who imagine where they'll end up," he countered, refusing to back down. "I know you're agitated, but there's no reason to get insulting."

I slowed my pace. "Does that mean you imagine where you'll end up?"

Landon cocked an eyebrow. "Did you think I didn't?"

I shrugged. "I guess I didn't think about it. In case you haven't noticed, I've been a bit self-absorbed of late."

"You've been overwhelmed with other things," he corrected. "No one blames you for that."

I blamed myself, but that wasn't germane to the conversation. "What do you dream about?"

"It's usually pretty simple." If Landon was embarrassed to talk about his dreams, he didn't show it. "You and me. A bigger house. A kid or two."

I pursed my lips. "Is the kid a boy or a girl?"

Landon snickered. "One of each."

"You know that boys are kind of rare in our family, right?" I felt the need to explain that to him. If his heart was set on a son, that might not be an option.

"I think we've discussed this before, but I'm fine with that." His tone was easy, pleasant, and there was no hint of subterfuge in his words. "I don't understand how you guys kept the name 'Winchester' for a hundred years if there were never any males, but I don't care either way. I think a little girl would be fun, too."

I decided to join him in his seriousness. "When do you see this happening?"

Landon's chuckle was long and drawn out. "Are you asking me when I'm going to propose?"

"Of course not," I sputtered, my cheeks flashing hot. "I would never ... you ... me ... we ... why would you assume something like that?"

"Oh, you really are a terrible liar." He gripped my hand and tugged me closer and wrapped his arm around my back. "I know you're not jealous of Clove, but you're anxious about her getting married before you. At first I thought Aunt Tillie was making it up, but now I realize it's true."

"I am not ... whatever it is you think I am."

"I don't have a name for it either. At least we're on the same page."

I wanted to make him see things my way. Ultimately it felt like a losing endeavor, so I could do nothing but sigh. "Fine. I might feel a little sad that she's getting married first. That's not the same as being jealous."

"No. People who are jealous want bad things to happen to others. You don't want bad things to happen to Clove."

"I'm the oldest," I reminded him. "I'm supposed to be the one who gets married first."

"You were all born within two years of each other. No one is really older than the rest."

I balked. "That's not true. I was born first, so I learned the rules first. I was expected to teach those rules to Clove and Thistle when we were growing up.

"Also, I was the first to drive ... and date ... and graduate from high school ... and leave home," I continued. "It was expected of me, to lead the way, so to speak."

"And you think you should still be leading the way now?" Landon's expression was hard to read. He didn't look upset, merely curious, but I couldn't be sure.

"No. I don't want you to think I'm marriage crazy or anything."

"I don't think that."

"I just don't want her to beat me."

Landon offered a hearty chuckle as he pulled me against his side. "I think that's a family thing. I don't want my brothers to beat me either. The thing is, I know we're going to get married. I simply don't see the need to rush it."

"I don't either."

"Are you sure?" His gaze was probing. "If you want to move faster, we can talk about it."

He was so sincere it soothed the nerves I hadn't even realized were frazzled. "I believe things happen when they're supposed to happen," I replied. "For me, the hardest part is knowing that others are going to be looking at me as if I've fallen behind. I know it's ridiculous, but people have always held us up against one another for comparison."

"And you were always first," Landon surmised. "Even though you were close in age, you were always first and you grew accustomed to your place at the head of the line."

"Pretty much," I confirmed. "Do you think less of me because of it?"

"No. I like that you aren't completely perfect. That's a normal human response. It's also good that you recognize it's a bit ridiculous to worry about. That's also a normal response."

"So ... we're not arguing, right?"

"Not even a little."

"Can we still make up when we get back to the guesthouse?"

Landon's grin was so wide it almost swallowed his face. "I like the way your mind works."

We increased our pace and were practically breathless by the time we arrived. Landon's hands were on my waist as he spun me, offering up a smoldering kiss as he grabbed the keys from my hand and tried to open the front door. We were so lost in each other I didn't notice someone moving toward us until the figure was practically on top of us.

"Landon ... !"

He must have sensed the interloper at the last moment because Landon abandoned his attempt to get the key in the lock and thrust me behind him as he turned to face our guest. Given the limited light, it took me a moment to make out the individual's features.

It was a woman. I knew that right away. The shadow was too short to belong to a man. When she finally moved to a spot where I could see the angles of her face, I almost gasped in shock.

"Mrs. Little?"

"Oh, this is not how I wanted to spend the rest of our night," Landon complained, his eyes narrowing. "What are you doing here, Mrs. Little? If you've come to lodge another complaint about what happened in your shop today, I'm not in the mood to take it. Bother Chief Terry."

"I've tried bothering Chief Terry," Mrs. Little sniffed, crossing her arms over her chest. She looked petulant ... and on edge. "I was hoping I could come inside so we could talk."

She had to be joking. "What?"

"Inside." She made an exaggerated face and pointed toward the door. "We need to talk, and it's too cold to do it out here."

"We were pretty warm before you showed up," Landon complained.

"So it's probably best that you invite me in," Mrs. Little noted. "The sooner we hash this out, the sooner you can go back to your fornication."

Landon slid me a sidelong look. "I know she meant that as an insult, but it sounds good to me."

I was right there with him.

MRS. LITTLE HAD NEVER VISITED the guesthouse — at least to my recollection — so it felt weird for her to inconvenience us tonight of all nights. She sat in the chair at the edge of the room, the one Landon preferred when he was watching a game, and rested her hands on her knees.

"I would offer you something to drink, but I don't want you to stay longer than necessary," I supplied.

"That's fine." She waved off the comment with a dismissive gesture. "We both know I wouldn't drink anything in this house anyway. I'm afraid of being poisoned. It's a reoccurring nightmare."

That was somehow fitting. "So, what is it that you want?" I was stiff as I sank on the couch next to Landon. For his part, he didn't look nearly as worried as I felt. He was hardly at ease, though.

"I want to talk to you about Mike Hopper," she started.

"Oh, wow!" My mind started buzzing at a fantastic rate. "Did you kill him? Did he try to have sex with you, too? As much as I'm not a fan of murder, I can see wanting to kill him. He's something of a pig."

Mrs. Little's mouth dropped open. "Of course I didn't kill him. I'm not a murderer!"

"You were seeing him," Landon pressed, his eyes sharp as they lasered into Mrs. Little. "I'm kind of curious how that happened given the fact that he usually sees couples."

"Oh, well ... ." Mrs. Little, visibly uncomfortable, shifted on the chair. "Is that really important?"

"I think it is."

"And I think it isn't." Mrs. Little was firm. "It has come to my attention that you've discovered certain files — documents that should've remained private thanks to Dr. Hopper's status as a licensed therapist — and I want my file back."

I wasn't expecting her to come right out and say it. She had to be desperate to appeal to us in this manner.

"We cannot release any files that we've confiscated during our investigation of Dr. Hopper's murder," Landon said.

"My file has nothing to do with your case," Mrs. Little argued. "I'm not a suspect, so that means my personal information should be off limits."

Landon snorted. "What makes you think you're not a suspect?"

"Because I'm not."

Her answer was so simple that at first I thought she was delusional. When she rested her hands on her knees and straightened her shoulders, though, I knew she believed it. "Why don't you think you're a suspect?"

"Because I didn't kill him."

"That doesn't mean you're not a suspect," I pressed. "Everyone is a suspect until we can rule them out."

"We?" Mrs. Little's thin eyebrows hopped. "Since when are you a part of the Hemlock Cove Police Department, Bay?"

"I'm not."

"Then why are you ruling anyone out?"

"Well ... ." As much as I hated it, she had a point. I wished I would've worded that another way. "Um ... ."

"Bay has been instrumental in this case from the start," Landon offered, taking up my cause without a second's hesitation. "She has good instincts, and while not privy to files or evidence, she's still come up with some solid leads due to her own investigation. An investigation that she's allowed to run thanks to her standing as the owner of The Whistler," he added hurriedly. "She's well within her rights."

Mrs. Little's expression was dubious. "Do you two really think I'm going to believe that?"

"It's the truth," Landon replied.

"You might fool the majority of the residents in this town, but they're sheep, and I know better. Bay is knee-deep in this case. She always is. I'm not sure why you feel the need to include her — although I have my suspicions — but she's just as involved in this one as she has been in the others."

Landon refused to back down. "I'm sorry, but you're mistaken."

"Mistaken my aching butt," Mrs. Little fired back. "Ultimately it doesn't matter. I don't care what Bay is doing ... or why she's helping you. That's your business."

"Then what do you want?" I asked, tugging on my limited patience. If I exploded now it would only make things worse.

"I want you to give back my file."

"Our warrant for the files hasn't come through," Landon said smoothly. "We don't even know who is mentioned in the files, which remain at Dr. Hopper's house. In fact, I really need to remember to get on that judge tomorrow. I don't know why he's dragging his feet."

"I do." Mrs. Little's eyes sparkled. "Would you like me to tell you?"

Landon was caught off guard. "Excuse me?"

"I know why the judge hasn't issued a warrant yet. I'll tell you in exchange for my file."

"Wait ... are you trying to bribe me?" Landon's eyes widened. "You know that's a felony, right? You can't bribe a federal agent."

"I'm not trying to bribe you." She shook her head with disdain. "Law enforcement officials make deals all the time. I can tell you exactly why your warrant hasn't been signed in exchange for my private information, which is of no use to you. And before you deny having those files again you should remember that I saw you entering Dr. Hopper's house after dark the day his body was found. I know darned well you have those files."

"Oh, yeah?" Landon wasn't ready to concede defeat. "Prove it."

"If you want me to call your boss, I will." Mrs. Little wasn't above a good threat and she whipped out her favorite — I'm going to tell on you — without batting an eyelash.

"Go ahead." Landon leaned forward and pinned her with a dark look. "My boss has met you. He was here this summer, in case you've forgotten. He knows all about you. He has a file on you, too, if you're interested."

"Why would he have a file on me?"

"Because you like to insert yourself in investigations and tattle on your neighbors," Landon replied. "You're a busybody."

"I am no such thing!"

Landon ignored her building fury. "You're a busybody," he repeated. "You fancy yourself the center of the world, privy to everyone's business, and yet you demand your own privacy. That's a dangerous combination. So, yeah, we have a file on you."

"Well, I want that file."

"You're destined for disappointment." As flirty and romantic as Landon was twenty minutes before, he was furious and irritated now. "We don't have Dr. Hopper's files." The lie rolled off his tongue. "You're not accomplishing what you thought you were tonight. In fact, all you've accomplished is to make sure that your file is the first I look at."

Mrs. Little huffed out an indignant grunt as she got to her feet, clutching her purse to her chest as she glared. "You'll regret coming up against me."

"I regret most things about you."

"Well, you're going to especially regret this," Mrs. Little stressed. "You're not the be all and end all of law enforcement in this town. You may be a federal agent, but Chief Terry is in charge. And, from what I can tell, he's no longer smitten with the Winchesters. He's moved on."

Oh, now I was in it. "You don't know what you're talking about!"

"Bay." Landon grabbed my arm before I could launch myself across the coffee table and reenact whatever sports movie revolved around football and brutal tackles. "Don't let her get to you. That's what she wants."

"What I want is for you people to mind your own business," Mrs. Little fired back. "If you won't listen to reason, I'll have to go to your superiors."

Landon wasn't about to be threatened. "Knock yourself out."

"I will."

"Great." Landon purposely strode toward the door and threw it open. "I believe your business is done here."

Mrs. Little wouldn't stop grousing under her breath as she stormed to the door. "You think this is over, but it's just beginning."

"Awesome." Landon stood to the side, refusing to look at her. "You can begin outside. We'll begin in here."

"You just want to fornicate." Disgust washed over her pinched features. "You're animals, that's what you are."

"And proud of it." Landon slammed the door in her face, leaving her complaining on the other side of the threshold as he flicked the lock to make sure she would stay out. His chest heaved as he snagged my gaze. "Are you ready for bed?"

It wasn't a funny situation and yet I couldn't stop myself from giggling. "Are you about to use all that excess energy on me?"

"You have no idea."

"Bring it."

"That's the plan."

TWENTY-FIVE

I solved several problems in my sleep, the biggest of which was the judge conundrum. I was excited when I rolled over and shook Landon awake.

"You can't possibly want to do it again," he murmured, his eyes closed. "I need nourishment before I can, Bay. You wore me out."

"I think we wore each other out," I said dryly, my lips curling. "But that's not why I was waking you."

"Unless you have bacon I'm not interested."

"I don't have bacon ... but I'm considering putting a small refrigerator in here so I can bribe you with the scent when I want something."

"Now you're thinking." He cocked an eyebrow and fixed me with a quizzical look. "Why are you up so early? And why are you so excited? We have thirty minutes more to sleep. Let's enjoy them."

"I had a dream."

Landon's smile was sly. "A naughty dream?"

"Ugh. You really are a pervert."

"You say that like it's a bad thing."

"Focus!" I snapped my fingers in front of his face to make sure I had his attention. "I know what Mrs. Little was talking about last night."

"So do I." Landon sobered. "She's well aware that we have her file and she's embarrassed by what she believes is in it. She should be. I've seen that file. Hopper clearly didn't like her."

"Which begs the question of why he was treating her," I mused. "She still hasn't answered that question."

"No, she hasn't," he agreed. "She evaded it. We need to find some answers on that front. Nothing I come up with makes sense."

"I'll call Hopper later and force him to answer," I offered. "I have some ideas on the necromancer front."

"I can do it with you if you're nervous."

"I'm not nervous." That was mostly true. "I have to do this on my own eventually. I'm a grown-up."

"That's what it says on your Witches 'R Us membership card," he teased, poking a finger into my stomach and causing me to squirm.

"Will you focus? I'm serious."

He heaved out a sigh and dragged a hand through his morning-mussed hair. "Fine. You're serious."

"I had a dream," I started again. "In it, Mrs. Little managed to get me arrested and I went on trial. It went the way of the Incredible Hulk's trial — if you remember that — and I managed to escape, but that's not the interesting part."

"Oh, no?" Landon deadpanned. "I was about to call a news conference on the Hulk dream. Continue."

I twisted my lips. "I don't have to tell you anything."

His expression softened. "Tell me."

"The judge in the dream was the visiting judge. You know, Judge Morton. He's retired but he still fills in when the current judge is on vacation."

"I know how visiting judges work," he said dryly.

"Judge Morton is Janet Hall's father. She was at Mrs. Little's store yesterday. She's also in Hopper's files."

Realization dawned on Landon's face. "Oh."

"There you go."

"The judge has been dragging his feet because his kid is in the files."

He thinks if he holds out long enough we'll solve it without having to drag her into things."

"Not only is Janet in the files, she's one of the women Hopper convinced to have sex with him," I supplied. "She has more to lose than most."

"Well, that makes sense." Landon rolled to his back and stared at the ceiling. "I guess I know what I'm doing today."

"Confronting the judge?"

"Nope. Going to a federal judge higher in the food chain. I'm going to cut Judge Morton out of the decision."

"That sounds like a plan."

"Yeah. What are you planning to do?"

"I'm going to deal with Hopper's ghost and get the answers we need."

"Are you sure you don't want me close when you do that?"

"He can't hurt me."

"I know, but ... you might need me."

I smiled, love washing over me. "I always need you. But on this one, I want to do it myself. It's important. I've got to start dealing with this."

"Okay, but if you need backup I'm only a call away."

"I'll keep that in mind. I'll be fine."

DESPITE MY BRAVADO, I was nervous when Landon departed for the day and I was left with nothing to do but the one thing I'd been dreading. In truth, the idea of being able to control ghosts sounded intriguing on paper. In reality, it was daunting.

I never fancied myself the sort of person who would try to control another soul. Sure, my family was all about controlling each other, but in a wholesome way. We wanted to manipulate and cajole like normal people. Doing it magically eliminated the fun.

I had a new reality, though, and it was time to embrace it. The ability wasn't going to simply disappear. I had to come to grips with the power and begin exerting some control.

With that in mind, I headed to the bluff on the far side of the property. As a Winchester, my magic was tied to our bloodlines. Because we were all earth witches to some degree, that meant I found my greatest strength on the property. I was hopeful that would benefit me today.

The weather was a balmy forty-eight degrees when I'd set out from the guesthouse. Winter was holding on with bloody fingertips, but it would soon be a memory. Once spring officially hit, the trees would finish filling out — our earlier burst of decent weather came and went far too quickly when winter decided it wasn't quite finished with us — and then we would be back to picnics and naked dancing under the full moon.

For now, though, I had a ghost to deal with.

I picked a spot in the bright sunshine and spread out the blanket I'd thought ahead to bring. The ground was still cold, so I didn't want to risk a frozen behind. I sat cross-legged on the blanket, rested my elbows on my knees, and turned my palms to the sky. Meditation wasn't necessary when dealing with ghosts, but Hopper served as a constant form of agitation and I wanted to maintain my cool.

I sucked in a calming breath, focused and called his name. This time there was no doubt I'd managed to engage the magic on the first try. Hopper materialized five feet in front of me, his eyes wide when he realized his proximity to the sharp cliff drop-off, and he started complaining the second he could open his mouth.

"Well, it's about time! I thought you'd forgotten about me."

"I could never forget about you," I said dryly. "You're all I think about."

"Oh, don't placate me. I know very well you've been dealing with personal issues rather than focusing on me. I'm not an idiot."

"How do you know that?"

"I just ... do."

Meaning he guessed. And, because he was feeling petulant, he turned himself into a victim. I recognized the effort from when I was a teenager. Hopper was far too old to give in to those urges, though.

"I need to talk to you."

"Well, great." Hopper mimicked my position as he lowered himself to the ground and faced me. "I need to talk to you."

Hmm. "What do you want to talk to me about?"

"I've been thinking about this whole necromancer thing," Hopper replied. "I think there's a reason I died in Hemlock Cove, a place where a powerful witch happens to reside. I'm guessing it's because I'm supposed to keep offering my services to the people in the area. My story isn't over yet."

I was horrified. "You want to keep having sex with people as a therapy? You're a ghost ... and that's disgusting."

Hopper rolled his eyes. "That's not what I meant."

"Oh." I was embarrassed. "Okay, ignore the sex comment."

"You have a puritanical streak. I find it odd because you're a witch and Puritans killed witches."

I wasn't happy with the direction this conversation was heading. "I hardly think that's something we should waste time talking about."

"And I think you're wrong." Hopper was firm. "I think that you're exactly the sort of person who could benefit from what I have to offer."

"Meaning?"

"Meaning that you have a lot of emotional issues, and it's always helpful to discuss those issues with a trained individual. I can help you shed the fear."

He managed to sound worried and condescending simultaneously. It was an interesting phenomenon. "I'm not fearful."

"You've been fearful since the moment I showed up at the news-paper office."

"That's because you told me my disembodied voice ordered you to abandon the afterlife and hang out with me."

"I think that's a sign." Hopper refused to back down. "Think about it. I could hang around and treat people. Sure, I'm a ghost, but you can make it so others can see me. I can keep my house — perhaps you can talk the townsfolk into making it so I don't have to pay taxes or some-thing — and things could go on exactly as they have been."

"Oh, sure," I drawled, dumbfounded disbelief rolling over me.

"Ghosts shouldn't pay taxes. That's a given."

Hopper's eyes gleamed. "Exactly. You're getting into the spirit of things."

"Spirit being the operative word."

"Oh, don't go getting cranky. It was merely a suggestion."

I inhaled deeply to calm myself. "Souls aren't meant to stay on this side after ... well, after they've shuffled off the mortal coil. There's a design to this — life and death — and it's not wise to break from the design."

"You have a ghost at The Whistler," Hopper argued. "You don't seem to have a problem with her sticking around."

"Viola? She chose to stay in Hemlock Cove. I'm still not certain why. I think she's simply not ready to cross over. I've tried talking to her about it, but she's adamant about staying."

"Why is it okay for her to stay and not me?"

"Because I didn't force Viola to stay." Although, now that he mentioned it, I had no idea when my necromancer powers kicked into high gear. I knew when I first noticed them. Viola died several months before that ... and in front of me. I was so traumatized by her shooting that Landon went into protective boyfriend mode and shut me away from the world for hours to make sure I processed things correctly. There was always the chance that the trauma triggered my necromancer abilities and I was the reason Viola opted to stay behind. That was something I would have to consider ... but at a later date.

"I don't care that you forced me to stay," Hopper argued. "I'm glad it happened. I want to be here. This is my home."

"This is what you know," I corrected. "You don't want to pass on because you're afraid of what's on the other side. I get that you're a pervert and you're probably worried you don't have a bright afterlife waiting for you, but I'm sure you can do some penance and arrange for that to happen. I mean ... it's not as if you're evil."

The second the words escaped my mouth I noticed a shift in Hopper's demeanor. He didn't cackle maniacally and rub his ethereal hands together, but he did acknowledge the statement. Unfortunately, it was with a smirk.

"Wait a second ... ."

Hopper didn't allow me to follow my natural train of thought, instead trying to force me to focus on something else. "I believe everything happens for a reason. You're a witch. That means you believe in karma, right?"

I nodded, my mind moving at a fantastic rate.

"Therefore, it's important for me to stay here," Hopper stressed. "I need to remain because this is where I belong. I want to help people. I'm a giver. Hey, who knows? If you get powerful enough maybe you'll be able to give me another body or something. I mean ... I know that's down the road, but I'm not sad being here without any way to interact with the living or anything."

That's when things clicked into place. Er, well, as close as they were going to get without him filling in the gaps. Realization washed over me in a cool, green wave that left me feeling sick to my stomach ... and a bit shaky.

"I didn't call you."

Hopper froze at my quiet words. "What are you talking about? Of course you called me. That's why I'm here."

"I'm not talking about today. I definitely called you today."

"Then ... what are you talking about?"

"The day you died." I worked hard to untangle the crossing threads in my busy brain. "I didn't call to you. You saw what was waiting for you on the other side and you ran."

"That is preposterous." He said the words but couldn't hide the lie in his eyes.

"No, I'm right." My anger began building as I rubbed my sweaty palms over my knees. "You understood you wouldn't be going to a good place, so you stayed behind. I'm not sure how you found me — maybe you were running from whatever was chasing you, or merely wanted to put distance between you and the threshold that terrified you — but somehow you found me.

"Maybe you did hear a voice at that point," I continued. "I don't like the idea that my disembodied voice is floating around ordering others what to do, but I don't believe the story you told the day you appeared is the truth. You stayed behind because you were afraid to cross over, and now you're trying to manipulate me to keep you here because what's waiting is worse than living in limbo."

Hopper didn't immediately respond. Instead he merely stared. He finally shook his head and raised his eyes to the sky. "Why can't you just do as I asked? It's not as if it hurts you."

"You're not a good person. I should've seen that earlier." I was talking to myself more than him, but I knew he could hear. "You manipulated those women into sleeping with you, abused your position, and I'm betting you were responsible for a few more immoral deeds. I mean ... why were you seeing Margaret Little?"

"I already told you. I won't break doctor-patient confidentiality."

I was sick of that song and dance, and unleashed a flurry of magic, allowing it to barrel into Hopper and causing him to widen his eyes. He wasn't corporeal. That meant he could walk through walls or things could pass through him without trouble. The magic I sent to rein him in was strong enough to cause physical pain to a body that no longer existed, though, and I wasn't even mildly sorry when his features twisted.

"What the heck is this?" Hopper's voice was laced with panic as he struggled. "What did you do to me?"

"I want to know why Mrs. Little was seeing you," I demanded. "She's afraid of something. She tried to blackmail us for her file last night. I can't understand why she was seeing you in the first place."

"I won't tell you that!" Hopper gritted his teeth as he fruitlessly struggled against the magical bonds I'd tethered him with. "There's nothing you can do to make me. My oath is my bond."

I snorted. "We both know that's a load of crap. I'm willing to test the theory that there's nothing I can do to make you talk."

For the first time, real fear flickered across Hopper's twisted features. "What are you going to do?"

"Take control. You had a chance to do the right thing and tried to manipulate me instead. I think it's time we evened the score."

"That sounds ... ominous."

"Oh, you have no idea."

TWENTY-SIX

I felt empowered after my showdown with Hopper. Not in an evil "I'm going to put you in a sleeping curse to get my own way" empowered, but stronger all the same.

Hopper didn't answer my questions. He was adamant. That made me realize I was on the right track ... yet still unwilling to go full-on evil to get my way. I was essentially a work in progress.

I texted Aunt Tillie and she met me on the bluff shortly before ten. She wasn't happy about being summoned, but when I informed her of what I wanted she brightened considerably.

"You want me to torture your ghost?" She was almost gleeful as she circled a furious Hopper. He remained trapped in the magic I tethered him with, unable to move. "I can't believe you finally gave me a gift that's truly magical. This makes up for all those years you made mugs with Twila and insisted they were good Christmas gifts."

I scowled. "I was a kid. A coffee mug is a great Christmas gift when you're a kid. I made it myself, for crying out loud."

"They were lopsided."

"Only the first two ... er, four."

"Whatever." Aunt Tillie clearly wasn't in the mood to reminisce.

"What is it you've done here?" She peered closely at the magical bindings anchoring Hopper to the bluff. "What spell did you use?"

The question caught me off guard. "I didn't use a spell."

"What did you do?"

"Um ... I just imagined what I wanted and it kind of happened."

"Really?" Intrigued, Aunt Tillie extended a finger and poked at the magic. "This is very impressive. I'm guessing it's because you're a necromancer and he's a ghost. Unless ... do you think you could do this with a live human being?"

I didn't want to even consider that. "No."

Aunt Tillie met my steady gaze. "Are you sure?"

"No," I admitted. "I don't know why it came to me. It just did. He's being a tool, so I need him to stay here until he decides he's going to answer my questions."

"What questions?"

"I want to know why Mrs. Little was seeing him."

"She's nuts."

"There has to be more to it than that."

"She's massively nuts."

I sucked in a calming breath. "This is serious." I told her about my run-in with Mrs. Little the previous evening, keeping the story succinct. "She's got her finger in a bunch of different pies," I finished. "I don't think that gathering we saw at her store yesterday was a coincidence."

Aunt Tillie's brow wrinkled. "What do you mean?"

"Of the people who were there," I explained, "at least two of them were having sex with this piece of walking garbage." I sneered at Hopper, which caused him to groan and twist. "Esther was there, and she had ties to Hopper. I don't think he was treating her, but something else could've been going on."

"What about Tori Corbin? She wasn't in the sex files."

"No, but I didn't pay attention to all the names in the files we didn't flag," I admitted. "I'm willing to bet that Tori and her husband were seeing Hopper regularly, too. I'll have to confirm that with Landon later this afternoon. He's going above Judge Morton's head to get the warrant for the files. His daughter, Janet, was definitely having sex with Hopper. We can't risk going through the files a second time without the proper paperwork in place."

"Okay." Aunt Tillie turned thoughtful. "Maybe Janet was the psychopath."

I didn't know much about the woman, but it was a decent guess. "It's a possibility. The other possibility is Melanie Adams. I mean ...why was she there? I definitely would've remembered seeing her name in the files."

"Maybe Margaret simply wants to add her to her cadre of losers," she suggested. "Margaret likes power. Given Melanie's relationship with Chief Terry, she could afford Margaret some leverage."

"I considered that, too," I admitted. "Mrs. Little complained about Melanie in her own file, but somehow they got over that. There's a chance Melanie didn't even know that she was being plotted against."

"Maybe they worked out a truce."

"Maybe."

Aunt Tillie pursed her lips. "You're going to ask Melanie about it, aren't you?"

"That seems to be the next logical step. I'd rather confront her than keep questioning her motives."

"I guess that's a good idea." Aunt Tillie said the words but didn't look convinced. "Be careful, Bay. I don't know that woman well, but she's relishing the power she has over Terry. That was clear last night. She thinks she's won because he went with her."

"He was her ride."

"Still ... she feels as if she's in the power position. When she realizes she's not — that you're still nearer and dearer to Terry's heart — she might not take it well."

"Do you think she would attack me?"

Aunt Tillie shrugged. "It's doubtful, but she's not nearly as sweet and innocent as she wants people to believe."

"I'm visiting her yoga studio. She wouldn't dare turn things into a physical confrontation there."

"Probably not." Aunt Tillie held my gaze for what felt like a very long time and then smiled. "I can torture the ghost however I want while you're gone, right? I mean ... can I tell him stories about my childhood and make him look at photo albums?"

"You can get as mean as you want." I meant it. "I want to know what Mrs. Little was doing under his care. There has to be a reason she was seeing him. Also, I want to know who the psychopath is." I fixed Hopper with a pointed look. "He might not know who killed him — and I'm on the fence about whether that's true — but he knows who the psychopath is. He's not leaving this bluff until he shares the information."

Aunt Tillie offered a hearty salute. "I'll get the information if I have to kill him a second time to do it."

"Good luck."

"Oh, I don't need luck." Aunt Tillie's eyes gleamed with evil intent as she grinned at Hopper. "I'm the wickedest witch in the Midwest. I have skill."

I'D NEVER BEEN TO MELANIE'S yoga studio. I was familiar with the building — it used to be a pizza joint, and before that a video store — but she'd put the facility through a massive overhaul. I was determined not to like her, but even I had to admit the space was cute.

She was finishing up with a class — I recognized a few familiar faces in the group — so I loitered at the back of the room until she finished with her demonstration.

At first glance, she seemed amiable. She chatted with her customers as they dispersed, offered them helpful hints and bathed them with compliments about their efforts. She was aware of my presence even though she barely glanced in my direction. She waited until her customers had left before she acknowledged me.

"Well, you're the last person I expected to see." She rubbed a towel over her sweaty face as she regarded me. "I was about to make a strawberry smoothie at the bar. Do you want one?"

I followed her gaze to the counter. It was basically a half-moon with eight stools placed around it. "Sure."

She headed in that direction, keeping distance between us, and slid behind the counter before indicating I should sit on one of the stools. "You're not allergic to coconut or anything, are you? I use coconut water in the smoothies."

"I'm not allergic to anything."

"Well ... great."

Melanie was the picture of efficiency as she began chopping strawberries. She didn't seem eager to deepen the conversation, which meant I would have to be the one to speak first.

"So ... about last night."

"Yes, that was a lovely evening," Melanie drawled. "I can't tell you how happy I was to be part of your happy family last night."

If she expected me to apologize, she was going to be disappointed. "What did you expect? You tried to get me arrested. They were hardly going to welcome you with open arms."

"I didn't try to get you arrested." Her eyes flashed with impatience, making them greener. "I simply pointed out that your actions yesterday afternoon were not acceptable. I can't believe that you think they were. Margaret Little ... ."

I held up my hand to still her. "You're new to town. I'll give you the benefit of the doubt because of that. But we have a long history with Mrs. Little that you're probably not privy to. I doubt very much she would tell you the whole truth when it comes to her relationship with my family."

Melanie pursed her lips. Her face was devoid of makeup because she'd been working out, but she was still attractive. That only served to irritate me more.

"Listen, I'm not going to pretend that I'm an expert on Margaret Little. She's been nothing but nice to me since I landed in town. She invited me to join the Downtown Development Authority. She's going to help me with my first booth at the spring festival. She's been warm and welcoming."

Obviously Melanie didn't realize that Mrs. Little had been complaining about her to the neighborhood shrink. "Mrs. Little is great at schmoozing people when she wants something," I agreed. "The second you cross her, she becomes a vicious enemy."

"And what did you do to cross her?"

"Oh, all manner of things."

"I prefer specifics." Melanie tossed the strawberries into the blender, her gaze never moving from my face. "If you expect me to cut ties with this woman, I want a good reason."

And there was the rub. "I don't expect you to cut ties with her on my behalf." That was the truth. "She's not an easy woman to get along with. Is she evil? There are times I wonder. Still, her dislike of my family is probably warranted. She's been enemies with Aunt Tillie since they were in grade school."

"Yes, your Aunt Tillie is quite the welcoming soul."

"Oddly enough, she has a good heart," I countered. "I would never pretend that she's perfect. She has plenty of faults. I mean ... a lot. She's headstrong and mean when she wants to be. She goes out of her way to tick people off. She's a master at revenge.

"She's also loyal to a fault," I continued. "She would die for any one of us. She listens when we talk, even though she doesn't always agree. She tries to help when we're in trouble, although sometimes her solutions are out there. That doesn't change the fact that she's a good woman."

"I guess I'll have to take your word for that," Melanie said dryly as she added coconut water to the blender. "She's been nothing but rude to me."

"Maybe that's because you tried to get her arrested, too."

"Maybe." Melanie hit the puree button before I could say anything else, so I bided my time and watched her mix the concoction. When she was finished, she poured it into two glasses and shoved one in my direction. "No sugar. Totally healthy and organic. It's going to be the drink of the future."

I preferred a chocolate malt or a good old-fashioned Slurpee. Still, I forced a smile and sipped the drink. It tasted like icy pieces of grit thanks to the strawberry seeds, but I feigned delight anyway. "Awesome."

Melanie's expression darkened. "You hate it."

"It's fine. I'm just used to richer food."

"Because that's what your mother cooks?"

And there it was. I wondered if Melanie would bring her up. If she was as innocent as she pretended, she would've avoided the topic. She was manipulative, no matter how she played things. She was about to see what buttons she could push by mentioning my mother.

That wouldn't end well ... for either of us.

"My mother and aunts are the best cooks I know," I offered honestly. "I've never tasted a bad dish that they've cooked. Okay, Twila once got it in her head to make Indian food, and that tasted like curry-flavored turds, but that's the only meal I've ever wanted to send back."

"You love your mother."

"Doesn't everyone love their mother?"

"I didn't like my mother, but I guess I loved her." Melanie sipped her smoothie. "You're upset because you want Terry to be with your mother. Don't bother denying it. He told me the whole sad tale."

I had no intention of denying it. "I always wanted him to marry my mother," I agreed. "It started when I was a kid. I stopped thinking about it as an adult, though, so I'm not sure it was exactly an active wish."

"It was active enough that you didn't like it when he told you he was dating me."

"I ... well ... ." I wasn't sure how to answer.

"You can say it," she prodded. "You don't want me in Terry's life because you know that means there's no room for your mother. I had hoped there would be room for you and me to share space in his heart together, but I don't think that's going to be the case."

And just what did she mean by that? "Excuse me?"

"You heard me." She refused to back down. "I tried to be nice to you. I wanted us to get along for Terry's sake. But after yesterday, it's abundantly clear that's not going to happen. We can't share the same space ... which means one of us must go."

I could tell from her tone that she thought I would be the one saying goodbye. "Have you mentioned this to Chief Terry?"

"I have." She bobbed her head. "He was obviously upset, but he sees the truth. We can't have a future if he clings to you and the past. It might be different if you were the same little girl who stole his heart, but you're an adult. You have a man of your own. You don't need Terry to coddle you any longer."

That might be true, but I certainly didn't need her pointing it out to me. "You can't just dictate to him. He has a choice of who he includes in his life."

"And I understand that you'll be around to some degree because of your relationship with Agent Michaels," she said. "But you're not his child. You have a father. I'm sure Terry will be friendly when you cross paths, but there's no reason for him to have dinner at the inn ... or race to your aid when you have something that needs to be taken care of around your house. That's what Agent Michaels is for, right?"

"I like to keep him around because he always smells like bacon, but I'm sure he can handle home repairs."

"Good." Melanie wrapped both her hands around the glass and rested her elbows on the counter. "You don't need him. We're happy ... at least when you're not around muddying the waters. I think that settles things."

She was nuts if she thought I would simply agree to her erecting an invisible fence to keep me out of Chief Terry's life. "That settles nothing."

"You're wrong."

"And you're wrong if you think I'm simply going to allow you to boss me around and dictate how things are going to go." I rolled off the stool, leaving my smoothie barely touched on the counter. "You're not going to tell me who I can and can't spend my time with."

"That was never my intention. You have a family. Terry is quickly becoming my family. There's no need for you to take over his life."

"I don't take over his life."

"No? Last time I checked, everything was about you where your relationship is concerned. He was so upset over something you did the other night that he sat in the dark with a glass of bourbon for an hour. I could hear him muttering to himself about annoying witches. He doesn't swear. I like that about him, but he was calling you a witch and I don't think it's because of your charming personality."

I had news for her. He wasn't complaining about witches simply because he wouldn't say the B-word. That was hardly important right now. "You're not cutting him out of my life." I was firm. "I don't know what game you think you're playing — although I'm guessing it has something to do with Mrs. Little and that's why you've smoothly side-stepped telling me why you were at her store yesterday — but you won't win."

"It's not about winning." Melanie looked tired. "It's about doing the right thing."

"Oh, no." I wagged a finger. "I grew up with Aunt Tillie. It's about winning ... and you're going to lose."

"How do you figure that?"

"Just you wait. I'm nowhere near done with you yet."

And the gauntlet was officially thrown. I felt both good and bad about it. It was too late to take back, so I rode the wave.

War was officially here.

TWENTY-SEVEN

*A*fter leaving the yoga studio I considered going to The Whistler to work. I went as far as to park in the lot and haul out my laptop. I never made it through the front door. I was far too unsettled.

Instead, I headed toward Hypnotic, where I marched through the door without greeting anyone and threw myself on the couch with a dramatic sigh.

"Oh, and it's lovely to see you, too," Thistle deadpanned, shaking her head as she looked up from the catalog she perused. "I'm so glad you stopped by to brighten our place of business."

Clove snorted and moved from behind the counter. "I don't want to encourage Thistle ... like ever ... but she has a point. Why are you making that noise?"

I made a show of picking at the fuzzy balls on my sweater. "What noise? I didn't make a noise."

"Oh, puh-leez." Thistle rolled her eyes and mimicked my earlier sigh. "If that wasn't a cry for help, I don't know what is."

She had a point. "I talked to Melanie Adams."

Clove's eyes widened to the size of saucers and Thistle abandoned the catalog and scurried toward me.

"You don't look bloody." Thistle looked me up and down with a studied gaze. "Did she punch you in the kidneys or anything?"

Clove made an exaggerated face. "Why would she punch her in the kidneys?"

"Because that's where people punch one another when they want to hide the evidence. Like ... abusive husbands. They punch their wives in the kidneys so it's easier to hide."

"That is horrible." Clove planted her hands on her hips and snagged my gaze. "Did you know that?"

Honestly, I didn't. "No. I think we should create a spell that punishes men who beat their wives, though. In fact, we can set it up so they punch themselves in the kidneys. Maybe we shouldn't limit it to just men. Maybe we should do women abusers, too."

"While it's not unheard of for women to beat their mates, they're more likely to abuse other women and children," Thistle offered.

"Wow. You're a real downer today." I gave her a smile before shaking my head. "I simply meant that maybe we could come up with a spell to punish all abusers."

"Sounds great," Clove enthused.

"It does," Thistle agreed. "I'll bet that if it could be done Aunt Tillie would've already done it."

"That's a fair point." I rolled my head back to stare at the ceiling, my energy level flagging with each passing moment. "Maybe I can use my new necromancer power to put together a pack of punching ghosts that can roam town to protect the innocent."

Thistle, always good at picking up on the emotions of others, recognized my melancholy attitude and pursed her lips. "What's your deal?"

"Nothing."

"Oh, you can't come in here and do the sigh thing without answering the question. You want to talk, and you know it."

She was right. I did want to share my misery. "Melanie Adams is just the worst. Do you know what she said to me? She said I was an adult and that it was time for Chief Terry to break from me and spend more time with her. She said she was going to force him to choose."

Thistle didn't react as I'd expected. There was no stomping of feet or swearing to warn the room. Instead, she merely shrugged. "Then she's going to have a rude awakening in her future. He won't choose to cut you out of his life."

"He won't." Clove was solemn as she sat on the couch and patted my knee. "I know you can't help but be worried because ... well, you're you and that's what you do ... but Chief Terry won't simply walk away from us."

"And it's not because he's too loyal for his own good," Thistle added. "He loves us. Sure, he loves you best — something you rubbed in all the time when we were kids — but he loves all of us. I'm including Aunt Tillie in that statement, which should tell you how far gone he is."

I turned sheepish. "I really shouldn't have told you guys I was his favorite when I was a kid. That wasn't fair. He loved us all equally."

Thistle screwed up her face into a scowl. "Don't turn into a martyr. It doesn't work. You were his favorite. We came to grips with it a long time ago."

"It was only because he thought I needed him most," I said hurriedly.

"That's true, but it doesn't matter. He spent time with all of us. He listened to all of us. He loved all of us. You needed more attention because your struggle was more profound and he was determined to help you learn to keep your secret. It is what it is."

"What's important is that he'll never be out of our lives," Clove stressed. "He loves us way too much. When Melanie tries to force him to make a choice, I have news for her: She won't be it."

I knew she was right, but remained unsettled. "I hope so." I rocked back and forth as a wave of nausea rolled through me. "I shouldn't have said some of the things I said to her. I was pretty mean. What if she tells Chief Terry how mean I was?"

"He won't believe it," Clove replied automatically. "He thinks you're an angel."

"He does," Thistle agreed. "It was totally annoying when we were kids."

I shot her a grin that faded quickly when my stomach did an exaggerated somersault. "Ugh."

Clove frowned as she leaned closer and pressed her hand to my forehead. "You're sweating like crazy. Do you feel all right?"

"I think I might be getting sick," I admitted, rolling my neck. "I'm not sure what's going on, but I feel shaky ... and like maybe I should go to bed."

"I'm always a fan of spending the day in bed, but I'm not sure we shouldn't take you to the hospital." Thistle sat on the coffee table in front of me and stared hard into my eyes. "What are you feeling?"

"I want to puke."

"Maybe you should," Clove suggested. "I always feel better after I puke."

"I haven't eaten anything to puke up. Landon made breakfast sandwiches before we left the guesthouse, but I didn't eat mine. He ended up having two."

"He's going to get fat, and I'll never stop laughing when he does," Thistle supplied.

"Then, when I was at the yoga studio, Melanie offered me a smoothie," I said. "It was just strawberries and ice, a little coconut water."

"Did you drink it?"

"I took one sip and then forgot about it."

Thistle's hand was back on my forehead. "Clove, get some mugwort from the herb rack. Grab some nettle and mayweed, too."

I was caught off guard. "What are you doing?"

"Making you feel better."

"But ... I don't understand. Those aren't the normal herbs to soothe an upset stomach."

"No, but they could stop poison," Thistle pointed out.

"Poison? You don't think ... ." I trailed off, uncertain. There was something about Melanie's demeanor that had set me off the second I'd walked through the studio door. I'd felt something bubbling beneath her veneer, and I'd doubted very much it was hurt feelings.

"I'm on it." Clove snapped to attention and rushed to the herb rack. "We need to brew some tea so we can mix everything together."

"I'm on that." Thistle's expression was serious as she stood. "You stay right there. It's probably nothing — maybe a delayed case of the flu or something — but better to be safe than sorry."

I nodded and swallowed hard. "Okay. I don't want to die from being poisoned, so I'm all for drinking the herbs no matter how much they stink."

Thistle's smile didn't make it all the way to her eyes. "Good idea."

TEN MINUTES LATER, the tea was ready and I wasn't feeling better. Instead, the sweating was worse and I was forced to lie on my side to keep from getting dizzy. That, of course, is when Landon decided to pay a visit.

"Hey." He seemed distracted and didn't so much as look in my direction. "Have you guys seen Bay? She's not at the office. I have to talk to her."

"She's right there, dingbat," Thistle snapped as she stirred the tea. "Are you blind?"

Landon followed her gaze and met my eyes. "I didn't see her." Concern replaced whatever he'd been previously feeling. "What's wrong with her?"

"Do you want me to lie or tell the truth?" Thistle asked as she skirted around the counter.

"The truth."

"There's a very small chance that Melanie Adams might have poisoned her."

"What?" Landon's eyebrows flew up his forehead as he rushed to the side of the couch and dropped to his knees. My body was on fire, and when he touched me the shakes returned with a vengeance. "Why haven't you called an ambulance?"

"We made this instead." Thistle attempted to nudge Landon away with her hip. "I need her to drink this, so ... get out of my way."

"Give me that." Landon snagged the mug and sniffed. "What is this?"

"An old remedy we learned from Aunt Tillie when we were kids," Clove volunteered. "It's supposed to be really strong and fast."

"Wouldn't a hospital be faster?"

"No." Thistle vehemently shook her head. "They would lose half the day doing tests. We don't know what she was poisoned with, and it couldn't have been a large dose because Bay only had one sip of the smoothie Melanie gave her. The tea should knock whatever it is right out of her."

"Then I'll give it to her." Landon was grim as he propped my head and moved the mug to my lips. "I want you to drink every drop. If you're not feeling better in five minutes I'm taking you to the hospital."

I opened my mouth to protest, but he stilled me with a dark look.

"I will not lose you. On this one, you're going to do as I say."

I nodded and closed my eyes as the tea hit my lips and I began to drink. It was hot enough that it took me a full three minutes to get it down, but when I did my stomach immediately began to settle.

"How do you feel?" Landon placed the empty cup on the coffee table before pressing his hand to my forehead. "Sweetie, you're hot."

"The tea will make that worse," Clove provided. "It'll burn through her fast."

"That's how it heals," Thistle added. "It burns out all the toxins."

"Right." Landon's eyes filled with concern as he leaned down and wrapped his arms around me. "Five minutes, Bay. If this isn't better in five minutes, I'm getting you help."

"It's going to be okay." My eyes remained closed as I stroked the back of his head. "I feel better already."

"I think you're just saying that to get me off your case. It won't work."

"No, I honestly do feel better." That was the truth. My body felt as if I was floating, and even though my stomach remained upset it wasn't an altogether bad feeling. "I'll be fine. It was just one drink."

"Yeah." Landon's lips brushed my cheek. "Tell me how this

happened, Thistle," he ordered, his hands busy as they moved over me. He was constantly checking my temperature and for injuries. "How did she get like this?"

"She showed up like this," Thistle replied. "She had some sort of showdown with Melanie Adams. She didn't go into a lot of detail other than to say that Melanie threatened to force Chief Terry to choose between them."

"Melanie won't have much luck with that." Landon's lips landed on my forehead. "I don't know if this is wishful thinking, but she's cooling off."

"The tea is working," Clove said. "I told you it would."

"I don't understand why Melanie would poison her. I mean ... that has to be some sort of mistake. She would have to be an idiot to go after Bay in such an aggressive manner."

"Or a psychopath," I murmured, causing Landon to stiffen.

He leaned closer. "Why would you say that?"

"I think she's crazy. There was something in her eyes. I was so worried about what she was saying about Chief Terry that I didn't notice even though it was right on the surface. She's not right in the head."

"Not that I don't believe you, but are you saying that because it's the truth or simply because you don't like her?"

"It's the truth."

"Well ... okay. I trust your intuition."

I wrenched open an eye and managed a smile as I stared into his concerned orbs. "Are you simply saying that because you think I'm dying?"

"If I thought you were dying I'd be prostrate on the floor. You'll be okay." He sounded sure of himself as he brushed my hair from my face. "You already look better. The color is coming back to your cheeks."

"She should be completely normal in a few minutes," Thistle offered. "I think that's good, because we're going to need her at full strength if we're going after Melanie Adams."

Landon balked. "I can't just sit back and let you guys hunt her down."

Thistle was blasé. "Sure you can."

"No, I'm going to hunt her down. But I need proof that she tried to poison Bay if I'm going to arrest her. You said she made you a smoothie, Sweetie. What was in it?"

"Strawberries, ice and coconut water," Clove answered perfunctorily, shrinking back when Landon scorched her with a dark look. "What? Bay told us."

"I doubt she would keep proof of a poisoning around her shop," Landon mused, his fingers gentle as they brushed against my cheek. "I need to get out there as soon as possible."

"How are you going to explain that to Chief Terry?" I asked. "He'll be suspicious if you suddenly show up at the yoga studio and question her. He'll think I sent you."

"I don't really care about that." He was firm as he met my gaze. "Your cheeks are pink. Your temperature is almost back to normal. You look adorable again. That's good."

"Adorable except for the way her hair is all sweaty and her makeup ran," Thistle drawled.

Self-conscious, my hand flew toward my face, but Landon caught my wrist before I could touch to see if Thistle was telling the truth.

"Ignore her," he chided, slowly shaking his head. "She's simply trying to agitate you."

"She's doing a good job," I muttered.

"You're beautiful. You always are."

"And you're definitely feeling emotional." I struggled to prop myself on my elbows. "I'm okay. I'm better. I'm even good enough to fix my makeup."

"You don't need makeup."

"I feel as if I do."

"Well, you don't." He pressed a light kiss to the tip of my nose. "You're okay."

"Yeah. I got lucky. I only took the one sip. Thistle recognized right away what was happening. I'm not sure I would've figured it out on my own."

"Then I owe her an ice cream cone or something," Landon said dryly. "I need to reward her for saving your life."

"And ice cream is the best you can do?"

"Don't push things too far, Bay." He dropped his forehead against mine. "You scared the life out of me. You have no idea how terrified I was seeing you on this couch. It looked as if you could slip away at any moment."

"He's exaggerating," Thistle countered. "You didn't look that bad."

"Thank you," I muttered, causing Landon to chuckle as he dragged me against him for a long hug. "As for Chief Terry, even if he takes our side — which I expect he ultimately will — he'll put up a fight at the start. We need to sit him down and explain things to him."

"He's not my first priory," Landon argued, pulling back. "You're my priority. If I have to arrest her against his will, I'll do it. Besides, he's not in the office."

I furrowed my brow. "What do you mean?"

"He's not in the office."

"But I ... you're investigating a murder. He's always in the office when you're investigating a murder."

"Not this time." Landon carefully combed his fingers through my hair. "I figured he was with Melanie, maybe running late. I left him three voicemails about Hopper's files. I told him about the judge stalling. I managed to place a call to a federal judge who promised to issue a warrant within the next hour, so ultimately it won't matter. I thought Chief Terry would want to know."

He would definitely want to know. In fact, he would be champing at the bit to take the files we stole days before and reunite them with the other files so he could get that albatross off his back. It was one less thing to worry about, and Chief Terry was a big proponent of whittling his worry list.

"Did he not come in at all today?" I asked after a beat.

"No."

"That's not like him."

"No, but after last night's dinner I figured he was soothing Melanie's hurt feelings," Landon explained.

"Melanie is at work. She had a class first thing this morning. Chief Terry wasn't there."

"Oh, well ... ." Landon licked his lips as his demeanor shifted. "You don't think she's done something to him, do you?"

"I think we need to track him down right now."

"Definitely." Clove wrung her hands as she stood at the end of the couch. "We need to find him right now. Bay's not the only one who loves him."

"I know that." Landon climbed to his feet. "I'm going to place a few calls. If he doesn't answer, I might need you guys to help me track him down."

"How?" I asked.

"That locator spell thing you guys do. We might need it."

That made sense. "You worry about your calls." My muscles felt slightly stretched as I stood, but I was rapidly returning to full health. "We'll get the spell ready."

Landon nodded. "We need to move. If she's unstable enough to poison Bay there's no telling what she could do to Chief Terry."

That's exactly what I was afraid of.

TWENTY-EIGHT

We were ready to cast the locator spell when Landon rejoined us at Hypnotic forty minutes later. He was grim.

"No luck?" I asked, my stomach sinking when he shook his head.

"No one has seen him since last night. In fact, I think we were the last ones to see him. It's as if he fell off the face of the earth after dinner last night."

"That's probably because Melanie backed him into a corner," Thistle mused. "She was probably melting down and demanded he make a choice. He either refused to do it or made the wrong choice ... at least from her point of view."

I didn't like the sound of that. "He could already be dead."

"Don't go there, Bay," Landon chided, his hand landing on my shoulder. "Don't let the fear in. Killing Chief Terry would net her nothing but trouble."

"She's not stable. I mean ... she poisoned me. If she's not stable, that means she's not rational. She might not be thinking about the bigger picture."

"I know, but I refuse to believe the worst until I have no choice." He pocketed his cell phone. "We need that spell. I have no idea where that woman lives and I can't find an address in Chief Terry's official search program. I went through his office. She must live around here."

"Then we'll find her." Thistle was firm as she clutched a baggie full of ingredients. "We need a private place to cast this. The last thing we need is other people witnessing us work our magic."

"Where do you suggest?"

"Well ... ." Whatever Thistle was about to say died on her lips when a hint of movement appeared at the front door. We all turned our eyes in that direction and I couldn't hide my frown when I realized Aunt Tillie was on the scene.

She stood on the sidewalk, a glowing orb of light hovering over her right shoulder. She had an impatient look on her face, and when she planted her hands on her hips her message was clear.

"Oh, geez," Clove muttered. "What is she doing here?"

"That's probably my fault." Landon looked resigned. "I called The Overlook to make sure none of them had seen Chief Terry. I tried to play things down, but I'm not sure how successful I was."

"If Aunt Tillie got them all worked up I'm surprised they're not here," Thistle said as she tugged open the door and fixed our great-aunt with a dubious stare. "People are going to notice that thing flying so close to your head."

"I'll tell them it's my pet bird," Aunt Tillie replied dryly. "I'll name it Thistle because it's a dodo."

Thistle rolled her eyes. "That was weak."

"I'll think of something else and get back to you." Aunt Tillie shifted her gaze to me. "Your buddy on the bluff started talking, by the way. I have some information for you."

Holy crap! I'd totally forgotten about Hopper. I left him under Aunt Tillie's watchful eye. I expected him to break sooner rather than later, and it looked as if I was right. "What did he say?"

"I'll tell you during the drive. It plays into what's happening now. I heard Winnie in the kitchen after Landon called. She thought it was weird he was looking for Terry. Given what that loony doctor told me, I realized what was going on."

"Oh, yeah?" Landon folded his arms over his chest. "What's going on?"

"Melanie Adams did something to Terry. He's missing, and you're worried enough to make calls. You guys need to find Terry, which is why I conjured this."

The sentry wasn't human, or sentient, but it seemed to glow brighter with her words. It was almost as if the spinning ball of light couldn't wait to be set free.

"We were going to do it," Thistle offered. "We were going to wait until we had privacy to do it, but this works."

"We don't have time to waste. When you hear what I have to tell you about Hopper's dealings with Melanie you'll wish we'd acted sooner. We need to go."

I often questioned Aunt Tillie's motivations and decision-making skills. The look on her face told me this was the time to do neither.

"So, let's go," I prodded. "We have a lot to catch each other up on."

"And we have to find Terry," Aunt Tillie said. "He needs us."

I didn't like the way she phrased it. "Yeah. We definitely need to find him ... alive."

"Then let's move." Landon didn't put up an argument about Aunt Tillie joining the team. That's how I knew he was legitimately worried. "The sooner we find him, the sooner we can take that witch down."

"Don't insult witches," Aunt Tillie chided. "She's not a witch. She's a ... ."

"Let's not go there." Landon held up a hand to cut Aunt Tillie off. "We need to move. Given what Melanie did to Bay, I have a bad feeling about what she has planned next."

Aunt Tillie made a face. "What did she do to Bay?"

"We'll tell you on the way."

"SHE DID WHAT?" Aunt Tillie was positively apoplectic when I related the tale of my poisoning once we were in Landon's Explorer.

"She poisoned Bay," Clove replied helpfully. "But we saved her."

"I saved her," Thistle corrected. "I realized she was acting wonky and figured it couldn't hurt to flush her system."

"See, you're not entirely useless when it comes to magic," Aunt Tillie drawled from her spot between Clove and Thistle in the back seat. "The locator sphere is heading to the east, Landon."

In the driver's seat, Landon scowled. "Do you think I can't see that?"

"I think you're crabby," Aunt Tillie replied. "Why is he so crabby?"

"He's upset about Bay being poisoned," Thistle replied. "He's not happy about Chief Terry going missing either."

"We're all upset about that." I craned my neck to see Aunt Tillie's face. "What happened with Hopper?"

"First, I just want to point out that you told me to torture him," she started.

"I'm aware of that."

"I did a few things, tests if you will. Ultimately I sang until he agreed to spill his guts."

"That's all it took?"

"I cast a spell so I sounded like a boy band."

"That would do it."

Aunt Tillie's grin was sly. "Once he started talking I couldn't shut him up."

I was almost afraid to ask. "What did you find out?"

"He's a sick man."

"We figured that out on our own."

"No, I mean really sick." Aunt Tillie wrinkled her nose. "He's been having sex with patients for years. The reason he moved to Hemlock Cove wasn't because he liked the town. He moved because he was getting heat from the Traverse City Police Department. They were investigating him for sexual misconduct."

"That sounds ... lovely," Thistle drawled. "Why wasn't he arrested?"

Aunt Tillie shrugged. "I have no idea. He didn't know either. The thing is, he wasn't just treating couples. He was also treating women on the side."

"We already knew that," I reminded her. "He was seeing Mrs. Little."

"Yeah, I know how that came about, and it's a good story." The evil flash in her eyes told me she was going to use whatever information she uncovered to go after Mrs. Little. While I was interested to know why Hemlock Cove's most upstanding citizen would sign up for therapy, we had other things to worry about.

"What about Melanie?" I asked, getting straight to the heart of matters. "What does she have to do with Hopper? I mean ... you made it sound as if she played into Hopper's story as much as Chief Terry's peril."

"She does," Aunt Tillie confirmed. "She's the psychopath."

Somehow I already knew that. How was up for debate — and at a later time — but it wasn't a surprise. "We need all the information you have, and we need it fast."

"Are you telling me to keep my story short?"

"I'm saying you can make the story as long as you want when you're telling it the second time around. For now, you need to keep it short."

"Fair enough." If Aunt Tillie was offended by the admonishment she didn't show it. She loved Chief Terry as much as the rest of us. She understood we were working on a truncated timetable. "Hopper started seeing Melanie as a patient two years ago. She owned a yoga studio in Traverse City. It was popular for a time, until it came out that Melanie was running special one-on-one classes with a few of the men."

I let the information settle for a moment. "She was a reverse Hopper."

"Pretty much," Aunt Tillie agreed. "She got in trouble because some of the wives found out and confronted her. The business went downhill quickly. Her studio was vandalized and she was in danger of going bankrupt.

"She started seeing Hopper for her mental issues," she continued. "Hopper agreed to keep it on the down low and fill out the appropriate paperwork, and they started meeting twice a week. It wasn't long until they recognized sexual deviancy in one another."

"Hopper told you that?" I was incredulous. "He doesn't seem the type to admit his faults."

"Oh, I embellished a little," Aunt Tillie admitted. "He told me that they were attracted to one another, and rather than fight the attraction they gave in to temptation."

"The language is getting a little flowery," Landon complained. "Get to the heart of the story."

"Fine." Aunt Tillie glared at the back of his head, making me think she had plans for retribution later. "They had sex for a bit and Melanie let a few things slip, like the fact that her parents mysteriously disappeared at a time she needed money. Their disappearances allowed her access to their bank accounts."

The sick feeling in the pit of my stomach I'd managed to shake earlier was back. "She killed her parents?"

"There's no proof of that. Hopper deduced it. He was willing to help her spend the money, but he was suddenly leery of her. She picked up on the change in his attitude."

"This glowing orb thing is heading into the woods," Landon noted. "Melanie must have Chief Terry in a cabin or something."

"Or he's already dead and she dumped his body in the woods," I muttered.

"Bay." Landon's tone was low and full of warning. "Don't be a defeatist. We'll find him. Alive."

I wanted to believe that with every fiber of my being. When I thought too hard about what we were facing, though, I couldn't shake the sensation of dread rolling through me. "Go back to your story, Aunt Tillie," I prodded. "I want to hear the rest of it."

"It's pretty simple. Hopper didn't stop sleeping with Melanie. He kept spending her money. Then, one day, it was gone. Melanie was getting progressively unhinged, to the point she was stalking him. She followed him after work, called him fifty times a day and pretty much made his life hell."

"So, she really is a psychopath," Thistle noted.

"Pretty much," Aunt Tillie agreed. "She did a lot of weird things to him. She broke into his house and stole his sheets. She left photographs of herself in frames around his house. Hopper said he was firm and ended things, but she refused to accept his decision."

"She sounds like a total nutball," Landon said.

"I believe I told you that the day I met her," I muttered under my breath.

He cast me a sidelong look. "You said that before you had any proof."

"It was a feeling ... one that turned out to be right."

Landon exhaled heavily. "I'm never going to hear the end of this, am I? You were right about Chief Terry's girlfriend. She's crazy. I should've let you step in sooner to get rid of her."

"Pretty much." I flashed a smile. "I think this should be a lesson that you should never doubt me again."

"I'll keep that in mind."

"I'm not done telling my story," Aunt Tillie barked, causing everyone in the Explorer to focus on her once again. "That's better." Her smile was serene as she folded her hands in her lap. "Anyway, Hopper thought he was smart and called the police. He claimed that Melanie was a former patient and she'd developed an unnatural attachment to him. Because he recognized the signs that she was going off the rails, he ended their sessions, but she continued to follow him around."

"I'm guessing he conveniently left out the part about sleeping with her," Landon offered.

"Oh, he totally lied to the cops and doesn't deny it," Aunt Tillie said. "He said he had to protect himself. Given how Melanie has been acting, that doesn't seem like such a bad idea. Anyway, the radio station hired security guards to protect him and he had a security system installed in his house.

"Melanie apparently set off the security alarm multiple times and was arrested, but she violated countless restraining orders and refused to give up no matter how many warnings she was issued," she continued. "About this time, Hopper had his own trouble with a few husbands and was looking to get out of Traverse City. He used Melanie as an excuse and moved to Hemlock Cove. The radio station set up a studio in his basement so he could record from there, and he had a fresh new crop of women to choose from."

"He simply moved his operation to a new location," I complained bitterly. "I shouldn't be surprised, but ... ."

"He's a total tool," Thistle finished. "I'm more interested in Melanie than him. He got what was coming to him. I'm guessing Melanie is the one who delivered that fate."

"No matter how hard I pushed, he couldn't remember the night he died," Aunt Tillie said. "I don't know if that's because he can't bear the thought or something else is going on. It hardly matters. Melanie is clearly crazy.

"She followed Hopper to Hemlock Cove and she settled in before he realized she was here," she continued. "She opened a new yoga studio and ingratiated herself with certain members of the community ... including several of Hopper's patients. When Hopper confronted her, she said she would out him to his patients if he spilled the beans about her. They were essentially blackmailing each other."

It made sense. It was sickening, but it totally made sense. "At some point Melanie must have decided to move on," I deduced. "She met Chief Terry. He was nice to her. She said she was impressed because he came out to check on her after a security breach. She was all fluttery because he did it himself and didn't send an underling."

"Melanie probably transferred her stalking to Chief Terry, and he didn't even know it," Landon added. "She hid what she was until he was already hooked and then started exerting control over him. Because his stories so often revolve around Bay, she probably saw her as a rival."

"I'm not romantically involved with Chief Terry," I pointed out.

"No, but you are the love of his life in different ways." Landon offered me a wan smile. "He adores you. There's no way Melanie would be able to dislodge you from his life. The more she tried, the more Chief Terry dug his heels in. He probably reached his limit last night."

Sickness flooded me again. "Why wouldn't she kill him if he refused to play along?"

"Because she needs him to embrace the fantasy world she's created," Landon replied, pulling onto a rutted driveway that had seen better days. "I think we're getting somewhere."

"She killed Hopper," I pressed. "She stalked him. She thought she loved him, but ultimately she killed him."

"Only after she found someone to replace the fantasy," Landon said, coming to a crawl and peering through the windshield. Slowly, a small cabin became clear. It was partially hidden by trees. "She's still obsessed with Chief Terry. She can't kill him because she needs a new obsession to move onto first."

"I hope that's true."

"It is." He squeezed my hand. "We're here. I'm guessing this is where she lives."

"Then this is where she has Chief Terry." I reached for the door handle. "I'll get him. You guys wait here."

Landon gripped my hand tighter. "Don't even think about it. We're coming up with a plan. Nobody is running off half-cocked ... and I'm in charge of whatever plan we come up with."

"Oh, does that make you feel manly, Sparky?" Aunt Tillie drawled.

"Why did we even bring her?" Landon's temper was on full display. "She's going to drive me crazy before this is all said and done."

"We need her," I pointed out. "She's the most powerful weapon in our arsenal."

"Not today," Aunt Tillie countered, a small smile playing at the corners of her lips as she stared out the window.

"What do you mean?" I followed her gaze, my heart giving a little jolt when two forms took shape in the shadows of the trees. "Are those ... ?"

"Ghosts," Aunt Tillie finished, positively giddy. "They're ghosts and they're trapped here. That means they're angry."

"I bet they're Melanie's parents," Clove supplied. "I can't see them yet – Bay, you need to get on that – but it makes sense. She supposedly killed them, right? She probably buried them out here so the cops wouldn't find the bodies."

Oddly, that made sense. "So, we have ghosts," I said, concentrating in an effort to make the ghosts visible to everyone. "What do you want me to do with them?"

Aunt Tillie rubbed her hands together, clearly relishing the adventure. "I told you I had a plan. You need to chill out and trust me."

Under normal circumstances I would find that was a terrible idea. We had too much to lose to ignore her instincts, though. "Fine. Lay it on me."

TWENTY-NINE

I didn't like Aunt Tillie's plan. I didn't see where we had many other options, though.

"Okay."

Landon turned apoplectic. "Okay? You're just going to agree to that plan even though it puts you in danger?"

"Do you have a better plan?"

He nodded. "I'll call the state police and let them go in. They can absorb the risk."

That sounded great in theory, but I knew it wouldn't fly. "Landon, we have no proof Chief Terry is here. Heck, we have no proof Melanie is here."

"That's her car." He pointed toward the sedan next to the cabin. "I know because I ran her license plate earlier. She's here."

"And what grounds do you have to call the state police?" I forced myself to be calm. "You have no proof she took Chief Terry. He could've voluntarily taken off on his own. You have no proof she killed Hopper. We're working on a hunch."

"Well ... ." Landon broke off and rubbed his chin. "I hate that you're right."

"We need her to admit what she's done in front of all of us," I supplied. "Besides, if you call the state police she might panic when she sees all the lights and hears the sirens. She'll probably hunker down and choose to go out in a blaze of glory ... and maybe take Chief Terry with her."

"I know you're right, but I don't like this." Landon flicked his gaze to the ghosts watching us from the edge of the driveway. "How do you know they'll work with you?"

"I'll make them do it." I sounded surer than I felt. "I'll make her see them."

"I still don't see why we have to hide," Clove complained. "Wouldn't it be better if Melanie saw she was outnumbered by real people instead of ghosts? She might be more likely to run if she thinks she has a chance to escape into the woods."

"And go where?" Aunt Tillie challenged. "Where is she going to go?"

"I don't know." Clove jutted out her lower lip. "She might not care as long as she can escape to stalk another day."

"It's too late for that," Thistle countered. "She'll be hunted until her dying day at this point. She'll realize that. She's crazy, not stupid."

"And just so I understand, the plan is to make her think that you're a ghost," Landon pressed. "If she sees you with her parents, she'll think the poisoning worked and she's free and clear, right?"

I nodded. "Yes. While she's focused on me you can slip around back and into the house. Chief Terry is in there. Once you get him out we can reveal the truth."

Landon shook his head, unconvinced. "Bay, I don't like this. She might have a weapon. She might try to shoot you or something. We know she's fine stabbing someone."

"She won't get close enough to stab me. If she tries, I'll have the ghosts swarm her. As for a gun, there's no reason to shoot a dead person. If this plan works the way it should nobody will get hurt ... including her."

"I don't care about her."

"No one does. This is our best shot of getting Chief Terry out safely. I'm not going to risk him. I can't."

"Okay." Resigned, Landon rubbed his hands over my shoulders before pulling me in for a hug. "I'll head to the back. You'll know once I get Chief Terry out. If you get in trouble, don't hesitate to send those ghosts to kill her. I'd rather come up with a convincing story to cover her death than risk something happening to you."

"I'll be fine."

"Make sure you are." He gave me a quick kiss. "Give me five minutes to get into position. I want you three to be hidden, but close," he ordered Aunt Tillie, Clove and Thistle. "If she needs help ... ."

"We won't let anything happen to her," Aunt Tillie reassured him. "I promise. This really is the best plan. You know it. Being away from Bay will be like torture to you, but rescuing Terry is the most important thing. You're the key player here. You're still in charge."

"Oh, now I know you're placating me." He rolled his eyes and shook his head. "If this goes south, I'll change the play on the fly and come at her from behind. Don't be surprised if that happens ... and don't send those ghosts after me if you can help it."

"I won't."

"Then let's do this." He gave me another kiss. "I love you."

"I love you."

"And I love myself," Aunt Tillie drawled. "Get moving, Sparky. Terry is waiting to be rescued. Make sure he knows it was my idea when he finds out you've come riding to his aid. I can't wait to collect on this favor."

I GAVE LANDON THE five minutes he requested. Aunt Tillie, Clove and Thistle dispersed to thick areas of foliage to hide, leaving me with the ghosts as my only company. I gave them each a long look as I gathered my courage and rubbed my sweaty palms against the knees of my jeans.

"You guys raised a real winner," I offered. "I can't tell you what a fan I am of your daughter."

Neither of them spoke. Perhaps they were too beaten down by circumstances. It didn't matter. I wasn't here to make friends.

"It's time," I said as I pushed away from the Explorer. It was far enough back on the driveway that I was hopeful Melanie wouldn't see it. If she did, the plan would fall apart and I'd have to come up with another way to distract her. For now, I was sticking to what I had. "Here we go."

I took short steps as I walked toward the cabin, the ghosts falling into formation on either side. They seemed to understand what was about to happen and didn't put up a fight, but they weren't exactly excited by the turn of events.

"Not big talkers, huh? I guess I can't blame you."

I moved as close as I could to the cabin without making myself an easy target, and then I began to sway slightly. I'd seen enough ghosts to know this was a regular occurrence and mimicking what I knew made me feel stronger. Aunt Tillie cast a glamour before I set out from the Explorer that made me appear ethereal like the real ghosts. It wouldn't survive upon close inspection, but I didn't plan on allowing Melanie to get close enough to figure out the truth.

"Melanie," I called out, adopting a singsong voice that I hoped was creepy enough to give her pause. "Melanie."

I watched the cabin closely for movement, calling out her name twice more before a curtain finally shifted on the other side of the window.

"You should come out," I taunted. "We need to have a talk."

When the front door of the cabin finally opened, Landon's worst fear came to fruition. Melanie didn't look happy to see me as she stepped onto the dilapidated porch. She was also armed, a rifle clutched in her hands.

"What are you doing here?" She was clearly baffled. "You should be dead."

"I am dead."

"So ... what? Are you saying you're a ghost?"

"You have a lot of ghosts." I hoped against hope I could utilize my magic without it backfiring and let loose a tendril of color. It wrapped around the ghosts that stood behind me, illuminating them to the point Melanie could make them out. "It seems you've been a bad girl."

Melanie's eyes went wide when she realized I wasn't alone. "What the ... ?"

"Your parents." I hoped that was true. If I'd guessed wrong and Melanie had killed more people to bury out here, the whole plan would be for naught.

"What are they doing here?" Melanie turned screechy as she clutched the gun tighter to her chest. "They've been gone for years."

"They've been *dead* for years," I corrected. "They were never gone."

"But ... how?"

"You killed them. They were your parents and you killed them. When a soul is hurt to the point it can't cope — like what happens when a child kills a parent — it remains behind rather than crossing over." That was basically a load of crap, but there was no way for Melanie to know that.

"And that's what happened to you?" Melanie's fear gave way to intrigue. "You're a ghost, and because of the way you died you're trapped here?"

"Pretty much," I confirmed. I couldn't see Aunt Tillie or my cousins because they were so well hidden. That didn't stop me from looking out the corner of my eye for hints of movement. I should've been relieved that I didn't see any, but I hated feeling alone. "You should be proud. You've managed to clear the way to Chief Terry, and all it took was poisoning me and killing Dr. Hopper."

Melanie balked. "What are you talking about? I didn't kill Hopper."

For a moment I almost believed her. Then reality set in. "You're right. That was the wrong word to use. Hopper got what was coming to him. He was a predator and you were protecting yourself when you ended him. That's why you stole your file, right? You were simply protecting yourself."

"That's right." Melanie brightened considerably. "Do you have any idea what he did to me?"

I nodded. "I'm a ghost. I can see everything now that I've passed." That was a total lie. Melanie had no idea about the afterlife, though, so I figured she would believe almost anything. "I know what he did to you. I know what you did to them." I gestured toward her dead parents. "You can't escape your actions forever."

"Oh, yeah?" Melanie turned haughty. "Let me tell you a little something about my parents. They were cheap. They'd been putting money away for as long as I could remember — some retirement fund or something — and when I got in trouble they refused to help me.

"More than that, my father had the audacity to tell me that opening a business in this economy was a bad idea and he thought bailing me out was an even worse idea," she continued. "He said I should get a real job and learn some real skills. He didn't consider yoga real anything. He refused to help ... so I had no choice but to help myself."

She was so entitled it made me want to punch her. I was supposed to be a ghost, so that wasn't an option.

"Hopper had no problem helping you spend that money," I said. "Once it was gone, he lost interest."

"He was supposed to love me."

"And the only thing he loved was himself."

"He had no right to treat me that way." Melanie's lower lip quivered. "I was a good girlfriend, a good partner. He just tossed me away the second the money was gone. Did he think I was simply going to allow that?"

"Of course not." I hoped my voice was soothing despite the fact that anger was bubbling close to the surface. "Hopper was a bad man. You have to know, you weren't the only one he was seeing when you thought he was monogamous. He had affairs with multiple women ... in multiple towns and cities. That's how he operated. You're not to blame for his bad decisions."

"He should've loved me the way I deserved to be loved," she sniffed.

"Is that why you went after Chief Terry?" I was honestly curious. "It is, isn't it? In him, you saw a man who would never disrespect a woman."

"He was nice," Melanie said. "He listened when I talked. I could tell that he would love me forever ... if he would simply see the light and cut you out of his life. It's funny, but it was the way he talked about you that caused me to fall in love with him. His refusal to let you go is what caused the problems."

"He's too loyal for his own good."

"All he had to do was cut you out of his life. Then things would've been perfect."

"That's what you told him to do last night, isn't it? You insisted he break ties with my family. You wanted him all to yourself."

"It wasn't a difficult request," Melanie snapped. "You're an adult. He's not really your father. You don't need him."

Her words made me angry. "I'll always need him ... and love him. You can't dictate to a person, order them to feel a certain way. Chief Terry's greatest gift is his acceptance. You should've accepted him."

"Oh, don't you worry about acceptance," she drawled. "He's going to accept me and what I have to offer if it's the last thing he does. Thankfully for him, we'll have a lot of time together to work things out.

"Nobody knows how to find me here," she continued, grinning. "You're dead, so you won't be looking for him. Your boyfriend must already be crushed by your death, so he'll be distracted. The same for your family. That means I get Terry all to myself, as it should be."

A hint of furtive movement at the back of the cabin caught my attention. I allowed myself a quick glance to see that Landon, Chief Terry at his side, was making his escape. Chief Terry looked beaten down, weary, but he was on his feet and alive. We briefly made eye contact, and then I turned to Melanie to put my second plan of action into motion.

"You're not going to get what you want."

Melanie was surprised. "Excuse me?"

"You're not going to get what you want," I repeated. "You can't force someone to love you. I'm guessing you've tried multiple times over your life. It's not something that can be manufactured. Love is kismet. It happens at the right time, when destiny exerts itself. You can't simply make it happen because you want it to."

"Do you want to bet?" Melanie's smirk was chilling. "Hopper

thought he could avoid my wrath, but I showed him. I snuck into his house, waited for him to come back from dinner, and then I taught him a thing or two about shunning my love."

I felt sick to my stomach. "You're not even sorry a little, are you?"

"Sorry? About killing a monster? No, I'm not sorry. I'm not sorry for killing you either. I tried to be nice, but you refused to accept me. You were a monster, too."

"I was unpleasant," I agreed without hesitation. "I was unwelcoming."

"Because you wanted him for your mother. Well, that didn't happen. I won."

"I wanted him for my mother ... and myself. I wanted him to be an official member of my family. I won't lie about that."

Melanie was smug. "You lost. You're dead and I'm in charge."

"I didn't lose. I was mean to you and I'll always wonder if that played a part in how things went down. I sensed what you are, though. I think I sensed it from the beginning. It wasn't just anger that he didn't pick the woman I wanted for him." At least I hoped that was true. "It was more than that. But as for losing, I'm not the one who lost."

"You're dead."

"Not quite." I leaned over and picked up a stone from the driveway, lobbing it so it landed with a sound *plunk* at her feet. "Your parents are dead. That's awful, by the way. I can't believe you killed them for money. But I'm not dead. I'm still here. Your plan to poison me didn't work."

Melanie blanched. "No ... you're dead. I can see through you. You're ... shimmery. You're definitely dead. I know it. You said ... I ... ." Her mind was clearly working fast. So were her hands. She gripped the gun, intent clear as she raised it. She planned to point it at me ... and then pull the trigger.

That didn't happen because Aunt Tillie was on her feet. She strolled out of the bushes as if she didn't have a care in the world and raised her hands to the sky. "Don't even think about it!" She bellowed.

I had no idea what spell she was going to cast or if Melanie would've been standing when she was done. Ultimately it didn't matter. This was my fight and I had a different weapon in my arsenal.

"Take her," I ordered the ghosts, who looked thrilled at the prospect. "Don't kill her. I think a life behind bars will be far worse than a quick death. End it, though. I'm done here."

I turned my back on Melanie as she began to screech. There was no need to see what was to come. The thing I wanted to see most was standing at the Explorer with Landon, and he had tears in his eyes.

"I knew you'd find me, kid," Chief Terry choked out when I drew closer. "I knew you'd be the one."

I threw my arms around his neck and gave in to the tears I'd managed to fight off since the moment I knew he was missing. "No one could've stopped me from finding you."

"I know." He rested his cheek on top of my head. "You're a good girl. You always have been."

Melanie continued to scream as the ghosts swarmed her.

"Not so good," I countered.

"Oh, no. She has that coming."

At least we could agree on that.

THIRTY

*A*s a victim, Chief Terry couldn't handle his own crime scene. That meant Landon was in charge, and by the time his co-workers swarmed the scene he already had a story in place. It involved me being panicked about Chief Terry going missing and forcing Landon to drive out to Melanie's cabin as a precautionary measure. He didn't expect to find anything. It was a happy coincidence that we found Chief Terry being held against his will, and we all worked together to free him.

It was a story that didn't necessarily make sense on the surface, but we knew no one would dig too deep because everything was tied up with a neat little bow.

Landon arranged for Chief Terry, Thistle, Clove, Aunt Tillie and me to be transported to The Overlook while he remained behind to take Melanie into custody and process the scene. I stood at the door of the vehicle that would drive us away from the horror in the woods, met his gaze over the hood of the Expedition, and smiled.

He offered a small wave and called out. "I'll be there as soon as I can."

That was all I needed to hear. I nodded, returned the wave, and happily left Melanie's cabin in the rearview mirror.

The second we arrived at The Overlook Chief Terry took over as the center of attention despite the fact that several guests had checked in the previous day. Mom didn't exactly ignore them, but Chief Terry trumped all else as he was escorted into the dining room and fussed over as if he were royalty.

"Are you okay?" Mom looked as if she was caught between crying and committing murder as she smoothed Chief Terry's hair and helped him out of his filthy coat. "I'll make sure this gets cleaned."

"You don't have to do that," Chief Terry protested.

"I want to do it." Mom was firm. "Just like I want to make sure you have something warm in your stomach. We're making soup and sandwiches for lunch. I'll get something out here right away for you."

"And I'm making warm bread," Twila offered, smirking. "I'll make sure you have some of that."

"Which will pale in comparison to the cookies I'm making," Marnie supplied, her lips curving. "I'll make sure you have a huge plate of those."

It seemed the competition for Chief Terry's affections was still on ... or perhaps they simply wanted him to feel welcome. Either way, I couldn't hide my smile as Chief Terry's cheeks flushed with color and Thistle scowled.

"I want some cookies, too," Thistle barked as Marnie disappeared into the kitchen. "I was part of the rescue team, for crying out loud."

I ignored Thistle and let her wallow, instead focusing on Chief Terry. I felt awkward and out of place as I picked at the tablecloth and scuffed my shoes against the floor. "So ... ."

"I'm sorry, Bay." He uttered the words without hesitation. "I'm sorry for all of it."

"You don't have to be sorry."

"No?" He cocked a dubious eyebrow. "In the past few days I've yelled at you, refused to talk to you, picked a crazy woman's side over yours, but you saved me. What should I be, if not sorry?"

"To be fair, I deserved to be yelled at. We broke the law and stole files."

"Yeah, well, you've done a lot worse than that over the years. I don't know why I got so bent out of shape over it."

"Probably because Landon was involved." I'd given the situation a lot of thought and come up with a hunch. "If it had just been Aunt Tillie, Clove, Thistle and me, you would've been annoyed but resigned because we're always impulsive together. Landon agreeing to break the law shifted things, made them more difficult to deal with. That's why you were caught off guard."

"I think you're using that as a convenient excuse."

"Do you have a problem with that?"

"No." Amusement flitted over his face before he sobered. "I'm still sorry about what happened with Melanie, the way things went last night. It wasn't your fault. I need you to know that."

However heartened I was by his words, I knew that allowing him to take the onus on his shoulders was unfair. "I shouldn't have done what I did."

"What do you mean?"

"Right from the start, I decided I was going to get rid of Melanie," I explained. "That wasn't fair to you. I knew it and yet I persisted. If I'd had the chance I would've manipulated her right out of your life."

"I see." He stroked his strong chin. "She was crazy, Bay. She planned to lock me in the basement until I saw reason and agreed with her assessment that we belonged together forever. That's what she said. She was all kinds of nutty."

"I know."

"She needed to be out of my life," he persisted. "She wasn't a good person ... or safe, for that matter."

"She was very *Fatal Attraction*," I agreed, causing him to scowl.

"I should never have let you watch that movie when you were a kid," he muttered, shaking his head. "I thought it was a simple romance."

"I had nightmares for days," I agreed. "Boiled bunnies and the like."

"You've never let me forget it either."

"That's what family does. They never let you forget anything."

His eyes watered and he blinked several times rapidly. "You're my

285

family, too, sweetheart. I'm still sorry for how all this went down. You deserved better. I just ... didn't handle things well.

"The truth is, I wasn't sure how to handle things," he continued. "I was nervous about you meeting her and I knew things wouldn't go well because you were bound to dislike her. From the start, I think I recognized that you were predisposed to dislike her, and that made me nervous. That's on me."

"No." I vehemently shook my head. "I reacted like a baby. Melanie is crazy and needs to be locked in a loony bin for the rest of her life, but when I first met her she was fine. She wanted coffee and conversation ... and I looked at her as the enemy from the start. That wasn't fair to you."

"Life isn't always fair, Bay."

"You sound like Landon."

"You're fond of the boy, so I'll take that as a compliment."

"Yeah, well ... ." I cleared my throat as I trailed off. "I was upset that you didn't want to date my mother," I admitted after a beat, opting to put everything out there so we could move past it. "I always assumed that the two of you would end up together. I don't know why. It was in the back of my head when I was a kid and it stayed there as I grew up. I thought it was inevitable ... like destiny that simply hadn't yet been fulfilled."

"Ah ... ." Chief Terry looked caught.

"I know it's not right to force you into something you clearly don't want," I said hurriedly. "I don't want you to be unhappy. I thought you liked her. After our talk at Christmas, I assumed you'd date her. I know that wasn't fair, but ... I just wanted you to stay close to my family."

"I know." He heaved out a sigh. "That's why I didn't want to date your mother."

"I don't understand."

"I didn't want to ruin things, Bay. You weren't imagining things as a kid. I was always attracted to her."

"Why didn't you act on it?"

"Because I was trying to do what was best for you," he answered honestly, causing my heart to tumble. "At first it wasn't the right time because you were still grieving the loss of your father and the divorce. Then, suddenly you were a teenager and it took everything I had to keep up with you.

"By the time you left for college it felt as if we'd missed our window, even though something was always there," he said. "When you came back it was awkward, and I used that as a convenient excuse. So, you see, it never felt like the right time."

I decided to meet his honesty with some of my own. "I think that's all in your head. The right time is when you make it. Look at Landon and me. We met when we were kids, had crushes on one another, and then completely forgot about each other. When we met as adults, that was definitely the wrong time to be attracted to each other — what with the murderers and drug dealers and all that — but we couldn't stay away. It was the right time for both of us even though it felt like the wrong time."

"Are you saying I should just get over myself and ask your mother out?"

My heart soared at the idea, but I didn't want to put too much pressure on him. "I'm saying that you should rest for a few days and then get your act together. You hurt her, kind of broke her heart, when you started dating Melanie. She was ... lost."

"That's not what I wanted." He rubbed his forehead, weariness taking over. "I thought dating Melanie would be easier. I was wrong."

"Oh, you think?" I shot him a grin. "That woman tried to lock you in the basement. I guarantee the only person who is going to try to lock you in a room here is Aunt Tillie ... and it won't be the basement, because that's where she hides things she doesn't want anyone to find."

"Thank you for telling me that." He patted the top of my hand. "I'll get myself together, Bay. I'll make this up to you."

"You don't have to make it up to me. I'm fine. I knew we would always find a way to move past the fight and be fine."

"Then I'll figure a way to make this up to your mother."

"That would be better." I grinned as I leaned my head against his shoulder. "I thought there was a chance we wouldn't find you in time."

"I would never leave you that way, kid."

"That's what I kept telling myself."

We lapsed into comfortable silence, Clove and Thistle sipping coffee at the end of the table as they stared at the wall. They weren't usually the silent types, but they didn't want to disturb the moment of tranquility.

Thankfully, as Winchesters, we had Aunt Tillie to do that. She was all bravado and bluster when she breezed through the swinging doors and pulled up short in front of Chief Terry. "I bet you'll have better taste in women from here on out, huh?"

Instead of frowning, Chief Terry chuckled. "You can count on that."

"Good."

The sound of footsteps coming from the opposite direction drew my attention, and when I turned I found Landon strolling toward me.

"Hey." I straightened. "Did your co-workers believe the story about me making you go out to Melanie's house?"

He nodded as he knelt in front of me. "Yep. No problem there. She woke up, by the way. She was telling stories about ghosts attacking her. Everyone thinks she's crazy, which is ultimately good for us."

"Unless they put her in a hospital instead of prison," Thistle pointed out. "She killed three people. She would've added Bay and Chief Terry to the number if pushed far enough. I don't think a hospital is the right place for her."

"She'll be in a high-security hospital for observation to start," Landon said. "We'll have to go from there. At least she's off the street."

"That's something," I agreed, holding his gaze for an extended moment. "I controlled the ghosts. They didn't kill her."

"You did so well." Landon was sincere as he pushed my hair away and leaned in for a kiss. "In fact, you were amazing. I always knew you were something special, but you blew me away today."

"Oh, geez!" Chief Terry shook his head and refused to look at us. "I haven't even eaten yet and I think I might lose my appetite."

"You and me both, Skippy." Aunt Tillie was all smiles as she sat at the head of the table.

"Why are you in such a good mood?" I asked, suspicious. Landon gently pulled away from me so he could sit in the open chair on my left. "You were with me most of the day. How could you possibly have done something that makes you this excited?"

"I'm a multi-tasker."

"You're ... something."

"Oh, don't be that way." Aunt Tillie wagged a finger. "I'm simply in a good mood. There's no reason to get worked up."

"I'm not worked up ... but, why are you in a good mood? You didn't do something to Hopper, did you? I still need to go out to the bluff and send him to the other side."

"Can you do that?" Landon asked.

"Yeah."

"Should you do that?"

"It's better than having him here."

"That's true." He linked his fingers with mine and focused on Aunt Tillie. "Seriously, why are you in such a good mood? It makes me nervous."

"Can't I simply be happy to be alive?" She adopted an air of innocence.

"No," Landon and I answered in unison.

"You guys are absolutely no fun," she grumbled.

"You're up to something." Landon slid his arm around my shoulders as he continued to stare at my great-aunt. "Does this have something to do with whatever you found out from Hopper's ghost regarding Mrs. Little's treatment?"

"No, but I'm looking forward to messing with Margaret about that in the future." Aunt Tillie laced her fingers together, prim and proper, and smiled so serenely that I knew she was about to drop a bomb of epic proportions.

"Oh, what did you do?" My stomach twisted. "It's something bad, isn't it? You've figured out a way to make the zombie apocalypse come to fruition, haven't you?"

"Don't be ridiculous. I'm still months away from achieving that."

"Then ... what is it?" I narrowed my eyes. "You didn't manage to clone yourself, did you? I know you were working on that a few weeks ago. I thought you'd agreed to give up that endeavor."

"Yes, because one of you is more than enough," Thistle drawled.

"Way more," Clove agreed.

"Ugh. You guys are starting to irritate me." Aunt Tillie rolled her eyes. "I'm simply an old woman enjoying the fact that a family friend was rescued from the clutches of a madwoman."

"Oh, crap!" Thistle's eyes flashed with annoyance. "Whatever she's done, it's big."

"That was a perfectly reasonable statement," Aunt Tillie argued.

"Even I'm getting nervous about what she's planning," Chief Terry admitted. "Maybe I should skip lunch."

"Don't even think about it," I warned. "If my mother and aunts don't get to dote on you they'll take it out on us. That's hardly fair."

"What did I tell you about life being fair?"

"Yeah, yeah." I waved off the statement, my eyes going wide when the inn doorbell rang to alert there was someone at the front door. "What was that?" The doorbell was only utilized for deliveries.

"That's my new pig!" Aunt Tillie was on her feet. "It's Peg. I told you about her."

In all the hoopla over the past few days, I'd forgotten about Aunt Tillie's pig quest. "You actually bought a pig?"

"Yes. She has spots and everything. I think she'll make a great addition to the family."

I risked a glance at the swinging doors. Thankfully my mother and aunts remained on the other side. "You know this won't end well, right? They'll freak out."

"That's only part of the appeal." Aunt Tillie's smile was serene as she sauntered toward the door. "Things are about to change around here, girls. I think you already know that. You'd better prepare yourselves ... because it's going to be a witchy ride."

Of that, I had no doubt.

Printed in Great Britain
by Amazon